. . . Thought That's Thin. . .

The Cliff Fulton Series
Book 2

Also by James William Peercy

Without A Conscious...

The first Cliff Fulton mystery (1 of 5)

...Thought That's Thin...

The second Cliff Fulton mystery (2 of 5)

The Wall Outside

The Xun Ove series Book 1 (Fantasy)

Partition Majik

The Xun Ove series Book 2 (Fantasy)

Moon Half Full

Short story (Science Fiction)

. . . Thought That's Thin. . .

The Cliff Fulton Series
Book 2

James William Peercy

Hydra
Publications

Hydra Publications
1310 Meadowridge Trail
Goshen, KY 40026

www.hydrapublications.com

DEDICATION

To those who seek to know because they are forced to, want to, or are driven from within.

May my brother rest in peace.

ACKNOWLEDGMENTS

I wish to express sincere appreciation to family, and friends. In particular: Claudette Peercy for putting up with me when I've said, "Come look at this..."; Clifford and Dianne Peercy who never set limitations on what I could become; Brian Miller and Darrell Miller with whom I used to swap stories and dreams as we rode to school on the bus; Elizabeth Mendoza whose excellence in photography is equal to her personality and friendship; Arash Mahboubi for reading, and commenting (to the point of asking, 'When is the next one?'); Doug Coleman for his timely aid in reading through the last edit; and Lana Bernardin for her enthusiasm to utilize her promotional skills; thanks to Tony Acree with Hydra Publications for the first printed edition, and Sarah Cheek for her editing talents.

To all of you, highest commendations.

. . . Thought That's Thin. . .

The Cliff Fulton Series
Book 2

THE CLUE SO FAR…
Without a conscious thought that's thin…

Chapter 1

Push me.

Cliff Fulton stared through bleary eyes. A tiny L.E.D. lit the note above him in bright, white light with the words, "Push me". Where was he?

His hands moved to the right and left. They bumped into red velvet material as his eyes focused in and out. A pillow lay under his head, the air tasted foul, and his lungs labored to breathe. Coffin? Why am I in a coffin?

Panic swelled. His heart thumped loudly. In both directions, he traced the sides and corners as far as his fingers could reach. They found no gap.

Push me.

He planted his hands on the ceiling and pushed with all his might. The ceiling above him did not budge. Sweat beaded on his forehead. It trickled down the sides of his temples. The bleariness returned as he stared back at the note. His thoughts were hazy. Think, Cliff, think.

"Push me," the words whispered from his lips. He remembered hearing those words in a different context. Cliff reached up, maneuvered his left hand above his chest, and peeled back the note. A single red petal fluttered down, and he spotted a tiny button stuck to the velvet cloth. When he touched the tiny button, it dropped to his shirt.

Unable to see where it went, he hunted fervently to find it. His fingers touched a vest and jacket—he wore a suit.

When his hand found the small button, he held it to the light. His fingers secured the two ends and pressed the tiny indention. An explosion shook his prison.

The lid shot up with a bounce, smoke issued from its hinges, and dank air swished in. He dropped the button and shoved the lid. The ground rumbled as a second explosion came from further away.

His chest lunged forward as white knuckles gripped the walls of the casket. The inside of a mausoleum quietly stared. A stained glass window in one wall spelled "Fulton."

Voices came in quiet echoes: two were baritones, and one held a higher pitch. They came from the outside, muffled, and become fainter by the moment.

A heavy mausoleum door stood closed. Reflected light from the stained glass window illuminated fresh, moist shoeprints that led toward the door. He climbed out of the coffin, dusted himself off, and took in the plentiful air.

The words "push me" echoed through his mind, but this time there were more. In a Japanese accent, the memory rolled back. "Go ahead, push me again."

He hurried to the door and threw his weight against it. Thick, solid, and balanced, it shifted outward way too slowly.

The path they had taken led from the mausoleum across dry grass. The water glistened off the dry grass in patches and reflected the sunlight in tiny bursts. The shoeprints went both left and right with a smaller pair going deeper into the cemetery.

Sprinklers operated by the church next to the parking lot. Odds were, whoever had done this had come from there. Cliff started into a sprint and followed the direction of the two baritone voices. Up ahead, he heard, "Come on, you coward, you heard the boss. How's he going to know it was us?"

He hurried past burial plots, some with great headstones and others without. The stone trail weaved toward the church. Two men were up ahead, but how far, he could not tell. Around the headstones and mausoleums, glimpses came. As the path curved, he caught his first good look. One wore a hat, and both dressed in dark suits. A second later, his view was blocked.

As he rushed forward, a strange thought occurred. What would he do when he caught them?

The path opened near the church's southern wall. He whipped around and caught sight of two startled men. Their eyes met. The one without the hat bolted toward the church.

"You fool." The second started after the first. As the church doors swung back, music played in the background.

The shorter, hatless man tore forward, charged across the wide hallway, and slammed into the service doors. The music rose in volume as the inner doors flew back. A line of people filed past a closed casket. On the casket, Cliff caught the picture of his grandmother.

A stunned silence dropped as all eyes turned to the hatless man. Heedless, the man ran down the center aisle. His companion slowed, removed his hat, and slipped down the corridor to the right as a slight smile crossed his lips.

Which man to chase? With only moments to decide, Cliff surged forward, caught the inner doors as they started to close, and yelled, "Stop that man!"

Albert, Cliff's best friend, placed one foot on the pew seat, the other on its top, and launched himself over the three people to his right. As he dropped through the air, he missed the hatless man. The hatless man reached the casket, realized the line of people blocked his way, and rushed toward the south exit door.

Chaos broke out. The line of people shifted without direction. The minister stepped to the podium and tried to bring order. Cliff's dad, Joseph, watched the hatless man shove people out of the way. Joseph, who sat on the front pew, stuck out his foot.

The hatless man tripped; he fell forward and down. Two others pinned him to the floor.

Cliff released the inner door and turned toward the right hall.

Dim light illuminated the frosted windows. No door opened or closed.

He stepped forward and listened for the second man. The women's bathroom stood to the right, and the men's sat to the left. Cliff had been here—before he had awakened in the casket.

Tears formed in the corners of his eyes. He had excused himself from the funeral, his heart could not take it, and had planned to wait the rest of the time here in the hall.

Scuff marks decorated the floor. As his eyes followed them, he remembered the bench by the wall. Footsteps had approached. He had not looked up. Thoughts of his grandmother had pushed everything else away.

Someone had dropped a black sack over his head while a second had wrenched back his arms. A phone had been forced to his right ear, and he had heard a man with a Japanese accent say, "Good morning, Mister Fulton. Go ahead, push me again."

His thoughts came back to the here and now. The hallway was silent. The man had come this way, but nothing betrayed his presence. And what of the smile as the man removed his hat? Did he wait for Cliff to follow, or did he know he would not? Cliff set his jaw and stepped forward.

Footsteps ran up behind him. Cliff spun around and raised a fist.

"Whoa!" Albert backed up. "We're friends. Remember?"

Despite her high heels, Penny rushed up behind Albert. "Cliff, are you okay? Your suit!"

"He went this way." Cliff turned toward the corridor.

Albert stepped forward to look past Cliff. "Who?"

"The second man."

Albert stepped back with his eyes open wide. "There are two of them?"

"Cliff," Penny's voice soothed, "you really should explain."

The inner chapel doors opened, and a large throng of people moved out. A wailing whine came from outside the church and grew louder by the moment.

"Cliff," Joseph's voice called behind them, "you need to get in here."

Cliff hesitated and then turned to Albert. "Watch this corridor for me."

"Me?" Albert turned to stare. "Why me?"

"Someone's has to keep an eye out in case he comes back. You're the only one I can trust."

Penny huffed. "Thank you very much."

"You know what I mean."

Albert shook his head. "Look, man, I'm flattered, but I'm not going to be much of a barrier if he shows."

The police walked through the front of the church.

His father called again, "Cliff!"

"I've got to go." He turned toward the inner chapel doors. "Just watch it. If you see anyone, note his description."

Penny hurried to join him as Cliff stepped into the sanctuary. Most of the people had left. The man without a hat was secure. He sat on a pew watched by several men and exclaimed very loudly, "Look, I told you I'm sorry. I had no idea I was breaking up a funeral!"

"You're lying." Cliff strolled forward; his face was hard. "You knew exactly what you were doing. You and your friend locked me in a casket."

A hushed silence dropped as all eyes turned to Cliff. Curiosity, shock, and disbelief crossed everyone's face, all except for his dad and mom who showed only concern.

"Joseph," his mom, Jessie, came forward and touched her son's suit, "he's telling the truth."

"I know he is." His father's jaw tightened as he turned to the hatless man. "I want to know what this is about, and I want to know now!"

A man stood up and gripped his father's shoulder. The graying temples and facial features made him look older than Joseph but nonetheless similar. "Me too."

Two police officers came forward. "We'll take it from here." One of the two pulled out handcuffs and locked them around the hatless man's wrists.

The hatless man shook his head. "It was a mistake, I tell you!"

"We'll find out at the precinct."

The other officer turned toward Cliff. "Can you take me to the casket?"

"Certainly." His eyes narrowed. "It's in our family mausoleum."

Joseph's eyes darted to Cliff. "I'd like to come too."

Jessie took her husband's arm. "We'd both like to come."

A man stepped up and barred their way. "Joseph, I'm George Sealman. We talked on the phone earlier?"

Joseph hesitated though he looked toward the man. "Elaine spoke very highly of you, but I don't think now is the time—"

"It is important that I meet with you now. Let your son go with the police." He turned toward Cliff and extended his hand. "It is a pleasure to meet Elaine's grandson." As their hands touched, Cliff felt a small wad of paper in the man's palm. George's eyes did a single glance toward the handshake. He gave Cliff time to covertly grab the wad of paper before releasing the grip. George turned back to Joseph and Jessie. "It is imperative I tell you both."

Cliff recognized the man. George Sealman was Gran's attorney and had provided the safety deposit key that had been essential to discovering Gran's killer. Cliff slipped the wad of paper into his pocket. The officer motioned for him to lead the way.

When they passed through the inner chapel doors, Cliff motioned toward Albert. "A second companion fled down there. That's where they took me hostage."

The policeman frowned. "I see." He reached for a cellphone and hit autodial. Someone on the other end answered, but Cliff could not hear their words. "Yes, sir. See you shortly." As the policeman hung up, he motioned Albert back and checked the restrooms one by one.

Albert exhaled, and they all watched the search. The police officer went systematically down the hall. When he reached the narrow corridor, he came back. "If he went that way, he's further into the building." The hatless man came by in custody and was led to a squad car.

The outside church doors pushed open, and in stepped Lenord Scott, the member of the FBI, who had helped Cliff. Lenord shook the policeman's hand. "Thank you for calling. With your permission, I would like to escort Cliff."

At seeing Lenord, Cliff let out a sigh of relief. "It's good to see you."

"And not surprising to see you." A slight smirk crossed the agent's lips. "I thought you were staying out of trouble."

"Me too." Cliff's voice dropped as he pointed. "The family mausoleum is this way."

He pushed the church doors back. The sun's brightness made him blink. They followed him around the right corner, along the southern wall of the church, and found the stone path.

It didn't take long. The door had remained ajar. Despite the stained glass window on the inside, the light was dim, but the casket was obvious. A deep frown formed on Lenord's face.

"No way!" Albert slipped left and hovered over the broken coffin. "They did not!"

Lenord pointed a finger at him. "Don't touch."

Both of Albert's hands came up. "It never crossed my mind." He leaned close and looked over the wreckage.

"You were serious." Penny clutched his arm.

"It wasn't meant to kill me." Cliff pointed toward the hinges. "Someone wanted to scare me, but I don't know why." He wrinkled his brow. "Could it be your sister?"

"Sister?" Lenord turned and narrowed his eyes at Penny. "Your sister was part of what happened to Elaine Fulton?" The accusation was plain; if Penny had a sister involved, odds were, she was involved, too.

Penny stiffened. Only two people knew what had happened, and those were Cliff and Albert. "She's not my sister."

Cliff's face flushed. The funeral, the casket, and the two men had thrown him off. He should never have mentioned that. "She's clean," he assured Lenord with closed eyes. "She wasn't a part of what happened."

"Which one?" Lenord pushed the point. "Her or her sister?"

To say Penny, meant the sister existed, and to state the role Penny had played would only incriminate her without need. "I think you should ask Richard Andrews the Third about that."

Lenord snorted. "I see. Cliff, you know I can't help you if you don't come clean, FBI jurisdiction or not. You're not playing with people who follow rules. You're toying with merciless killers. Remember that."

Cliff swallowed. Less than three hours ago, he thought all this was behind him. Why were they dragging him back into it now?

Lenord bent down to investigate the casket. Cliff's eyes went to the mausoleum. This place had been bought by his great grandparents. Every family member had a spot.

He moved toward the area and noted the preparations made by the cemetery. In less than a few hours, Gran would be placed in that slot. She would then be entombed forever.

When he touched the cold stone, it drove home the finality. The loss stabbed him and twisted its blade inside his heart. As he moved past the two-foot posts which separated each column of slots, a pattern caught his attention. Though the shadows tried to hide it, something had been engraved in the stone of Gran's slot. He pulled out a handkerchief and cleaned the area. The carvings became numbers. He mentally noted them down: 0394-981.

Those were the same numbers used on the safety deposit box key Gran had given him. They were the same numbers as the key to Gran's code. Curious if all the burial slots had numbers, he checked the others and found they did. Sequentially, his grandfather's came first, and his uncle's came third. Even his father and mother had one.

Penny stepped near him. "What are you doing?"

"There are—" He remembered Lenord stood in the room and dropped his voice. "—numbers on Gran's slot." His fingers touched the pocket that contained George Sealman's note.

"Of course there are numbers. They are used to indicate which slot belongs to whom. Do you honestly think she planned this too?" Concern flickered across her face as she sighed. "Cliff, not everything is a secret code."

"No—" He refused to believe her. "—this is not a coincidence. The number on Gran's slot is the same as the code she left for me, and I'm going to find out why."

Chapter 2

The mausoleum door swung back in a rush, and a woman in a dark suit stepped quickly in. "Lenord," her oriental accent called as everyone turned to face the door. "There's another casket—" The woman spotted Cliff, Albert, and Penny; her eyes narrowed. "I mean, there's something else you ought to see."

As Lenord rose from the casket debris, he threw a look at the trio. "Cliff, this is Chrys Xu, on assignment from Japan's Ministry of Defense. We have been ordered to extend her every courtesy. The ICPO with homeland security selected her to help get to the bottom of this matter." He turned back to Chrys. "Go ahead; these three know more than they're telling. They don't realize that I'm going to find out anyway."

The woman gave a nod. "A second casket had a man inside." She glanced down at the remains beside Lenord; her eyes were quick to notice the details. "Only, his explosives didn't knock off the hinges. His killed him."

"Push me," Cliff whispered. Though his voice was inaudible, Ms. Xu's eyes met his. He spoke louder. "When I was in the casket, the words 'Push me' were on the lid's ceiling. That was also part of the warning before they put me in it, 'Go ahead, push me again.'"

"Perhaps—" Lenord gazed down at the casket ruins. "—it would be more prudent to have Chrys escort the three of you back to the church. I'll go check out the other casket."

"Wait a minute." Cliff stepped forward. "If something is

going on that concerns me, shouldn't I be involved?"

Lenord gave a grin. "That was my argument, but you three are keeping secrets. It goes both ways, you know. Now, is there anything else you'd like to tell me?"

No one volunteered.

"Very well. Chrys, please take these three to the church."

The trio moved out of the dark into the bright day. As Ms. Xu stepped to their left, Cliff noted the size and shape of her shoes. She stood poised and kept equal weight on both feet. Shoeprints which matched hers led further into the cemetery. That had to be the way Ms. Xu had come.

She noticed his gaze, and a slight smile crossed her lips. "You are a foot person."

Cliff jumped. "I'm sorry. I was just thinking."

Albert smirked, and Penny glared.

"This way." Chrys led them along the stone path toward the church.

Penny took Cliff's arm, slowed their stride, and created distance between them and Ms. Xu.

As Albert dropped back to join them, he drew in a breath. "Isn't she awful young for an agent? On top of that, that girl isn't much bigger than a stick, and with that waist long, black hair—" He whistled. "—she is gorgeous."

Penny pinched Cliff. "Just thinking?"

Cliff cleared this throat and tried to keep the color from his cheeks. "It's not what she implied. I was figuring out the direction she came from."

"Why?"

"When the explosion went off, I heard a second explosion. The other casket with the other man went off about the same time. Three possibilities exist for this: one, we both woke up, found the button, and pushed it together; two, someone else initiated his; or three—"

Albert's voice fell. "When you pushed the button, it caused

his to go off."

Silence dropped, and Cliff slowly nodded. "What if, when I got out, it killed him?"

"No." Penny shook her head. "Nobody would do that." As she glanced toward Cliff, her eyes opened wide. "Would they?"

"And why not?" Albert shrugged. "It would be the perfect setup. You get the message that these people mean business, which I've been telling you all along, and you get the blame for killing another man."

Cliff swallowed.

"Albert," Penny's voice became firm, "you're not helping."

"I don't want to believe it either, but it is a possibility."

With reluctance, Cliff nodded and noted they could not see Ms. Xu in front. "It is a possibility, whether I like it or not. We need to see the other mausoleum."

The trio gradually slowed to a stop and listened. Ms. Xu must have moved out of earshot. Why would she get that far ahead?

Albert pointed the way they had come. "You think you can find it?"

Penny shivered. "I'm not sure we want to find it."

Cliff nodded.

"Well then—" Albert turned and took a step back. "—what are waiting for?"

Ms. Xu stepped out from behind a large headstone. "Lost already?" Her smile gave no indication as to what she might have heard, or if she had heard anything, but Cliff had no doubt. Her eyes took them all in. "The church is this way." She pointed.

"Of course." Cliff nodded. "Penny? Albert?"

They started forward again, but this time Ms. Xu stayed behind them and made it uncomfortable for them to talk. She did exactly as Lenord indicated. The words "on assignment from Japan" crossed Cliff's thoughts.

"Ms. Xu—"

She smiled. "You can call me Chrys."

In a flirtatious voice, Albert asked, "Is that C-h-r-i-s? K-r-i-s? C-h-r-i-s-s?"

A smirk crossed her face. "C-h-r-y-s will do nicely."

"Gotcha," he winked. Cliff elbowed him.

"Chrys, Lenord stated you are on assignment from Japan. Can I ask why they called you?"

"You may ask, but I may not answer."

Her wit was quick. It reminded Cliff of Richard Andrews the Third; he was the "spy" that had worked with his grandmother.

She pursed her lips in consideration. "I'll be frank, Mr. Fulton—"

As Cliff's last name came off her tongue, her voice felt familiar.

"The situation has international implications that could endanger the peace between the United States and Japan. I'm here to trace down those implications and eliminate them."

Cliff's chin rose, and he nodded. "The rest of the cover-up?"

"What one country wishes to conceal, another keeps hidden—sometimes for a favor." She smiled. "It is the way of the world."

"It is bogus," Albert threw in as they reached the end of the path.

She walked them to the church steps.

"Albert's right," Cliff insisted. "The cover-up is wrong. People need to know."

"Know what, Mr. Fulton?" The smile never changed on her face. "There is nothing to know. We are investigating an attempted murder outside the boundaries of the local police. Go home. Leave this to the professionals." Her eyes were stone-cold. "You may live longer." She turned and walked toward the cemetery.

Penny tugged Cliff's arm. "Did you see that? Did you see her eyes? It was just like—"

"The assassin who tried to kill you at Charlie's." Cliff

nodded. "I hope Lenord knows the type of person he is working with."

Albert grabbed the door and swung it open. "Who says Lenord is any less guilty? Just because he stopped his partner doesn't mean he's not involved."

"I won't believe that of Lenord." Cliff shook his head as they walked in. "Even if his duty is to the powers that be, I saw the look on his face that night. He was shocked and betrayed."

Gunfire echoed where there should be none. The first thoughts in Cliff's mind were "family." He hit the inner chapel doors and noted the debris of smashed benches and broken fixtures. What had happened? The last he knew his parents were going to speak with George Sealman, but where? Albert and Penny were right on his heels.

"Where are you going?" Albert grabbed his shoulder and pulled him back. "Those are gunshots. We've been there and done that before. This is not the time!"

"Albert's right," Penny pleaded. "We don't know what's going on here."

"Right time or not, I don't care." Cliff released the doors and turned to the right. It was the same area the police officer had searched. "I don't get it. It was just a funeral. It was a simple funeral for my grandmother. You would swear she had started World War III."

Richard Andrews the Third slipped in from behind. "Somebody has, and despite Division A's attempt to keep it quiet, they not only want what was in that briefcase, they want everyone involved eliminated."

Cliff's face lost all color. "My family?"

"There's a safe house not far from here. I need to get you to it." His eyes swept them. "All of you. Other agents are retrieving your parents."

Cliff didn't like it. "They were right here." A lump formed in his throat. "They're okay?"

"We have all gone dark until we reconvene at the safe house."

An explosion shook the church; smoke billowed from the chapel.

Richard waved toward the exit. "And that's our cue." He hit one of the front doors with enough force to open it, while he indicated for everyone to stay low. Two shots pierced the thick oak doors and sent in rays of sunlight. He let it slowly close. The position of the gunman could be seen in the reflection of the cars parked near the church.

"When I count three, I will draw their attention." Richard removed a sidearm, checked the magazine, and undid the safety. "I want you to head toward the left and get in the black sedan." He reached into his pocket and tossed Cliff the electronic key fob. "I've just unlocked it. If I'm not there in one minute, you are to start the car and go to where it tells you. Got it?"

Cliff gave a nod.

"One, two, three." The door slammed open while Richard moved down the steps and fired. "Go!" He raced toward their assailant.

The three moved. Wood splintered behind them as they hurried down the steps. They shifted to the left, but where Cliff had expected one black sedan there were three.

"I knew we should have gotten the license plate." Albert urged everyone to move faster.

"You forget," Penny pointed at Cliff, "we have the key fob." They slipped to the side and put at least one car between them and the firefight.

Cliff frowned. "Which we can't use."

Albert's voice rose. "What do you mean we can't use the key?" A shot rang out and he ducked then lowered his voice. "Hit the button!"

"Do you know if the car will make a sound, flash its lights, or be silent?"

"Well, no, but—"

Penny bit her lip. "He's right. If it does the first two, it will give us away. If it's the last, we will never know. We'll have to try the handle on each one, and hope no one else left their car unlocked." The shots died for a moment as they worked around to the end of the nearest car. "There are three black sedans and three of us. I say we each try one. I'll take the closest."

Albert nodded. "I've got the one to the right of you."

Cliff tossed Penny the electronic key fob. "And I'll take the far corner."

"What's this for?"

"If you find it first, I want you inside. If we can't get there in time, drive away."

She threw them a look. "Oh, come on. Do you really think I would leave you guys?" She studied their faces. "You're serious?"

Cliff nodded solemnly. "Okay, everyone, let's move."

Penny huffed at them. "But what if I don't want to drive off?"

Cliff headed toward the left, stayed low, and stole looks over the top of the car he hid by. Had he done the right thing? Richard had given the key to him; he had expected Cliff to find the car. This whole day had gone crazy, and nothing made any sense.

He remembered the facts about Gerhard Von Richter as he stole forward. Two others had worked with him: Claretta "Talia" Badoglio, and Fushimi Taruhito. The three had created a circumstance which had ended in his grandmother's death. Gerhard was dead, he assumed Claretta was in hiding with her daughter Tish, and Fushimi was not around. Well, maybe "not around" was too definitive a statement. He, or someone like him, had called Cliff on the cellphone right before they had knocked him out.

His hand found the handle on the car; it was locked. As he turned to leave, someone hurried in his direction. A glint of light sparkled briefly off something in the man's hand.

Cliff slid beneath the black sedan. The fit was tight, but it was the only place to hide. It worked, that is, until he heard the doors unlock and knew what was about to happen. He had two choices:

hang tight, keep his head down, and pray something underneath did not hit him, or try to slide out the other side. He went for option two.

The engine started when he was three-quarters there, the front tires turned as he made it to the edge, and the car took off as he rolled out. His hands were no sooner under him, he could clearly see the back end, when the car jerked to a stop.

It all went in slow motion. He launched to his feet, watched the driver's door swing out, and took his first step as the driver swung a gun in his direction.

A horn blared from the center black sedan; Albert had found the right car, and Penny raced toward it. The driver shifted his weapon toward her.

Cliff charged. "No, you don't!"

Caught between the blaring horn and charging college student, the man hesitated a single moment.

Cliff rammed into him and hit the gun wrist. The weapon sailed high as Cliff elbowed for the throat. He missed, hit the man directly above the heart, and forced the breath out of him. It only lasted a second.

The man snapped back, grabbed Cliff by the hair of the head, and jerked him sideways as he brought his own fist toward Cliff's throat.

A shot rang out and pierced the man's hand. It burrowed through to score in his left bicep. The bone in his arm snapped. The grip on Cliff's head released. Cliff followed the man's example, launched a right punch, struck the throat, and knocked the man back into the car.

Richard shouted across the way. "Cliff! Car! Now!"

Cliff bolted for the car and caught sight of Richard doing the same. More men raced around the corner of the church. Flames licked the sky at the church's far end. Where the police were, Cliff had no idea.

Three thuds sounded; they bounced off the black sedan only

moments after Cliff got there. A back door opened. He jumped, dropped inside, and managed to get his foot in before it slammed shut. He found his head in Penny's lap.

She stared down at him with a mixture of relief and terror. "Thank you."

As he rose up, their lips met.

"Hey!" Albert turned around in the front passenger's seat. "I helped too!"

Richard grinned and checked the displays on the car. "Me too, lovebirds, but you don't see me wasting time." Bullets bounced off the windows and doors.

Cliff rose and buckled his seatbelt. "Your car is bulletproof?"

"Comes with the job." Richard hit the ignition, and the car came to life.

The crowd assembled around them grew, but despite their numbers, they kept their distance.

Albert peered closely. "What are they waiting for?"

Chapter 3

Around the corner of the church walked a man. Richard nodded. "That."

A bazooka lay on the man's shoulder. Nonchalantly, the weapon shifted and took careful aim.

Albert's eyes opened wide. "But what are we waiting for?"

"Now." Richard floored it, headed straight toward the man, and pressed a spot on the steering wheel. The bazooka launched and blew by the sedan with lightning speed. The men closest to them leaped to the sides. Others opened fire. He swerved to the left and hit the gas to put as many obstacles in the way as possible. "It will take a second or two to reload, depending on how close the rockets are, and another few seconds to stabilize and aim. By then, we'll be gone."

Albert came unglued. "You played chicken with a rocket launcher!"

"It was that or let them tag us. I knew he would not hit us if we went straight at him."

"Why?"

"Regardless of what you see in the movies, people on a mission like to come back alive. A direct hit that close would have killed them all."

Richard pressed another spot on the steering wheel, and two digital displays appeared in the center of the windshield. One showed what went on behind them while the other gave a diagram of where they were headed.

"Albert," Richard pointed at a series of numbers on the screen, "I want you to keep an eye on those. If they decrease faster than ten at a time, let me know." He reached the next corner, barely slowed, and turned sharply to the right.

Cliff leaned forward to study the display. The numbers bounced between one and two decrements. "What is it?"

"Radioactive tagging. I did a widespread marking on everyone within range as we drove toward the bazooka."

"When you tapped the steering wheel." Cliff nodded. "Wow."

"You will see a faster drop the closer they come within range of the car. A drop of more than ten in a row shows they are closing in quickly. At Zero, you can see the whites of their eyes."

"They are following, but the numbers are staying the same."

Richard frowned. "Yes, but how I'm not sure." He adjusted one of the displays and initiated a diagnostic check. "They are following, but not us. It's one of ours going in the same direction." His frown deepened. "We've all gone dark so I can't send a warning." His fingers drummed on the steering wheel and then tapped. A display of satellites appeared as he reached to enter a code. A third display responded as lines and circles triangulated the location of what they tracked. It estimated its basic path based upon known routes and gave its ideal location. The car deviated from the digital map and cut to the right.

Cliff's eyes stayed glued to the displays. "You're going to intercept."

"I am. If I can stop that vehicle from reaching the safe house, it will certainly make things easier." Richard grinned. "Elaine was right. You would make a good agent." The car turned only inches from the corner of a building and hurried down an alley.

"But an agent for whom?" Cliff glanced toward Richard. "I don't want to lose my soul to a group who only cares about themselves."

"That's not it at all. People have to have rules; they cannot exist without them. To claim all a group's decisions are correct would be saying they are perfect; they are not."

"And yet, they let people die every day in the name of profit."

Richard nodded. "Point taken; no agency is flawless. If your grandmother believed in our cause, don't you think it has some merit?" The car accelerated despite the cramped accommodations of the alley. They flew by trash bins and garbage cans. Stray papers and loose items whipped into the air. "In about thirty seconds, we are going to collide with a moving vehicle. Please make sure your seatbelts are locked."

"What?" Albert pushed back into the passenger seat, and despite the seatbelt, grabbed the sides for dear life. "Whatever happened to the words *safety* and *passenger*? Where are the airbags? I don't see airbags!"

Cliff sat back with a worried look on his face. "You're joking?"

"I never joke when it comes to my car. Hold on."

A black sedan like theirs appeared as the car shot out of the alley. Richard spun the steering wheel to the right, the wheels smoked raking black marks on the pavement, and they slammed sideways into the other vehicle. Both cars slid with the momentum as the other car struck against the curb on its left, bounced up onto the sidewalk, and rammed sidelong into a light pole.

Horns honked and swerved around the collision. People ran in all directions. Richard touched the steering wheel, and part of the roof slid back. He grabbed hold of the edges, stood up in the car, and held out a small black device. The other car did the same. A red-faced man stood up and boiled with anger. "Why the car? Why is it always the car?"

"In five minutes a number of hostiles are going to be coming to this same spot."

"You're saying they marked me?" The anger drained from the man's face. "I'll check." He dropped back inside, swore, popped his door open, and motioned to someone in the backseat. "From here, we walk."

Richard dropped back into his sedan.

Albert nodded toward the other car. "Are they hurt, or are we hurt? Don't we get out?"

"Nope." Richard put the sedan in gear, turned the wheels, and flowed into traffic.

Penny watched the pair out the rear window. "Aren't you going to give them a ride?"

"Do I look like a bus?" Despite the damage to the car, the mechanics seemed unaffected.

"No, but—"

Cliff touched her hand. "I think what he's saying is that the passenger may not be a passenger at all. They may be a spy."

Richard's face sobered. "The driver will know soon enough."

The traffic thickened. At the next corner, they took a left, caught a curve, and headed out of town. As the map adjusted back on course, it estimated their distance.

The numbers Albert watched vanished from the display. "Gone." He pointed. "It feels like the calm before the storm."

Richard slowed and stayed with the speed limit. A sign with the words "Shady Oak Lane" came into view. The car slowly pulled onto a gravel road. "Watch what you wish for."

About a mile down the tree-lined sides, the road broadened into a parking area. At least five black sedans and two limos were parked. Richard pulled in and stopped.

As Albert stepped from the car, the door closed behind him. "Come on! Spiffy spy cars and limos? Where's all the high-tech security?"

Richard clicked the lock on the electronic key fob. No lights flashed and no sound issued. He ran his hand over the crushed side of the car and whistled. "They're not going to like that." He turned toward Albert as he walked around the car. "You have been scanned and probed ever since we entered the gravel drive. Sensors under the road measured your weight, checked for additional armament, and even monitored your pulse. Had they found anything amiss, we would never have made it here."

Albert swallowed as they headed toward the house. "That's—comforting." He glanced down at his waist." They do know I want kids, right?"

Richard laughed. "They know more than that."

Albert froze in mid-step.

With a grin, Cliff pushed him to start him up again. "Just remember, we watch the watchers."

A grin returned to Albert's face. "That's right. We, U.S. of A., citizens, watch the watchers. We, the people, in order to form a more perfect union, we watch you!" He pointed up at a discreet camera placed under the porch to the house. "That's right, Jack. Got it?"

As he stepped to the front door and reached for the handle, the door opened of its own accord. Just inside, two armed men stood at attention. Albert held his head high as he took in both.

"We." He nodded and turned back to find another man waiting in uniform. "Got it?"

"Got it." The man's voice became deadly serious. "And my name's not Jack. Up against the wall, smart-ass. You're getting searched, and if you're lucky, we may check your body cavities."

Albert backed up quickly. "Richard!"

Penny and Cliff turned toward their driver with eyes wide open.

Two of the guards fought to hide their smiles as Richard burst out in a laugh. "Hold up there, Steve. You're scaring the kids."

A grin cracked Steve's face. "We've got to have a little fun."

Albert inhaled. "Fun?"

"It's not every day we have someone quote the Preamble to the Constitution."

"Right." Albert stepped behind Cliff and Penny. "I'll be quiet."

With a chuckle, Steve led them toward two large, closed doors all in white. The ornate carvings and designer handles implied this was more than a safe house. Then again, that was obvious by the security under the road.

As the two doors swung open, Cliff spotted his mom, dad, and uncle along with someone else. The man Cliff had met in Albert's house; the man in charge of Division A. Cliff's face fell; the excitement of seeing his parents changed into an emotionless mask.

"Cliff!" His mom hurried toward him as his dad and uncle stood up. She grabbed him, hugged him, switched to Penny, and then to Albert. "We had no clue what happened. They wouldn't tell us anything!"

Richard noticed Cliff's sudden change and stepped forward. "They were fine, Mrs. Fulton." Cliff's dad walked up. "And Mr. Fulton. We had them safe."

Joseph's face reddened. "What I want to know is why this happened to begin with."

The man Cliff recognized as the leader of Division A cleared his throat. "I'll answer that."

Everyone turned except Richard, who bowed politely and stepped back into the foyer.

"Please—" The man motioned toward the seats they had left. "—be seated." A friendly smile crossed his face, but Cliff did not believe it. They all headed to the table.

"Now then," the man spoke amiably, "let me introduce myself. I'm Karl Duncan. George Sealman asked me to read the codicil if he could not be present."

As he listened, Cliff noticed other things about the room. A set of windows were in the wall to his left. Through them, he could see a single paved driveway almost out of sight. Why paved when the road that led here was gravel?

Vegetation in large planters was positioned around the room. Several decorative dividers stood a little taller than his height, and two smaller doors, one behind Karl and one directly opposite existed in addition to the main entrance. He tuned back into Karl's speech.

"Since the occurrence of this unfortunate incident, Mr. Sealman cannot be located. Because of this, I will be the one to read Elaine's codicil. "He reached to his side and lifted a small briefcase to the table. As it opened, he removed a file and an electronic key fob, closed the briefcase, and placed it back on his right side.

Silence gripped the room. Jessie, Cliff's mom, fought back tears, and his father, Joseph, put his arm around her. "I'm sure he's fine. Communication is sporadic at best."

"Indeed," Karl agreed with a smile that seemed a little too reassuring. "I have no doubt he will be found. The question is only when."

Cliff raised his hand, wondered why, and lowered it.

"Yes, Cliff?"

"Why not wait? Why the hurry?" His eyes met Karl's, and he saw the steel behind the smile.

"Based upon Mr. Sealman's own recommendation, he felt it was imperative that it be addressed after the funeral."

"I see."

"Well then." Joseph ran out of patience. "If it's that important, let's get on with it. This day has been trying enough, and I for one would like to relax with my family."

Karl nodded and shifted his gaze from one adult to the other, expectant. No one volunteered. He cleared his throat again. "Perhaps, if one of you would present Elaine's codicil?"

Cliff's uncle narrowed his eyes. "You don't have it?"

A strange feeling of foreboding hit the room; Karl's face clouded as his voice became hard. "No, I was given to believe he gave it to one of you."

The wadded up paper came to Cliff's mind. No, it wasn't the size of a codicil, but did it have something to do with it? He had to find a safe place to take a look at the note.

With only a second's pause, Karl called, "Guard."

The white doors opened, and in walked Steve. Cliff caught sight of Richard chatting in the foyer though his eyes never strayed far from the white double doors.

"Sir."

"It's been a long day and will be a longer night. Please show these guests to their rooms."

"Wait a minute." Joseph stood up. "I thought this was only temporary. We were told we could go home once everyone was safe."

His uncle followed suit. "It is important that we leave."

"And you will, I assure you." Karl smiled. "Once we understand the nature of this situation, I'm sure our friends here—" He motioned toward Steve. "—will be glad to escort you back. In the meantime, you will be guests of this house and under their protection." Karl's eyes hit them all but lingered a second longer on Cliff's uncle; a thoughtful look crossed his face.

Cliff mumbled, "You mean prisoners."

Steve's eyes shifted toward him with no emotion at all.

Karl did not address the statement. "I believe the kitchen has lunch prepared. Feel free to enjoy. Dinner is at six this evening. We will talk later." Steve ushered them into the foyer, and the large white doors closed.

Chapter 4

A disturbed look crossed all their faces, and Richard's smile dropped. "Trouble in paradise?"

Cliff met his gaze. "They won't let us leave."

Richard waved it away. "Of course they won't let you leave. It's all part of the protocol. No worries. Just enjoy the time off and relax."

Jessie exhaled. "That's good to hear. After Karl found out we didn't have Elaine's—"

Richard's gaze swept to her. "There is plenty of time to discuss those things. Right now, you need to relax." His smile brightened, and he waved toward the kitchen. "The food is ready, and I know you must be hungry. Why don't we stop there first?"

Steve stepped forward. "Karl said to show them their rooms, first. Are you taking the responsibility?"

Richard laughed. "Next floor up? All in a row?"

The guard nodded.

"Got it." He grinned. "Come on, Steve, lighten up. These folks were at a funeral when the whole world blew up. Cut them some slack."

With reluctance, Steve nodded, but he, too, visibly relaxed. He turned toward the group. "I'm sorry if things seem a little tight around here. My condolences; no offense was meant."

Joseph inhaled. "None taken. It seems like yesterday when we found out she was murdered, and then we had trouble with the body, and—"

Cliff's uncle watched Joseph.

"Dad—" Cliff caught his eye. "—I don't think Steve wants to hear the whole story."

His father sighed. "I'm sorry." He shrugged it away. "We just never expected all this."

"Nor should you," Richard jumped in. "Please, the kitchen is this way."

He stepped toward the left and led them to a wide hall entrance. Closed doors were on both sides. The kitchen was at the end.

What they called the kitchen was really a formal dining area. It was equipped with an old-fashioned phonograph. Richard proceeded to it and selected an album. He glanced back at Cliff with a smile. "You should see the selection. Digital just isn't the same."

Cliff stepped beside him to note the titles neatly stacked. "I would have thought with all the toys you have, digital would be your preference."

"Ah, but you see, young Mr. Fulton, some things are better without modern enhancements. Records mirror the original waveform without compression loss. This makes it harder to filter out." He dropped his selection on the phonograph and moved the needle over. His fingers turned on the power. The music played. "You see, if we speak below the music level and stay close to the phonograph, we not only create a countermeasure for the listening devices in this room, but we can talk in peace." He smiled at Cliff. "Keep your head turned toward the curtains and blinds when you speak. The cameras are behind us."

Cliff nodded and followed his instructions. "So they have lip readers, too?"

"Most certainly. I dare say you are in one of the most sophisticated technological buildings around. Many are brought here to learn their secrets."

"So it is a prison?" Cliff frowned.

"I call it a *protected paradise*. Your mother said Karl wanted Elaine's codicil?"

Cliff nodded.

"Keep your voice low and reduce head movements. Your reaction can say a thousand words."

"Understood." Cliff fought not to nod. "George Sealman, my grandmother's attorney, has vanished. Karl expected us to have the codicil."

"You have met George Sealman."

Cliff's voice slowed. "How did you know?"

"I saw it in your eyes when your mother mentioned him. If Karl wants Elaine's codicil, he believes there is a tie-in to the briefcase. A second set of papers, perhaps? The last thing he wants is this information getting into the wrong hands."

Cliff remembered their conversation the night Gerhard was killed. "I thought you said it didn't matter without proof?"

"The right papers are proof, and she could have included other things."

"If I had such papers, do you think I would tell him?"

Richard chuckled. "If you did have them, the smart thing to do would be to bury them so deep that they never would see the light of day. Your only other choice would be to go so public it would not matter anymore. Either way, if third parties get wind, it could cost your life."

"I hadn't considered that."

"An old friend of yours, Lenord Scott, contacted me today. He explained what happened in the mausoleum."

"Then you know about the second casket?"

Richard's face lost all emotion. "I know."

"I want to know about that casket."

A sad smile crept onto Richard's face despite his instructions for Cliff to hide his expression. "Why?"

"I need to know I didn't kill him."

"Cliff—" He inhaled. "—sometimes it is better not to know."

"You think I killed him?"

"I am not saying that, and even if you did, you did not knowingly do it. You couldn't."

Cliff's eyes stared into nothing. "How do you know?" After what they did to his grandmother, could he kill?

"I'm not blind. I saw what you did to save Penny. You had no chance of winning against that trained killer, yet you took him on as if you did. That takes guts, stupidity, and luck. You would have sacrificed yourself to save her. Thank God I kept you from it."

"It had to be done."

"I can't get you back to the cemetery. If you take one step out of this house, they will know."

"Then find a reason to get me out."

"Hmm, but it would have to be a very good reason."

"Can you do it?"

"You do not have any idea what you are getting into, do you?" Cliff didn't answer.

"I thought not." Richard sighed. "I'll see what I can do. In the meantime, you better go eat." He turned and nodded toward the table. Food had been brought, and the others had taken their seats. Cliff strolled over to them.

Albert looked up and grinned. "It might be a prison, but the food's good."

As he sat down next to Penny, Cliff scooted up his chair.

She leaned near him and whispered, "I didn't know you had such a fascination with records. Maybe I should show you mine."

"That could be arranged." Cliff reached under the table and took her hand. The touch was reassuring. "Just as soon as we get away from this safe house. It's *only* a matter of time."

She looked at him and caught the change in his voice. "Yes, I think it is."

Chitchat drifted from what they had for dinner last week to the frustration of working with the funeral home, but none of it came back to the events of the day. Cliff's parents never brought up Elaine's codicil, nor did anyone mention George Sealman's disappearance. They did not have to; everyone understood Richard's hint in the foyer.

Cliff remembered some of the things he had read about audio surveillance. Whole walls, as well as anything solid, could be used as a listening device. Speakers that were not producing sound could as easily send it. Video could be used for lip reading. Analog phone lines could transmit signals even if they were on the hook. An air conditioning vent could send enough sound that a digital-signal-processor filter could translate it into voice. The best protection against all of it was not to face a camera when talking, make sure the blinds were closed with the curtains drawn, and use sound masking. That was what Richard had done while talking with Cliff. However, if everyone did that, it would look rather obvious.

Penny poked him. "You're doing it again—going off in your own dream world. Everyone else is finished."

She was right. He had not even touched his food. As a matter-of-fact, they rose from the table as Penny spoke. He pushed the chair back and stood up.

Jessie noticed. "Cliff, you really should eat. It will be a while before we sit down to dinner."

"Mom," Cliff assured. "I've got this."

"I know, but it's a mom's right to be concerned."

He grinned and looked around the table. Despite the crazy events, he wasn't hungry.

Albert stretched and stifled a yawn. "So what now? Do they have any fantastic video games or maybe a computer we can play with?"

"That's a good idea." Cliff nodded. "What do they have for entertainment?" He turned toward Richard, who had also not eaten.

The agent smiled. "Let's show you where you'll be staying. There's a game room on the same floor."

"Great!" Albert headed toward the hall.

"You're in a hurry." Joseph grinned. "I, for one, am feeling tired."

"It's the strain of what happened." Jessie took his arm. "I feel like a nap."

They reached the foyer, received a nod from security, and followed Richard up the stairs. Cliff noted that the guards had changed although Steve stood by the white doors as if waiting.

At the top of the stairs, Richard pointed out their rooms. "Adults on the left; kids on the right. The game room is directly ahead."

"Going there now." Albert affirmed as Cliff joined him. "Penny?"

"Be there in a moment." She stopped a yawn and looked surprised. "I want to see the room."

As they stepped into the game room, it was a little hard to take it all in. Familiar things were there, of course. A pool table, a manual hockey game, and a few other items stood out beside an entrance to an exercise and weight room. However, what caught their attention was the digital display of a curved screen, twelve feet wide by four feet tall, with two futuristic seats in front.

Albert crossed to it and ran his fingers over the controls. He glanced at Richard. "Can I?"

"Sure."

Albert spun around the arm of the chair and sat down. "Now what?"

"Touch the top control."

He flipped back the plastic cover, hit the button, and watched as the screen lit up. A long list of games scrolled. "Hey—" Albert's eyes opened wide. "—there are prototypes for games in here that haven't been released for beta."

"Who do you think authorizes the release of the games before the copyright?"

"No way." Albert shook his head. "You mean you guys monitor—"

"—the games you play." Richard nodded. "How do you think we catch so many hackers? The average person never hears about the hackers caught—unless it's beneficial. We use them."

It made sense; it made too much sense. Cliff eyed the interface nervously. "If they can do all that," he cautioned Albert. "Are you sure you want to touch that thing?"

"Oh, come on." Albert adjusted his grip. "It's just a game."

What Richard had told him of the surveillance in this building rolled back. How could he let Albert know the importance of this without giving himself away? He couldn't, at least at the moment, so he turned to something else. "I'm going to see what's holding up Penny."

"Yeah, right." Albert adjusted his pointer and selected a listing. "Have fun, lovebirds."

Richard turned toward Cliff with a grin. "Sounds like I better stay with Albert."

"I want to find out what's keeping her."

"Sure," Albert teased as Cliff walked back. "Fancy room, low lights, I get it."

Cliff shook his head though his cheeks did flush as he made it to her room. He knocked once, waited, and knocked again. No one responded.

He tried the knob, found it unlocked, and pushed. As the door swung back, he spotted her lying on her front across the bed; she was sound asleep. That was odd; she had never mentioned a nap. Although, as he thought back, she had yawned before entering.

He felt a little drained as well and a little hungry. Mom had been right; he should have eaten something, but he could wait. A consistent eating time was never his thing anyway.

On a curious thought, he shifted to his parent's room, found their door unlocked, and pushed it open. Both had fallen asleep on the bed, fully dressed, and lay on their backs. What made the situation unusual was that Mom had fallen over Dad—backwards.

He turned toward his uncle's room as if nothing were unusual. The situation was the same; his uncle was out and lay across the bed.

As he closed the door, he continued to the end of the hall. At the game room, he spotted Richard hovering over Albert. Albert had slumped forward, and Richard checked Albert's pulse.

Warning signs flashed in his mind, and he remembered Richard encouraging them all to eat the food. Was it a farce? Had he only pretended to get a favor from Steve? Although Gran, his grandmother Elaine, did work with Richard, it was Cliff she had turned to with the information about the briefcase, not the agent. Without waiting for Richard to see him, he backed up and started down the hall.

He had no idea what to do. Why trick his family into eating food that would knock them out? They already had them locked up.

At the bottom of the stairs, the two guards at the main door had slumped to the floor, Steve was nowhere to be seen, and the two white doors were wide open. No alarm blared. Shouldn't a safe house, especially one this well protected, indicate when things were amiss?

He stepped into the center of the foyer and heard three voices. The voices came from the dining area, and one of those was Karl.

The name of the man, if that were his real name, reminded Cliff of the electronic key fob he had seen in the room with the white doors. He glanced back and spotted it. It sat beside the folder on the table. Only now, the folder was open.

He stepped to the right, passed into the room, and went to where Karl had sat. The folder was marked with a security level Cliff did not recognize. On a quick glance, in it was a dossier on his family. Penny's, Albert's, and George's were there too.

The voices came closer; Karl's voice was loud and distinct.

Cliff grabbed up the electronic key fob, felt a sting, and almost dropped it. With dossier and key fob in hand, he slipped into the half-open door and crouched down out of view.

A gruff voice sounded in the room. "Prove it."

Karl strolled with no care in the world. Behind him were two men, both with guns. He glanced at the table but did not miss a beat as he shifted the chair back, reached down for the briefcase, and mouthed words silently that only Cliff could see. "Stay alive."

Chapter 5

Cliff almost choked. If Karl knew he was here, why didn't the two men with the guns?

Karl stood up and handed over the briefcase. "This is what you want. You'll find everything neat and tidy."

One of the men took the briefcase. "Thank you. You've been most hospitable. Too bad we cannot use you again; your termination has been arranged." The man motioned toward the foyer. Karl nodded as he led them away from the room.

The voices grew lower, the front door opened, and Cliff heard two spuds from a silencer. The front door closed.

The folder in Cliff's hands shook as the knowledge of what he had heard penetrated his soul. "Killers," Lenord had called them, and this time they wanted to kill his entire family.

He fought to focus on something else—anything that would give him back control. Everyone counted on him since they could not help themselves.

The shaking stopped, and his eyes narrowed. It had been silent now for a good five minutes. He peeked around the half-open door and saw the room was clear.

Stay alive; the mouthed words burned into his conscious mind. If there was one thing he had learned since Gran had been killed, that was at the top of the list. However, in order to do that, he had to set priorities: one, secure a safe place, two, move family and friends to it, and three, find transportation out of the safe house.

He checked out the windows first, stood up slowly, and noticed the small elevator behind him. Directions pointed up and down. He pressed up, the door silently slid back, and he stepped in.

No controls were present. As the doors closed, a red light kicked in. A panel at eye level opened, and a lens appeared. Cliff stared at it. The elevator did nothing else. He waved his hand in front of the lens, but nothing changed.

"It has to be a retinal scan. So what happens when it reads the wrong eye?"

The doors would not reopen. No emergency stop was visible. He had effectively stepped into a steel trap and locked himself inside.

What was he thinking? He shook his head and realized he wasn't. He explored an environment not his own. With no other choice, he looked into the lens.

The red light vanished, and he heard a hiss of air. As the fumes entered his nose, his head reeled. He hit the wall and smashed his left hand as he fought not to drop the key fob and folder. The elevator dropped and the hiss stopped.

As the air cleared, so did his head. He gulped air as the motion halted and doors slid open. Basement lights faded on. A row of black sedans stood in front.

His hand pulled out the key fob, and he studied the pictures. Most of them applied to the cars, but several did not. His eyes took in the elevator. Why design a key fob that bypassed security? The answer was clear: because sometimes agents didn't drive the cars.

It made sense. Richard had thrown him his key fob. If the key fob were equipped to be traced, or if an agent had to send in an asset without his presence, this would be a way. Yet, surely security was tighter than that? What if a key fob was lost and someone picked it up?

He hit unlock, and his expectations came true; to find out which car, he would have to try the doors. The second one yielded at his touch, and the driver's door opened. Now that he had secured transportation and a potentially safe place to hide, he could head back for the others.

Elevator. He exhaled at the thought and looked around for stairs. Apparently, Division A did not have to follow standard building codes. Either that or the door to the stairs was well hidden.

He stepped inside the elevator and gazed down at the key fob. The pictures made no sense, but then he changed his point of view to a five-year-old child. He clicked the appropriate button.

The doors closed. The elevator rose. It bypassed the first floor and arrived at the second. It was elementary, literally. Only an adult could over-think it.

As the elevator door opened, a bedroom came into view. It was smaller than those they had been given, and he was sure its simplicity belied its function, but there was no time to study it. As a temporary safe point, it was perfect.

He laid the folder down on a small dresser and put the key fob in his right pocket. The note in his pocket crossed his mind. Did he dare read it in this building? What if he were being watched? No, he would check it when he was far from here.

With only one other way out, he approached the single door, grasped the handle, and eased it open. It looked into the hallway next to Penny's sleeping quarters. The air in the hall was warmer than that of the room. If it weren't a matter of being closed off, it could mean this room was climate controlled which implied possible electronics.

He shifted out into the hall and pulled the door closed. Voices came from the game room.

"Where is the boy?" A man with a Japanese accent demanded. "Find him, now, and get into the security center. I want them to think twice before they push me again."

Cliff ducked into Penny's room, saw she was still on the bed, and slipped into her closet. His breath held as he counted the seconds. He knew how long it took to go from the game room to downstairs. When he decided they were gone, he gently pushed the closet door open. A voice called loudly, "The girl's here. Let's verify the others."

He fought the desire to pull the door closed. A person shifted on the carpet, a brief investigation took place in the room, and then the person walked out. Without further delay, Cliff opened the door and peered around the edge. No one was in the hall, but if they were searching door to door, he would have to be quick. He moved to the bed and whispered, "Penny!"

She did not stir.

"Penny, wake up!"

The mumble of her words was way too loud, and Cliff winced. He glanced nervously at the door. "Okay, we'll do this the hard way."

His arms went around her, and he heaved backwards. Despite the awkward angle and deadweight, he leveraged her to the edge of the bed. His hands adjusted their position, and he twisted her around. With a deep breath, he heaved her up on his shoulder.

His left arm stabilized the top part of her body. His right arm grabbed her legs. With careful steps, he avoided the walls and doorway as he moved out of the room and into the hall.

The other voices were silent, and his secure room stood only a few feet down. As he balanced her on his shoulder, he reached for the handle and twisted. It did not move.

Locked—the word rolled through his mind, and he started to panic. If it were locked, he would have to carry her to the first floor, enter the room off the foyer, and catch the elevator.

Voices came up the stairs as someone stirred in the game room. Options—he needed options. Key fob, car, and elevator: the three words entered his mind. With a grip on her legs, he reached into his right pocket, pulled out the key fob, and hit a button.

The door handle turned silently. Cliff pressed quickly in but could not turn to close the door. With his balance on one leg, he used his other to push the door closed.

Sweat trickled down his temples. He laid her gently on the bed, rotated to the door, and opened it to listen. Silence. He slipped into the hall.

With quiet steps, he moved toward his parent's room, saw the door open, and stepped inside. Neither was there. He proceeded to his uncle's room.

His uncle Matt still lay on the bed though someone had moved him closer to the side. He heaved, but despite his best effort, he could not get him high enough. Forced to bend lower, he slipped him onto his shoulder and rose. His legs trembled as he stood. The way was clear. The voices were quiet. The first few steps held. Sweat started down his face.

At three strides, a man with a Japanese accent called, "Did you find the boy?"

Cliff swallowed. He took another two steps.

The voice spoke again, deadly serious. "You—carrying the uncle. I asked you a question."

Cliff froze. He knew the voice behind him; it was the man on the phone in the church. If he answered, would the man know who he was? He deepened his voice. "No."

The man sighed. "Keep looking. We have to be out in ten minutes."

Cliff picked up the pace as voices filtered from the stairs. His heart thumped wildly as the distance stretched out before him. Ten feet, seven and a half, five feet—

Two heads poked above the floor. He could see them through the banister. In slow motion, they turned in his direction.

"Hey! You!" The men sprinted up the stairs. Cliff reached the door and fumbled for the key fob. The knob turned. As his assailants raced around the corner, Cliff did the only thing he could think of. "Forgive me, uncle." He thrust the body at the approaching men.

One went down. The other staggered. Cliff shoved against the door, skidded in, and slammed it. They struck the outside, but the door held firm.

"Time to go, beautiful." He picked up Penny, snatched up the file, and made his way in the elevator. When the elevator doors opened again, he rushed to the black sedan.

As the folder landed on the dash, he placed Penny in the front passenger's seat and secured her with a seatbelt. Under the steering wheel, he locked all doors and started the car.

It roared to life while he checked for various icons to press. A few matched the symbols on the key fob but more did not. Other than being able to hit the gas pedal and drive, he couldn't be sure of anything else.

The lines on the cement in front of the car made a path like a single-lane road. His foot hit the gas, and he followed it. When it came to the end of the line of sedans, the exit was obvious. Unfortunately, it was closed.

A light brightened as a door opened at the other end of the garage; someone had found the missing stairs. Cliff hit the gas.

The car raced forward. A warning dial flashed up on the windshield. The impending collision counted down in metrics. He scanned the steering wheel one more time, saw a symbol, and tried it. The door to the garage opened.

He shot through the rising garage door as it scraped the top of the car. Sparks flew and gunfire sounded. The bullets bounced off the rear window and trunk.

The car swerved to the left as it followed the paved road. It looped around the side of the building and ended at the gravel parking lot.

Most of the cars were gone. Richard's could not be seen. A second vehicle, one he had not seen before, stood nearer the front of the building. The back of the vehicle was open, and two men carried out his uncle. At least he had not been killed like Mr. Karl Duncan.

His vehicle raced up the gravel drive; rocks bounced and struck beneath it. White smoke plumed into the air as it created a smokescreen behind him.

Others raced to their vehicles; he caught glimpses through the haze. One by one, they came to life, turned up the road, and followed.

When the "Shady Oak Lane" sign appeared, he slowed, gave a signal, and felt like an idiot; he had just told them which way he was going. His wheels cut onto the highway, and he floored it.

Cliff studied the symbols on the steering wheel. The approximate areas Richard had pressed came to mind. His fingers moved over the regions and tapped the ones most promising.

The views flickered to life. A radar device and a number of tiny blips appeared. He counted them off and exhaled. There were many, and they accelerated fast.

Think, Cliff, think. On a straightaway, he was outmatched, not because of the car, but because he had no clue how to use it. It was all a matter of understanding, like the way he had figured out how to use the key fob. Only, this was not elementary; the creators did not intend everyone to understand what the higher functions meant.

As well as he could, he studied them and kept a watch on the road. Penny was out, and he had no idea when she would wake up. He glanced toward the folder on the dash. An alert flashed on the screen. Another car approached from the front and barreled straight for him. Did all cars show up as blips, or only those that chased him? How could he tell?

As he rose over the next hill, the one in front came into view. With its crushed-in driver's side, it could only be one person.

Another warning flashed on the windshield and showed a pending collision with a countdown in metrics. A second screen appeared; something had locked on him, and it came in fast.

Chapter 6

Cliff floored the accelerator and watched as a third blip flashed into existence. It glowed bright red and quickly separated from the others. A countdown on the screen showed six seconds with intercept predicted at five miles. Only a missile could move that fast.

Seconds stretched out. The car rose and fell as it hurtled over a small rise and headed toward the next. Warnings flashed; the distance closed. Based on screen graphs, he could not outrun it.

His eyes sped over the controls and looked for some sort of logic. A curve with an arrow pointing in, a curve with an arrow pointing out, a half circle, a whole circle, and a bottle stared back. Bottle? Maybe nitrous oxide? What did he have to lose?

The button pressed down. His body slammed back into the seat as the car surged forward. The missile slowed but still gained. Schematics flashed onto the screen.

Three seconds. Vulnerability readouts pointed to locations around the missile's body and suggested counter-measures. He glanced at the controls. Where were the counter-measures?

Two seconds. The car rose as he hit the next rise and dropped down the steeper side. The straight road gave the missile an unhindered course, but the rise forced a search.

The display showed motion sensors along with a UV detector; its path wavered up and down as it searched for its prey. He gained one second.

A message flashed across the bottom of the screen, "Automatic counter-measure deployed." The brakes initiated of their own accord. The steering wheel spun. The backseat side windows rolled down, and the wheels squealed as the car slid sideways. Black smoke billowed on both sides of the car. The warning screen showed one and half seconds.

A five-foot tube with fins and a cone blew through the two open backseat windows and shot out into the open air. The warning countdown reset to thirty seconds as the missile started a tight circle. The wheel spun a second time, and the car raced down the road.

Cliff's eyes opened wide; he no longer had control of the car. The counter-measure made sense although it took a computer to time it right. As he topped the crest of the next rise, a missile launched from Richard's car. It headed straight toward him, curved away at the last moment, and collided with the other in the air.

The explosion shook both cars. Cliff grabbed the wheel, but control had not released. His driving instructor's voice boomed in his head, "Pump the brakes. Back off the speed." The car skidded left and right. It braked and slowed to the side of the road.

He breathed despite the fact more blips were on their way. Richard's car did not slow. A green indicator flashed onto the windshield.

What did that mean? Cliff scanned the controls and spotted a tiny speaker with three small curves in front of it. He tapped the icon, the control of the counter-measure released, and Richard's voice boomed. "Go, I will deal with these. Once you get to the city, touch the symbol with the eye and use the arrow keys to enter seven-three-five. I will find you."

The agent's car rocketed toward the other blips. It was suicide; he could not tackle them all on his own. Cliff did not know enough to help nor did he completely trust him. In this shady world where friend could be foe, anyone could have an agenda.

"Go," the agent's voice boomed.

Cliff hit the accelerator, and the car took off. The blips on the screen played out in slow motion. Red blips left Richard's car. Red blips left the others. Flashes of light lit the sky behind him over a rise that hid the details. One by one, blips vanished off the screen, and as Richard's meshed with the others, he lost sight of him entirely.

Was Richard dead? A firefight with car to air missiles? No one would believe this!

All the blips vanished. Either he was out of range or no one was left. How in the world could anyone clean up a mess like that? A shiver went down his spine as he glanced at Penny. She was still out. The intercept screens vanished from the windshield leaving only two: an empty monitoring screen that showed his speed, and a view of what was behind.

The city limit sign appeared, and traffic increased. He cut his speed to normal. This was not that far off one of his pizza routes. He followed the signs toward the inner city and passed by the spot where Richard had slammed into the black car. The car was gone. Other than scratches on the pole and black tire marks, no other evidence existed. A block down he turned, remembered a cross street that intersected the road he wanted, and headed in that direction.

It was quiet; no blips appeared on the screen, and Penny slept. He kept to the speed limit, found the road back to the cemetery, and drummed his fingers on the steering wheel. After the adrenaline boost of the last two hours, it almost put him asleep.

He woke to a horn blare and cut the wheel back to his own lane. What was wrong with him?

The elevator; it had to be the sleeping gas. While he had shaken off the initial effects with adrenaline, his system still contained it.

The road to the church appeared on his left. Deep ruts and flattened grass showed where others had parked. Further up the road, wisps of ash still swirled in the air.

The fire had died out. Only a portion of the church continued to stand. The area at the back had blackened outside walls.

Penny stirred but did not wake. He pulled near the church behind some trees, stopped the car, and touched her face. "Penny?" No answer. Whatever they had used, it must have been bad.

He turned back to the controls on the car. Richard had said to touch the symbol with the eye and use the arrow keys to enter seven-three-five. The agent had also disappeared when everyone fell asleep. Of course, he may have had to escape himself, but could Cliff really trust him?

Cliff tapped the eye. A display flashed up to allow him to enter the numbers. His grandmother had trusted Richard only to a point. She understood the allegiance he held to Division A. Instead of entering the numbers, he tapped the eye again and watched the screen vanish. Too many people knew exactly where he was, and every time they did, others turned up. He would have to do this on his own.

The key fob dropped into his pocket as he swung the door open. The sun plunged closer to the horizon. In an hour or so, it would be dark.

A gentle breeze rustled the trees as a bird whistled through the smell of ash and soot. The car door closed and locked; he would rather someone not carry off the unconscious Penny.

Past the trees, he made his way quietly to the backend of the church. The fire had torn through it. The area of the chapel had been consumed. A look through the debris showed nothing of his grandmother's casket. He hoped they had brought her out before it was too late.

Not that it mattered; to save the living from the fire was most important. Yet, he felt the indignity. They had destroyed her funeral as a last insult.

Each step brought up ash and soot. Though the fire did not

burn, he could feel the warmth all around him. He lifted an angled two by four and pushed it aside. The ash turned his hands black; the board felt warm to the touch.

A breeze rushed through and forced him to cover his mouth until swirling black ash settled. It wasn't until he stepped into a small hall that he realized why this part of the church stood. A walk-in, fireproof safe made of cinder blocks sat at the back. It should have been secure despite the fire, but the door stood ajar.

Quietly, he crept up to it. Someone moved around inside and dropped items on the floor. A drill kicked in and screeched against metal. Holes had been drilled through the outside lock.

He backed up carefully, avoided pieces of the charred wood, and stepped onto the green grass. Curiosity teased him, but he could wait. Other places could be searched first for the answers.

The path to his families' mausoleum appeared devoid of other people. With a little luck, no one else would be around. Then again, why was someone robbing the church?

Why, indeed? The funeral, the casket, and the explosion all played back through his mind. The footprints on the grass would have dried, but maybe a depression had been made.

At the area in front of the mausoleum, he looked over the grass with what sunlight still shown. Nothing disclosed; the blades of grass had stood back up, and the water was gone. He turned to the closed door and found crime scene tape over the outside. The other would be same.

He followed a path to the left. The trees became thicker. Shadows created dark corners, but the burial plots were fewer. The mausoleums stood further apart.

The yellow and black strips were hard to miss. Had Lenord let him go earlier, it would only have taken a minute to reach.

One minute. It would have been so easy for someone to place him in his casket, and the other man in this one. Cliff reached up to break the tape but paused. To interfere with a crime scene was a criminal offense, and despite what he had done so far, he had not crossed that line. With a deep breath, he reached up and carefully undid the ends; maybe he could secure it back.

The door swung open but not easily; it had been damaged by the explosion. No body parts were present, but blood splatters had dried around the walls.

Cliff gagged, not so much from the smell, but from the thought of what had happened. What if the man had been given the same choice and Cliff had pushed his first? Why give Cliff the option at all? If he was that much of a nuisance, why not get rid of him and be done?

The wood of the casket had been blown to bits; they didn't intend this man to live. The explosion for Cliff had been set for the hinges only.

A second clue, a shredded piece of Levi material, caught his eye. The man had not been wearing a suit. He may not have been there to attend a funeral.

A piece of leather had stayed intact and had not been picked up by the investigator. When overturned, he noted the design and part of the stitch. It reminded him of cowboy boots.

A card stuck sideways in a crack. With the dim light from inside the mausoleum, it would not have been obvious unless looked directly at it. As he retrieved it, he flipped it over and read an address with a suite number. The name was Michael Bishop. Could this be the name of the man that was murdered? He slipped the card in his pocket. The door creaked and moved outward. With no place else to go, Cliff slipped into a bottom slot and hid in the shadows.

As he held his breath, shadowy legs entered. Between each motion, they paused as they searched the room. The shadowy figure walked to the far wall, reached down, and picked up a small metallic object. A moment later, they slipped out.

Breathe—the stench resumed along with a deep, musky smell. Everywhere he moved in the slot, the dust stirred in swirls.

With a covered nose, he let the dust settle, grabbed hold of the side, and slid slowly out. If he didn't find a change of clothes soon, they would definitely smell him, too.

He climbed to his feet, noted the wall the person had approached, and found the spot where the item had been picked up. A roundish oval with a faint eagle design showed in the dust. It could be a badge, but whose? How did the FBI miss all these clues?

Levi's, boots, and badge: it all added up to an official of some type. Either someone had stumbled into the plan of the killer, or the killer had no more use for them.

No other clues revealed themselves so he headed to the door. Albert said it didn't matter; Penny claimed it was not his fault. However, it did not explain the why, and that was something Cliff determined to know.

The door swung out slowly as he watched for others. The crime scene tape was gone. A shoe impression pointed back toward the church; it had not been there before.

With a cautious gait he followed, listened for footsteps, and stepped lightly on the stones. As the path cut back into the middle of the cemetery, he spotted his family mausoleum.

The tape had been removed; someone had searched both. The sun waned closer to the horizon and cast dark, long shadows.

"Cliff."

The whispery, low voice was almost out of hearing. Cliff turned his head to follow the sound. Someone stood in the darkness.

"Cliff." The man stifled a cough. He leaned against the outside mausoleum wall.

"George?" Cliff glanced toward the door of the mausoleum, made sure his voice was low, and approached cautiously. "George Sealman?"

The man nodded and waved him further into the shadows. With the bruises and cuts on his face, the lawyer did not look good.

"George, Division A has looked all over for you!"

George motioned for him to keep it down, leaned away

from the wall, and planted his body directly in front of Cliff. This effectively hid anything behind him as he controlled a cough. "Do you still have the note I gave you?"

Cliff reached into his pocket and pulled out the note. "Yes, but—"

"Give it to me."

With a curious glance, Cliff extended the note toward him. "I never had a chance to read it."

George pretended to take it and added a second. "Good, it is better that you didn't."

"I don't understand."

"Cliff, I have tried to fulfill all of Elaine's wishes, but this one should be avoided."

"Gran had another message for me?"

George nodded and never took his eyes from Cliff.

"Then why would you hide it?"

The lawyer's eyes narrowed. "For your own safety and mine."

A branch snapped behind George. The man tightened his fist as if expecting something to happen, but nothing did. As the fist gradually relaxed, the lawyer exhaled.

"Division A asked about the codicil. They thought that one of my family members had it."

The fist tightened again. "Elaine's codicil was in the church when it burned; I could find no way to save it." It released once again. "I am sorry, Cliff."

"And my grandmother's body? Did they get it out before the fire?"

This time the fist did not tighten. "Yes, the casket is fine. They placed it into storage until the police clear up the crime scene."

"Thank you." Cliff nodded. "I know this ordeal has been stressful. It is nice to know the details have been handled."

"They have—" The lawyer's fist tightened again. "—right down to the smallest detail. You should go home. Let the professionals take care of it now." The fist relaxed. "It will be safer."

"I see," Cliff nodded. "Thank you, George."

George nodded. "Perhaps one day we will meet again."

Finality showed in George's eyes. Someone hid behind him, and after this conversation, they planned to kill him.

So why let them have this conversation? They wanted to convince Cliff to stay out of the way, and they were using the only person available. George had given more than enough clues, but the whole thing didn't make sense.

George turned to go.

"Wait," Cliff stepped forward.

George stopped and held perfectly still. His eyes watched someone else, but Cliff could not see who. "Yes, Cliff?"

"I found something I think you should see."

The moment was timeless. In less than a second, the person watching George had to decide to allow this or not. Cliff's eyes searched for a weapon. A branch lay beneath the trees, but it was not large enough. If he could get George out of the expected and keep the watcher off guard, they might be able to escape.

"Cliff—" George cleared his throat. "—perhaps this is not the best time."

"Oh, but you must." He stepped closer to George and slipped around him, his back to the person he could not see. It was risky but the only chance George had. "I insist. You are the only person I can trust."

Their eyes met, and George nodded. The tightened fist relaxed. "Very well, lead the way."

"After you." Cliff motioned to the front of the mausoleum. On his first step, he heard a branch snap behind him, and then whoever it was left.

As they stopped in front, George turned toward him. "You've taken quite a risk. They are still deciding what will be your fate."

"I had to save you."

"For the moment, I am safe. In their eyes, your actions have increased the value of my life."

"Are you sure Gran's codicil was destroyed in the fire?"

George shook his head. "I am sorry Cliff. Nothing could be done."

So they still listened? How? Did he wear a wire, or were they within hearing distance? One or the other had to be the case for George used head signals to indicate the truth.

"George, who are they?

Chapter 7

George nodded toward Cliff's hand with the note. "I wish I could help you, Cliff. I am as much in the dark as you. Whoever they are, they prefer not to include you as a casualty, but they will not let you get in the way."

The words, push me again, came to mind. Three individuals were involved in the cancer plot against the United States of America: Gerhard von Richter, Claretta Badoglio, and Fushimi Taruhito. Gerhard had died, killed by his own son, Claretta was never located, and he suspected Fushimi was the caller on the phone. If Claretta and Fushimi knew he had exposed their plot, why didn't they want him killed?

"Cliff?"

If these people were reluctant to kill him, maybe they would let go of information if he offered some of his own. He shook his head. "I'm sorry. I'm trying to get my head around this. So why were my parents kidnapped?"

George's eyebrows rose. "When?"

"Before I arrived here. Somebody drugged the food at the safe house. I was the only one not drugged." Cliff purposefully did not mention Richard.

"I see." George tapped his lips and cautioned Cliff.

Twilight slipped across the sky as the last rays of sunlight faded away. A cool wind blew, and twigs cracked out of sight.

"What if there are more players in the game," Cliff thought out loud. "What if one group was after the other?" A branch snapped distinctly to the right hidden in the darkness.

"Cliff—" George no longer gave any facial response. "—what was it you have to show me?"

"It is this way," he motioned to the path.

Without the sun, the shadows along the path were black. The tombstones stood out as dark against a slightly lighter sky.

People were about; Cliff could feel it though how many he could not tell. As they worked their way down the obscure path, the movement continued behind them.

The path ended at the church. He led George around several trees and hedges as he chose the most indirect route. If he could confuse those that followed, he might save George yet.

The car came within reach though he could not see it. He weaved George through a series of turns and twists and then plowed through the foliage. When they turned to the right, they stopped beside the car.

With a finger to his lips, he turned to face George and then hit the key fob. As he did, he reached for the back door and opened it.

George gave a single nod and sat down in the back then pulled the door closed. Cliff went around to the driver's side and climbed in. Warning screens flashed upon the windshield as the surveillance mechanism was effectively blocked. "Now we can speak."

With a nod, George gazed around. "This is the car you arrived in?"

Cliff nodded. "It was one of the vehicles at the safe house."

Penny fluttered her eyes. "Where am I?"

"In a car outside the church that burned."

"But how?" She squeezed her eyelids tightly shut and rubbed her eyes. "The last I remember—"

"They drugged everyone. You were the only one I could get out."

"Cliff—" George leaned forward. "—perhaps it would be

better if we left. This is no place to hide with the others still out there.”

“If we leave, we will only draw attention. Right now, they don’t know where we are.”

Penny turned to look at George. “I saw you at the funeral.”

“Yes. I am George Sealman, Elaine’s lawyer.”

“He was being tracked,” Cliff threw in. “They were going to kill him. Why, George?”

The lawyer paused. “The more I tell you, the more chance they will not let you live. It would be better for you to do exactly what I said: go home and forget about it.”

Cliff shook his head. “I can’t. Someone kidnapped my parents, my uncle, and my friend.”

A sigh escaped George’s lips as he nodded slowly. “I understand. The day before the funeral the FBI approached me. They were curious as to the contents of a certain codicil and requested I allow them to see it.”

“My grandmother’s?”

The lawyer nodded. “I refused, of course. Without a court order, I would never do such a thing. Your grandmother’s instructions were very clear; they listed when and where it should be read. It also specified by whom.”

“That doesn’t explain what happened today.”

The lawyer took a deep breath. “Last night someone broke into my office. They made it look like an ordinary theft, but the only files they went through were Elaine’s. I did not call the police, nor did I let anyone else know.”

“They stole the codicil?”

George shook his head. “The codicil was kept securely at the church—sealed in an airtight container. My instructions were to meet with your parents first and explain Elaine’s requests. I was then to meet with you; she said you would know how to retrieve it. No one knew that the codicil was here except for Elaine and me. To the best of my knowledge, I am the only other person who has seen it."

"Someone knew." Cliff glanced in the direction of the church though he could not see through the trees. "When I first got here, somebody had breached the lock on the walk-in safe."

Penny threw him a glance. "I may still be druggy, but even I can see you can't possibly know they were after your grandmother's codicil."

"She's right." George gave a nod. "As I said, only two people knew it was there."

"Think about. A fire the very day of the funeral? I'm warned and placed in a casket? My friends and family are seized?" Cliff shook his head. "No, someone knew. Someone wants it."

The conversation dropped. The silence was loud and clear.

"I have to check that walk-in safe."

George's voice strained. "No, Cliff. Nothing good can come of you going to the safe right now. Give it a day or two, maybe even a week, but now is not the time. If you walk in there, you are asking for trouble."

"If I don't go now, we may lose the codicil."

"It is better than losing your life."

Cliff thought on the words but refused to believe them. "Which box is it?"

"Nine-Eighty-One."

The number made him remember. Gran's key had been 0394-981. Her slot in the mausoleum was the same. Coincidence? He thought not. "How do I get it out?"

"The code to open the lock is zero-three-nine-four."

This was definitely no coincidence.

"Okay, I'll be right back."

"No." George reached for the door handle. "If you are going, I am going too."

Cliff's voice stayed firm. "You can't. The moment you open the car door, you run the chance of the surveillance device connecting again. Right now, you have vanished."

"But I can." Penny turned toward him. "You will need backup." She shook her head and blinked several times. "Just give me a minute."

"Until you are less groggy, I can't have you there either. It is risky enough with only me."

"But you can't go in alone!"

Cliff grinned. "If anyone's there, I'll leave and come straight back. I'm not about to take unnecessary risks."

"Says the man who's going in without backup."

"Says the man going in under the cover of darkness."

"What are you going to use as a light? Stardust?"

He held up his phone. "This, of course." The memory of how they had traced him with his cellphone came rolling back. His eyes studied the cellphone. That had been Gerhard's doing, not Fushimi or the FBI. Not even Division A had tagged his phone—that he knew of.

His fingers touched the file he had taken from Division A. The brief glance had told him they knew almost everything which included his cellphone numbers. "Penny, check the glove box and see if something is in it."

She looked around for a button to open it, but found none. "How?"

The symbols on the steering wheel were no help. What he needed was an instruction manual. Richard's directions for the locator had been very specific: press the button with the eye and enter the code seven-three-five. "Hmm, I guess I'll have to wing it." He pulled his cellphone out and laid it on the dash. "I can't take the chance that they are following my cellphone."

"They could be following anyone's cell." Penny pulled hers out. "I mean, look at the technology in this car alone. However, mine is the least likely."

"I doubt that, young lady." George put his hand on the passenger's seat. "They are after anyone who is connected with the Fultons. Anyone at all."

"George, let me borrow your cellphone."

The lawyer turned to Cliff.

"Think about it. They want you dead, not me; if the phone is the bugging device, I will help lead them away. If it is not, no harm, no foul. On top of that, you both will be safe in the car."

"But you will not be safe."

"I suspect it is a listening device, not a tracker. Otherwise, they would have found us."

George considered. "It is logical, but I don't like it. They were going to kill me, Cliff, not rough me up."

Penny shook her head. "I don't like this."

"Either we get the codicil or we don't. Without that codicil, we'll never know why it is so important. I've got to go. I will do it with or without a light." He opened the door.

"Here." George handed the cellphone to him. "Good luck."

"Is there a password?"

"A pattern. Make an S on the screen."

As his finger moved over the screen, it shifted to reveal the main page. He searched for a flashlight app, found it, and turned it on then off. It would only be used as a last resort. "Thanks."

He moved the phone outside the car door, but he saw no change in the surveillance blocking indicator. It had to be somewhere else on George.

As the car door closed, he hit the lock button on the key fob, and then turned to make his way through the trees. The cool breeze chilled, and the tops of the trees rustled. He ducked a few branches. The way through of the foliage to the edge of the church lawn was fast. Despite the darkness, he saw no one in the area.

He stayed low, kept to the edge of the trees, and worked his way closer to the church. Stars came out one by one though the city haze hid the weakest.

When he could go no further, he cut across the lawn to the church and slipped into the shadows of the standing back section. To see here was difficult, but rather than turn on his light, he looked more closely at the surroundings. The burnt wood appeared as a blacker shade than the darkness around it.

The trail he had walked earlier that day was familiar. The black ash stirred as he moved further in. It made the details harder to see.

He reached the edge, stepped around the corner, and reentered the short cinder block hall. He could not tell if the door stood open or closed. His hand had just touched the phone when boards stirred behind him.

He froze. Was it the wind or a burnt board falling? The movement became louder, and it shifted in his direction. His body pressed against the wall, looked back, and waited.

Something stopped at the corner. Somebody fumbled in the dark. "Cliff?"

"Penny?" he whispered back. "I told you not to come!"

"Since when do I have to take orders?"

He exhaled. "This is dangerous, and you are not awake yet."

"Speak for yourself," she threw back. "I'm not letting you go in there alone."

The air felt cold as he inhaled. Without another word, he guided her through.

They stood in the cinder block hall and gazed into the darkness of what should be the door. With a step forward, he reached out and tested it with his right hand. The big metal door stood slightly ajar, but not fully open. The safe door pulled back.

Despite the heat that the fire had generated, the door moved soundlessly. When it swung out about two feet, he slipped in with Penny and closed it behind them. The phone light turned on.

The room glowed to life. Metal storage units spread out on three walls like a bank's safety deposit box room. In the midst of this, boxes had been drilled out from the front to the back. The drillers had stopped in the two-hundreds and spot hit the rest.

"General theft or covering up a crime?" Penny gazed down at the floor. Box contents were scattered around a black satchel; someone had left in a hurry.

Cliff remembered the numbers he had seen on the slots of the mausoleum. His grandmother's box sat untouched, but the two around it, nine-eight-zero and nine-eight-two, had been opened. "It looks like they ran out of time." He moved toward his grandmother's and studied the locking mechanism. A slight wind entered the walk-in safe.

The locking mechanism used a numerical input. A type of iris moved over four individual columns. Where the iris stopped, up and down keys were used to adjust the number.

Cliff shifted it to the first column. A zero showed up. On each of the other columns, he adjusted the number up or down. As the last number appeared, the door moved out with a click.

The box contained a sealed bag. He slid it out and looked for an opening, but found none.

"That must be it." Penny reached over and touched it.

"What better way to know if the bag had been tampered with than to hermetically seal it?" He turned it over and spotted the seam. "Gran went to a lot of trouble to lock this away."

A gust of wind blew into the safe and stirred the debris on the floor. Cliff turned the light toward the door. A person stood there all in black. In his hand lay a gun with a silencer.

"I'll take that." He motioned to the bag in Cliff's hand.

Cliff focused on the man's eyes. "It doesn't belong to you."

The man laughed. "Mr. Fulton, you either give me the bag, or I will kill you, orders or not."

"Orders?" Cliff noticed other details on the man. He wore a heavy vest with many pockets and a black belt with packs around his waist.

"Yes, orders. Somebody thinks you are more useful alive." He extended one hand. "The bag, please, or I'll start with her." The silencer pointed toward Penny.

"No." Cliff stepped in front of Penny. "Leave her out of it."

"Then give me the—"

Chapter 8

The man fell forward. George stood behind him with a two-by-four.

"George! I mean, thanks. I mean, George, what are you doing?"

"You don't think that when a young lady runs off after her young man that an old codger like me would stay, do you?"

"But that was the only place you were safe."

"And I will be again, but first things first. That package is not your grandmother's codicil."

Cliff looked skeptical.

"Her instructions were very explicit. While that bag is hers, her codicil was not hidden in it."

Cliff turned back to the wall unit and reached inside. The floor was smooth. Metal existed on all four sides. As he tapped each one, they all sounded the same. The image of where he had found the briefcase flashed into his mind. Gran had hid it at the back of the locker; she had been careful to put it out of sight. Not only that, but when she had hid the letter at the bank, it had been in a false bottom.

He reached his arm further in and touched the back of the unit. It felt cold and reflected the light like the other sides. He tapped it, and the sound echoed. How did he get it out?

No latches or protrusions showed. It had been pushed in, all the way to the back, and fit exactly. He stared at the two units around it, nine-eight-zero and nine-eight-two. Those two numbers were part of the sequence on his grandfather's and uncle's slots in the mausoleum.

Neither unit had been cleaned out; they had only been opened. In his grandfather's unit, a group of papers were held together by a special wrap along with a small box and a small leather bag that jingled. His uncle's stood more barren with only a small bag; something was in it, but he could not tell what.

Cliff considered the false back on his grandmother's unit. Rather than investigate the items of his uncle and grandfather, he reached a hand further into his uncle's unit. His fingers felt a depression at the back on the left wall. He pushed it and nothing happened. He did the same for his grandfather's unit and found a depression on the right wall. A push did nothing.

A memory of his grandmother rolled back. At the age of seven, she had brought out a puzzle box. She held it up and pressed somewhere on it. The pieces loosened in a given pattern, but before he could touch it, she slid them back into place.

Without instruction, she handed the box to him. When he could not find the place, she took it back and patiently repeated the process. He found it on the third try.

With thoughtful brow, he stepped forward, put his right arm in his uncle's unit, his left arm in his grandfather's, found the depressions, and pushed. The back of his grandmother's unit issued a soft click. The false back slid forward until the lip extended about a half-inch from the unit front.

It smoothly pulled out. A spring and rod had pushed it forward; the depressions had released the spring. On the hidden side of the false back clung a sealed vinyl envelope.

"That is your grandmother's codicil." George nodded.

"When was it placed?"

The lawyer raised an eyebrow. "Does it matter? The point is, she intended for you to find it and knew you could."

"You have avoided the question."

"I have."

Cliff's brow wrinkled as he looked down at the vinyl envelope. "In other words, she intends me to know, just not now."

"Precisely."

Penny pointed at the open door. A single light floated in the darkness and moved closer.

"Time to go." Cliff reinserted the false back, closed his grandmother's unit, and adjusted the iris to make sure the numbers were scrambled.

Penny lifted the satchel and unzipped it. "Other things are in here, but we can use this."

With a glance at the door, Cliff dropped his relative's items into the open satchel. She zipped it up and swung it over her shoulder. More lights appeared from various directions. With his free hand, Cliff picked up the man's gun.

George turned toward the exit. "Hurry." A group of lights swung toward them.

Cliff shined the light over the ash and allowed them to move more quickly. As they reached the outer church wall, he turned it off.

"Run to the car. It's a straight shot and our only hope."

"He's right." George pushed both Cliff and Penny forward. "Go, I'll be right behind." A shot bounced off the cinder block wall. "Go!"

Penny and Cliff ran, barely able to spot the trees against the skyline. Either they reached the car or they would be caught.

A second shot hit the trees followed by a third. If it was the same people who were deciding whether to kill him or not, a decision must have been made.

The trees in front were less than fifty feet. The lights had swollen to more than twenty, but the coordination was off. One group had reached the church safe area. Two others had fanned out systematically as they checked the forest and the yard between. If whoever held the lights searched, who did the shooting?

A bullet ricocheted; a snapped branch rustled its leaves. Penny and Cliff passed into the trees, worked their way through the foliage, and came to the car.

Where was George? Cliff hit the key fob. "Get in. I'll be right back."

Penny dashed to the passenger's side. "What about you?"

"I need to check on George."

She tossed the satchel into the car. "Lock it. We can both check on George."

"Penny!"

She folded her arms. "You want to stay and discuss it?"

He hit the key fob button, and the doors locked. "Come on."

As they neared the edge of the churchyard, they could make out two bodies. One lay on the ground and the other stood over it with a gun. Cliff raised his weapon.

Penny panicked. "Cliff, what are you doing?"

"I'm trying to save George's life."

"With a gun? Are you crazy? Do you even know how to shoot?"

He lowered it and glowered. "Does it matter? That person is going to kill him."

"And if they don't, you may, and if you do shoot the right one, you will never be able to live with yourself." She put her hand on the barrel and pushed it to the ground. "You saved me more than once. It is my turn to help you." She ran toward the figure in the darkness.

"Penny! No!"

Cliff threw down the gun and bolted after her. The shadow turned but not quickly enough. Penny rammed into the shadow and knocked it off its feet. Both tumbled to the ground.

Cliff leaped over George and landed near the person Penny had knocked down. He pinned the gun by grabbing their wrist and sword-handed the person's throat. The individual gasped as he dropped an elbow to the solar plexus; they went silent as he hit the temple. Gerhard's thugs had taught him a few things about fighting.

"Penny, get up." As he rolled off the still form under him, he stopped at Penny's side. "Up! There's no time!" He felt for a pulse and found one, but when he lifted her head, he encountered a warm liquid. Gently, he laid her down and went to George. The searchers with lights came closer. George lay unconscious, too.

Cliff hit the ground in frustration. He had to get a hold of himself. If she had only stayed in the car—he stopped. If she had stayed in the car, he might have committed murder.

His head hurt; the relief and frustration collided. He could not carry two unconscious people. What was he to do? He went back to the person Penny had knocked down and searched for something he could use. The person wore a mask, a heavy vest with many pockets, and a black belt. In the dark, he found a holster and ammo pack.

A group of five lights turned in his direction. George and Penny needed medical help, and only one option stood open. Cliff made his way toward the lights.

Chapter 9

A hand came from behind and covered his mouth. The person whispered, "Damn it, Cliff, next time I give you a tracking code, enter the bloody code!"

Cliff relaxed; the hand dropped away. "Richard?"

"No thanks to you." He turned Cliff around and stared him in the eye. "I take it all back. You are not like your grandmother; you are worse. Do you know how long it took me to find you? That car is still in stealth mode."

Cliff stifled a chuckle as relief flooded through him. "I'm sorry. With what went down at the safe house and then the missile—"

"You thought I tried to kill you." Richard nodded. "I got that, and I don't blame you, but there was no other way. Had I not left the house when I did, I would never have been able to help. The missile made it look like you were destroyed."

Cliff turned and pointed at the searchers. They were almost on them. "You've got to help me. Penny and George are knocked out."

"George Sealman?" Richard bent down and checked the old man. "He's fine—clipped by a bullet, but nothing serious." He moved to Penny and frowned. "She hit her head and could have a concussion. Both need to be looked at."

"You are not listening to me!" Cliff pointed again. "The searchers are almost here!"

Richard tapped something in his ear. "I've got this area covered, but we do need a medic. Check the next section over."

The lights moved to the right and skipped them entirely.

Cliff's shoulders relaxed. "Division A?"

Richard nodded as a single light headed toward them. "When I determined you were here, I assembled a team and had the area checked. Too many unknowns are looking for you."

"So the lights are not searching for us?"

"We are here to help, Cliff, no matter what you think. We took back the safe house five minutes after you left."

The medic approached, stopped at Penny, and examined her.

Richard motioned Cliff behind him. "Keep your voice low. They don't know who you are."

Cliff's brows furrowed, but he obeyed. "Why, and what about the others?"

"Which question first?"

"The second."

"We haven't found them yet. We still don't know who hit us."

The medic administered a shot to Penny and then moved on to George.

Cliff pointed. "They have a monitoring device on him, but we don't know where."

Richard went near the medic and spoke quietly. The medic nodded, pulled out a handheld device, and swept it over George. Richard came back to Cliff.

"And the person we stopped—" Cliff turned to where the body should be and his voice dropped. "—is gone."

Richard bent near and checked the ground. "We have an intruder moving off into section Eight-A. The intruder is hostile and armed." He looked up at Cliff. "Description?"

"Black clothes, black mask, black vest with pockets, black belt, black holster, and a gun with a silencer. You may or may not find another in the church safe area. Oh, and—" Cliff remembered when he grabbed the person's wrist. "—small boned."

Richard called it in. "What happened?"

The medic finished with George. Out of hearing, the medic spoke to someone by tapping his ear. Four more lights headed in their direction, and Richard took Cliff further away.

Cliff told the tale though he left out a few details. He did not talk about the notes, nor did he talk about the false back in Gran's unit.

Richard nodded and did not interrupt. Cliff knew exactly what the man looked for. It wasn't just the details he mentioned; it was the details he had not.

Two stretchers were brought, and they picked up Penny and George. Cliff pursed his lips; a knot in his stomach had grown. "Where are they taking them?"

Richard grinned. "Don't worry. They'll be safe. What did you leave out?"

"That's what you said the last time."

"And you didn't answer my question."

Cliff looked at him. "Not anything of importance to Division A."

"You should know by now, Division A wants to know about everything, but I'll let it slide for tonight. Where's the car?"

"Hidden behind some trees. You need me to bring it in?"

Richard chuckled. "Bringing you in is the last thing I want to do."

"Why?" That explained why Richard had him step away from the others. The lights around them thinned.

"The only way they could have infiltrated that safe house is if they had an inside person. We have a traitor in our midst."

Cliff's eyes opened wide. "That means Penny and George are in danger."

"Not necessarily. You were their target. The rest are reserved as pawns."

The knot in his stomach became worse. "I don't like it. I feel like I have been pushed down a waterslide without being prepared."

Richard's eyebrows crossed. "Do you have a place to crash? Someplace off the radar?"

"Maybe."

"That means no." Richard shook his head. "Here's the deal—" He reached in his pocket and pulled out a key. "—go to twelve twenty-two East Woodard. We sometimes crash there in emergencies. Use the back door. There's food in the fridge and a bed to lie down on. Nothing fancy, but it is good for the night. I'll meet you in the morning." He handed the key to Cliff.

Cliff started toward the trees.

"And enter the code!"

A smile cracked Cliff's face as he passed into the trees; in a situation like this, you found humor where you could. His mind drifted to the others. He had tried so desperately to keep his family out of this situation. Until today, he thought he had succeeded.

As he reached the car, the key fob was already in his hand. He unlocked the vehicle and stepped in.

The silence as the door closed reminded him of how alone he felt. Along with Albert, his family had been taken, Penny was hurt, and Gran's lawyer was a target. He looked over the interior and spotted the satchel Penny had tossed on the seat. A thought hit him: satchel, safe unit, and George. The listening device on George had heard every word in the walk-in safe.

As his head dropped back, it bumped into the headrest. How could he have been so stupid? Whoever they were, they knew all about the airtight envelope, and they knew his grandmother's codicil had survived. Pressure built with every thought. He was tired, exhausted, and sleepy.

The car started smoothly. He backed out, turned around, and headed for the address that Richard had given him. As he moved away from the cemetery, he caught a main street and followed it further into the city.

He kept watch behind him, but no one appeared. The quiet night and the consistency of the night lamps were hypnotic. He remembered where one of his pizza routes deviated, followed it down a few blocks, and turned right. The house should be a block or so down.

A plain brown house, with no lights turned on, held the address of twelve twenty-two. The driveway connected to the alley. He turned, went to it, and parked. The unobtrusive neighborhood held white picket fences only a foot tall. Nobody would think twice about this place unless they knew he was here.

He grabbed the satchel and threw it over his shoulder. Penny was right; a lot of items were in it. It would certainly need a closer inspection.

A narrow sidewalk led through the picket fence, up a single step, and to the back door. The key went easily in, and the door creaked open. He locked the car as well as the back door.

The kitchen light glowed to life. He checked the fridge. Juice, lunch meat, and a few other items stared back. It was enough to satisfy him. He grabbed two slices of lunch meat and swallowed them down.

Room by room, he checked the house. It contained one bathroom, three bedrooms, a living room, and a kitchen. Albert would have loved it.

A shower and a change of clothes called to him, so he stepped into one of the bedrooms. In various sizes, the dresser had socks and underwear, sealed and still in packages. The closet contained shirts and pants, even some dresses, also sealed and packaged. He dropped the satchel beside it. A collared shirt with a pair of jeans, he laid upon the bed. On the floor were shoes in various sizes; a pair of sneakers fit the best. These he carried to the bathroom.

It took only a moment to transfer his wallet, George's cellphone, miscellaneous items, the business card, a pocketknife, and the two notes to the new clothes. His own cellphone lay in the car. For the moment, that was the safest place for it.

He undressed, stepped in, and started the shower. The dust,

grit, and grime washed off and down the drain. The warm water helped his muscles, and the things which had seemed insurmountable before found hope.

It was a matter of perspective. He knew someone wanted Gran's codicil, he knew someone else had been murdered, and he knew at least one group, though reluctant, sought to kill him.

Cliff shook his head. Water drops bounced to the sides of the shower. As the drops struck and caught the light, he saw many facets of color.

More than one issue existed, but somehow they intertwined. The house creaked. Had the back door opened? He stepped out of the shower, dried quickly, and slipped on the new clothes.

The house seemed quiet as he peered out. If someone had entered, they were silent now. The door opened enough for him to get through, and he slipped into the bedroom. A female with an Italian accent laughed lightly as a whiff of perfume hit his nose. "That didn't take you long."

Cliff turned to see Tish lying across the bed. Her head, white hair cropped short, was supported by her hand and elbow.

"I had expected to see a little more skin."

"How did you—"

"Know you were here?" She winked. "What girl wouldn't keep watch over a cute guy?"

His face turned red.

"And he still blushes? How quaint. This may be more fun than I thought." She patted the bed. "Why don't you sit down and relax? I will make it worth your while." With her tongue, Tish touched her lips.

"You know your sister and I are together."

Tish pouted. "And it could have been so much fun."

Cliff didn't like this. He had enough trouble without her presence. "Why are you here?"

"Men—" She rolled her eyes. "—no foreplay at all. They are all straight to the point. Although, it might be nice to try that, too." She smiled seductively. "I might even teach you something." Her smile increased as his blush came back.

"Tish."

"Can't a girl have a little fun?"

"I'm not your type."

"And you think my sister is?"

"We've been all through that."

She rose from the bed, moved beside him, and whispered, "I won't tell if you won't."

Cliff sighed. "Why are you here?"

She laughed playfully. "If I tell, I'll need a favor in return." Her lips brushed his cheek. "Deal?"

"It depends on the favor."

She moved in front of him and pressed her body close. "Maybe we'll throw that in, too."

His cheeks turned warm. "You're enjoying this, aren't you?"

"But of course." Her voice was alluring. She touched her lips to his lightly. "At least think about it." She pulled back and looked him in the eyes. "My brother may have been the instrument, but he didn't do it alone."

The thought of what her brother had done chased all the blush away. His voice became hard. "I know he didn't do it by himself, but he planned it."

"No." Her voice became serious. For a moment, she saw right through him. "He was not the planner; he was manipulated. By the time I settled everything down, I knew others were behind the assassination of your grandmother."

Cliff's world stopped. He could hear the throb of his heart and feel the pulse quicken. She was lying; she had to be. The color drained from his skin. "No." He looked into her eyes and saw only pools of darkness. "No. You're lying."

"I am not." She shook her head slowly. "You know I am telling the truth."

You think you're telling the truth, he told himself. You think you know the answer.

"Cliff, you must believe me." Her voice pleaded. "It is vital that you understand. If you don't—" Her voice faltered, and all the confidence and innuendoes fell away. "—if you do not, they will find you, and they will kill you, too."

"Who are they?"

Tish bowed her head and pursed her lips. "If I tell you, you will never believe me. If you discover it on your own, you will understand why."

"Did you—" He swallowed. "Do you know what happened at the funeral today?"

"I was informed. I am truly sorry." She reached out to touch him, and he flinched away.

"Did you do it?"

In an instant, her voice became hard. "I see." The mocking voice came back. "You have been warned, and you will do me the favor when I ask."

"I agreed to nothing."

"You agreed by default. I will have what is mine." She turned and strolled out of the room. Cliff heard the back door creak, and she was gone.

Was she right? Was her brother, Adelric, truly set up?

The thought enraged him. For someone to do such a thing was unforgivable. If what she said was true, there could even be more than one.

Chapter 10

Both hands twisted into fists as he fought the anger. He was beat; exertion with little food had worn him down, and he still did not know enough to piece together what was going on. Pieces, papers, notes: those three words grabbed his attention. He reached into his pocket and pulled out the two pieces of paper given to him by George. He was not sure of what order they were given, but at least he had them. The first read, "Beware the flower." As the second unfolded, he read the numbers, "0394-979."

Beware the flower. The image of the red petal falling from the casket roof still burned into his conscious mind. When he and Albert had gone to the hotel in search of his parents, he had seen red petals there, too. A red flower was also on the lapel of a Japanese man who had entered the elevator with his wife. Could he have been Fushimi?

The numbers he did not recognize though they were close to what Gran had given him. Did this correspond to a slot in the mausoleum? His grandfather's ended in nine-eight-zero, and his uncle's was nine-eight-two, but what relative had nine-seven-nine?

His eyes drooped. Part of him wanted to go find out now; the other part wanted to rest. Thoughts faded and then returned. For what good it would do, he had better make sure the back door was locked.

It was not locked. He checked it to see how Tish had gotten

in. The door showed no damage and did not appear to have been picked. That would mean she had her own key, but who would have given it to her? Richard's name came to mind. However, it could have been Division A since the two weren't seeing eye to eye.

With a quick turn, he locked the door and headed back to the bedroom. The insult to Tish had not been intended, but the question had to be asked. Once a criminal, always a criminal? Did he really believe that?

Tish was all about her family. Yet, there were times he saw something else. Just because she could be humane didn't mean she could be trusted.

A little voice in the back of his mind stirred; he had fallen asleep. His eyes focused on the bed. It would be better to fall asleep on it rather than off. He removed his shoes, lay down, and dropped into a deep sleep.

· ● ·

The ceiling of the coffin stared at him. The message "Push me" glowed in the tiny light. As his fingers pressed the button, the coffin jerked. In an instant, he floated in the air while he stared down as the other casket exploded. Bits and pieces went everywhere as a single piece of metal bounced to the right. His body dropped closer. The item appeared to be a badge.

"No!" Cliff shot straight up and found himself sitting. As he labored to breath, his body dripped in sweat. "I did not kill that man!"

The room was unfamiliar, yet he remembered it. A glance to the side of the bed showed the sneakers. That's right, I am at a safe house; I was told to get some rest.

His pulse raced as he lay back, reached up, and rubbed his eyes. The damp hair stuck to his scalp. If this continued, he would have to take another shower.

Why was he convinced he had killed that man? Why did they want that man to die?

Fact one: someone had wanted to scare Cliff witless.

Fact two: true or not, his mind was convinced he had killed him.

Fact three: someone wanted his grandmother's codicil.

Fact four: they were desperate enough to kidnap his relatives and friends.

Fact five: Tish had tried to help him.

Of all the facts, number two disturbed him the most. To kill was not something he would ever have considered in the past, yet he had picked up an assassin's gun.

It was the anger: the anger that someone had killed Gran, the anger that the person behind it may have gotten away, and the anger that they would not leave his family alone.

Breathe. Cliff took a deep breath and let the air out. Only a short time ago, he had been nothing more than a college student. Friends and family were happy, and no one had been murdered. Yet, here he was going to the funeral of his grandmother, running as they destroyed it, and trying to figure out if he was a murderer. The word murderer led to the funeral and the codicil: Where was the satchel?

Cliff threw his legs over the side of the bed and searched the room. It had been beside the closet door, but now the satchel could not be seen.

How in the world had she done it? He thought back over every detail. She could not have taken the satchel without him knowing. That meant it had to be here.

He threw open the closet doors and spotted it against the wall. A note was attached to the top. His voice read, "Cliff, if you want the codicil, meet me at the restaurant. Nine-ish is good. We'll have breakfast. Till then, Lover." It was signed by Tish.

The only restaurant associated with Tish was Dino's, an Italian restaurant and bar. He picked up the satchel, took it to the bed, and dumped out its contents. Of the items he had taken from the church, only the vinyl envelope was missing.

He shook his head and chuckled; he had been played. She knew he had the satchel and had used their conversation as a distraction. This begged the question: was she telling the truth?

The rest of the contents caught his attention. Two gun magazines were fully loaded. A handgun lay in the bottom along with a battery-operated drill and a transmitter. His eyes held the transmitter; it blinked with a red light. Why hadn't the car picked up on it? What if it had, and he had not paid attention? Penny had tossed it in.

What if Tish's thugs had broken into the safe and the transmitter let her keep up with them? The man George had knocked out could have contacted Tish when the satchel was taken. That left the person in black that had attacked George; that person could have been with someone else. Otherwise, they would have let the trio go and followed them wherever they went.

He held up a hand and counted off the groups he knew: one, Fushimi's group; two, Tish and her organization; three, the FBI with Chrys and Lenord; four, Division A; and five, the group who had kidnapped his friends and loved ones. The first and second groups could be the same as number five though he doubted it; it didn't *feel* like Tish had kidnapped them. Division A could have staged their own kidnapping though that did not *feel* right either. Who could he trust? Did he know the difference?

All the items were returned to the satchel, but he left the transmitter out. If he turned it off, it would let whoever owned it know that he had found it, and he could not be sure who did. Regardless, it was no longer safe to stay here. He put on his shoes, hefted the satchel, and headed to the closet.

The shoes interested him. With the transmitter placed in one of his old shoes, he slid it down to the toe. By his feet, he pushed the shoes in a pile and hid them in the depths of the closet. It wouldn't make them look hard, but at least they would have to search. He adjusted the satchel, turned off the light, and headed toward the back door.

The cold wind had not changed; it whistled a tune as he pulled the door open. Since the moisture on his face and neck had not dried, the wind chilled him to the bone.

Slowly, he scanned the area. Two shadows outlined against the inky blackness. One stood outside the picket fence next to a tree. The other sat to his left in the backyard of a neighbor. He could have easily overlooked both if he had not searched.

The time had come to end this. Cliff walked toward the car, opened it, and tossed the satchel in. He turned and strode toward the shadow by the tree.

The first saw him coming and straightened. A female voice challenged, "Well, it seems Lenord was right. You are observant."

Though he gave a slight bow, this surprised him. "It seems I am watched by many tonight, Chrys."

She gave a slight grimace as if smiling was difficult. "You remember. What a good memory you have. Perhaps, too good?" She nodded toward the other shadow.

"Some things are better off understood. How is it that the FBI, a major crime syndicate, and Division A all know I'm at a Division A safe house?"

She raised an eyebrow. "Crime syndicate? You must feel very important."

"Why?"

She leaned toward him. Dim light through the tree leaves lit her face. A slight discoloring existed on the left side of her head near the temple. "I've a secret," she whispered. "You like secrets, don't you, Mr. Fulton?" Light flashed off the metal of a gun as it slid from its holster.

He did not move. "What will Lenord say?" He remembered the thugs in the university tunnels and pieced together a defense. If he angled to the right and stepped in closer, he could knock the gun from her hand.

Her voice remained calm but forceful. "Move." With her left hand, she shoved him down as the other hand came up, centered, and fired. The other shadow dropped but two more replaced it. Shots rang out in the darkness. Chrys dropped beside Cliff.

"We need to get you out of here—" She gave a threatening smile. "—before you get hurt."

Two spits came in their direction and hit the tree above. He nodded. "Thanks."

She spoke through gritted teeth. "Anytime, Mr. Fulton, anytime. Stay down until I run!" She jumped to her feet and raced toward the two gunmen.

Cliff dashed for the car as something stung him on the side of the neck; he slapped at it and found a tiny dart lodged in his skin. It came out easily but dropped through his fingers. The dart took effect. He staggered toward the driver's door.

The car contained a shadow. By the time he pulled the door open, the shadow had vanished. The world stretched out in odd directions as he dropped in. The door closed with a click that sounded like thunder. In the mirror, three shadows chased a fourth into the darkness.

He wasn't thinking—that he knew. His head bobbed forward and back. He could not leave; he did not want them to see him leave.

When they were out of sight, he backed up into the alley and pulled toward the street. The car turned left, went straight for five blocks, and caught a main thoroughfare.

Where to now? His head dipped, and his eyes snapped open as a horn blared. He swerved.

"Stay awake!" He slapped himself on the arm, but it did no good. He drummed his fingers, bounced a knee, and pinched himself. However, nothing helped keep him awake.

He spotted a convenience store as his eyes went in and out of focus. Charlie's materialized—the place where he had first met Penny. The glass had been repaired in the front, and additional bars had been installed. In the store, a few people moved around. A clerk cleaned up a mess where one of the bottles had fallen.

The place where Penny had parked her car came to mind. He turned down the side street and pulled up beside the curve.

The voice of his father shook him. "Cliff, lock the door." He found himself only seven years old and sitting in the passenger seat of an old truck. "Cliff?"

He reached over and tried to hit the lock, but his arms were so heavy, they would barely move. "Dad? Dad, I can't."

"What did I tell you?" his father demanded.

With a heavy arm, he reached over and hit the door locks. A message flashed on the windshield. "Locks engaged."

"Dad?" His head jogged back and forth.

His father vanished; Richard appeared. "I told you to enter the code."

"Code?" He blinked several times, but it did not clear up the fog. His eyes started to slide shut. "What code?"

"Enter the code."

The image of an eye came to mind; it looked at him through the windshield. As he stared, it moved toward him, dropped to the steering wheel, and shrank until it vanished.

His right hand would not hold still as it tried to press the icon. When he grabbed his right with his left, it barely slowed down the motion.

Both his hands gripped the wheel and then loosened enough to slide their way across. It worked. The icon came closer. As the tip of his right finger touched it, he pushed his whole body forward to apply the right pressure. A screen appeared on the windshield as it waited for the numbers.

His vision blurred; each line looked like three. The right hand dropped and tried to find the arrow keys. When it found them, a seven appeared in the first column.

It took three tries to get the cursor to move to the right, but it finally slid over. A three came up on the second column.

Three. It stared at him, but he could not figure out what to do next. Three what?

Mentally, he counted three-one, three-two, three-three—his head fell back and the screen faded from view.

· • ·

He stood in darkness and ran from something he could not see. Something screamed. The screaming became louder. It rounded a corner and stared at him, mouth agape with the face hidden by a hood. As the hood slid back, he saw the face of the man he believed to be Fushimi and heard the infamous words, "Push me again."

Chapter 11

Red. Something red and blue moved back and forth. Cliff opened his eyes only to be blinded by a man outside the car with a flashlight.

With his right hand near the arrow keys, he spotted the screen on the windshield. The numbers seven-three-four had been entered. The last digit should be five.

With a click to the keys, the four changed to five, and he hit enter. The special screen disappeared as someone rapped at the window.

What should he do? If he sat tight and refused to answer, they could not get in. However, was that the type of precedent he wanted to set as a law abiding citizen even if everyone else appeared above the rules? Cliff pressed a button and the window slid down an inch.

"License and registration."

Cliff swallowed. While he had his license, he was not the owner of this car and had no idea where the registration was. Also, while he knew there must be a glove compartment, he had no idea how to open it.

"Sir, do you understand me? I need to see your license and registration."

Cliff nodded as he looked over all the symbols to figure out where the glove compartment was. One symbol caught his eye: a flap with a curved arrow pointing to it. He raised his finger. What if he guessed wrong? That button might do anything. Another stood out as a curved, tray-like icon with a straight arrow above it. Which one was right?

"Sir, please step out of the car." The police officer's hand moved closer to his gun. A second officer came up from behind.

Cliff pressed the second icon. A dash tray slid out with a badge, a magazine, and a handgun.

The police officer saw the gun. "Hands on the wheel! Now!"

Cliff grasped the steering wheel. "May I show you my badge?"

"Step out of the car with your hands up." The officer reached for the handle, but found the door locked.

Cliff held perfectly still. The window was only an inch down, but more than enough for a bullet to enter. "All right, I'm coming out. I'm lowering my left hand to unlock the door."

He kept his right hand up and away from the tray while his left hand came down, but instead of hitting the lock, he pressed the button for the window. The window rose, both officers pulled their weapons, and Cliff hit the gas.

The car took off and raced into the neighborhood. Behind him, both officers scrambled to their car. He couldn't outrun them; every patrol car in the area would be alerted in about a minute. His only option was to find a place to hide.

But where? He still felt the prick of the dart though the effects of the drug had worn off. A garage with a door would be great. It had to be something easy and quick.

Gran's came to mind, but her car already sat in it. Albert's had no garage. The area Cliff drove through contained nothing but homes.

A parking garage might work. It would at least get him off the street. Or—an alley? An alley might work. The one he used to walk through when he lived in his apartment—the shortcut to Albert's house.

The red and blue lights shined behind him though they had yet to gain any distance. He turned to the left, sped up for several blocks, and swung to the right down a street with heavy trees. It was left again and then right, followed by five blocks in a straight line. At that point, he slowed down.

The red and blue lights grew fainter, but their absence did not fool him. More than one patrol car would be on watch.

Right again, he went several blocks. With a left, he caught a street that curved around the university. The buildings came into view with their empty windows of darkness. Not long ago, he had been in that building and faced Gerhard von Richter.

He took the street to Albert's house, passed the house, made two more turns, and found the alley. The car pulled slowly up, picked a spot hidden by large, green dumpsters, and backed in. No one in the apartment liked to park here because of its concealment. The odds of someone noticing him were nil to none.

For the first time in a while, Cliff relaxed. It was pleasant to relax. It could have been a result of the dart, but he felt rested, too.

At least three groups had been at the second safe house: Tish, the FBI, and one other. If Chrys had led the third group away, the others had to be on the same team. Why had someone shot the dart? He remembered the shadow that had been in the car. The car had been unlocked when he went toward Chrys. He checked the contents of the satchel but found nothing missing. Was the shadow an illusion?

A couple of stray cats slipped in to investigate the dumpsters. They appeared to show no interest in the car, yet he knew they were watching.

What was the time? He looked at the controls; four a.m. approached fast. No wonder the police had checked out the car. A lone man asleep, parked near a business that was closed, would be nothing but suspicious.

He reached over and picked up the badge. An eagle decorated the top with the letters FDA around the shield's edges. Why was an FDA badge in a car owned by Division A? The mausoleum came to mind. Could it be connected? With the badge placed back, he picked up the file folder and thumbed through it.

They hadn't missed much about him. How did they get his fingerprints? The information on his parents looked thorough, but his uncle, grandfather, and grandmother came up short.

Their sheets were a quarter of the size of the others. Oh, they had the usual: birth, death, age, build. Yet, it did not contain details before they came to America. The facts about Gran included her work at the University. It did not mention the destroyed briefcase.

His uncle had an occupation, but the details were sketchy. He worked for a mining company in the Colorado Mountains though his exact position was not named. Shouldn't Division A know more details than this? Add to that Karl's words, stay alive, and it became stranger still. How had Karl known he would be there? Why had the key fob stung him?

He tapped the symbol with the curved tray. The badge, clip, and handgun slid back into the dash. Manipulation—he was set up. Someone directed him by knowing his character.

But who? Karl, Richard, Tish, George, Lenord, or Fushimi? Gran? No, not Gran. She had prepared him to use his talents in ways that would save his life.

Fushimi had used him and caused him to kill but left him alive. Lenord had saved him. George had warned him. Tish, though manipulative, didn't seem hostile.

Richard and Karl? Everyone wanted something from him, but what were they looking for?

When Gran had first died, they sought the evidence of Gerhard; Division A wanted it destroyed. This time, it was a codicil.

He opened the satchel and looked at the contents. His grandmother's small, airtight bag had shifted to the top. The bag felt light and airy. The seam appeared almost invisible.

With his thumbnail, he ran back and forth across the seam. The soft material cut deeper with each pass. In a final effort, the seal broke, and the package hissed. His thumbnails pushed tightly into the slit and pulled it apart.

A gleaming platinum ring lay inside. A mold of velvet

wrapping held it in place. He picked it up and raised the ring to the light.

A street lamp played across its top and reflected off the raised projections. The word Fulton lay inscribed, but other protrusions rose as well. The protrusions were taller, although not by much, than the word Fulton. The ring's outer rim held a circle. The ends of the circle met at a sideways v. The pattern matched the stained glass window in the mausoleum.

He started to wrap it up but noticed writing on one side of the paper. Though very crinkled, the numbers were clear: 0394-979.

Cliff stared at the numbers. Those numbers had been given in one of George's notes. If this represented a slot in his family mausoleum, who lay there?

The ring went into his pocket. Along with the two notes, the packaging material ripped into tiny pieces as he stepped out to the dumpster and sprinkled them into the garbage. If the first note had been so important that George had been ordered to retrieve it, none should be kept.

As the pieces fluttered down, two glowing eyes appeared in the dimness of the garbage. They studied him but did not run. As he turned away, a cat hissed from his left; another darted across the car. Two, human-like shadows moved in his direction.

No one parks back here for a reason, the thought echoed through Cliff's mind. Maybe it wasn't his smartest move. The car was still running, and the key fob was not in his pocket. The doors were unlocked, and the satchel sat in the passenger seat.

Four quick steps brought him to the driver's side. As he opened the door and started to slip in, someone pinned him with the door.

"Who do we have here? Rich little boy out for a drive?"

Cliff turned and stared. He had faced down assassins, looked into the eyes of his grandmother's killer, and watched Division A destroy the briefcase Gran had saved. He wasn't about to back down now.

A butterfly knife danced in the man's hand. "You like knives?"

Cliff studied how the guy held the knife. "I do. Although, I think you haven't had it long."

"You don't say?" Another shadow moved around the car toward the passenger's side.

Even in this light, Cliff could see the details of the knife's handle. "The catch isn't worn. Either you haven't had it long, or you aren't very experienced." As he talked, he maneuvered his leg for better leverage.

The man grunted. "Think you're a smart-ass, don't you?" He started around the car door. "Let's see how smart you really are."

Cliff shoved the door forward and rammed it into his groin. The man gasped while Cliff dropped inside and slammed the door. He hit the lock button, but not before the passenger side pulled open. The second person ducked his head in, and Cliff hit the gas.

The car jumped forward. As the second assailant lost his footing, he bounced against the seat. The man's hand found the satchel; Cliff grabbed it, too. The steering wheel rotated left and whipped a tight curve. The hand on the satchel strained. The car raced for half a block down the alley, and then Cliff hit the brakes. The passenger door bounced out and slammed back.

The second man swore as it hit across his legs. His grip lessened, but he did not let go. The first one who had been hit in the groin rose to his feet and hobbled down the alley toward the car. Cliff grabbed the satchel with his left hand and back-knuckled with his right. The man's head snapped back, but the hold did not break.

"Let go!" Cliff grabbed the man's fingers and peeled them off. The first assailant came closer. Cliff tossed the satchel into the backseat. He grabbed the wheel, hit reverse, and shot backwards. The second man slipped but clung. The car thudded as it hit the first; the first man dropped from view.

Cliff turned and hit the icon with the curved tray. As the tray slid out, he grabbed the gun and pointed it at the second man. "You have two seconds to get out of my car! One—"

The man shoved backwards, hit the door, and bounced away. Cliff dropped the gun in the seat and took off. At the end of the block, he hit the brakes. The door bounced out and slammed shut. Without giving his signal, he turned to the right and drove.

It had been foolish to get out of the car in the dead of night and in such an unwatched alley. The numbers 0394-979 came back to mind. While the police might be expecting to see this car around town, they were less likely to be looking at the cemetery. It would be a good place to park, and Division A had swept it.

He turned to the left, went down several blocks, and caught a major street. The time went quickly as his mind rolled. A red light reminded him of where he was.

The streets were basically empty. With so few cars on the road, it would be easy to see if someone followed.

The light changed green. He accelerated across the intersection, caught a freeway, and started the last stretch. Five minutes later, he drove up the cemetery road and pulled beside the church.

As the engine went silent, his eyes checked the grounds. Trees limbs waved gently against a sky that twinkled with stars. The moon had not risen; that would happen in an hour or so.

His cellphone caught his attention. It sat on the dash, and a green light flashed; someone had left him a message. The only people that would do that were Penny or Albert.

He touched the middle, made a Q with his finger, and checked the messages at the top. A text message, not a voice message, had been received. With the strange ID at the top of the message, it said, "Bring codicil unopened. Will trade loved ones. Waterfront, bay fifty-two." The message had been sent only moments after he had been rescued by Richard.

Bay fifty-two, the same location Gerhard had used, added

multiple possibilities. Tish was Gerhard's daughter. Division A had helped rout Gerhard's men. The FBI had been there. Fushimi had been part of the conspiracy with Gerhard. And now another, unnamed group had appeared who might be a part of anyone.

The fact that Tish had the vinyl envelope ruled her out of the mix. The fact that Division A's safe house had also been compromised played in their favor. With Lenord, he had no doubt though Chrys wavered. Fushimi could be anything and seemed to be the most likely suspect.

He could not go to the warehouse until he had the codicil. He could not get the codicil until he met with Tish. The cemetery beckoned him as he waited for morning. With the phone on the dash and George's cell with him, he pushed the door back. The cold wind confirmed the front had blown in.

Door and key fob, he shut and locked the car, respectively, then turned toward the burnt church. In the dark, the small branches slapped at his body until he stepped onto the lawn.

No lights—not only were the searchers gone, but power had been shut down for this side of the cemetery. Until the mess could be cleaned up, the safety measure was necessary.

The path to the walk-in safe could have been done blindfolded. As he stepped in, he pulled out George's phone, made the pattern, and turned on the light. The units reflected brightly. As he traced the numbers, he scooted to the right and found Gran's.

No units appeared to be touched; Division A must not have done anything to them after he had left. He spotted the unit for nine-seven-nine. The box did exist, but nothing said what the combination might be. If Gran had set it up, it might follow her pattern.

As the iris moved over each column, the numbers fell into place. With a soft click, the door opened, but when he checked inside only dust stared back.

Did the number have no meaning? No, Gran had sent a message, and then verified the message with the ring itself.

With a hand inside, his knuckle tapped; no side gave a hollow sound. The unit closed and locked. If the secret wasn't here, only one other place could be checked.

With a touch, he turned off the light. Darkness enclosed him as he dropped the cell in his pocket, made his way out of the safe, and worked his way to the cemetery proper. He shivered and wished he had chosen a long sleeve shirt.

The stones which made the path into the cemetery broadened out and formed a half-circle entrance. His feet felt the stones as he walked. His eyes used the headstones which lined the path to guide him. The cell light came on briefly to spot the mausoleum door.

His body moved to the center of the mausoleum as the door slowly closed. The stained glass window with the word Fulton glowed faintly. Each point that made up the word had a tiny, clear piece of glass in its center; the points stood out like stars in the night.

It matched the platinum ring concealed in his pocket. The ring around the stained glass window had the sideways v as well.

The light on George's phone came on, and he checked the slots: 0394-981, 980, and 978. He checked it again to make sure it had not been missed, but number nine-seven-nine did not appear. Why give a clue to an empty unit and to a slot that did not exist?

Using the light, he floated over them again: nine-eight-one, nine-eight-zero, and nine-seven-eight. The next slot over was supposed to be nine-seven-seven, but it was too far over.

Cliff stared; two nine-seven-eight's existed. Had someone miscounted?

His hands ran over the letters, and he could feel an irregular indention in the bottom circle of the last digit; the nine had been shaped to look like an eight. Tiny indentions pressed into the smooth surface. If a person didn't look close enough, one would think the engraver had simply made an error.

The indentions followed a pattern, and that pattern stared from the stained glass window. He pulled the ring from his pocket and pressed it into the indention.

Chapter 12

Points of light glimmered as something in front of the ring lit up. This was more than a mechanical response; micro technology had been incorporated.

That was impossible. The first microcircuits were not in use until 1949. And yet, the concept was first developed by a radar scientist in 1909. Could someone have known back then and developed a product in secret?

As Cliff removed the ring, a musky whiff of air drifted into the mausoleum proper. A panel slid up to reveal a hollow in the column between the two slots marked nine-seven-eight. Objects within caught the light of his cellphone and flashed multiple colors.

On a small ledge toward the back sat a small medallion. At an inch in diameter, it hung on a silver necklace and looked exactly like the stained glass window. Beside it lay an eyepiece three inches long; it contained rings which spun around the center. The rings were numerically numbered and consisted of ten.

As he picked both up, the two appeared made for each other with other covers that could be lifted to add more medallions; the medallion slipped into the eyepiece. Though he raised it to his eye, he could see nothing. The phone light shifted in his left hand. A part of the light beamed through the eyepiece and illuminated the opposite side. Like a kaleidoscope, there had to be a light behind it.

Now was not the time to do this. As he turned from the

column, the hidden panel closed of its own accord. It had to have a sensor or timer.

The eyepiece went to his left pocket so that nothing would scratch it. The medallion dropped around his neck and hid inside his shirt. The ring he placed all by itself on the right. If he kept finding more strange items, he had better get some cargo pants.

Colors—as he stepped out of the mausoleum door and into the cold night, a faint memory came back. Gran had laid out some pictures on the table for him. Each time he colored one, she would give one a number.

"Zero's for red; it will come to mind. One is for green and all that is thine. Two is a wonder for bright as the sun, its yellow and orange with purple that's spun."

That wasn't all of what she had said; ten colors and ten numbers were stated in total. Did it have something to do with the eyepiece?

He reached the church, skirted it, and came around to the car. The car door unlocked. As he slipped in, his cellphone flashed. Cliff picked it up, swiped it, and stared. This time it was a text from Richard. "Where are you?"

For Richard to send a text message did not make sense; he had entered the code into the car. A lost or stolen phone? A dead Richard or one held hostage?

He cleared the alert, placed the cellphone on the seat, and stared. They waited for an answer. If it were not for the message about bay fifty-two, he would have turned it off.

The watch said 5a.m., and daylight had yet to stream across the sky. To close his eyes did no good. His mind fought to piece together the facts.

Everyone sought the codicil. Richard had said if a second copy of Gran's papers existed, he should never let anyone know. Then it hit him; everyone wanted the codicil because they thought it was a second copy of Gran's papers.

He took a deep breath and breathed out slowly. This whole thing, burn down the church and take his family and friends, had occurred because of those papers—at least in part. After talking with Tish, he had the impression there could be more.

In fact, he did have a copy of the papers. He had found them under the squeaky step and hid them in the underground room between the house and the garage. To the best of his knowledge, nobody else had a clue.

It wasn't the plan to keep it that way. Though he intended to spread it around the world, he hadn't found a good way to do it.

Any computer or internet access they had ever worked with could not be used. Despite the fact that Division A had taken care of their records, he knew they were being watched.

Not openly, of course. Division A rarely did things in the open, which is why it surprised him when Richard showed up at the church. Not only did they expose themselves to those in the church, but they had taken his family and friends in, too.

It didn't make sense. He understood the implication of the papers, and he understood that it could cause a major economic change. However, all this would happen only if they were believed. In order to be believed, there had to be a way to authenticate them. Without the briefcase that connected them to the government cover-up, how could they be validated?

In the car, he and Penny had tried to look at the papers. What had stopped him? That's right. A neighbor had come by to give condolences about Gran and welcomed him to the neighborhood. They had also wanted assurance that he would have no wild parties; they had looked straight at him and Penny when they had said it. Were all adults concerned about the same things or was it because they had done it themselves?

After that, they had run out of time and decided to hide them. He had gone to the underground room, placed the papers back in the original protective bag, and hid them. As Gran's funeral plans were worked out, all thoughts of the papers left.

Cliff closed his eyes. These people were crazy. Even if he gave them the papers, they would never leave him alone. Someone would come again; his family would never be safe.

Fushimi's remark, "push me again", made sense. He had stepped on the man's toes by exposing what the three had planned. It also implied possible other activities, too.

The senseless started to make sense—some of it at least. The clues Gran had given about the medallion and colors implied a code. And the man that had died? He had to find out why. Yet, how could he do that and deal with the codicil?

His eyes opened and stared out into the night. The first glimmers of the rising moon struck above the horizon. The light shone through as the leaves moved. The car creaked, and he shivered. He placed the key in the ignition, turned it on, and adjusted the heater.

As he did, his eyes caught sight of the cellphone; it flashed again. He picked it up and stared at it. This time it came from Penny. "Where are you?" Someone appeared desperate to find him. He decided to take the bait.

"Hiding till morning," he typed back. "Where are you?"

An expected pause came. "A little sore. Big bump on the head. Wish you were here."

That had to be Penny, though he did understand someone else could be doing it, so he continued. "Sorry about that."

"It wasn't your fault. Just didn't want you to use that gun."

Cliff relaxed. No one could have known that except for Penny—unless maybe Richard. He stopped; someone could be pretending to be both. His muscles tensed. If someone had Penny and Richard, he had no way to help them.

The phone flashed again, and George's number appeared. It, too, was a text message which said, "Where are you?"

Cliff nodded and pursed his lips; his hand held George's cellphone, and they did not know it. He typed back, "Where are you?"

After a pause, Cliff saw exactly what he expected. "Just a scratch from the bullet. I will be fine. Penny and I can meet you. Tell us where you are."

"I am," his fingers hesitated over the keys as his mind swirled through different scenarios. Could he turn the tables and learn who these people were?

Backspacing over what he had typed, he resumed, "Meet me at Hoy Hall entrance in forty-five minutes." His finger pressed the send button.

"We will wait for you inside the front entrance."

They were smart. They would not be out in the open, and without that, Cliff had less of a chance to determine who they were until it was too late.

Four entries led into Hoy Hall: the emergency door, the back door, the front door, and the hidden tunnel entrance. If he could use the fourth, he could figure out who they were. It would only take twenty minutes to get there. He backed out, turned around, and started down the road.

The police still looked for him. University patrol would be around, too. Rather than concern him, the idea reassured him; if things got tricky, he would need all the help he could get.

University security opened the back gate as the car pulled up. He showed his pass, and they let him through.

Three parking lots were in the back with only sparse trees. The best would be the middle; it had material stacked to one side due to renovation.

With a bound, he left the car and rushed toward the auditorium. A few others were about. They were mainly teachers that came in early. As he moved around a tree, he caught himself before he collided with another in the shadows. "Excuse me."

She kneeled beside a tree trunk to pick up leaves. "Early bird gets the worm?" She smiled. "No worries."

As she stood up, he noticed a bag full of leaves.

"Teaching aid." She nodded toward the bag. "If you end up in my class, you'll learn all about them."

He could feel the seconds as they ticked by but did not want to appear rude. "I'm sorry. I should have watched better."

"As I said, no worries." She turned at the sidewalk and headed toward a building.

A glance at his watch showed 6:35 a.m.; he had twenty minutes to get in place. If he remembered correctly, while the majority of the auditorium remained locked at this hour, the furthest door to the right was not. The door opened without a hitch.

He passed through the foyer, swung back the inner door, and headed down the aisle. The red carpet and seats combined with the dim lights to give the room a cozy glow. One or two students moved about, but no one paid any attention.

The short stairs up were clear. He bounded them in twos, hurried toward the back of the stage, and turned toward the downstairs where all the props were stored.

"I don't remember seeing you before."

Cliff turned as he tried to remember the voice. On orientation day, the man had been one of the speakers who welcomed the students. "Just getting some props, Dr. Slocum." He caught sight of the clock behind the teacher; he had fifteen minutes left.

"So, you aren't in my class?"

"No, sir, but I like helping out." Cliff smiled. "It's a great break from my law studies."

The teacher nodded. "I imagine it is. Very well."

Cliff went quickly down the stairs, shifted around the various props, and spotted the door that led to the tunnel entrance. A number of support items blocked it so he moved them away.

"We don't need those," a student walked in behind him. "It's the ones on the opposite wall." He waited for Cliff to comply.

"Sorry." Cliff grinned and moved toward the correct location.

"Is there any certain number?"

"As many as we can take." The student grabbed up a handful and waited for Cliff to go first.

Cliff reached down, grabbed them up, and headed for the stairs. At the top and out of the walking path, he stopped with his back to the student. "Loose shoestring. Just a moment."

The student nodded and walked by. Cliff picked up the props and followed.

He could have just left them, hurried to the entrance, and scrambled down the tunnel, but what if he needed to come back this way? It would be better to have an ally than an enemy.

They reached the practice area on the stage. As the student put his down, Cliff hurriedly sat his on the floor and spun to go get more.

He passed the clock as he turned toward the stairs; only ten minutes were left. With the door unblocked, he slipped through quickly. The door shut behind him.

The heavy hatch lay closed. With both hands, he grabbed the wheel on top, turned it, and with one massive effort, heaved it back. It rose slowly from the top of the vertical tunnel. Cliff dropped onto the spring-loaded ladder and leveraged the hatch shut.

So far, so good. The ladder squealed as his weight brought it down to touch the cement floor. A voice with a Japanese accent called quietly, "Good morning, Mr. Fulton."

A switch clicked and bathed the hallway in light. Five people gathered around him with guns although the guns were holstered.

The accent matched the same voice that had called him the previous morning. It matched the same man he had seen in the elevator at the hotel his mother and father had stayed in. On the man's jacket pocket sat a red carnation.

"You must be Fushimi." No fear appeared despite the chills that ran down his spine. This man had tried to kill him once; correct that, he had tried to scare him. If he played his cards right, he might be able to find out why.

The man gave a single nod. "We each have something the other wants."

"I want you to leave me and my family alone."

"That, we can agree on." Fushimi bowed. "The question is, can we agree on the price?"

"We want nothing to do with you. You leave us alone, and we will leave you alone."

Fushimi smiled sadly. "If only it were that easy, Mr. Fulton. Unfortunately, your grandmother became part of a war that has drawn you and your loved ones into it. It has taken time and resources to track this down."

"The war began when the three of you decided to take revenge on the United States. Gran only exposed it."

"You are much like your grandmother: ready to pick a fight you cannot win. I have warned you once. I will not be so kind again."

"So you did have me placed in the casket?"

"Consider it a time of contemplative thought. You will stop your meddling, you will back off your infernal quest, or I will kill you, son of the chosen or not." His eyes bore into Cliff's and did not blink. "Push me again."

Son of the chosen? Cliff wrinkled his brow. "I don't understand. If I am that much of a nuisance, why even wait?" Yeah, it wasn't the smartest statement, but Cliff needed to know.

"You are an irritant, Mr. Fulton, but by staying alive you keep at bay something of greater power. Rest assured, it has nothing to do with you personally. If you were any other soul, I would simply get rid of you."

"Like you did to my grandmother?"

Fushimi tilted his head. "Even now I see you doing the same thing. You are evaluating and sizing up how far you can go. I can hear the voices in your head. What can I do to keep this man talking? What information can I gain?"

"You didn't answer my question."

In the back of Cliff's mind, he could feel the need to know gain force. Did this man help orchestrate the death of his grandmother? Was Tish right, and others were involved? What type of people would hate her so much to do that? Cliff's face held no emotion.

The man clapped his hands as he studied Cliff. "Well played, Mr. Fulton, but I have been at this game much longer. So I will answer your question with a question: why does a burying beetle eat its own kind and not suffer loss? Answer this, and you will have your answer."

The implications exploded in Cliff, and one sat at the top of the list. His studies had never been about burying beetles, but the meaning could not be missed. He did not speak loudly, but the words were laced with venom. "My grandmother was *nothing* like you. She would *never* have anything to do with your *kind*."

Fushimi shook his head. "Pedestals are for heroes; we sit on thrones. Be careful on which you place her."

Thrones and pedestals? None of this made sense, and they had yet to get to the point. "Why did you call me here?"

Silence dropped, and Fushimi gave a slight chuckle. "We have both been fools, Mr. Fulton. We did not call you, and you did not call us." He nodded to those at his right. "Two of you head to the entrance. Verify the area is secure." At a sprint, two hurried off.

"We were set up." Cliff pursed his lips and looked back at Fushimi. "Why?"

"Why kill a baby bird when the adult is available?" The man nodded toward the others. The three left fanned out as they drew their weapons.

"They want you?"

"Does that surprise you, Mr. Fulton?"

"I don't know."

"Of course, you don't. A whole world lies beneath your feet of which you are unaware."

An explosion shook the hallway. "Go!" Fushimi pointed toward the explosion.

"No. Wait!"

Fushimi turned toward Cliff.

"I can get us out of here, and no one has to die."

Chapter 13

Cliff's eyes stayed firm, and Fushimi saw it. The man snapped his fingers to stop his men but spoke to Cliff. "Do not disappoint me."

Anger tried to rise into Cliff's cheeks, but he hid it. Without saying a word, he headed into the darkness toward the right. Fushimi and his three men followed.

The map Gran had given him existed in his head. "Stay to the center of the hall, and you won't hit anything." He counted paces, slowed in the dark, and found the switch for the next section of the hall. The lights came on; those behind turned off.

With a dark hall behind them and a lighted hall in front, they picked up speed. At the next change in direction, he switched off the light and flipped on the next. The hall turned and ended at a vertical tunnel. Fushimi's hand came down on his shoulder as he grabbed the ladder.

"We'll take it from here." Fushimi nodded toward his men; one man went up the ladder.

"You don't know where it goes."

"I think I can guess." Fushimi followed the man and at the same time motioned behind him. "Bring the boy." A man gave a nod and pushed Cliff toward the ladder.

The small room at the top was dimly lit, but not dark. Cliff climbed out of the circle and onto the floor. As the man came up behind him and stepped away, another closed the hatch. Without waiting for permission, Cliff pushed the door open.

Light flooded in from a quiet walk area. He stepped forward and turned toward Gerhard's living room. The television sat silent; the chairs and sofa were empty.

Fushimi looked uncertain. "Which way?"

"Go to his study. The doors to the right come out in a hallway. The stairs are down the hall."

Fushimi caught his eye. "You have been helpful, Mr. Fulton, but do not think this will end my threat. If you push me again, this alters nothing."

Cliff held the stare. "If I push you again, you won't have to find me."

"Bravery becomes you, Mr. Fulton, yet it may very well be your death." Fushimi laughed as he opened the study doors and passed through.

Cliff closed the doors and turned to look at Gerhard's apartment. His steps stirred up dust as he entered the living room. He remembered Gerhard had come from the kitchen as he had dried his hair. Could Gerhard have left some artifacts that might be useful? After all, he ruled the school, even to the point that no questions were asked of his activities.

He stepped into the kitchen. A short hall led to a bathroom and two bedrooms. The search of the first bedroom went fast, but all Cliff found was a small locked chest. Unless the man had a hidden panel, nothing else showed in the room. The second bedroom proved fruitless as well.

His fingers drummed on the chest; it had a small lock, and he could probably knock it off, but a hammer would be the best. Did Gerhard have a toolbox?

Down at the end of the small hall sat a door that opened to a closet. In the closet were three shelves stacked so high with linens he could not see behind them. The linen closet stared back. Why did a man living by himself have so many linens?

The top shelf revealed nothing, the middle was no better, but the lower had a strange depression at the back. With George's cell in hand, he shined the light and saw it had a keyhole. Where would Gerhard hide the key if it wasn't on his person?

The kitchen came to mind. He took the chest with him and rummaged through the kitchen drawers. After several, he found a silver-plated knife, stuck it between the shank and the top of the lock, and leveraged quickly. The lock popped and fell off. He lifted the lid.

What met his eyes surprised him. Gems of various colors decorated the bottom of the chest. He picked up a small diamond and cleaned it. As he breathed upon it, the fog stayed until he wiped it off. This could not be a real diamond; real diamonds did not hold heat. So why the chest if the gems weren't real?

With a paper towel laid on the counter, he carefully dumped out the gems. The towel helped them not to bounce as they formed a small pile.

His fingers checked the lining of the box and felt a small depression. Too small to touch, he used the silver knife to push it.

A click issued from the chest. A small panel slid about a quarter of an inch out. His fingers pulled it the rest of the way. The panel had a cutout, and the cutout held a key.

Cliff used the paper towel to pick up the gems and funneled them back into the chest. The lock and chest he placed back in the master bedroom. He headed toward the closet.

The key slid in and turned all the way around, but nothing happened. He removed the key, stepped back, and stared. On a hunch, he closed the closet door with him inside and tried the key again. The shelves and back wall pushed forward into a narrow hall. Dim lights set flush within the walls turned on. A set of wooden stairs curved down.

No railing existed, so his fingers touched the sides. Three steps down, he turned and looked at the back of the secret door; a handle stood on this side. As a precaution against those who might follow, his fingers took hold and pushed the door closed.

Something clicked to his right. He pulled the handle, but it did not move. His hand ran along the back of the door as he searched for a keyhole. With nothing else on the plain walls, his fingers played over the flush set lights and gently pushed each one. Nothing happened.

His mind flashed back to the direction of the sound. Almost everywhere on the wall the wood grains matched with only one exception. Two inches off the floor, the wall showed an indent of a fraction of an inch.

As the key pressed against the indent, the indent moved smoothly back to reveal a keyhole. When the key slipped in, the secret door moved toward him. Muffled footsteps met his ears.

The linen door was still closed. He stepped forward and pulled the secret door toward him until it fell quietly into place. From the variation in footsteps, it sounded like three people. One walked in front and moved slowly. Another stood behind but came up fast, along with the third.

A man yawned. "They're not here. I told you they didn't get this far."

A grunt came from a second. "I thought your friend was smart. Now we'll have to search the underground halls." The footsteps became fainter. A smack sounded. "Well, wise guy, speak up." Someone mumbled before the words became clear.

Albert's voice almost shouted. "I said, if you'd get that gag out of my mouth and untie my hands, it would be a whole lot easier to figure out where he went!"

Cliff put his ear closer.

"You better," the first warned. "Your life depends on it."

Metal pinged on a counter; one of them had gone to the kitchen and played with the knife. The voices got fainter.

"Perhaps you need to sit down—" Something made a soft thump. "—until you do."

A second man huffed. "I'll go check the tunnels, but this might take a while."

"We've got all day." The first grumbled sarcastically. "Take your time; I like babysitting."

The second man snorted. "Time is all we've got. Why can't the boss let someone else do this? We need the other kid, and I don't like dealing with boys."

"His name is Cliff." Albert's voice elevated. "And I'm tired of being called a boy."

"Are you, now?" The second man laughed. "Well, pardon me, boy. Just be glad we're not through with you yet. That's when the real fun begins." The voices dropped. Someone moved further away. They swung a door back and slammed it.

Cliff counted to ten slowly; this gave the second man time to go down the vertical tunnel. To explore the stairs was now secondary; he had to rescue his friend.

Voices and music kicked in. The closet door pushed out slowly. With his feet as quiet as possible, he made it to the end of the hall and looked across the kitchen.

Albert sat on the sofa. He could see part of his body, but not the face. A guard had his back to Cliff and stared at the television.

The guard's cell rang. The man tapped the interface and put it to his ear. "Yeah?"

The response could not be heard.

"I'm not sure. If something happened, it would be our skins."

More words came, but they were indistinct.

"I don't like it either." The man grunted. "Fine. I'll be there in a minute." He turned toward Albert and pointed. "Don't go anywhere." He headed toward the vertical tunnel.

Albert's eyes caught Cliff. Cliff placed a finger to his lips, and motioned for Albert to come to him. Albert started to rise.

The man walked over and pushed Albert down in the seat. "What part of *don't go anywhere* do you not understand?"

"I just wanted to get some water."

"With your hands tied?"

Cliff bumped a chair; it scooted forward with a slight squeak.

Albert grinned. "It's a specialty of mine."

"Okay, wise guy—" The man turned around slowly as Cliff scrambled to the hall. "Just a second." He stepped into the kitchen and looked the room over.

Albert yawned. "This place got you spooked? You already checked the kitchen, and it was empty. I promise; undo my hands, and I won't leave through the front door. Deal?"

"What do you take me for? A moron?" The man turned toward Albert. "Have your fun. I'll have mine later." He tapped one fist into the open palm of the other. "Don't get up again."

Albert adjusted his body and leaned back with closed eyes. "Whatever you say, boss."

"That's better." He stepped into the living room, turned to the right, and headed for the vertical tunnel. The door opened and closed. Albert's eyes were shut, so Cliff crept up to the corner where the kitchen met the living room.

Albert opened his eyes which darted to the left, Cliff pulled back as the guard leaped around the corner. "Gotcha!"

Cliff's right fist shot out and caught the man on the side of the jaw. The man's left hand came forward, grabbed for Cliff, and snagged his shirt. Using his right hand, Cliff knocked the arm away. With both his hands, he grabbed hold of the man's shirt and dropped backwards toward the floor with a jerk. The guard catapulted up and over. As the man's legs and arms shot out like a cross, he slammed onto the floor back first.

A groan escaped the man's lips. Cliff rolled to his feet, turned around, and hit him on the chin. The man went silent.

"Quick! My hands!" Albert launched off the sofa toward the kitchen.

Cliff struggled to work the ropes free. "Who are they?"

Albert shrugged. "Man, I fell asleep in the game chair, and I woke in a wooden box."

"A box? Like a crate?"

He nodded. "At a warehouse of some sort. Your parents and

your uncle were there. We were all gagged and tied until they pulled me in for questioning. I never saw Penny." His foot tapped the man on the ground. He whistled. "How hard did you hit him?"

"Hard enough. We need to leave." A rope loop worked free. He started on the next.

"Did you hear what I said? I never saw Penny."

A second loop came loose. Cliff glanced at the unconscious man. "I got Penny out."

"Then where is she?"

"Division A—" With a third loop, the whole thing loosened. "—unfortunately. We got in a jam, and Richard helped us. She was hurt but not too bad. Richard had me hide. Something's up, but he didn't say what."

With his hands free, Albert massaged his wrists. "Thanks; it had started to rub."

"What about you?"

"They took me in and started questioning me. I figured they were looking for you and Penny. The next thing I know, they tossed me into the back of a car. Things must not have gone right, because they took me to the entrance of the underground tunnels, blew the lock, and told me to show them where we went the first time."

"So they know about Gerhard and the school?"

"They know something, but they didn't tell me."

"Come on." He led Albert toward the secret door.

"Wow."

"Yeah, I found the key in a secret compartment. I don't know where the passage goes yet—" He stepped through onto the stairs. "—but it has to be better than here."

"Maybe." Albert stayed beside him and tried to gaze down the stairs, but the curve cutoff his view. "It might be better if we got out of here. The other goons could show at any time."

"It is taken care of. Push that handle."

Without a thought, Albert reached over and pushed it away. The secret door clicked shut. He turned around, pulled on it, and shoved; it did not move. "I don't like this."

Cliff pulled out the key. "I told you, it's all taken care of." He didn't want to put the key in either pocket, so he dropped it in his sock and waved toward the stairs. "After you."

"No, no." Albert waved. "You found it."

Cliff chuckled. "Not curious?"

"Are you crazy? Every time I stick my nose in something, someone tries to cut it off!"

With a laugh, Cliff started down the stairs. They continued to circle around and ended at an ivory door. He placed his eye to a keyhole, but the darkness gave up nothing. The key he had found fit with a click. The door swung slowly back.

A dim light turned on but gained in brightness. It lit the room as pictures and artifacts turned from black and white to color. Wood crates sat in corners with some unpacked and others not. Two other doors existed: one in the wall straight ahead, and one in the wall to the left.

Albert touched one of the old frames. As his fingers shifted over it, so did a bit of dust. "Paintings and pictures." He turned and looked more closely at the artifacts.

Cliff touched one. "There were many artifacts stolen by the Nazis during the war."

Albert nodded. "It looks like Gerhard may have had some." He touched the edge of another frame. "This looks like what we studied in historical art. Metaphysical, I think they called it."

"Odds are, it was by De Chirico."

"Why do you say that?"

"Look at the train vanishing behind the wall in the background. Look at the angles at odds with the perspective. And of course, there is the name."

Albert chuckled. "Yeah, I should have caught that, but it could be a self-forgery. He did get outraged that they did not praise his work after 1918."

"Forgery or not, someone gave it value." Cliff gazed around

the room and touched a box marked enigma. "It seems too easy. I understand the value of these pieces could be in the millions, but—" He stepped toward the door ahead and turned the handle.

As the door pushed in, the hallway went straight for about five feet and then cut a right angle. It stopped at an elevator. Cliff hesitated. The last time he had entered an elevator, the gas had almost knocked him out.

"What are you waiting for?"

"Let's check out the other door."

Albert shrugged but followed. When they tried the other door, it was locked.

Cliff used the key, and the click happened again.

"I don't get it." Albert rubbed his chin. "Why lock the door with the same key used to get in. That isn't very secure."

"Maybe it's a slowdown tactic." He turned the knob and watched the door swing in. More stairs appeared, but this time they were not lighted. "In the unlikely chance something happened, and the secret door was exposed without the key, they would have to get through every locked door. This would certainly give the person time to escape."

He pulled out George's cellphone, turned on the light app, and stepped onto the stairs. The battery showed fifty percent.

"That's not your phone."

"Nope." Cliff took each step carefully and used the light to make sure of their footing. "I suspected someone might have tagged my own."

When they reached the bottom of the stairs, it took the key to unlock another door. As the door swung back, their light revealed a Maybach limousine.

It felt strange to see this vehicle again; Gerhard's driver had used the car to hunt him. He bypassed it and headed toward a closed garage entrance. Beside it stood a smaller door.

"Aren't we going to take the car?"

Cliff threw a glance at his friend as he went closer. "Why?"

"We need wheels. No one is going to think twice if the dean of the university leaves."

"The dean is dead." His eyes studied the garage controls; the servo unit operated by remote. The remote had to be in the car. He turned toward the smaller door; no keyhole showed. Magnetic locks appeared to hold it in place.

"Have you seen his obituary in the newspapers?"

Cliff gave the words some thought as he turned toward the car. "No. I think they want it covered up just like my grandmother."

"Precisely. And from the looks of that room, Division A doesn't have a clue what's down here. They may not have connected the day job thing with Gerhard."

"I can't believe that." He shook his head. His hand tried the car door; it was unlocked. "Not that they're infallible, but they knew way too much about that briefcase. If they haven't made an issue about this, it means the time is not right."

"I don't think they know. If they did, they would have surveillance all over this place, and I'm not seeing any."

As the door swung back, Cliff spotted a remote clipped to the visor. He started to push it. "What if someone is waiting outside the door? We'll not only tell them we are here, but we'll draw attention to everything else. Do you know where the garage opens up?"

Albert shook his head. "But knowing Gerhard, it wouldn't be in the open, and the device will be as quiet as possible. Otherwise, everyone would know when he was coming or going."

"Maybe." Cliff bit his lip. "Maybe not. He controlled the whole school, remember? Nobody sees anything they aren't supposed to see."

The remote had three buttons. Ideally, one was necessary to raise and lower the garage door. What were the second and the third buttons for? He stared at the smaller door, took a chance, and hit the second button. No noise issued, but the smaller door swung out. He plucked the remote from the visor and closed the door. "Come on."

"On foot? I am not walking!"

"I have a ride—" Cliff chuckled. "—and it's safer than this one."

They stepped through the door and out into the early morning. The sun had not risen. With his free hand, Cliff pushed it closed. It fit so perfectly, the door appeared to vanish.

"Nice." Albert nodded. "I bet the garage door is the same way."

They stood on a cement driveway surrounded by buildings. It curved to the right and came to a metal gate. Light trickled across them; twilight would soon fade. Cliff hit the third button.

The gate swung back as soundless as the door. They moved to it and saw the driveway went another fifty feet, exited from between buildings, and curved around the school. Where the buildings were not, thick foliage grew to the height of ten feet as the driveway wove toward the back of the school. Cliff grinned. "Now we know how he came and went."

They followed it to the end and found the back parking lot. As they reached the finish of the hedge, they saw the reflection of red and blue lights.

Chapter 14

"Police?" Albert threw his friend a glance. "What did you do?"

Both leaned forward and stared out at the lights. Two cars sat by his.

"It's strange that security brought in the police."

"Beyond strange. Gerhard would never have allowed it. Even when he had my classroom instructor shot, he covered it up." Cliff hesitated. "Let's take a closer look."

"What?" Albert's eyes opened wide. "You are crazy. I say we go back, get Gerhard's car, and drive out. Let them have the car. It's not yours anyway."

"If we don't understand what's going on, who is to say they won't stop us?"

Albert nodded slowly. "Point taken. So what now, Sherlock?"

"They might have my description. I don't know how much they could see through the windows. I do know they could see the gun."

"You—" His friend grabbed his shoulder and pulled him behind the foliage. "You pointed a gun at the police!"

"No," Cliff's head shook quickly, "you think I'm crazy?"

"I am beginning to wonder."

"It sort of came out when I hit a button." He shook his head. "There's no time to explain."

"Does it look like I have to run?"

"Look, we'll talk about it later. Right now, we have to find out what is going on, and if we have any chance of getting that car."

"Right, and in the meantime, we'll all point guns at the police."

"Albert."

"Okay, okay, I get it." He inhaled. "So?"

Cliff slipped forward and looked around the hedge. "Stay with me." A quick step brought him to the nearest sidewalk. It led away from the car and the police.

"See, nothing to it."

"Yeah, right. So how do we find out what's going on?"

They moved up to a group of students, and Cliff grinned. "What's happening out there?"

One of them turned. "Somebody reported a stolen car. Security called them in."

Cliff cringed; his cell, the satchel, and the file folder were there. If they got in— "Really?"

"They think one of the students took it; the police claim the student pulled a gun."

Albert jumped in. "No way. Wow!" He leaned near to get a better view. "Someone would have to be stupid to do that." A quick glance went toward Cliff. "Well, we better get to class." They headed toward the back of the auditorium.

Cliff shook his head. "That doesn't make sense."

"What doesn't?"

They turned at the corner and walked down a back alley.

"How did they know the student pulled a gun?"

His friend considered. "The newspaper?"

"It happened only a few hours ago."

Albert gave a slight nod and slowed his step. "Then the only way is if someone told them."

"Bingo."

Cliff's outstretched hand pointed toward Hoy Hall. Two black cars had parked along the street. One had two men in it.

Albert's eyes followed. "Those are the ones who brought me to the school. The others—"

"—are in the underground tunnel."

The sky brightened; twilight would soon be gone. "Are you thinking what I'm thinking?"

"Doc," they said at the same time.

They dodged to the left and kept to the right of the garbage bins. It didn't appear those that watched knew Albert had escaped, or if they did, they took a subtle approach. The two boys hurried up some steps, went past the library's door, and wove between two buildings.

One by one, cars turned into the university and parked. The parking areas along each side of the street slowly filled up. Students walked along the sidewalks and into the buildings.

The key was to be nonchalant. If they could pass to the side closest to the lake without drawing attention, it would be easy to slip between the hedges. From there, they could stay downhill until they made it under the bridge.

However, though the students came from across the street, none went the other way. The cars thickened. The parking filled up. Very soon, the students would disappear into their classes, and to hide in plain sight would become difficult.

The watchers in the cars kept a low profile. They would turn upon occasion while their eyes scanned the crowds. Minutes ticked away as the sky became brighter. The students started to thin. Those in the car turned to watch the campus.

"Let's go," Cliff started across. From the corner of his right eye, he could see their watchers, but neither appeared to pay attention to the street.

One swung his head to the right as they made the opposite side of the road. Cliff and Albert crossed into the foliage. Two car doors slammed.

"Run!"

They bolted down the hill toward the large rocks around the lake and hit mud. Cliff slid right as Albert slid left. They dropped behind the nearest rocks.

"Doggonit, Cliff, this is way too familiar!"

"Shh!"

Both ducked.

Cliff's heart beat like a drum. He sat with his back to a large rock and stared out over the lake. The wind wasn't still; small ripples bounced across its surface. He dared not look around least the hunters spot the movement.

Leaves stirred in the trees. The water bounced back and forth on the shore. Small bubbles rose and burst on the lake's surface. The distinctive sound of shoes on wet grass came closer.

The words "keep calm" ran through his mind. "Stay still and they won't know where you went." As he breathed quietly through his nose, he exhaled through his mouth in a rhythmic pattern. His heart beat slowed though the footsteps were almost upon them.

What to do? If they were found, they had no weapons. Wait— yes, they did. Smaller rocks were all around, and a slick slope lay beneath them. Sand formed from the rock's deterioration had piled on both sides. Nature had given them a defense.

Two men walked toward them. The sound was slight, but he could hear them. They must have found their skid marks in the mud.

He looked toward Albert while he made a motion as if to pull something toward the lake. He then pointed at Albert.

Albert frowned. His eyes grew wide as he pointed at himself and shook his head. He pointed at Cliff and made the same hand motion Cliff did.

Cliff shook his head, pointed at Albert, made the same hand motion, and stared at him. Albert repeated the whole thing again.

A head appeared between them, looked at each, and smiled. "Boo. You can come out now." Both Albert and Cliff reached up, grabbed the man by the shirt, and jerked him toward the water. The man plummeted.

Cliff grabbed sand. He brought it over the rock and hurled it toward the second man. The man threw an arm up to protect his eyes. Cliff slammed into the man's feet.

The man fell forward, passed over the top of Cliff, and headed straight toward Albert. Albert threw himself to the left, grabbed with both hands, and shoved the man after his friend. The first man struck the water followed by the second; waves shot into the air.

Albert dropped beside Cliff. "Man, we have got to do something about your sign language!" He laid there and breathed.

"Come on!" Cliff grabbed Albert by the shirt and pulled.

"I'm coming!"

The two men thrashed in the water as the boys broke into a sprint.

Albert pulled up beside Cliff. "They know exactly where we're going."

"No, they don't." As they approached the bridge, Cliff climbed higher until they reached the street corner. "Walk at the top; don't run."

His friend's voice barely contained a whisper. "Walk?"

Cliff nodded as they stepped up. He slowed his breath and put a smile on his face in case anyone came close enough to notice. "What a great morning." His voice resumed a normal tone. "There's fresh air, a nice sunrise—"

"And two goons chasing us." Albert flashed a bright smile as a student caught his words. "Man, this writing class is getting to my head."

Cliff laughed and nodded toward the student. He kept his smile and watched the person turn away. "That was close."

"Like it's going to make any difference?" Albert continued to smile, too. They stepped toward the crosswalk that went over the bridge. Traffic moved in both directions. Cliff pressed the button that would let them cross.

The seconds ticked by. A glance behind showed the men had made it to shore.

"Come on." Albert mumbled without breaking his smile.

"We haven't got all day."

"We have to be normal."

"Normal as in caught again? That isn't an option."

"Walk" flashed from the opposite side; they headed across the street. The countdown began when they were almost there.

The men could no longer be seen; line of sight was blocked by the side of the bridge. Both stepped out of the street, kept to the sidewalk for a few feet, and slipped down the other side.

Cliff peered under. The makeshift houses had not changed. However, no one appeared to be about. He moved to Doc's makeshift quarters. The pallets were as he remembered, but no occupants lay inside. "Doc said he could never leave so long as Gerhard held power."

"Cliff," Albert glanced behind him, "now might not be the best time to stay in one place."

"How did he know Gerhard died?"

As they moved further under the bridge, Albert peered around. "Doc is not the issue right now." One of the men who hunted them headed to the top of the bridge; one could not be seen.

"Come on." Cliff headed back toward the school.

"Wait a minute." Albert grabbed his arm. "We go to all the trouble to get over the bridge and you're headed back to the school?"

"Doc's not here. Where else would you suggest?"

"But not back!" his voice rose though he brought it under control. "Back is not good!"

"The quickest way out is to take their car." Cliff looked around cautiously as they reached the side of the bridge. "It's up along the foliage. We'll cut in about halfway down."

A voice whispered above them. "You're looking for Doc?"

With a slow turn, Cliff spotted a frail-looking man in the highest reaches of the bridge where the light did not shine well. "I am."

"No, we aren't." Albert rolled his eyes. "My brilliant friend would rather steal a car."

The man's eyes turned toward Albert; they did not blink.

"Yes," Cliff iterated, "we are looking for Doc. Do you know where he is?"

The frail man coughed with a nod, and the echoes traveled under the bridge. He caught a glimmer of the chain around Cliff's neck. "It will cost you. What's hanging around your neck?"

For a frail man, he had very sharp eyes. "No."

A noise approached from the far side of the bridge; someone moved toward them.

"Cliff."

"No." Cliff touched the medallion through his shirt. "This is a family heirloom."

"Fine." Albert glanced toward the noise. "Make a decision then. To the car or find Doc?"

Chapter 15

Was it worth giving up the medallion? Doc might know the new group who wanted Gran's codicil. He looked the frail man in the eye and pulled out his pocketknife. "I can give you this." The pocketknife caught the light.

The frail man came forward, paused, and took the knife. "Done."

From the other side, the voices of two men echoed under the bridge.

"But we need to see Doc now."

The man glanced in the direction of the voices and nodded toward the right. He led the way to a blanket that hung over a rough wooden frame.

As they hurried through, sleeping quarters came into view, followed by a second vertical blanket. They lifted it and found a sewer drain about fifteen feet in diameter. A rusted lock lay in a trickle of water that flowed down the center. With a low creak, the grating used to keep people out swung open.

The boys stepped in first. The grate closed with a screech, and the frail man slipped past them into the dim light. The light became fainter; their sight diminished until all was darkness. Footsteps and gurgling water played upon their ears until an orange glow appeared. The glow danced; it reflected off the right side of the tunnel and sparkled as the water flowed.

The closer they came, the more details were visible. The distortion of the image came from an open door set into the left wall.

Doc's familiar voice called as they reached the door. "I suspected you would be back." The man nodded as the three turned toward him. "It is not safe for you here."

"We didn't have a choice." Cliff stepped into the doorway and noticed the equipment.

Doc followed his eyes. "This is a supply room left over from the building of the underground tunnels. Before it became a sewer, supplies were brought at night so no one would notice."

Cliff's eyes narrowed. "That means there is another way into the school."

The man nodded. "The way is sealed but there. However, that's not why you're here."

"No. I need to know if there is anyone else who might be interested in the papers Gran had."

"I don't understand."

"Gerhard wanted them; Fushimi and Division A wants them. Is there a fourth group?"

"So Gerhard *is* dead." Doc looked down. "I had suspected but wasn't sure."

Cliff's eyes centered on him.

"About a month ago—" He waved at the other homeless around him. "—my friends and I noticed unusual traffic at the school. Gerhard always kept a tight reign. These new people hunted for something—so we kept watch. They found the tunnel entrance beneath Hoy Hall."

"Who are they?"

"There have always been rumors that Gerhard, Fushimi, Claretta, and your grandparents were part of an organization that has been around for a very long time."

"Claretta?" Albert turned toward Cliff. "That's the first time I've heard that name since we discovered the plot. Cliff, that's Talia referring to the Italian fairytale."

"My grandparents?" Cliff's face flushed with anger. "You've put my grandparents in the same boat as those murderers?"

Several of the homeless stepped forward along with the frail man. The frail man didn't act so feeble now, and the pocketknife had been replaced by a gleaming nine-inch dagger.

Doc's eyes locked with Cliff's. "Leo, Phil, Stick, it's okay. He is not a threat." The three moved back, and Doc caught sight of the medallion's imprint against Cliff's shirt. "I think you know there is something hidden here. Do you think it was an accident that your grandmother picked you? Why do you think Division A has such interest in you and your family?"

Cliff looked away. Yes, he had noted the slot numbers in the mausoleum. Yes, he had found the hollow column with its contents. However, to include his grandparents with those murderers—that was unthinkable. Fushimi's accusation had been enough, but to hear this from Doc, too? He turned to stare. "Why didn't you tell me before?"

Doc's eyes gazed back. "Would you have believed me?"

"No." He glanced down. "No, I wouldn't."

"Elaine was wise. Her world went beyond what people know exist. It is the darkness. It is the reason why stories are told of demons in the night."

"If this is true, if my grandparents were a part of this, why wasn't my father involved?"

"On your father's birth, Elaine and her husband made the decision to try and keep at least one son from being consumed. For your uncle, it was too late; as the older, the group swept him in before it could be stopped. By then, your grandparents had come to the United States, established a home, and left the old life behind—or so they hoped."

"Your grandmother went to work for the school. The government caught wind of her credentials and drafted her into the program. I suspect Gerhard maneuvered that."

"This—" Cliff swallowed. "—this doesn't make sense." His mind took the new information and merged it with everything he had learned. "If Gran wanted Dad out, why bring me in?"

"It was the papers. Elaine must have felt those papers had to get out, and you were the only one that could do it."

"Why not my uncle? Why my family?"

"You would have to ask him about that."

Cliff sighed. "And to do that, I have to free him."

Doc nodded slowly. "I take it, they have been kidnapped." He did not guess; the man knew.

"How did you know?"

"Standard operating procedure: why chase the mouse when you can bait him to the trap."

"What do I do?"

"You take the bait, you watch your back, and you don't give them what they want."

"But they'll kill them."

"Maybe, but that's not the point. Elaine trusted you to do something only you could do. She prepared you in ways you are only realizing now. Trust your instincts; she did."

"I can't let my family die."

A groan from the grated entrance echoed up the tunnel. Doc turned to a device behind him. Infrared showed two bodies coming up the drain; night vision showed they had guns. "It appears your hunters are here." He turned to one of the homeless. "Stick—" The frail man stepped forward. "—take the boys up the tunnel to the third exit. The third, do you understand?"

Stick nodded.

"The rest of you take the first and second. I don't want anyone to get hurt, and I don't want them to find us. Move."

Albert shook his head. "You have this kind of technology, and you live under a bridge?"

Stick pushed Albert and Cliff toward the door; there was nothing frail about him now.

"This was here a long time before I was." Doc grinned. "I just know how to tap into it. Safe journeys. May we never need to meet again."

They stepped out into the sewer tunnel and hurried forward. Behind them others rushed regardless of the darkness.

The footsteps helped; the echoes went in all directions. Add in the facts that Albert had hold of his belt and that he had hold of Stick, mix everything together, and the situation was complete.

How in the world did Stick see so well? A metal door echoed closed.

After two hundred feet, they reached the first exit; a reflected glow bounced from above to illuminate a ladder. The last in line went up this ladder while the others continued straight.

The tunnel branched to the right, Cliff assumed toward the school, and to the left. Stick headed left, went down about a hundred feet, and turned left at the next branch. When they came to more reflected light, Cliff released his hold, and Stick waved them toward the ladder.

"We need to go to the school. We have to get transportation."

Stick shook his head. "Doc said the third exit; no one can see you from here. The others have confused your hunters, but what you do now is up to you." He held out Cliff's pocketknife.

"Thanks."

Stick grinned and then hurried further down the tunnel. "You need it more than I."

"If I didn't know better—" Albert stared after the man. "—I would swear they weren't homeless at all, but Doc's own bodyguards."

"And what better disguise?" Everything Doc told him rolled back through his mind. Nothing was as it seemed, and nobody was who he thought they were. Was this the type of life Gran had tried to save his family from?

"Up or back?" Albert read his mind.

"Doc said the other tunnel led to the University."

"Doc said it was sealed. Is it worth the chance?" The footsteps were almost gone.

"Do you know any other way to get back into the school without being seen?"

"No, but we're students. We could stroll right in and—"

Cliff stared at him.

"I know that look. The last time you did it, we tried to storm the school to look for Penny."

"If we can get as close as possible to my vehicle, it would help."

"And what part of *still watched by the police or towed* entered into your equations?"

"We could always take Gerhard's."

Albert leaned back and stared at the top of the tunnel. "Now he wants to take Gerhard's."

Cliff pushed Albert's shoulder. "Then you come up with something."

"We're out of sight of the school and happen to be close to a road. Taxi anyone?"

Taxi—he was right.

"It beats going back and running for our lives."

Cliff pulled out the cellphone and wallet. The watch said eight-thirty in the morning, and his wallet revealed he had the cash. "Okay, let's see where we are."

The ladder took them up into a small room. Several drain holes led down into the sewer with a manhole directly above. A view into the outside world existed at street level.

The lock to the manhole had been removed; it was a courtesy of Doc, no doubt. They both reached up and shifted it. Though heavy, plenty of elbow room helped as they lifted it off.

The air that wafted around them smelled better than the dank air of the tunnel. Both scrambled out. They replaced the manhole cover and looked around at the street.

The tunnel had taken them about a block to the right of the university's front. The street sat in a quiet neighborhood. No one stood about.

He pulled out George's phone, found a map app, and looked up taxi services. Yellow Taxi appeared in the list. When the telephone number appeared, he tapped it.

"Location?"

Cliff checked the GPS on the phone and gave the address.

"We've a dispatch in your area. They should arrive in about five minutes." The call hung up.

Albert sat down on the curb. "So we wait."

"Yeah." Cliff frowned and sat down beside him. He looked back at the phone. "Don't you think that call was a little strange?"

"What do you mean?"

"First off, they didn't identify themselves."

"They could have been new."

"And second, they didn't ask how many."

"Maybe the cab's empty."

Cliff shook his head. "It doesn't feel right." He checked the phone and brought up the number, but instead of dialing it, he switched to a different taxi service. When the phone answered, the same type of voice said, "Location?"

"Sorry, wrong number." He ended the call and tapped Albert on the shoulder. "Come on."

Albert got to his feet. "Aren't we waiting for the taxi?"

Cliff started to walk. "No."

"Oh, come on!" Albert rolled his eyes. "They can't know we're here!"

"They do."

"Prove it."

"Call the number. Call any taxi number. Five dollars says it will be a girl's voice simply asking for a location, and they won't identify the company."

Albert raised an eyebrow. "You're on." Cellphone in hand, he picked another. The phone rang twice before a female voice picked up.

"Location?"

"No, we're good. Our ride is on the way. Thanks." He hung up, reached in his pocket, and pulled out a five. He hesitated before handing to over. "It could be coincidence."

Cliff accepted the five and stuffed it in his pocket. "I don't like the odds."

As they turned at the corner, part of the university could be seen. Albert grabbed his arm. "No, not back there. We could head to the pizza place."

"Doug Chills would love that." Cliff chuckled. "Last time, Tish's people beat him up."

A black car travelled past them on the cross street. It hit its brakes with a screech.

Cliff spun to the right and wove his way back to the corner. "Time to go!"

Albert stayed on his heels. "You don't say!"

A second black car turned onto the street behind them. A third materialized from the right as they changed course to cut between two houses. They hoped a fence and dropped into an alley.

Cliff inhaled quickly. "We've got to lose them!"

"Not on foot." Albert shook his head and took a breath. "We can't run fast enough, and if we hide, they are bound to find us."

"Can't run and can't hide," Cliff mumbled. "What about fight?"

"What?" His friend's eyes went round. "Do I look like I'm nuts?"

"Not a fist fight." He motioned at a trash can. "Have a seat."

"And what?"

"We wait."

Chapter 16

Two black cars appeared, one at each end of the alley. They pulled in and started slowly toward the boys. About three feet from them, they stopped, and men got out on both sides.

"Mr. Fulton, I've heard so much about you." The man in front removed his dark shades; his blue eyes contrasted against to his dark, gray-striped suit. "You lived up to your name."

Cliff knew exactly to what he referred: his last name, Fulton, and the life his grandparents had lived before they came here. "And you to your persistence."

The man nodded. "The question now is what do we do with you?"

"You're Division A?"

"The same." The man smiled. "You've been off our radar for almost a day. You have two friends waiting in a secure location."

"I have parents and an uncle who need to be rescued. I can't do that with you around."

The man laughed. "Do you realize how much danger you're in? The people who have them will not hesitate to kill each one should the need arise."

"I realize if I don't help them, they won't live to see tomorrow morning." Two additional black cars pulled in behind those already there. Four cars to catch two boys? What were they up to? "You have to let us go."

The man turned toward Albert. "And you feel the same way?"

Albert's eyes became like steel. "Where Cliff goes, I go."

Cliff stepped in. "What of Penny and George?"

"As I said, they are in a secure location."

"Tell me something." Cliff's eyes narrowed. "How does a safe house that is secure become infiltrated in less than four hours after we arrive?"

The man never twitched. "It doesn't, Mr. Fulton."

Cliff nodded slowly. "You knew I would not eat. You knew the others would. The folder, the car, they were setups. Why?"

The man slipped on his shades, interlaced his fingers, and tapped his two thumbs together. His voice became very serious. "Why do you think?"

Time slowed down. The beating thumbs were all Cliff saw. The truth was close; they hid something. They had kidnapped or helped to kidnap his family. What did they have to gain by leaving him on his own?

They tested him; they were trying to find out how much he knew, but about what? The codicil? Maybe. Gran's past? Maybe. He glanced back at the files in his mind and remembered details on the pages. If they had set him up, then they were manipulating him. Every action, every reaction, they poked and prodded until he did what?

A second truth stood out. From the beginning, Division A had never gone directly against the mysterious other group. Only when Richard had been involved did they have any direct conflict. Even when he had brought the briefcase to them, they had simply destroyed it. There could only be one of two conclusions: no other group existed, or they worked with them.

Psychology—the word echoed through his mind. If they understood what he had figured out, no second chance would come. "I think someone tried to make Division A look like the villain, and they did it from within the ranks."

The thumbs stopped. The seconds felt like eternity. The man reached up and removed his shades. "An excellent deduction, Mr.

Fulton. We suspect an agent whose name is Richard Andrews. I believe you know him?"

Cliff nodded.

"We have received intel which indicates this agent is responsible for the infiltration of the safe house and the loss of certain counteragents at the cemetery last night. If you encounter him again, we ask you to please let us know."

Cliff remembered the card Karl Duncan had left; it was nowhere near him now. "How?"

The man pointed to Albert. "George's cellphone has been bugged. Regardless of the number you call, it will come straight to us."

They knew. They were the ones at the cemetery, they had kidnapped George, and they were after the codicil. Unfortunately, he had delivered Penny and George right into their hands.

So why blame their own? A ploy? Something that might make Cliff more apt not to trust Richard? There were too many lies to know the truth, and not enough truths to expose the lie.

With a nod, he drew back the man's attention. "The kidnappers have said to meet them at bay fifty-two, but they want the codicil. Albert and I have to find it first."

Almost imperceptible, the man's head twitched. "You don't have it?"

"No." Cliff watched for any other reactions; the man's pointing finger and thumb twitched together. "It was stolen. Before you stopped us, we were trying to get it back."

"By whom?"

"I'd rather not say. It could endanger me retrieving it."

The man's eyes caught Cliff's as he sized him up. "I see." The pause was too long. "How can we help?"

Cliff had waited for this question. "You wouldn't be able to get the police off a certain car which belongs to you, could you?"

A knowing look crossed the man's face. "The one you took from our garage?"

"The same. If I'm going to find the codicil, I'll need transportation."

The man snapped his fingers, and a person to his right disappeared inside a car. A moment later, he came back. The blue-eyed man resumed, "It is taken care of. But Mr. Fulton, we expect you to find it, and we expect you to make the trade."

"I understand better than you know." Cliff nodded. "Do you know if the school is safe? Some men attempted to track us."

"The area is secure."

The words confirmed Cliff's thoughts; they did work with them. So who were the others, and what part did they play? "Thank you." He slid off the trashcan and onto his feet. Albert followed his lead. "We'll contact you as soon as the trade is complete." Both boys turned, cut between two houses, and headed for the university.

They heard words behind them. "I hope so, Mr. Fulton. For your sake, I hope so."

. • .

The walk was quick. True to their word, the cars that watched Hoy Hall vanished, his vehicle stood unwatched, and the police were gone. Division A had taken care of everything. That scared Cliff; to hold such absolute power was more than any group should have.

As they reached the car, he pulled the key fob from his pocket and tapped the unlock button. The car gave no sign. Yet, when he grabbed the handle, it opened.

Albert went for the passenger seat. "You're carrying luggage?"

"Hop in; I'll explain."

As the satchel pushed toward the center, Albert slid in beside it and pulled the door shut. Cliff dropped behind the steering wheel. With the doors closed, the outside noise cut off.

"Better." Cliff watched the screen indicate that a bugged device had entered the car and had been jammed. Albert handed back George's phone, and Cliff studied it. "Much better."

Albert noticed the screen. "Shouldn't their own surveillance be immune?"

"They are not Division A."

"What? Wait a minute, they drove the right cars and wore the right suits. They even got the police off your tail."

"They are the traitors, Albert. They have to be. Too many things don't add up. Richard had me take the car that night as a protection from them. Nothing else makes sense."

"That assumes Richard isn't a traitor."

The things he knew of Richard came back to his mind along with Richard's relationship to Gran. "No, Gran did not entirely trust Richard, but I don't think he would betray her. Not after what he has done to help me."

"You think he'd go against them?"

"Not directly, and not unless it was for a good cause." He looked out the rearview mirror; no one drove behind. A glance down at his watch showed almost nine o'clock.

After the car started, he looked back, reversed, and put it in drive. Despite it being in drive, he held his foot on the brake. "Can you look in the satchel for a file folder?"

Albert tilted it and his eyes opened wide. "Guns? Ammo? Cliff?"

"It's not mine." Cliff rolled his eyes. "Just give me the file folder."

He handed it to Cliff.

Cliff went through every page to make sure he would remember the details. He handed it back and drummed his fingers on the steering wheel.

"Thoughts?"

"The file is incomplete. This cannot be everything Division A has on my family."

"They want you to fill in the blanks."

Cliff nodded. "Those were my thoughts."

"But I don't get it." Albert stared into the satchel. "Why you guys? I sorta understand the briefcase, and I understand the reason they want it all to go away, but it feels like—"

"My family is being targeted. Didn't you hear what Doc said?"

"About all that old country stuff? Come on, this is the United States of America. You don't believe in that theory about a handful of people who rule the world? That's not possible. No small group has that much power."

"Division A is close."

"Division A doesn't rule the world."

Cliff whispered, "But what if they want to?"

"What was that?"

"I think we need to go. Tish is waiting."

"What a minute. Tish, as in Tish von Richter, Gerhard's daughter?"

The car started forward and followed the road toward the street. "The same."

"She's hot. I mean—" Albert blushed "—in a sort of, I'm menacing, dark, and I'm going to kill you, type of way. We wouldn't be going to an open field with lots of witnesses would we?"

After they turned at the corner, they continued straight. More students had arrived; the cafeteria had opened for breakfast. Not long ago, that was all he had to worry about. "We're going to Dino's."

A sigh escaped Albert's lips, "Man, I really don't like this. Just because she flirts doesn't mean she is not like her dad."

They pulled up to a stop sign and turned onto the street in front of the school. As they crossed the bridge, Cliff remembered the conversation they had previously had with Doc. Albert's words finally hit him. "I don't like her."

"You could have fooled me." Albert's eyebrows rose. "You certainly are friendly."

"That's her choice, not mine."

"Come on, man, criminal or not, a hot girl throws herself at you, and you feel nothing?"

They crossed the bridge and pulled onto a thoroughfare. The cheeks on Cliff's face flushed. "I like Penny, not Tish. Tish flatters to get what she wants. You know the type as well as I."

"I think there's more to it. She does like you."

"No. It's a ploy."

"It is not."

Cliff's jaw muscles tightened. "No, it is a ploy."

"She didn't have to help us. She showed compassion to Penny. She is all about family."

"Let it go."

"But it's important."

"Let it go."

"I'm just saying."

Anger flooded Cliff's face. "Why are you pushing me like this? Don't you think I have enough to worry about without some crazy woman coming on to me?"

Albert opened his mouth, held it, and closed it. Very quietly, he whispered, "Sorry, bro."

Cliff focused on the road and let the anger drain away. "I'm sorry, too. I shouldn't have reacted that way."

"No." Albert shook his head. "You're right. I guess it's the situation. I mean, come on. All these people want to know what may be in a codicil that belongs to your grandmother. On top of that, you're the only one with the key." He sighed. "That would wear on anyone."

They rode in silence.

Two stop signs later, Albert cleared his throat. "Uh, by the way, why are we visiting her?"

"She has my grandmother's codicil."

Albert pointed at Cliff and then toward the road. "How?"

"She stole it while I was in the shower." Cliff bit his lip.

A slight grin passed over Albert's face. "No interest in Tish, eh? Oh, come on, even you can see the implication of that statement!"

The red cheeks started to rise. "I went to take a shower. She came in and stole it."

"So, she steps in when you're in the shower, finds the room you are in, finds the satchel, knows where the codicil is, takes it, and slips out. How did you know she was there?"

"No." He paused at a yield sign. "I was taking a shower, heard a noise, *got dressed*, went to my bedroom, and there she was on the bed." That didn't sound right either. The sign for Dino's came into view. He gave a signal and pulled into a parking place.

"That doesn't sound at all convincing." Albert rolled his eyes.

Cliff killed the engine and removed the key. "She distracted me."

"I bet."

With a grin, Cliff opened the door and stepped out. "Are you coming or waiting in the car?"

"Do I have a choice?"

"No."

"I thought not." Albert grinned back. "Nice to have you back."

"Thanks for reminding me to have a little fun."

They pushed open the front doors and entered the main room. A petite young girl met them. "The reservation was for two, but I see you brought a friend."

Albert leaned toward him. "Told you. You should have left me in the car."

Cliff whispered back. "And let you dream up more rumors? Not on your life."

"Follow me, please." She guided them toward the back where a candle flickered in the middle of a table. The lights in this section were dim.

Tongue-in-cheek, Albert grinned. "Nothing romantic in this."

Cliff threw him a look. The hostess guided Albert to a table next to Cliff's, bowed, and headed to the front. "Ms. Von Richter will be here shortly."

"You were saying?"

Cliff leaned near. "Will you stop with the jokes? This is serious!"

Albert's eyes riveted to the left. "I can see what you mean."

Tish walked into the area wearing a sheer, red, hip-hugging dress, diamond necklace, and red knee-high boots. The sheer dress had enough material to reveal all the right places without showing anything. A smile curled her lips. "Cliff, darling, you did not have to bring a chaperone. After being in your bed, we are way past that." With a walk that accented every curve, she elegantly took the seat in front of him.

Chapter 17

Albert tried to avert his gaze; it drifted back.

Cliff met her eyes; it was way too provocative to look anywhere else. "Not hardly." He smiled back. "If you recall, you were pilfering while I was in the shower." Inside he groaned. If anyone else heard, boy, would they get the wrong impression!

"Pilfering what?" She stroked the table slowly in a circle. "Your family jewels?"

Despite the knowledge of the truth, Cliff fought a blush. "You took a small envelope which belonged to my grandmother."

She laughed. "There is nothing more sensuous than heirlooms passed from one generation to the next—by bloodlines of course. Do you like sharing bloodlines, Mr. Fulton?"

"That's enough for me." Albert stood up. "Perhaps I should go wait in the—"

"Sit down, Albert." Cliff did not dare look below Tish's face.

"Are you lonely, Albert? What a terrible host I am." She waved and another girl walked out in a similar dress but with a lattice pattern across the front. Sheer and well fitting, the girl slowly imitated the walk Tish had performed. She sat down in the chair next to Albert. With a lean toward him, she whispered in his ear, "What's your name?" Albert swallowed.

Tish's voice resumed. "You didn't answer the question, Cliff."

Cliff's gaze came back to Tish. "With the right girl—" He gathered his emotions and placed them firmly in hand. "—anything is possible."

A broad smile spread across her face. She leaned back, crossed her legs, and made sure he could see them. "I have something you want, and you have something I want." She studied him with knowing eyes.

"You have me at a disadvantage. While you know exactly what I want, I have no clue what you desire."

"Really?" She smiled playfully. "Am I not obvious enough?" She waved her hands slowly out to draw attention to her body.

A thousand thoughts flew through his mind at the same time. This had to be part of a game.

Tish caught the response, and her eyes sparkled. "What shall it be, Cliff Fulton? Did you not enjoy the other night?"

Albert choked. Despite the distraction beside him, he had heard every word.

"More than you know," Cliff went with it. "However, I cannot grant your request."

"Even at the cost of your grandmother's codicil?"

"You wouldn't do that."

"Why wouldn't I?"

"Because that's not how love works."

Tish laughed seductively. "You mistake my intentions, Mr. Fulton. This is not about love; this is about bloodlines."

It was the second time she had mentioned the word. What did she hint at? "But love makes it better. It is the bond between two that can only be broken by them."

Tish paused. "Your point is well taken. My mother and father were in love; though bent, it never broke."

"Then you understand?"

"You intrigue me, Mr. Fulton. So I'll give you the time you need. I will have your bloodline, and the day will come when you will freely give it to me. So here is my wedding gift."

With a flip of the wrist, the vinyl envelope appeared. She couldn't have carried it on her; it was hidden at the table the entire time.

"A man was murdered in a mausoleum on the day of your grandmother's funeral. The secret he holds can save your family. Expose it at your own risk."

She rose in slow motion and directed his eyes with each and every movement. "Until we meet again." With a provocative smile, she turned and strolled from view; once out of sight, the second girl rose and followed.

Cliff turned the vinyl envelope to see if someone had opened it. A sigh escaped his lips as he saw the seal intact. He glanced toward Albert.

"I—I—" Albert let out a whistle. "Wow." He looked at Cliff. "Now do you believe me?"

"She said bloodlines. Why?"

As the blush drained from Albert's face, he shook his head. "Who can know?"

"Someone has to." Cliff's eyes narrowed. "Why give me the secret that can save my family?"

"She wants live relatives for the wedding? Dead just isn't the same."

"Think about it. You have three people who banded together to get revenge by introducing cancer to the United States. If they were that determined, they wouldn't have stopped there."

"Why put all your eggs in one basket?"

"Exactly. The man who died in the other mausoleum was part of the FDA."

Albert turned with open eyes. "How do you know?"

"A depression in the dust—it could faintly be made out. I also found a badge that fit that depression in the car Division A gave me. On top of that, an address was found."

"If Division A knows all this, why don't they take Fushimi down themselves?"

Cliff nodded. "That is a very good question."

The door between the kitchen and the dining area bumped open. A cute, blonde waitress brought out two plates of food. She placed one before Albert and the other in front of Cliff along with silverware. Another brought out two cups and poured a liquid into them. A steamy wisp rose from the cups as the smell of coffee struck their noses. "Compliments of the house."

"Breakfast?" Albert eyed the meal that contained a pastry, two slices of prosciutto, fruit, and coffee. "Did you order this?"

"Apparently, my invitation included this."

"Well—" Albert's eyes brightened. "—no sense in letting it go to waste." With his fork and knife, he cut a portion of the prosciutto into several smaller pieces, stabbed one with his fork, and raised it to his mouth.

Cliff slid the envelope into his back pocket, reached for his silverware, and undid the paper wrap. Words written on the inside band appeared: Beware the assassin; beware the one who is red. His head darted toward the waitress, but she paid him no attention.

Tish's dress had been red. The color red reminded him of the red petal. It also brought to mind the stained glass window in the mausoleum. His fist crumpled the paper band. It had to be from Tish; the handwriting matched the first letter she had given him. Why would Tish send him a message when they had just met in person? There could only be two conclusions: the information had only now arrived, or someone watched her. As he finished separating the silverware from the napkin, he followed Albert's example.

The dried, cured ham had a delicious flavor. It crossed his mind that the food could be drugged, but what purpose would it serve? Her objective had been to give information.

He chewed slowly and took a second bite. Fushimi had warned him to stay out of his business. Division A knew about the FDA's involvement. Tish guided him with clues. On top of that, he had to use the codicil to win back his family's freedom.

The four facts swirl in his mind. Like the colors on the medallion, he remembered what Gran had said. Zero's for red;

it will come to mind. One is for green and all that is thine. Two is a wonder for bright as the sun, it's yellow and orange with purple that's spun.

Zero's for red. Was it the beginning of everything? The danger they were all in before his grandparents had come to America?

One is for green and all that is thine. The safe life, maybe, given to them in their new home? The exclusion of his father from the things of the past?

Two is a wonder for bright as the sun, it's yellow and orange— he stared at the meal in front of him. Wonder could be defined as amazement or discovery. Though he understood Gran had prepared him without his realization, it amazed him about the timing. She knew the family would be involved again. She knew the danger could not be avoided forever.

Albert nudged him.

When Cliff looked over, his friend's plate was clean. "That was fast."

"You're slow today." He grinned. "If you don't want it, I'll take it."

Cliff looked down at his plate; only two pieces of the ham had been touched. "Sorry, I was putting pieces together." He stabbed another portion, put it in his mouth, and chewed.

"What pieces?"

"While you ate, we received another message."

Albert looked both directions. "By who?"

"Tish, I think."

His friend raised a skeptical eyebrow. "It's okay, Cliff. I know there has been a lot of pressure."

Cliff took another bite and rolled his eyes in Albert's directions. "Ha, ha. The words were written on the band around the silverware. I crumpled it so no one else would notice."

Albert picked up the crumpled paper and unfolded it as best he could. "I see. Is it referring to two people or one?"

"That's a valid point. Also, does red refer to a color, or is it symbolic of something else?"

They dropped into silence as Cliff finished his meal. Albert sipped coffee. Cliff's mind continued to swirl. Each of the facts hovered like pieces to a puzzle, and though they might appear to fit two or three ways, he knew only one solution existed. As the utensils were laid on his plate, he made a decision. "Michael Bishop. We have to go see him."

"And where does this Michael Bishop live?"

"Not live, work." Cliff pulled out the business card. "Another souvenir I found."

Albert read off the address. "So we are going to the FDA to ask about a man that was murdered. Should I be worried?"

"Let's find out." Complimentary or not, Cliff estimated the cost, added a tip, and left it all on the table. He didn't like owing Tish more than he had to.

They headed out the front doors and around the building to the car. Traffic had been light when they had arrived, but as the morning went on, it picked up.

They backed out and started down the road. The address on Michael Bishop's card lay closer to the new business district. Do Chi Pizza, Doug Chills' place, existed in the old, as well as the warehouses around the lake. The new business district sat to the east of town; the skyscrapers were there.

A red light stopped them. The traffic became heavy. The short run of twenty minutes to the address grew longer by the second. When the light changed, they took off.

This was exactly why Doug Chills had them ride mopeds. They were small, quick, and could zip through traffic. Though the car was nice—well, perhaps nice was an understatement—he found himself missing the moped.

They arrived in less than forty minutes. Though they did deliver pizza to this part of the city, it wasn't the norm. The parking spot lay at the end of the block one building down. As he pulled in, Cliff noticed a landscaper by the hedges; the man never looked up from what he did and always faced the windows. In the reflection, Cliff caught a goatee with a mustache.

With change in the parking meter and the car locked, they went down the sidewalk to the FDA building. Though the structures on either side had shiny windows all the way to the top, the FDA building appeared older, not as tall, and trimmed in brown and gray. Construction signs decorated the side closest to them. As the dual front doors swung in, they stepped onto a marble floor that shined to perfection. A security guard looked up. "Can I help you?"

Cliff pulled the business card from his pocket. "We are looking for suite two-zero-three."

"Take the elevator on the right. When you come out, it should be the second door down."

"Thank you." They stepped toward the elevator. Security cameras stared around the room. One stopped as it pointed in their direction.

Albert hit the up button on the elevator. Inside, Cliff hit the button for level two.

The elevator rose; neither spoke. As the doors opened, they spotted at the end of the hall a doorway with thick, clear plastic hung as a divider. Beyond it, they could see scaffolding and ladders. They entered the door of suite two-zero-three.

No one sat at the front counter, so Cliff stepped forward and hit the small bell that lay on top. The small ding sounded like a horn in the quiet of the room. Just when they thought no one would come, an elderly woman walked to the front.

"Can I help you?"

It was only then that it hit him. What was he going to ask? Pardon me, I believe I have the card of a dead man who died in a mausoleum, and oh, by the way, I found it there myself? He decided to change it up. With a big smile on his face, he gave a single nod. "I'm looking for Michael Bishop."

Cliff held up his card. "We have some information he might be interested in."

The lady did not blink. "Michael has stepped out, but I'll be glad to let you wait in his office." She smiled kindly. "This way."

Cliff caught Albert's questioning glance as they followed behind their guide; his thoughts were the same. If the man in mausoleum wasn't Michael, then who was he?

She opened a door and motioned toward two seats. They were leather with armrests and rollers. As they sat down, she closed the door.

The clock ticked on the wall behind the desk. The second hand moved steadily over a digital display that glowed at the bottom. Interestingly enough, the center point where the hands connected reflected a tiny bit of light.

"Stepped out." The words played in Cliff's brain. How long had Michael been gone? If Michael were the man in the casket, anyone could take his place, and the two of them would never know the difference. If Michael were not, how did they explain their visit?

Albert strummed his fingers on the arm of the chair.

Cliff turned toward him.

"What?" Albert stopped and looked back. "Can I help it if I'm bored? We're sitting in an office waiting for a dead man—"

The door opened, and in came an older gentleman with a file folder; the name at the top could not be read. The man's dark hair and mustache had a touch of gray. He wore a sport's jacket, jeans, and a pair of dress shoes. Without a glance, he sat in the chair that faced the clock and studied the folder. After a moment, he turned toward them. "What can I do you for you?"

Cliff watched the man's face. "Michael Bishop?"

The man blinked. "Have you never seen me before?"

"No." Cliff noted the question had not been answered. "We are looking for Michael Bishop."

The man's eyes went from Cliff to Albert.

Cliff pushed the point. "Are you Michael?"

"Why do you want to know?"

"Because I believe Michael is missing, and you don't know where he is. Because I believe you are trying to find out if we had anything to do with his disappearance."

The man leaned back and studied them. "Hypothetically, let's say I agreed with your assessment. What information would you give me?"

Cliff remained stubborn. "Please, answer my question."

"And if I say yes?"

"I would ask to see your badge."

The man opened his jacket and slid out a leather wallet. As it flipped back, the badge appeared new, shiny, and recently polished. It had the same number as the one Cliff had seen.

"So either you are Michael or you have secured a copy of Michael's badge."

"Guilty as charged. My turn to ask the questions."

Chapter 18

The man's answers were elusive. Cliff's gut feeling said this was not Michael Bishop. If not, who was he? The young man's eyes narrowed. "Please, ask your questions."

"Where did get the business card?"

"I found it."

"Why did you track it down?"

"Some things are worth saving."

The man glanced toward Albert with a smirk. "Do you have anything to add?"

"Hey, man—" Albert raised his hands. "—I'm just enjoying the ride."

"I see."

The man sat back in the chair and folded his hands. "We seem to be at a quandary. You want answers from me, and I want answers from you, but neither wishes to give out information."

Cliff sat back to hide the nervousness building. What did he think he was doing? Going head to head with a federal agent was sounding a lot less palatable, but he could not back down now. "And what do you propose we do?" He centered on the man's face and could hear his voice speak as if separate from his body. "It might be better if we leave."

The man's voice stayed even, but his eyes were darts. "I can't let you do that—not until we have answers."

Albert's eyebrows rose. "Uh, Cliff? Don't you think—"

Cliff threw a glance at Albert and forced his voice to become more congenial. "I'm sorry. We came to you trying to find Michael Bishop. That was our only intent. If you cannot help us, then we should go somewhere else." He rose to his feet.

The ice in the man's words stopped him. "I don't think you understand. I have the power to detain you as long as I see fit." His finger tapped a place on the desk, and the door clicked. "Now, if there is any information you need to tell me before incarceration, this is your last chance. What do you know about Michael Bishop?"

The man had laid the cards on the table; this was not Michael Bishop. However, the information came at a high cost. He had no choice but to answer now.

"The business card was found in a mausoleum with an exploded casket."

The ice melted only slightly. "How is it we have not heard of this?"

"I don't know. The FBI investigated the incident."

"I see." The man eyes caught the telephone as it lit up. "I'll be right back." As he stood, the door lock clicked open, and he laid the file folder on the desk as he headed to the door. The door closed behind him.

Relief from the man's stare flooded through Cliff. He glanced toward the folder. The name at the top read Michael Bishop.

The shiny center of the clock came to mind. The arc of light convinced him it was curved like a lens, and with all the security in this place, he suspected it was a camera.

The door bumped open, and Richard walked in. His elevated voice was not happy. "Do you both know how much trouble you are in?" He lifted a device from his pocket and held it in front. His voice dropped to normal as the door closed behind him. "Their surveillance is jammed within fifty feet of this device; we have two minutes before he comes back. I want you to take this with you and listen to the recording. I'll ask you about it later."

Cliff's face tore through multiple emotions ranging from joy to concern. "What's going on?"

"There's a mole in the FDA. They're trying to find the leak, and so am I. Somehow, it's tied to the people that are after you."

Cliff's eyes went to the folder. "Can I see it?"

He handed it to Cliff. "You have one minute."

The very top sheet held a confidential mark and listed the penalty for unauthorized viewing. He went to the next. Michael Bishop's age, height, and additional stats were listed. His occupation at the FDA came next with the number of years employed. The last case he had been involved in had to do with the chemical called magnesium stearate.

Cliff had heard about this. Supplements and certain drugs used it as a flow agent. Unfortunately, based upon time and dosage, it could cause damage to the intestines and potentially prevent nutrient absorption in the body.

He closed the folder and started to lay it down on the desk when a yellow note slipped out and landed on the floor. As he reached down to pick it up, he saw the words:

Originally of the golden hue,

Its petals to catch the sun bent rays,

Position, power,

All to a few,

As death does change to blood red days.

A single initial "C" was at the bottom.

Red—once again the color brought back memories: the petal, the stained glass window, and the notes he had received from George and Tish. He could see the words in his mind's eye: beware the flower, beware the one who is red, and beware the assassin. Without saying a word, he picked it up and placed it in the folder. "Thank you."

The door opened, and the man they had met before walked in. Richard turned toward him. "Mr. Gibson, I'm taking these two with me."

"On whose authority?" The man's face turned red. "I agreed you could speak with them, not take them with you."

Richard's manner darkened. "Do you really want to go there?"
Silence dropped. "No."

"I didn't think so." He turned to Cliff and Albert. "It's time to leave."

In the hallway, Richard made sure the door had clicked behind them before they turned toward the front. "Agent Michael Bishop disappeared a week ago. The information surrounding his disappearance was conveniently misplaced, and though no real evidence of foul play materialized, the implications were there. What few facts were known, you saw in that folder. The rest you will hear on the recording." His hand gave the device to Cliff. "Turn off the jammer when you get to the car—not before." His voice dropped to a whisper as they approached the front desk. "This building has eyes."

The elderly woman watched a computer screen. She looked up briefly, noted each one, and smiled as her eyes stopped on Cliff. "Good luck."

As the hall door clicked behind them, Richard headed the opposite way at a jog. Cliff and Albert continued toward the elevator as the look from the woman toyed with Cliff's mind. The elevator dinged. Cliff grabbed Albert's arm as he started to enter. "She said good luck."

Another hall door opened, and two men headed in their direction. One gave a nod as they passed, stepped into the elevator, and held the doors.

Cliff smiled. "Thanks, but we'll take the next." The doors closed.

Albert watched the elevator's floor lights change. "And?"

A sign on the wall showed where the stairwell was. "She knew why we were there. She knows what's going to happen."

"Of course, she knows. She's an agent, too."

"No. She knows what is *about* to happen."

A grin crossed Albert's face. "Come on, Cliff, everyone that comes into the FDA's office is working out a problem. She was being polite."

"Maybe," Cliff frowned, "or maybe it's something else."

Albert folded his arms. "So what do you suggest? We climb out the window or something?"

"Most people take the elevator. Let's take the stairs." He headed for the stairwell.

Albert rolled his eyes. "Cliff, people take the stairs, too. Maybe not as often—"

"That's my point."

The door was not far. The gray cement steps were marked at the edge with orange, reflective tape. Each step echoed. Security cameras watched in the corners, but the jammer still functioned. They reached the ground floor, pulled the door back, and stared.

Cliff saw it in slow motion. A heavy folding screen shifted over the front doors so that no one outside could see in. Through the glass of one door were two bullet holes. His eye swept to the left. The two men who had entered the elevator in front of them lay on the marble floor. Beneath them, a pool of red formed. Someone had shot them as they exited the elevator. If Albert and he hadn't changed course, it could have been them.

No one had noticed them yet. His left hand shot out, caught the stairwell door before it closed, and pulled Albert back inside.

A security officer turned toward them. "Stop!" The stairwell door closed with a click.

"Come on. Second floor!" They started the climb.

Albert shook his head. "We'll be right back where we started!"

When they reached the door, Cliff jerked it; the door came open without a hitch.

Someone opened the door below. "I said stop!"

Cliff led to the left toward the renovation. As they passed through the heavy plastic, they could smell the outside air. The room had been stripped down to the old stone walls. Sheetrock had been stacked in piles. Open, gaping, square holes waited for window frames and supports.

Cliff hurried around obstacles and leaned a little way out one window. The view caught part of the street. Outside the window opening, a bosun chair bounced lightly in the wind. Though it wasn't big, both of them might be able to use it.

"No." Albert backed up from the window. "I'm not getting on that thing."

"We're only on the second floor." Cliff gazed down; cement stood between the two buildings with a single hedge in the middle; the buildings were not that far apart. "If the landing was softer, I'd say we jump."

With a glance over the edge, Albert shook his head. "That contraption cannot be safe."

"If it weren't, do you think the window washers would use it?" Cliff reached out, caught the rope, and pulled it toward them.

"You're serious?"

With a grin, Cliff placed Richard's jammer in his pocket and then studied the pulley device. Adjusted one way, it went up; adjusted the other, it went down. He slid his legs across the plank seat and held onto the building to keep close. "Ready?"

The stairwell door closed. The image of a security officer flashed across the plastic.

"Now! Time's up."

Albert glared at him, leaped forward, and grabbed the rope. As he did, Cliff's precarious grip slipped, and they soared out away from the building.

"Don't just hang there. Sit on the seat!"

Albert's legs flailed. The bosun tilted back and forth. He grabbed at the control rope.

Chapter 19

With a snap, the bosun dropped; they spun toward the skyscraper. Cliff caught the control rope and slowed their descent. Faces from the skyscraper stared out the windows. A security officer's voice shouted from above. The bosun's arc reached its peak and swung back.

Despite the spin, Albert secured one foot to the plank seat; his left arm clenched around the primary rope. Cliff kept drag on the rope while he tried to avoid rope burn. He watched the rotation, positioned his legs, and cushioned the blow as they hit the side of the FDA building.

The bounce back lessened with the arc not as deep, but the spin would not stop. The mechanism that held them away from the building jerked.

Terror filled Albert's face. He grabbed the rope with both hands and shifted the weight more toward Cliff; his foot slid as the bosun lost balance. A shot rang out and bounced from the side of the building.

Cliff watched the world spin. "I think we've found our assassin."

"You think?" Albert's voice rose. "And we're sitting ducks!"

Another security guard appeared above them; they tried to use a long device to grab hold of the rope. As Cliff and Albert swung toward the wall, Cliff knew only one way out. He pushed off the side of the building and let go of the control rope.

The bosun dropped; it was slower than falling but not by much.

He raised his legs up straight and leaned back to try and make sure the plank hit first.

The ground raced toward them as they angled toward the hedges. He hoped they hit the hedges before they reached the bottom.

A second shot rang out. The bullet split part of the main support rope, and it snapped. They tumbled backwards as a metal jingle sounded above their heads.

The plank barely hit the ground as they slammed into the hedge. With nothing to hold onto, Albert tumbled in as Cliff dumped backwards.

Everything went quiet; they could no longer see the security guards at the windows above.

"Nothing's broken. Thank you, God!" Albert let his head drop back as the smaller branches and leaves held him up.

Cliff struggled out of the hedge and bosun. "Come on. It's not over yet!" He grabbed Albert by the arm and hauled him out. A third shot hit the wall.

"What are they shooting at?" Albert ducked down to make sure the hedge remained taller than he. "For someone who just picked off two guys at an elevator, they are not very good."

"Are you complaining?" The sound of the jingle above them became louder.

Albert glanced up, his eyes opened wide, and he shoved Cliff to the right. A device with part of a rope crashed down beside them. "Nope. No more bosuns for me!"

"Aw, come on. It's only a big tire swing."

"Yeah, you go with that."

They rose but heard no more shots. As law enforcement came down the road, police lights flashed. None of the security officers had yet to leave the building.

Three options existed: follow the hedge to the sidewalk and chance going around the front, pass through the hedge and follow it to the sidewalk, or head toward the back and gamble there was a way through. They headed toward the back of the building.

A tall, wooden privacy fence separated the back of the FDA building from the one directly behind it. A containment area had been set up for the dumpsters.

Cliff closed the lids to the dumpsters, grabbed a side, and hopped up on top. From this angle, the front part of the building remained obstructed, and he hoped the shooter could not see them.

Over the fence they hopped to land on a small area of grass. They reached the sidewalk and started their journey around the block.

Five minutes later, they spotted their car. Red and blue flashing lights reflected off the sides of the skyscraper. Traffic had been rerouted, and no more shots were heard. When no one appeared to pay attention, Cliff unlocked the car. They headed toward it.

As the engine started, a detection window flashed up on the windshield. He reached into his pocket, pulled out the device Richard had given him, and turned it off. The horror of the murders hit him as an officer directed their car away from the area; two men were dead and it could have been them.

The phone had been with him when he went inside; Division A probably knew they were there. Had Division A killed them, or had they just happened to show up the day of this murder?

If Division A did work with others, to trace them would be easy. Had someone changed their mind about wanting them dead? The possibility existed. Fushimi had warned him not to push again. He handed the jammer to Albert. "I think it's time we hear what Richard gave us."

Albert's hands turned it over and spotted the controls. As his finger pressed play, they heard a voice with the faint tick of a clock in the background.

"This is agent Michael Bishop. As per my handler's instructions, I have left this message on my own recording device set to call the office in the morning." The distant screech of a chair on a hard floor met their ears. "I will make contact in several days." The recording stopped.

"Can you play it again?"

With a nod, Albert repeated the message.

Cliff glanced toward Albert; the more he focused, the more he heard. Like the ceiling fan rattle when he had first learned of his grandmother's death, details of the recording leaped out at him. In a faraway voice, he spoke, "The folder I saw said Michael lived alone, yet that chair screech was too far away to be him. The noise of the wall clock in the FDA's office and the one on the tape sound similar. That gives us an idea of the distance. On top of that, Michael's voice sounds controlled as if someone listened. I think the recording was coerced."

Albert glanced at the street. "Cliff?" He pointed toward the road.

Cliff swerved back into his own lane. "Sorry."

"What just happened to you?"

"I—I don't know."

"I've seen you do that before but never like that. If you're going to think that hard, I'll drive."

The address of Michael Bishop popped into Cliff's mind; he had seen it at the top of the man's personnel sheet. He gave a signal and turned to the left. "I know where we have to go."

"We're going to his house, aren't we?" Albert sighed. "You do know we don't have a key?"

The traffic became heavy. At last, he spotted the street. "We have an invitation. Richard let us hear that tape; he invited us to go."

"How did Richard know you would pick up the details?"

How did Richard know? As the traffic cleared, he pulled past the few businesses at the beginning of the block and found the neighborhood. The dominant houses were brick and single story. They had well-manicured lawns. Privacy fences blocked off the back.

As he pulled into the driveway of a corner home, Cliff noticed a light with a motion detector above it. "Better turn on the jammer in case he has cameras."

"That won't stop an alarm."

"If it's cellular, it might." He pushed the door open, slipped out from under the wheel, and looked in at Albert with a grin. "Locks never stopped you before."

Albert's eyebrows rose as he stepped out and turned on the jammer. "Only in a good cause."

They headed past several trees and found a side door. It stood ajar. Either Michael had left in a hurry or someone else had come by, too. With only a slight creak, the door came back. A clock ticked loudly in the silence.

The kitchen had a tile floor with a black wooden table and chair set in one corner. The top of the table showed white marble set with a trim. One of the chairs had been pulled out.

A large entrance looked from the kitchen into the living room—in direct line of sight stood a desk with a computer. Beside the computer sat an answering machine.

Cliff went to the desk and listened. In his mind, he walked through the events on the tape.

"Cliff, don't you think we should have gloves?"

The notion had not occurred to him; a chuckle escaped his lips. "Yeah, try not to touch anything. If you do, use the tail end of your shirt."

The clock hung in the kitchen. The kitchen's turned chair faced the living room desk. The screech the chair made was caused by the tile floor. Someone had been watching Michael.

Albert bumped a lamp, and his hand shot out as it toppled. The shirttail immediately followed to wipe off any prints.

The kitchen table sat clean, and the tile floor gave up no tracks, but a single strand of long black hair had been caught where two joints of the chair met. Cliff picked it up and held it out.

A glint of sunlight hit the windows; another car came down the street. A door closed further in the house.

Cliff's heart leaped; it had not occurred to him that someone else might be here. Albert already stood by the side door with a frantic wave to leave.

They hurried out, cleaned the doorknob, and put it back the same distance they had found it ajar. They jumped in the car and backed out. Albert hit the dash. "Go, go, go!" With a side glance toward the house, Cliff caught a shadow move into the kitchen. The car took off.

"Did you see that?" Albert's eyes opened wide. "They were there at the same time we were!"

Cliff slowed his breath. "I know." He couldn't help but laugh. "I didn't think—"

"Man, maybe that's part of our problem. We jump in when we should pull back. Your pal Richard is better equipped for this!"

Cliff drove with no particular destination. "He's not my pal." A car behind him, a dark blue one, turned at a corner.

"He sure seems encouraging to me. Look what he did when he helped at the funeral."

Another car took the dark blue one's place; it was dark green.

"Look at the car you drive, man. Do you think everyone gets a set of wheels like this?"

Albert had a point. His mind went back over the facts.

Michael had been forced to make that recording; Cliff was sure of it. Tish said he had to find out about Michael before the trade for his parents. On top of that, he had been told to show up but not trade.

However, that wasn't all. The magnesium stearate stood out in his mind; somehow it tied in. "We need a computer."

The dark green car pulled to the right lane and passed them. A red Cavalier took its place.

"You're crazy, man. Where do you think we'll find one?"

The red Cavalier slowed and parked; another lighter green

trailed in behind them.

"Your home?"

"Nix. For all we know, it's being watched."

"University?"

Albert stared at him. "I don't care if Gerhard is dead, I wouldn't take the chance."

"Another friend?"

"You really want to involve them?"

Cliff sighed and watched the cars change again in the rear-view mirror. "No, we have enough people caught up in this."

"My thoughts exactly." Albert tapped his chin. "Although, I might have a place in mind. You remember that Internet cafe back toward our part of town?"

Cliff nodded. A dark blue car turned in behind them. No, not a dark blue car; it was the dark blue car, but the driver appeared different. He shook his head. Penny may have been right; although certainly with cause, he could see conspiracy everywhere.

"If we can get a computer there, it might give us what you're looking for."

At the next corner, he made the block. They passed a church; its stained glass windows glowed in the light. The cars altered behind him, but this time the pattern did not repeat.

Their car passed under a catwalk, not far from the church, where a few people crossed. A short time later, the Internet cafe came into view.

The parking areas were full, and the sides of the street were restricted. By a cross street, they found a parking lot down the block. As they turned in, the dark blue car passed.

The neighborhood seemed quiet with most of the traffic on the thoroughfare directly in front of the cafe. College kids ambled toward it carrying books and laptops.

"If we buy coffee or tea, they'll let us use a computer for free. Just be sure and buy at least one cup every thirty minutes."

Cliff nodded as they strolled through the doors. Albert stepped to the back and found an empty computer table while Cliff moved toward the drink counter. "Two Earl Greys, please."

"Hot or cold?"

A mirror hung from the ceiling above the counter and showed the street. A second dark blue car drove up as a yellow car pulled out from a parking place.

The guy behind the counter waited. "Well?"

"I'm sorry, hot."

With a rattle, cups, saucers, and teabags dropped onto a tray. The cups contained hot water. "The spoons and napkins are on the condiments counter."

"Thanks." Cliff's eyes watched the blue car park as he paid for the drinks. With the tray in hand, he stopped, added spoons and napkins, and took a seat beside Albert.

He tilted his chair to watch the big window in front. The guest login for the computer stood beside the monitor, but what Albert had so quickly pulled up caught his attention. "They took magnesium stearate off the market based upon the World Health Organization's evaluation on its toxic levels." He stopped and stared. "It was reinstated a year later."

Albert scanned the rest of the document. "They don't give a reason why."

"We can guess why. Someone lined somebody's pocket and paid them to make it look like further research was necessary." He pointed at the screen. "They claim it cost the drug companies more money not to use it. It wouldn't surprise me if Fushimi did this." A glance at the window showed the dark blue car had left. The dark green one pulled in its place.

"So how does this tie-in with Michael's death?"

Cliff stared at the dark green car; it did look like the same one. Were his eyes playing tricks? No, the make and model were the same. He needed to see the license plate.

"Cliff?"

He turned his attention back to Albert. "What if Michael had discovered that Fushimi had paid to have it reinstated?"

A second car drove away from the front of the cafe. The dark blue car came back and pulled into the parking slot.

"Albert, is there a back entrance?"

"What?" He looked up from the screen. "Back entrance?"

"How about a restroom window?"

"Nothing large enough for us. Why?"

The driver doors on both cars opened, and the drivers stepped out. They casually walked toward the entrance.

"Because it's time to go." Cliff stood and strolled toward the restroom; he spotted the door to the kitchen. "This way."

The door swung back, and a startled cook looked up. "Hey, what are you doing?"

Without a pause, Cliff rushed toward the back door. Albert glanced at the cook as he followed after Cliff. "Sorry, it's an emergency!"

The cook looked skeptical, noted the serious look on their faces, and stepped out of the way.

The door dumped out into a back alley. Two dumpsters sat close with a small parking lot for employees beyond them. They crossed the alley, cut across the lot, and hurried toward the car.

Cliff pulled back at the sound of an engine; he had no idea how many hunted for them. At least two cars had parked up front, and he remembered both as they drove. A car moved slowly down the street with darkened windows and an unusual license plate.

Their car sat parked a good distance away. In a matter of moments, the two men in the building would likely come out the back door. He spun the other direction and headed toward the Internet cafe. "Come on."

Albert stayed at his heels. "You can't be serious. We just came from there!"

"We can't get to the car from here."

When they reached the building, Cliff ignored the back door and followed the right wall.

"We're not going in?" Albert's face brightened, and then he frowned. "What are we doing?"

Cliff reached the right corner of the building's front. "We need transportation." The green and blue cars were still there. "I want you to head to the right down the sidewalk." He pulled out the key fob and handed it to Albert. "Find a good place to hide, wait five minutes, and head for the car. Pick me up near the back corner of the church we passed."

"And if you're not there?"

"Keep going and hide until Richard finds you. He knows how to track the car."

"Why aren't we both going?"

"We need a distraction. We have to get them off our scent."

Cliff peered around the corner. One of the men sat at the computer they had used. The other could not be seen.

His friend's eyes went from Cliff to the cars out front. "All right." He nodded slowly. "If you think it is the best way." He tossed the key fob in Cliff's direction; Cliff caught it. "I'll distract them; you get to the car."

Albert bolted to the main door of the Internet cafe and opened it. At the same time, the man at their computer turned toward the front. Their eyes met, and the man started to rise. Albert burst from the door and headed straight toward the dark blue car, opened it, and jumped in. Cliff dropped back. The car's side showed a reflection of what occurred within.

The man at the computer rushed to the front door, slammed it back, and while still hurrying forward raised a key fob at the dark blue car. Cliff stuck out his arm and caught him across the throat. The man jerked back, the key fob flew from his hand, and he fell with a crash.

Albert jumped out of the car. "What are you doing?"

"Saving your neck." Cliff swept the key fob up and tossed Albert the other set. "How did you think you were going to start his car?"

"I was working on it!"

"Go, I'll take care of this." Cliff waved toward the right.

Albert glared at him.

"We don't have all day."

In the Internet café, the second man had returned. The man's view shifted to the front door.

Albert saw it too. "Fine, but don't you get killed. Your parents would never forgive me." He took off at a sprint, while Cliff jumped into the dark blue car. A thud sounded against its back. Had someone shot at him?

The driver's mirror showed the man on the ground rising as the second came out. Cliff locked the door, put the key in the ignition, and heard it roar to life.

They would reach him in seconds, and the traffic would not give way. He hit the horn, punched the gas, and swung out. Tires screeched, horns blared, and one car dodged toward the left. His rearview mirror showed both men. One raced toward the dark green car as the other raised a gun. Was this car bulletproof?

The rear window shattered as a bullet burst through. He floored the gas pedal. The smell of burnt rubber wafted in as the tires squealed.

The man with the gun rushed forward. A passenger window shattered as a second bullet passed through and out the front windshield.

The cracked glass made it hard to see through, but Cliff kept the pedal down and roared past those beside him. Though the windshield had been penetrated, it had not fallen apart.

The dark green car rocketed into traffic heedless of those in its way. Cliff swung to the left, ignored the turn signal, and roared across the road. The green car spotted him, turned a street before, and matched him on a parallel course.

Which way would it go? Did this car have a tracking device? Cliff clenched his fists on the steering wheel. Whoever drove the other car could anticipate his moves.

Chapter 20

He had intended to turn left at the next corner, but that would put him meeting the other car. Instead, he swung right, went down one block, and swung right again.

A stop sign loomed. With a roar, the car rocketed across the thoroughfare. Horns blared, cars hit their brakes, and more than one swear word hit the air. The dip between streets bounced the car harshly as metal scraped the road.

At the end of the block, he bounced into a quiet neighborhood. The groan of the car echoed off the houses. A few cars parked along this road, but the traffic appeared light.

A car with darkened windows turned at the corner and started in his direction; it matched the one that had passed him and Albert when they had hid. If he didn't know better, he would think it was out on a Sunday drive.

The rear window collapsed part way; the dips he hit had taken their toll. He spun the wheel to the left, squealed the tires again, and smelled the rubber as it burned. The front end of the car narrowly missed another. He hit the gas and accelerated.

A corner came; he swung to the right, ignored the stop sign, and rocketed forward. Where could he go to get away from them and still be near to the church?

He had to think. Was it really Fushimi, or someone else? They had avoided killing him before, but after Tish's note, the whole game had changed.

At an intersection, he continued straight and then turned. Through the trees, the catwalk caught his eye. As no more cars came behind him, the tension in his body relaxed. He spotted the entrance to the catwalk and pulled over next to the curb.

The engine died and sat silently. Thank God no one paid attention. He stepped out of the car, closed the driver's door, and started to toss the key fob inside when a thought came to mind. He opened the door, reached over, and checked the glove compartment.

Nothing of consequence showed. The registration belonged to an Elliot Winston. He reviewed the rest of the details and went to search the trunk.

A click of the key fob opened it, and his lungs inhaled. A man lay in the trunk; his chest did not move and his eyes were closed. Odds were this was Elliot.

His lips quivered as he closed the trunk softly and let the keys fall through the remnants of the rear window. They hit the back seat, bounced once, and dropped to the floor in silence.

Another man had died, and it was his fault. With a queasy stomach, he headed toward the catwalk. How many more would Fushimi kill just to get at him?

At the end of the block, he turned and angled toward the catwalk's entrance. The stairs wound up in a circular manner around a central support. Chain-link fencing covered the sides and top above the cement walkway. He knew the reason for this; it kept people from accidently falling off the bridge.

The word *accidently* played in his mind. These things had not happened by accident. Gran had prepared him; she knew he could handle it. He had been fed the secrets to uncover what his grandparents had hidden. Part of this concerned his uncle, and he fully expected to talk with him at the first possible moment.

The sun struck the tops of the cars which drove beneath the catwalk. His stride slowed and watched them pass. From the corner of his right eye, someone approached from the opposite end.

Black clothes, a hoodie to hide the face, and boots, not tennis shoes, decorated this person. Though they walked casually, they headed right for him.

Was it paranoia? With nowhere to hide and no place to step out of the way, all he could do was play it cool and hope it was his imagination.

The figure slowed. An amused, male voice asked, "No more running, Mr. Fulton?"

Cliff forced himself to smile. "Who are you?"

The man laughed and the hoodie slid back to reveal part of his face. "I don't want to kill you; you've given a great chase. Unfortunately, my employer doesn't agree."

Cliff's heart thumped harder. "Who is your employer?"

The man focused on him with a smirk. "I can see the thoughts now. You think, I'll find out what he knows and somehow get out of this, but it's not that simple. The only thing simple is the business transaction you and I must perform."

Cliff steadied his heart rate. "I would still like to know." For the first time, he noticed a car parked down at the end of the catwalk. It matched the car that had passed him—the one with the darkened windows. "You knew my location all the time."

"And the real question you should ask is?"

"How did you know?" The man toyed with him, but Cliff played his game. "But no one knew I would be here except—"

"Albert?"

The muscles in Cliff's right fist clenched as he shook his head rapidly. "No, Albert would never betray me. Albert is my best friend."

The man stepped closer. "Realization dawns, does it not?"

"No, you're lying."

"Am I? You asked the question."

Cliff's body shook. "You're a liar!"

The man folded his arms. "Look at yourself, Mr. Fulton. You're falling apart. Your family has been taken, your girlfriend's captured, and your best friend has betrayed you. What do you have left? What are you still fighting for? A grandmother that's dead?"

Cliff's face flushed in anger. "You have no right to speak of any of them!"

The man stepped forward and stared into Cliff's eyes. "I have every right, Mr. Fulton." As the man's arms unfolded, he tapped the outline of a gun on his right side. "Only one thing is left for us to resolve. Where is your grandmother's codicil? After that, your misery will be over."

The codicil—it hid in his back pocket, and the man didn't know. It was his only ace left.

The shaking stopped, and the anger drained away. "Kill me. You'll never find it."

The man took a final step. From this angle, he could pull his weapon, and it would be out of sight of the cars below. "I intend to, Mr. Fulton, but you will give me the codicil before you go."

"Or what? You've said it yourself. I am completely alone and no one is coming to my rescue. I do believe we are at a conundrum; I now have nothing to lose." A bitter smile crossed Cliff's lips. "And I will make your day a bad one."

For the first time, the good humor in the man's face cracked. He pulled out the gun with a silencer already attached. "Oh, but you will give it to me. If I have to make you scream in pain for hours, you will give it to me."

Cliff lunged and twisted as two shots spudded into the cement. His left hand pinned the gunman's right as he brought his right fist down to score directly on muscles that controlled the gunman's grip. The man's reflex released the gun. It hit the walkway and skidded.

Without a pause, Cliff's right elbow rammed it into the man's solar plexus. The man bent forward involuntarily, and Cliff slammed a back knuckle between the man's eyes.

The man knocked backwards as Cliff plowed into him; his left hand clutched the man's throat. The Adam's apple bowed inward, and Cliff knew the end result; the muscles in the throat would begin to swell. As the man slammed into the chain-link behind him, Cliff pinned him to it. "Why won't you leave me and my family alone?"

The man gasped. Between the solar plexus hit that had locked his chest muscles and the swollen throat, he could not breathe.

"I want answers; a single nod will do. Do you understand?"

The man gave a single nod.

"Did Fushimi send you?"

The man shook his head though he gasped for breath.

Cliff gritted his teeth. "Did Division A?"

The man shook his head.

Who else? Cliff racked his brain to think. Doc had mentioned another group but had never given it a name. How could he ask the question? "Is the person who sent you the same one who kidnapped my family?"

The assassin wheezed and shook his head.

No? The people who had his family were not the same ones who hunted him? The person was not Fushimi? How could this be?

Tish's note flashed in his mind: beware the one who is red— beware the assassin. If this assassin was not from Fushimi or Division A, then who sent him?

The poem found in Michael's file came back to his mind. Red was the key; red meant assassin. An assassin that had once been golden? An author with the initial *C*? Was it someone who had once been good?

The poem and Fushimi's clue were two of the things he had wanted to research on the computer, but they had been forced to run. Was that orchestrated by his friend?

Only Albert could have known where he went. If a tracker had been on the car, they would have stayed on the same side of the thoroughfare and searched there first.

Division A could have tracked the car Albert drove, but if what Richard had said could be believed, only Richard had the code. His top two suspects were the secret group and the red assassin, but why try to kill him?

The man recovered but slowly. The gun lay ten feet to Cliff's right. Cliff kept his eyes on the man while he backed toward the gun and picked it up. If they planned to kill him, did he have the right to do the same? If he didn't fight back, would they ever stop?

The man's eyes watched as he regained his breath. Cliff counted the seconds. He had to protect his family, his friends, and himself from this scum. The gun pointed toward the man as Cliff came forward and pressed it against the man's chest. His hard voice spoke, "Remember this. Remember that I showed you mercy. I suggest you get another job."

He had half a mind to hit him, but Cliff relented. He placed the gun in his belt and pulled out his shirt to hide it. The last thing he wanted was additional attention.

The walk seemed short down the other side. The church lay a block or so up. At the corner, he swung back into the streets away from the thoroughfare.

His mind swirled with confusion; he had almost done it. It would have taken no skill to pull that trigger and end the man's life. Penny had raced in front to stop him; Albert had been appalled to see a gun in the satchel. Was it wise to keep the gun?

Through the trees, he spotted the back of the church. With each step he took, it loomed nearer, and the dread settled in his stomach.

Part of his mind said Albert would never betray him; part of his mind said the facts could not be denied. By only one way could the man have known his location; it had to have come from Albert. The red brick and tall steeples loomed like daggers which stabbed at the sky. If Albert had betrayed him, then no reason existed to show up at all.

A sidewalk led to the back of the church, and beside it were cement benches. He took one and waited. What choice did he have? Either Albert showed up or he didn't.

The back of the church opened, and a man came out in street clothes. He nodded toward Cliff, paused, and turned back toward him. "Can I help you, or are you waiting for someone?"

Cliff gave a short smile. "Waiting."

"But not too happily, I see."

Cliff gave a sad chuckle. "No. I'm not sure the person will show up."

The man studied him. "You know, it seems to me you want to believe him, but you're having a hard time. You've been betrayed before, and you're transferring those feelings to this person."

Cliff wrinkled his brow. "You're a priest?"

"I'm a man of faith." He patted Cliff on the shoulder. "Don't lose yours too quickly. Life has a way of making things right." The man continued his walk, turned to the left, and headed down the sidewalk.

The words, *man of faith*, held his attention. Penny had betrayed him but had proven herself in the end. Albert had never betrayed him, at least not that he knew of. In this game of cat and mouse, who could he trust?

More than fifteen minutes had gone by. Either Albert had found trouble or the man had said the truth. No matter how much he wanted to believe, the events of the day weighed on him.

A horn sounded. As he turned, a black car rolled up and stopped at the curb. A smile cracked his demeanor as he rose and walked. In a rush, he grabbed the passenger door and swung it back. "Albert, you don't know how good it is to see you." Cliff froze as his eyes narrowed. "Where's Albert?"

Chapter 21

The eyes that met him were familiar, but Richard's voice did not reassure. "Was Albert supposed to meet you?" The man shook his head. "The car he drove vanished off my tracker about ten minutes ago. Someone changed the code." His eyes watched Cliff carefully. "You want to tell me what's going on?"

Cliff sat down in the passenger seat and closed the door. A warning went off on the windshield that showed a weapon had entered the car. "I take it you've been tracking us?"

"Since when did you start carrying guns?" Richard held out his right hand. "They aren't toys, and even adults should be more careful."

Cliff's eyes narrowed as he turned toward him. "No."

"Cliff, you remember our first encounter? What did I tell you then?"

"They are too noisy and loud. Anyone can hear them."

Richard nodded. "Unless you are prepared and know how to use them, I suggest you leave them alone. In a gunfight, just by having one, you will immediately become a target."

Cliff slowly pulled the gun and handed it to him. Richard laid it on the seat. "To answer your first question, it hasn't been easy at all." He pointed to the side of Cliff. "Seatbelt, please."

Cliff brought it around him and clicked it in place. "Division A says you are the mole."

"Which Division A?"

Cliff looked toward him. "So they are divided?"

A sad look crossed the man's face. "Divided is a strong word, but not strong enough. A segment of our department feels we should cooperate with the group that kidnapped your family and friends. In order to facilitate the change, certain lives were lost."

Cliff's mind went back to Karl, the voices, the door, and the shots. "They killed the man who gave me the car fob and folder, didn't they?"

Time slowed as Cliff waited for the answer. The question was loaded, and that had been his intention. If Richard had escaped, he should not have been around when Karl died.

"I don't know. A number of agents haven't been heard from. Most don't even know about the coup." Richard glanced in his mirrors and started to drive. A red blip showed up on the windshield, but he cleared it by pressing a triangle symbol.

"How did you find me?"

The man chuckled. "You do know a shootout around an Internet cafe is a little hard to miss, especially if I tracked the car you took."

"So you were there?"

"I drove up as you raced off. I hit you with a tracer."

"The thud," Cliff remembered. "I had no time to see who did that. However, it doesn't explain how you found me here."

"I traced your car and spotted another that waited across the bridge. After I saw the gun you carried, I could surmise the rest."

Cliff's eyes took on a faraway look. "He tried to kill me."

"But you didn't kill him."

Cliff turned toward him. "How do you know? I wanted to."

"No, you didn't. No matter how angry you felt, I know you didn't want to, not really. By the time I got there, the man had vanished. I don't know what you did, but he did not go to his car."

"It was probably stolen anyway." All the emotion rushed back to him, and he could see the dead man in the trunk of the car. "They were sent to kill me."

"They underestimated you. If they come a second time, they won't make that mistake again."

"That's why I had the gun." He turned to stare out the window and watched the trees go by.

Richard broke the silence. "What do you want to do about it?"

"They have my parents, and they want to exchange for my grandmother's codicil. Richard—" Cliff bit his lip. "They are not part of Division A, but someone who knows things works with them. If I trade, they will kill us, and if I don't, they will do the same. On top of that, we have another mystery group; I was warned to watch for them."

Up several blocks, Richard spotted a park. He pulled up beside it. "Who warned you?"

"Tish."

Richard nodded. "It makes sense. Why didn't I see it before?"

"What?"

"It is a cabal, Cliff. This particular group has been around a very long time, and they are very patient. What they don't like is when one of their members leaves. Elaine and her husband stopped being active members. That makes them nervous. They want her family back."

"And you know this how?"

"Between what you have told me, and what Elaine said in the past, I just put it together."

"And now her family is being hunted."

"No." Richard shook his head. "You don't know enough to be a threat. It is the information Elaine left that they don't know. In order to get it back, they've called in other groups."

"So their hands remain clean?"

"Relatively speaking."

"Someone is hunting Fushimi, too."

It took a few minutes to bring him up-to-date. Cliff left out the part about the secret door in Gerhard's office and his conversation with Doc under the bridge. He did not bring up everything about Tish and Albert either. He was certain the man knew he had left something out.

Richard pretended not to notice. "Two birds with one stone. So we are back to the original question: what do you want to do?"

"I want to save my family, catch the assassin, and bring the person who set up the FDA man to justice."

Richard nodded slowly.

Accusation rose in Cliff's voice. "Division A knew about the FDA man. So did you."

Richard continued to nod. "I had hoped to spare you, but when I followed you to the FDA offices, I knew you had to discover the truth."

"So I did kill him." The blood drained out of Cliff's face. "I don't understand. How could Gran have been part of these people?"

Richard inhaled. "Your grandmother and grandfather were good people. They wanted a better way for their children. Do not let these revelations distort that picture."

Buried emotions surged toward the surface. "A picture of death at every corner? A picture of murder because someone found themselves in the wrong place at the wrong time?" His face burned, and he shook as tears fell. "They destroyed my grandmother's funeral and burned the church to the ground. They've attacked my family and friends. I hate them. I hate them with all my heart. You asked me what I want to do, and now I know. I want to take revenge."

Richard's voice became solemn. "No Cliff, revenge is not the way."

"They will never stop."

"They will stop." Richard kept his eyes ahead. "We simply convince them it is not worth their time to pursue."

The shaking dropped off, but the anger still burned. "How?"

"First off, we get your grandmother's codicil."

"And then?"

"We have to ensure there are no more secrets."

"You want to expose it all?"

"What better way to stop the killing? Why kill if there's nothing left to kill for?"

The solution held possibility. But how? As the anger left his mind, he started to think again. The foolishness of his outburst brought relief and embarrassment. He knew why he felt this way. This cabal tried to take everything from him. They wanted to make his psyche fragile. They wanted to make him feel alone. If you can strip all support away from a person, that person might give up hope. He would not. Never trap a dog in a corner, for he will surely fight back.

"I know where to start." Cliff continued to cool down. "We start at Gran's house."

Chapter 22

The silence thickened as they came up the block. Gran's house loomed with those vacant windows and closed blinds. The last two days had brought Gran's death vividly back.

His emotions were out of control. It had happened too much that day for him to trust himself. That scared him; if he couldn't trust his instincts, he might easily make the wrong decision.

They pulled into the driveway. Richard glanced at him. "The ball's in your court."

The passenger door swung out, and Cliff closed it behind him. Richard had kindly allowed Cliff to reveal only the secrets he wanted to show. Trust had begun.

Was that wise? In a world that flipped from this side to the other, could there be any real trust? Gran had trusted Richard; she had trusted Richard to be himself. Perhaps that was the real secret to understanding people. One did not put them on pedestals or expect them to be heroes.

The wooden steps did not creak as he made his way to the door; he had done that for Gran. As the screen door swung back, he reached in his pocket for the key. It was gone, but he didn't remember its removal; it had been in his pocket before the casket. When he emptied his pockets at the safe house, he could not remember seeing it.

If someone had taken it, it could only be for one reason. He reached forward and turned the doorknob; the door swung back.

The clock ticked on the mantel, and all appeared quiet in the house. Someone had been here; he could feel it. Now he understood how his grandmother could tell.

He gazed around at the living room furniture for clues to confirm his suspicion. The upstairs creaked although that was normal. As a precaution, he headed upstairs.

Only two people had access to this house now: Penny and him. She stayed the night, but in a separate room; he wasn't ready for a relationship beyond that.

The idea of marriage had crossed his mind. He liked Penny, but he wanted to finish school first. If he didn't, the added commitment might cloud his judgment about completing it.

Gran had made sure money was not a problem; he didn't need a job. However, to accomplish his goals was a must. It made him feel normal in a world that had turned upside down.

The top of the stairs revealed nothing unusual. Gran's door sat open in the same way she had left it; he didn't have the heart to close it off.

As he passed down the hall, he went to his room. The bed, dresser, and laptop had not been touched. However, the closet door stood ajar. Who had been in his closet?

The idea of dusting for prints came to mind, but he had nothing to do that with. Besides, for all he knew, the people could still be inside the house. He moved to the closet, grabbed the handle, and whipped it open. Penny screamed, saw him, and collapsed in his arms.

He struggled backwards with the sudden weight; she had gone completely limp. When he laid her on the bed, he checked her pulse and made sure that she breathed.

"Penny." He touched her face gently. "Come on, girl. This is not like you at all."

As her eyes fluttered, she centered on him, and her arms grabbed him. "You're here!"

"Of course, I'm here. It's my house."

"No, I mean." She loosened her grip but did not let go. "They're gone." Her eyes moved wildly from side to side.

"Has someone else been in my house?"

"Yes, I mean I—I don't know. They chased me, and I got away not far from here."

"You got away?"

"We were in a car. They were taking me away from the safe house."

"So you were at a second safe house?"

She nodded quickly. "Some men came and said we had to be moved. George and I were together, but they put him in a separate car."

What Richard had expounded upon drifted through his memory. Division A was torn in a civil war, and most of the agents didn't know it. "Where were they taking you?"

She threw a glance at the open door. "They chased me. I didn't know if I could get away."

"Penny, where were they taking you? What made you want to run?"

"Bay fifty-two."

Cliff's jaw set. That warehouse belonged to Gerhard, and his family was supposed to be there.

She started to shake.

He lifted her up and held her close. "It's okay; they're gone now, and I'm here to help. I do want to ask you one more question."

"Yes?"

"Did you lock the front door?"

"I can't remember."

"That makes sense." Cliff nodded. "You hurried in as you tried to get away, closed it quickly, and rushed upstairs. Am I getting the facts straight?"

She nodded but stopped and looked at him. "Why?"

To tell her of the key would only make her worry. "The door

was unlocked when I got here."

Her eyes opened wide. "Cliff, I'm sorry. I didn't mean to leave it unlocked."

He stroked her hair. "It's okay. I want you to rest. I'll be back in a moment."

Her grip tightened. "No."

Gently but with firm hands, he rolled back her fingers and placed her arms on the bed. "It will be fine. I want to check out the rest of the house."

She shook head. "No."

What had they done to her? "I'll be right back."

As he rose, she sat up. "Cliff, they won't make the trade. They plan on killing us."

"I know. It will be okay. Just rest."

He searched the last rooms upstairs. None had been disturbed. Penny's appearance explained the unlocked door, but not the missing key. Fushimi's men had put him in the casket; they could have taken it. At the time, Fushimi had no gripe with him except he wanted Cliff to leave his projects alone. Who else had access to his person?

The image of a shadow came to mind; the shadow had shown up in the second mausoleum. It had lifted the FDA's badge from the dust, and that badge had found its way into the car he drove. The shadow's build had been small.

He saw the scene in his mind. A shadow, yes, but what other details had he seen? Then it hit him—it wasn't a shadow at all, but a person dressed in black.

Two other people in black had appeared that night. One had come to the boxes stored at the church, and the other had attacked George. However, before that there had been another, hidden in the shadows behind George as he talked. The image had been unclear, but the narrow build could not be missed. The two shadows were the same person.

The set of footprints he had seen on the grass that came from the mausoleum—they had been narrow, too. Small build and narrow shoes meant possibly a thin man or woman.

He stopped by his room. Penny's wide eyes caught his as he looked in.

"I'm good. Everything's good." He smiled. "I'm going downstairs to check the rest."

She rose from the bed. "I'm coming, too."

"It would be better if you didn't."

The fire returned to Penny's eyes. "I'm not frail, you know. Just because I was caught off guard, doesn't mean I can't handle it now."

Cliff put up both hands. "Whoa, let's backtrack a little. No one said you couldn't handle it. You've been through a quite a shock. I'm giving you space to work it out."

"What if I don't want space? What if I want to help you check out the house?"

"Penny—" Cliff closed his eyes. Whatever had scared her had worn off; he had to keep that in mind. "I have no problem with you searching the house. I just want you to be safe. I love you."

Penny stopped and stared with an incredible look on her face. "You do?"

In his mind, the last three words startled him. They had not been there when he had started the sentence, but they had popped in. "I—do, apparently."

"Apparently?"

He raised his hands again. "It slipped out."

"You didn't mean it?" She slid slightly back.

"No, no, I had to have meant it. Otherwise, I would never have said it."

"Do you love me or not?"

Cliff leaned back against the doorpost and stared into nothing. "Yikes."

"Yikes?" Her face filled with confusion. "I don't understand. I don't like hearing those words thrown around lightly. Either you do or you don't. What is it?"

The doorbell rang.

"I'll be right back." Cliff spun around and hurried down the stairs.

"Oh, no, you don't." Penny took off after him. "I want an answer."

Without a look to see who it was, Cliff threw open the door. "Come in, Richard."

On the stairs, Penny's steps slowed as Richard walked in. Cliff closed the door behind him.

Richard took in their facial expressions, and his eyebrows rose. "Did I interrupt something?"

Penny jumped in. "Yes."

Cliff was adamant. "No."

"Okay, at least I know what took so long." He winked at them.

Cliff shook his head. "It wasn't like that."

"Definitely not!" Penny's voice was laced with venom.

A frown hit Richard's face. "Perhaps someone should tell me what is going on?"

Penny started the explanation, and Cliff finished it though he left out, of course, the *I love you*. She noted that he did so with a glance but held her tongue.

"It confirms what we thought." Richard nodded "The segment which has taken over Division A has moved up the stakes."

Penny stepped closer to Cliff. "Division A is divided?"

Richard looked around the room and took a seat on one of the plush chairs. "They call it a coup, and yes, one section has taken over the other."

She sat down in the nearest chair. "So they really want to kill us?"

"No." Cliff caught her eye. "We have a plan; we are here to get Gran's papers."

"Papers?" Richard's eyebrows rose. "*The* papers? The papers we thought were destroyed?"

He nodded. "Gran left a second set. She suspected what might happen with the first."

Richard grinned affectionately. "That little witch. I knew there was a reason I liked her." As he rose, his grin spread wider. "That makes this situation a little bit easier. Don't get me wrong. It is still deadly but with a better chance of success."

"Wait here. I'll get them." Cliff moved to the door under the stairs and swung it back. In front, the cement stairs led down. His finger found the light switch, and the stairway glowed to life. The door above closed of its own accord as the musky smell of mildew hit his nose.

At the bottom the stairs, he turned to the right, found the old worktable, and slipped under it. On the back wall, he removed a loose brick and found a hollow spot. His fingers touched a plastic bag, pulled it, and felt the assuring thickness within.

His intention had been to take them to Richard. Instead, he placed the plastic bag on the table, opened it, and pulled the papers out. As he separated them, he laid each down and read.

On the last page lay a drawing of a snake eating its own tail with other markings set in the center. Some were pictorial while others looked like random marks on the page. Why did Gran include it?

The words *random*, *circle*, and *snake* clicked together in his mind. His right hand grasped the medallion he wore, lifted it off his neck, and placed it on the table beside the paper. Where the v appeared around the circle of the medallion, so was the mouth of the snake.

Time was of the essence; he needed to get to the warehouse soon. He separated this sheet from the others, rolled it up, and put it back into the plastic bag. On second thought, he removed the two inch eyepiece from his pocket and added it to the bag along with the medallion. Once the bag laid hidden back in the wall, he crawled out and dusted off his pants.

Sounds came from above; they echoed faintly down the stairs.

To hear them down here, someone was very noisy. He crept up the stairs. Elevated voices met his ears, and since he was sure Richard and Penny were not shouting at each other, he quietly went down to the cellar rethinking his entrance. The papers formed a neat stack, so he rolled them up, slid them in his pocket, and headed toward the garage.

The stairs which came up inside the garage had not been disturbed since the last time he had been there. With a cautious push, he opened the door that protected the entrance.

Gran's car sat where he expected it. The building creaked as he stepped toward the garage's side door. Without a noise, he turned the knob and opened it a tiny crack.

Behind Richard's car parked a light green Cavalier. Light green—his eyes recognized it as one of those that had followed them to the cafe. He released the knob and let the door drop back. His eyes turned toward the rest of the garage.

The papers were in his pocket. They had to be hidden until he knew all was clear.

The door shut with a loud click; every muscle in his back tensed. His head swung around, but no one appeared. He slipped the papers out of his pocket and stuck them behind the edge of a pegboard mounted to the wall. The fit was tight but adequate to hide them.

With a gentle touch, he turned the doorknob and pushed it out slowly. No one stood between the house and the garage. The wind stirred the trees. The muscles in his back relaxed.

The distance to the back of the house went fast; no one appeared to be watching. He passed over the sidewalk and kept lookout toward the front. None of the cars were occupied; they had to be in the house. The unlocked back door reminded him of the way he had found the front; someone had been in the house before Penny had arrived.

A turn of the wrist opened the door; no sound issued, but his pulse raced. The door swung open slowly; he could hear voices from the living room. Penny's and Richard's were distinct, but he did not recognize the third though it sounded female and had an accent. As he turned to close the back door, something hit him.

Chapter 23

Cliff blinked as a bright light shown in his eyes. To the left and right he could see shadows.

A female voice spoke, "Welcome back, Mr. Fulton. We've been waiting for you."

Coarse ropes gripped his left hand as he tried to raise it to block the light. It was the same with the right; the wrists were tied to the arms of a wooden chair. His eyes closed tightly as he looked away. "May I ask who I have the honor of meeting? A little less light might help."

Humor laced the female's response. "Are you uncomfortable, Mr. Fulton?"

A male voice interrupted. "Enough. I've had enough of these games." A shadow to Cliff's right stood up. "Where is the codicil?"

Fear swelled up in him; he had thought to hide Gran's papers but not the codicil. Wait, they hadn't found it? Cliff blinked several times; it should be in his left back pocket but from the pressure of the chair, nothing was there now. "You don't have it?"

The click of a gun sounded as the barrel rotated into place. "No more games."

"No—" The female spoke as if she listened to something the male ignored. "—he really doesn't have it. Killing him would be useless."

"But it would make me feel better."

A thin shadow whipped up from nowhere and snapped against something. The man grunted as a metallic item bounced away across a wooden floor. "Those are not our instructions."

The man stifled a curse. "Then why is he here?"

"Why indeed?" the woman spoke. A button snapped as a pouch opened. A light came on that helped to compensate for the brightness focused on Cliff. With it, he could see some details.

The shadow that had hit the floor had the outline of a gun. The male's shadowy features were larger than the female's. Of the smaller ones, they were similar to those he had seen pick up the badge.

The woman had a whip from the sound of it and knew how to use it. Her cellphone came from the belt pouch. He remembered the black utility belts carried by the assassin's at the church. He nodded toward the guy. "How's the head? Those burnt church boards pack a mean wallop."

"They do, smart-ass. I'll be glad to show you."

The female pointed in the male's direction and whispered, "You've been warned." Her head moved up and down with the cellphone in her hand. "I understand." As the call ended, she turned back toward Cliff. "Where is the codicil?"

Cliff shifted in the chair. It had a slight wobble. "You're the ones who knocked me out. Shouldn't you know?"

The male exhaled. "I told you—"

"We did not knock you out, Mr. Fulton." The female's voice remained controlled. "We found you on the floor."

"Where?" Other objects started to seem familiar as he looked around the room. The primary light distracted his eyes, but the brief phone light had been enough to compensate. He sat in his own bedroom strapped to one of the wooden chairs in Gran's house.

The woman paused. "In the kitchen."

He listened but heard no other noise. Where were Penny and Richard? Where were the people from the light green car?

At least two had been there: one had been talking to Richard and Penny, and the other had knocked him out. But why leave him on the floor of his house and take the others?

"Mr. Fulton, we have been very patient."

"If you will bear with me, I will tell you what I know."

"Very well."

"I came in the back door of the house and was struck from behind. At the time, the codicil sat in my left back pocket. It is not there now."

"Check him."

The man advanced, grabbed the back of the chair, and tilted him forward. With Cliff's hands tied down, he gripped the arms and pushed his feet against the floor to keep from falling out.

"He's right. It's not there."

The chair dropped back, and the legs slammed onto the wooden floor. His seat tilted dangerously backwards but stabilized.

The cellphone dropped back into her pouch, and a snap sounded again. "So, it was stolen, and you don't know by whom."

Cliff nodded. The abuse the man had given the chair had made it wobble worse.

The man chimed in. "Now, can we kill him? It's the only way."

The woman shook her head. "Get the sack. We'll leave him tied up. Those are the orders."

With a grumble, the man moved behind them and pulled out a black, cloth sack. It slid over Cliff's head. Though dark, he could still faintly see the bright light.

"You have a reprieve, Mr. Fulton." He felt the woman's hand stuff something in his shirt pocket. "Find the codicil and call this number. We'll know what to do from there."

The bright light clicked off. Footsteps exited the room and went down the stairs. The front door opened and closed.

Cliff sat there and listened. When enough time had passed, he shook the chair side to side. The wobble got worse with each jerk. The wood gave a distinct crack, and then, all at once, the chair fell sideways. "Gran, forgive me."

He pulled his head away as it crashed to the floor. His right arm stung from the impact as the legs splintered and knocked the chair arm inward. With his forearm, he shook it until the pieces pulled apart. As the ropes loosed, he slid his arms out, pulled off the sack, and turned toward the light switch.

The light switch clicked on. They had removed covers from his bed and hidden the windows. A lamp shade and an aluminum emergency blanket had been used to create a makeshift screen. The rope they must have brought.

Nothing else appeared touched; the items that had been in his room were still there. He checked his pockets. His wallet, the ring, and other items still remained where he had placed them. Even the key to Gerhard's secret door could be felt in his sock.

They had only wanted the codicil, and they were the second group. The first had been the ones to take Richard and Penny while he was unconscious. If neither of these two groups wanted to kill him, who were the others that did?

On the stairs, he halted and stared at the living room. The plush chair, the one Richard had sat on, did not look right. Where the back of it met the seat, something forced a quarter inch gap.

At the chair, his fingers felt the smooth surface of rounded plastic out of sight. He worked the item up and watched as a key fob slid into view. Richard had left him transportation.

Someone had shifted an item on the mantel beside the clock. Another had been in the dining room and pulled out one of the chairs. A curtain had been pushed back. That's how they had caught him as he entered the back door; they had seen him sneak from the garage.

He played back the scene right before the hit. The dining room chair had been pulled out already. Why had they done that when Penny and Richard were in the living room?

Carefully, he sat down and dropped his gaze to the table. Cliff ran his hand over the varnished wood and felt small indentions in its surface.

Someone had written a note in this exact place. The writing material had been thin with the pressure hard enough to go through the paper and into the protective varnish.

He could not get paper and pencil to do a rubbing; to do that would destroy the light scratches with more of his own. Some fine dust or sand might also work if he could spread it lightly and then remove the excess without undue pressure. Both ways were risky.

The kitchen had the answer. In the utility drawer lay a small flashlight. Once back at the chair, he used the light from various angles and observed how it refracted. At the correct angle, the words became plain.

"Bring the codicil. Fifteen twenty-three West Paul Road."

Cliff's eyes opened wide. If it was no longer in his back pocket, and none of the people who had been there had taken it, where was it?

The floor in the kitchen and dining room proved fruitless. The last time he thought about it was on the catwalk, and that was only a thought.

Out the back door, he retraced his steps, followed them to the garage, and entered. Gran's papers were still there. He rolled and placed them in a front pants' pocket. From now on, these would stay with him until Richard could do what had to be done.

The trail backtracked around the car, through the door, and down the stairs. At the worktable, he checked around and under it. Every step on the stairs was searched. His mind went to Richard's car, so he exited the house. The ground showed another vehicle had pulled up beside Richard's; the tracks must have represented the second group.

The passenger seat of Richard's car was empty. How long ago had the envelope disappeared? With each place he could not find it, his heart beat faster. He had assumed—the very word *assumed* made him cringe. How could he have been so careless?

He made his way to the driver's side, slipped under the wheel, and closed the door. The next stop would be at the church near the catwalk.

The ride took forever. He had to force himself to obey every law. That codicil had become the key to everything. Without it, he had no idea how to save anyone, if any could be saved.

The codicil wasn't at the curb or the sidewalk. It wasn't at the cement bench. In his mind, he retraced his steps and caught sight of the catwalk. It would not have been lost there, right?

Back in the car, he drove down the street. The assassin's car had vanished. He pulled into the spot it had parked, got out, and looked around before heading toward the catwalk stairs.

Red and blue flashing lights caught his eye. Across the thoroughfare, at least one police vehicle sat parked. The circular stairs took him up, and he journeyed toward the other side.

A second police car arrived, and now the view improved; they parked beside the dark blue car.

Cliff slowed his walk until it halted completely. Someone had reported the car; someone would find the body in the trunk.

The sick feeling came back and hit the pit of his stomach. He looked at his hands and remembered he had not worn gloves. If they dusted for prints—

He breathed in deeply and let it out slow as his feet turned around and walked back toward Richard's vehicle. Though he had never been arrested, his prints had been in the file folder for Division A. If nothing else, they could recognize them.

Don't panic—the words echoed through his mind. With all that he had gone through, with all that he still had to do, nothing would come of this. Richard had pulled him out of harm's way before, and all Division A, the real Division A, had to do was make a phone call. He had even watched it happen. The car headed toward the Internet cafe.

But what if they didn't? Up until now, it had been to their benefit to bail him out. At any time, they could stop, wash their hands of him, and walk away.

The Internet cafe came into view, and when he turned the corner, a police car had blocked the driveway. Without a pause, Cliff continued down the street.

There was no going back to the cafe; whoever had called it in would recognize him. With all the commotion going on outside the front windows, it would have been a spectator's sport.

His throat felt tight. What was going on with him? Ever since yesterday morning, his emotions had been out of sync.

The car braked at a stoplight and waited for the light to change. What was he going to do? Richard and Penny had been taken, the dark blue car had been confiscated, and he could not go back to check the Internet cafe. The world closed in around him.

A car horn blared and brought him back to reality; the light had changed to green. He hit the gas and took off down the road. A radar flashed up on the windshield; it matched the one Richard had shown them when they had escaped from the cemetery. On the outer fringe, a red dot showed; someone tracked him.

How? He pressed the eye symbol on the steering wheel and watched the digits seven-five-nine appear on the screen. Richard had set a code so his own car could be tracked. Were they using the code, or tracking him some other way?

At the next corner, he swung to the right, sped up for the next few blocks, and turned to the left again. He needed context, he needed stability, and he wanted to go home.

After two groups had invaded Gran's house, he knew it should be the last place to go, but he couldn't help it; her house helped him to focus. As a main thoroughfare came, he slipped on.

The address written on the table came to mind, and the oddity of it hit him. They knew he would find the note. They implied that they did not have the codicil. They appeared to have taken Richard and Penny. Could it be a test?

As his mind went back over the facts, he pulled into Gran's driveway. It had to be a wild-goose chase, but first he had to prove it. He bounded up the front porch. With a step inside, his eyes studied the kitchen area.

The hit had stunned him, and he had staggered toward the dining room. Though the memory was fuzzy, his body had fallen to the floor. On one knee, he checked the floor carefully. If his body had hit the floor as dead weight, there would be some evidence.

Small scratches showed where his fingernails hit the waxed, wooden floor, and despite his clothes, revealed marks made by his body. The scuffs showed what he looked for—an inch long scratch. Based upon the position, it could only have been made from one item: the edge of the vinyl envelope. Someone had removed it.

Chapter 24

Anger flared. He hurried toward the upstairs. When he reached his room, his hands picked up the laptop. It was risky to use it for this type of research. Up until yesterday, he had thought they were no longer monitored by Division A; now, he knew better.

Not only was he on the radar, but anyone else associated with him would receive the same treatment. On top of that, Division A had fixed up the house after the first shootout. If they suspected anything, their surveillance would be in Gran's home. That may not have included the cellar or the garage, for if they did, they would have already found Gran's papers.

Those thoughts had never occurred before although they should have; they only made sense. When the briefcase had been destroyed, he thought everything was over. Scratch that—he wanted to think everything was over. He lulled himself into believing exactly what they wanted him to think. Gran's death had caused the start of a possible information avalanche, and until it hit the bottom, nothing would keep them away.

The laptop asked a question; it needed his password. He used his thumb to gain access and watched as it finished its boot up. With the loading complete, he opened a browser and thought about the poem he had found in Michael's folder.

What type of plant had gold petals that turned red? He entered the keywords *gold petals that turn red*. Petals implied flower, but none of the flowers listed appeared to do that. What if the process took time as a person might turn from good actions to bad? Breeders could have done it.

The poem implied position and power, but only to a few. Could the position and power have been earned because of the evil deeds done? *Beware the flower* came back to mind. He sat back and stared. Without Albert to help him, this might take a while.

Another question came to mind. Why does a burying beetle eat its own kind and not suffer loss? The implication had infuriated him. Though the facts pointed toward his grandparents being part of Fushimi's group, he still could not accept it. For Fushimi, their involvement was absolute; the man had given the answer of why his grandmother had been killed.

Cliff looked up burying beetle, read down the page, and stopped. The answer stared at him; the beetles gave the strongest of their young the best chance to survive. A new generation rose from the old. The players of the past insured their young's continued existence.

"Bloodlines." His grandmother and grandfather had tried to get out, but that wasn't enough for Fushimi; he had organized a plot to get rid of the competition. If you weren't directly in the game, he didn't want you to come off the sidelines. Then why didn't he kill Cliff in the tunnel? The answer was clear—it had to be done indirectly or others would make him pay.

The facts separated into three different layers. One, Fushimi had killed Michael who tried to interfere in his business. Cliff had no doubt the additives used in the making of prescription drugs had played a part. From what he had read, magnesium stearate sat at the top of the list, and there were probably more. On top of that, an assassin had tried to kill Fushimi.

Two, everyone looked for Gran's papers to resurface. Some would stop at nothing to keep that from happening. These were the ones who had sent the assassins.

Three, a battle in an old world order was taking place, and Cliff had become a part of it.

He closed the laptop and watched it shut down. It would suspend the screen. If Division A did watch, he would let them think he didn't know it. The warehouse and the address written on the dining room table had not left his mind. How long would these groups wait for him to show up? Did a time limit exist? What if showing up would trigger the killing?

The constriction of his throat returned as his stomach muscles clenched. No, he would not give in. With measured breath, he breathed in through his nose and out through his mouth. As he did, his body relaxed. She had trained him—nothing had been done by accident.

Other pieces of the puzzle fell in place. Just as he had realized the three layers, so the layers had to be washed away in the same order. To save his family and expose Fushimi, the assassin had to be revealed.

His heart said differently. He wanted to help his family first, and Penny was a major part of that. The word love had come unexpectedly, but he knew it to be no less true. On top of this, Albert had vanished, and he had no idea where to look. Strike that—he did know where Albert fit. Albert fit at layer two, and despite the facts they had fed him, he refused to believe that his friend had been disloyal. The mental list helped him sort priorities. To discover the assassin, he had to find a botanist.

Gran had been part of that field. Richard, Doc, and Gerhard had worked with her. Who else at the college might be able to answer his question?

With the laptop on the bed, he hurried down the stairs. One o'clock came fast, and not knowing the class schedule of the science building put him at a disadvantage. For all he knew, the teachers could be done for the day.

He locked the back door, not that it would do any good; he had no key to lock the front. No sooner had he stepped out when he noticed two people approach from the sidewalk in the reflection of the front glass door. He turned around. "Lenord and Chrys."

Lenord bordered on anger. "You are in trouble, and you need our help."

"I'm—" Cliff threw a glance at Chrys. "—fine. Everything has been handled."

A frown formed on Lenord's face. "It is not fine. You were at the second mausoleum." They stopped on the steps to block his path.

"I—"

"Don't deny it. Richard notified me."

When had Richard had time to talk with Lenord, and why would he do such a thing? The answer came back loud and clear: in the car when Cliff had gone into the house.

Cliff threw a worried look at Chrys.

"And don't go telling me you don't trust her. She saved you the night you stayed at the second safe house."

Though the dart had made the events hazy, he brought the memory back. Yeah, Lenord had a point; maybe he had misjudged her. "I'm sorry about that." He cleared his throat. "At first, I had no idea it was you."

"But I knew it was you. I was doing my job, and you compromised it." Her tone implied a double meaning.

"Yeah—" Cliff looked away as his jaw tightened. "—there's been a lot of that lately."

"Cliff," her tone softened a little, "we are here to help, not hurt."

The words were there, however, the eyes did not show the same feeling. His gaze scanned the neighborhood and stopped on Richard's car. "I would feel better if we talked in there."

They followed his eyes, and Lenord gave a nod. Cliff unlocked it, went around, and slipped under the steering wheel. Lenord took the passenger seat; Chrys slipped into the back with eyes that never left them. The car indicated that a tracking device had been blocked; Cliff cleared it before they noticed.

"It might be faster if you tell me what you know first."

Lenord turned toward him, and his voice rose. "Where shall I start, Mr. Fulton? One, last night a call came in about a young man who ran from the police in a black car; the call vanished out of the logged reports this morning with no reason given. Two, the police are looking for two young men who escaped from an FDA's office after others were gunned down by an assassin's bullet. Three, at an Internet café, two young men rushed through a back door hunted by others; bullets were fired. One of the boys drove off in a car later found to have a dead body." He pulled out a piece of folded paper and held it up. "The police have issued an APB for the person matching these fingerprints, and a description of both young men. One of them matches you." He stared at Cliff. "Need I go on?"

Cliff cleared his throat. "When you put it that way, it does sound like a bit of trouble."

Lenord clenched a fist. "Not nearly the trouble you will be in if you don't explain things."

Cliff took a deep breath and let it out slow. "Okay." It wasn't only a matter of telling the story; it had to be told in the right way. He started with the drive from the second safe house; Cliff kept it to the basics. He skipped Gerhard's secret passage and Doc. He resumed when Division A found him and relayed how they had called off the police.

The meeting with Tish remained unmentioned. He lightly hit the FDA and said nothing about Michael Bishop's house. To explain his reason for the FDA, he talked about the mausoleum and the badge found in Division A's car. His grandparents and the life they left behind stayed out. As it ended, Lenord's eyes dropped. "I see."

Chrys leaned forward and touched Cliff's shoulder. "And you don't know who abducted Michael Bishop?"

"No." Cliff sighed. "I've tried to figure it out, but I don't have enough pieces. I have to find out to save my parents."

She sat back; debate flickered across her face as he watched her expression in the rearview mirror. "Perhaps it would serve you better to focus on your parents and friends—" The words were sympathetic. "—rather than participate in something you do not understand." Her eyes met his with deadly calm. Cliff held her gaze until she turned toward Lenord. "I'll help him."

Lenord's eyes narrowed. "That isn't why you're here." He threw a glance at Cliff. "I'll make arrangements for him."

Her eyes hardened. "You remember the mandate?"

Lenord's face turned red. "I know my orders."

"I am doing my job as you are required to do yours."

"I don't like this."

"Noted. Consult your superiors if you wish."

Cliff looked toward Lenord as the implications sank in. "Hold it, what if I don't agree? You act like I don't have a choice."

Chrys turned her stern gaze on him. "Then, I will take you in right now, and your goal to save your parents will be over."

That would be a death sentence for everyone, and Cliff knew it. "You can't do that!"

Chrys lifted her cellphone. "Shall I make the call?" Her finger moved toward the screen.

"No. Wait!" He restrained himself from reaching for her phone. "I'll cooperate, but you have to let me do this my way. If I ask you not to do something, I need you to listen."

Chrys smiled. "I always listen, but the decision is mine on any action. I have been doing this a long time, Mr. Fulton." Her words were sharp. "*Your* quest is only beginning."

The last sentence struck him; Lenord noticed. Cliff slowly nodded. "I accept the terms."

The frown had not left Lenord. "You will be responsible for Cliff's safety. You will report in every hour on the hour. Otherwise, mandate or not, you will be recalled."

"So, it comes to threats?" Her eyes became soulless. "I'm here on a mission of peace."

"It comes to you pulling rank in a situation that makes no sense and with no explanation."

"I will do as you ask, so long as it is safe to do so."

Chrys and Lenord exited the car. A brief message flashed on the windshield as a tracking device left the vehicle. They spoke words out of Cliff's hearing. When Chrys slid into the front passenger seat, the windshield warning flashed. Cliff cleared it.

She eyed the spot where the message had been. "What was that?"

Cliff didn't bat an eye. "Richard had an accident—every once in a while the car glitches."

She nodded slowly though her eyes narrowed. "So, where to now, Mr. Fulton?"

"To my college. I need to speak with a professor."

Lenord had reached the car he and Chrys had come in. As he started down the street in front of them, Cliff put his own in reverse and pulled out.

Her eyebrows rose. "About what?"

"A poem." He continued to feed out the facts in bits and pieces as they traveled. How much could he tell her? He decided to chance a little more. "It is a clue from Michael's folder. I think a botanist could answer it."

A lull dropped between them. Chrys broke it with a far away voice. "Cliff, I know what you are going through. I know the road you are facing."

He glanced toward her and saw her staring at the street in front. "What road?"

"It is dark, and it is lonely. It is one that will steal all the loved ones you have. It is the only choice for the power of revenge."

He frowned. "I do not want power. I want my family back."

The voice became even further away. "I am not unsympathetic."

For a moment, he thought she would reach out and touch his arm.

Her face became dark. "Unfortunately, we don't always get

what we want."

"Who are you?"

Like a talisman protecting a hidden secret, his three words brought her back. She turned toward him with soulless eyes as her voice held vivid, dark emotion. "I am on loan from Japan to help the FBI. That is all you need to know. I can be your guardian angel, or the devil that destroys your soul." The words sent shivers up his spine as she turned to watch the cars.

The familiar street beside Hoy Hall came into view, and they pulled into a parking place. He locked the car as she joined him on the sidewalk. Out of the corner of his eye, he spotted a few students which stared, but they looked away the moment she turned in their direction.

He took a right, went up some cement stairs, and passed through the front doors of the building they sought. His eyes swept the hall noting classrooms, a computer lab, and restrooms. An index of the room numbers displayed on the wall. The transparent plastic of the index held back his finger as he slid it toward the bottom. "Room three-twenty."

Chrys added, "A professor by the name of Meredith Clomer."

The name was important, but why did she say it out loud? It was a memorization technique to associate what you looked at with an emotional event. The emotion of it helped make it more vivid so it stuck in the person's mind. Gran had taught him that.

Elevator lights went up, not down. A stairwell sat to their left. Gran's papers in his pocket came to mind, and something clicked as he thought of the computer lab. With Gerhard gone, would it be safe? "Just a moment."

Her eyes waited for the reason.

"Just give me a moment before we go up. I need to make sure of a class assignment." Without a pause, he hurried down to the computer lab. Most of the computers were free, so he grabbed the nearest one. Someone had left a thumb drive beside it.

He hit enter to reset the system. When requested, his fingers typed in his username and password. The desktop loaded. The folder labeled scan stood on the right. One by one, he scanned in Gran's papers.

His eyes watched the door; the last thing he wanted was for Chrys to walk in. When they were all scanned, he rolled them up and placed them back in his pocket.

The folder on the screen stared back at him. Now what? He transferred the scanned documents to his account.

Richard had warned him about using the system at the school, but that was before Gerhard had died. If the man wasn't watching, who else could possibly know? Doc's speech about the cabal came to mind as well as the rogue part of Division A. Had he made a mistake?

His eyes went back to the thumb drive. It wasn't his, but if he managed to live long enough, he would gladly give it back. With the thumb drive in the computer, he copied off all the scans. As he turned toward the door and reached for the thumb drive, Chrys entered.

"Done." A smile lit his face. "Now, let's go find out about that poem." She watched him deposit the thumb drive into his pocket.

Instead of toward the front stairs, he led them to the back. As they climbed, Chrys broke the silence with a dark foreboding. "I don't understand your fixation with this poem. For all you know, it is just a poem."

"Michael was investigating it." He opened the door to the third floor. "It has to have a meaning." A group of students turned toward them, and her persona changed. The shards of darkness washed away replaced by a pleasant smile.

As he checked the room numbers, he realized a large number of students were leaving the room he needed to enter. Cliff pressed through the door. The teacher stood on the left side. She wrote something on the chalkboard beside the picture of a large leaf. When she turned around, recognition lit her face. "So, you do want to learn about leaves?"

He met her invitation. "Ms. Clomer?"

She noticed Chrys, and her smile changed slightly. "I am. How can I help you?"

"Ms. Clomer—" Chrys stepped forward and extended her hand. "I'm Chrys Xu working with the FBI. This is Cliff Fulton, a student at the university. We'd like to ask you a few questions."

Meredith gave a funny smile. "What's this about?"

Cliff drew her attention. "I need know about a certain flower; at least, I believe it's a flower. I am trying to find the name."

The expression did not change. "That's not much to go on."

"There isn't much to tell. Let me write what we know on the board." He picked up a piece of chalk without waiting for her agreement and wrote the poem word for word.

Meredith studied the puzzle. "Many flowers were yellow and turned other colors through breeding. Daffodils, ilimas, marigolds, and mums are a few. This is not enough to go on."

Cliff caught her eye. "How about flowers associated with power or royalty?"

She frowned. "Are you looking for a botanist or a history teacher?"

Chrys gave a quiet chuckle. "We apologize. It seems we have wasted your time." She moved beside Cliff, picked up an eraser, and wiped the board clean. "Thank you for your indulgence." She placed a hand on his arm. "It is time to go."

Cliff needed help, and he knew Chrys would not provide it. He remembered George's phone in his pocket. "Wait." He slipped from Chrys' grasp and picked up a pen. As his body blocked her view, he spotted a scrap of paper. In a quick scribble, he wrote down the phone number. Below the number, he printed the words, "Please help me!"

Meredith's eyes dropped to the paper. Her eyebrows furrowed.

With a turn, he ushered Chrys out of the room. "Thank you for your help."

The moment they cleared the doorway, Chrys came unglued though her voice stayed low. "What did you write?"

"What does it matter?"

"Your freedom is based upon your willingness to cooperate."

They reached the front stairs, and Cliff started down. "I am cooperating. I'm putting together clues that will lead to Michael's murderer." They passed the second-floor landing.

Her voice became less harsh. "You asked her questions she had no idea how to answer."

As they reached the bottom, he spun to face her. "If you don't believe the poem is relevant, what does it matter?"

Their eyes met, and both wills lashed out. He could have sworn she would reach for her gun, but at the last moment, she leaned forward and kissed him.

Chapter 25

Cliff jerked back unsure of what had transpired. "I didn't see that coming."

She smiled. "It was either shoot you or kiss you. Surely you are not afraid of a little kiss?"

The solid wall behind him touched his back, and he realized he had continued to back up. "From my experience, women aren't that forward." The words he spoke rang oddly in his ears; his mind went back to Tish. "Usually."

Though she teased him, the darkness returned on the fringes. "Oh, come now, Mr. Fulton. We are both adults and can do as we wish. Is this not America? Our natures are the same; we have a fire within us."

"This is not what I wish."

"I have watched you from the first time you saw me. You were intrigued by me. Even your girlfriend saw that."

His thoughts went back to the mausoleum when he had noticed the small shoeprints which led deeper into the cemetery. The shoes she wore were the same size. She caught the direction of his eyes. "As I said, intrigued."

"It's not what you think. Intrigued is one thing. To force yourself on another is different."

She moved closer. "To know the sweet from the bitter you must taste the waters."

A door above them opened, and the voices of students filled the stairwell.

He had to get her out of her. "The car might be a better place to talk."

She nodded, but as he reached for the doorknob, she whispered, "Remember, I hold the keys to your freedom."

The door opened of its own accord. Cliff caught it and held it as a student passed through. Chrys stepped into the hallway.

His first instinct told him to close the door and race back up to the third floor. There had to be an entrance to the tunnel system within this building. If he could locate it, he could temporarily find a safe haven and try to work out a plan.

It was risky; the dark side of this woman had the capability of anything. He moved out behind her. "I'll be right back."

The voice held a curious smirk. "To where?"

His index finger pointed to the restroom. "It will only take a minute."

"Take your time, Mr. Fulton." She moved to a bench by the wall, sat down to wait, and crossed one leg over the other. The smirk had not disappeared.

With her eyes upon him, all other ideas of escape vanished. She was unpredictable. Surely Lenord had seen this?

The restroom door loomed closer. No one lay within, but that would not last for long; too many students moved within the building. He had to use the time to think.

Bloodlines, why did the word keep coming to his mind? It came from the darkness he saw in Chrys. Tish had it too although not as dark. Tish had family; Chrys did not. Was that the only difference? Was there a connection between the two?

Mentally, he repeated the words to the poem. Somehow, this involved Chrys. Otherwise, she would not try so hard to derail it. The red petals came to mind, and the red petals always brought him back to Fushimi.

George's phone rang; a number appeared he did not recognize. At first he thought to let it ring, but— "Hello?"

Meredith's voice nervously responded, "Cliff?"

"Yes."

Her voice became stronger. "I have some information that might be of interest."

His heart rate went up as he listened; the last teacher who had helped him had died.

She named off additional flowers and their connection with various royalties, but only one caught his attention. ". . . Mums were adopted as the royal flower of Japan. The original coat of arms shows a golden chrysanthemum with sixteen petals."

Cliff blinked and his voice rose. "What did you say?"

The nervous voice came back. "The mum was adopted—"

His voice became softer. "No, no, what was the other name you gave the flower?"

"It's called a chrysanthemum."

Everything stopped as he listened to the word. The notes came back to his mind: beware the flower, beware the assassin, and beware the one who is red. What if the flower was a chrysanthemum?

"Cliff, are you okay?"

The teacher was in real trouble, and it was his fault. He relaxed and spoke calmly, "Ms. Clomer, thank so much. Now, I need for you to do one more thing. Forget everything you heard today, destroy the number I gave you, and pretend it never happened. Can you do that?"

The much too pleasant voice of Chrys responded on the cell. "Of course she will. When you are finished, please meet us at the car." The call cutoff.

With deliberate slowness, he lowered the phone and put it back in his pocket. The restroom door pushed in, and the room filled with the talk of two students. He turned and walked out.

A breeze stirred the leaves as the entrance to the building pushed open. Two figures stood at the car. A pleasant smile lit Chrys' face although Ms. Clomer was not so merry. As he reached the car, he unlocked the doors and slid under the steering wheel.

Chrys made Meredith open the back door, pushed her in, and slid in beside her. The car blocked the tracer, but Cliff hid it. "Very good, Mr. Fulton. You will be a chauffeur today."

In the rearview mirror, Meredith held rigidly still with her back straight despite the seat. The situation had to stay calm to help her. "Where do you want to go?"

"Your grandmother's house. It is as good a place as any."

The car started. He checked both ways and headed down the street.

After a moment, Chrys spoke, "It's a shame, really. I wasn't even after you."

That statement did not completely ring true. At the corner, he turned left and headed over the bridge. "But you were after Michael?"

Her voice stayed matter-of-factly pleasant. "I used Michael as bait to attract Fushimi, just as I used you to bring Fushimi to the school. Unfortunately, the FDA agent found out my true intent and planned to reveal it. If he had, the mole inside the FDA would have picked up on it, and my cover would have been blown. Michael brought his own death—" She made her next words very pointed. "—and you pulled the trigger."

"No." Cliff felt his cheeks flush. "I was setup to kill him. You and Fushimi put me in a casket, sealed me in, and tricked me into pushing the button."

"I did nothing," her voice became pleasantly cold. "Fushimi wanted to warn you off and get rid of a meddling investigator. Two birds were taken care of with one stone."

The stoplight in front turned red. He hit the brakes, screeched to a halt, and barely avoided the rear end of the car in front.

"Careful, Mr. Fulton. Any undue attention and I'll end it all right here." She nodded toward the gun she had pulled from her holster. "I would rather not. The cleanup is not so easy."

Cliff's eyes narrowed. "But I'm sure you could."

The light went green. Their car pulled forward into the flow of traffic. "If your intention is to kill Fushimi, why have you waited so long?"

The rearview mirror showed the soulless eyes. "In each case, he managed to slip away, but it will not happen again. It will not be lost because of you." She threw a glance at Meredith. "Either of you."

He stared at the road. The word bloodlines bounded into his mind. Her family belonged to the same cabal as Fushimi; it had to be. Fushimi had wiped out her family. The thought of what they had done to Gran surged back and threatened to overcome him. Strangely, a piece of him sympathized. "I'm—I'm sorry about your family."

Meredith's voice spoke quietly, "But it's wrong. Killing him won't bring back anyone. It will only make you feel worse."

Cliff watched the soulless eyes of Chrys change as the voice became more pleasant. "What do you know of worse? What do you know of pain?" A smile tugged at Chrys' lips. "Too long he has roamed this earth. I will be the one to end it." Her eyes took in Cliff and Meredith. "Unfortunately, innocents suffer in war."

She was a martyr on a mission, and if he couldn't find a way to alter this, neither he nor Meredith would leave Gran's house alive. "Chrys, let me help you."

Meredith's head twitched at his words; Chrys' eyes narrowed. "How?"

"I want him brought to justice. Tell me, what can I do to help?"

She stared, and he knew exactly what she looked for. She wanted to know if he told the truth. "You would never help me kill him."

Cliff's voice went hard. "He had my grandmother killed and used Gerhard and his son to do it. He destroyed her funeral and has threatened me and my family at every turn. Why wouldn't I help? Until he's gone, we will never have peace."

Meredith gasped; her eyes focused on Cliff in the mirror, and she shook her head. "No."

He didn't intend to scare her, but it could not be helped. To win Chrys over, it had to be believable. It wasn't that hard; part of him wanted Fushimi dead. "I have to."

The faraway look flickered across Chrys' face. "I believe you."

"No." Meredith shook her head again. "This is wrong. You can't do this. I won't let you."

Chrys' gaze snapped to her and glared; the gun stayed steady in her hand. "You won't?"

"I—" Meredith's chest heaved. "No, please! I don't want to die. My son—"

The glare softened. Without saying a word, Chrys raised the end of the barrel to her lips and gave it a kiss. The smirk returned. Meredith went silent though her chest still heaved. Chrys turned to Cliff. "I don't know what he looks like."

The 'in' Cliff needed had appeared. He had met the man not only on the phone, but in person as well, twice: once at the elevator and once in the tunnels.

"Fushimi is very cautious."

But not with me, Cliff thought. Could it be because of his grandparents? Did the man really trust him? No, he had said it himself; others observed him.

Meredith's eyes watched the pair. Despite the terror on her face, she remained silent.

With a deep breath, he made the final commitment. "I can bring you to him. I have seen his face, and now he owes me a favor."

Chrys' eyebrows lifted. "Does he?"

Cliff kept his expression sober. "Thanks to you. Thanks to the fact I helped him get away when you called us to meet in the tunnels." He started to add *at the university* but knew it would freak Meredith out.

Chrys' eyes narrowed. "Before I could act, others interfered." Her persona changed, and a laugh escaped her lips. "The paradox is amusing."

The car turned toward the right and made its way onto the

thoroughfare. That explained Albert's presence in the tunnels; the group who had captured him had interfered with Chrys' plans. "We knew we were tricked; we had to work together or be caught."

"And he trusted you?"

Cliff did not bother to answer.

The smile broadened on her face. "Yes, he would trust you. After all, you are no real threat. You are an innocent who has never played in the darker side of reality." She leaned toward him. "I heard about your adventures in finding the briefcase. You are way too lucky for someone so naïve. Perhaps that is part of the attraction." She sat back and the smirk returned. "Perhaps you are my soul mate after all."

The word soul mate made him uncomfortable. He turned onto Gran's street. "If you can set up the meeting, I will get you in." Could he be so sure? Would Fushimi let him walk right in?

The gun dropped into its holster. She picked up her cellphone and ran a caressing finger over it. The system read the stroke, analyzed her fingerprint, and granted her access. "I agree."

Casually, he threw in, "But I have one condition."

Chrys stopped. Her finger sat ready to call the number. "And that is?"

"We leave Meredith tied up but unharmed."

Her eyes dropped to the gun. "I don't like loose ends. I don't like taking chances."

His voice stayed soothingly smooth. "Meredith will not say a word." He remembered Chrys' reaction to the word *son*. "She has a son to take care of. She doesn't live in that world."

"But you will—" Chrys smiled with delight. "—and you will never want to go back."

A shiver ran up his spine as he pulled into the driveway. The anger he felt about his grandmother's death fueled his plan—that scared him. "Are we agreed?"

Chapter 26

Chrys considered with a faraway expression. It didn't appear promising.

"If you don't believe me, you might as well raise the gun and shoot us both."

Meredith's eyes opened wide. Cliff sat there as his words sank in. If she wanted to get Fushimi, he held the key.

"Yes," she said as her eyes came back. "Let's get Ms. Clomer into the house."

It didn't take long. They were back in the car when Chrys connected the call.

"Chrys here. There is a guy named Cliff Fulton with me, and he wants to see Fushimi." Voices came through, but they were indistinct. At last an affirmative response came, and she thrust the phone to Cliff.

The voice was not Fushimi's. "Cliff Fulton?"

Cliff wasn't sure it would work, but he played the only card he had. The word favor had never been used. As a matter of fact, Fushimi had stated the opposite. "Yes sir."

"What's this all about?"

"Is this line secure?"

"No."

"Then I suggest we talk in person. This may take a while to explain."

The man grunted something to someone and then returned. "We'll call you and let you know." The phone hung up.

Chrys, who sat in the front seat beside him, leaned back and smiled. "Stop looking so worried. You did well."

"I'm not sure they believed me."

"If they hadn't, you wouldn't have gotten that far, and in a matter of minutes, they would have traced the call and showed up on your doorstep. Fushimi doesn't like being played."

"Which explains why it's so hard to get near him."

Chrys nodded. "I've been working at this for five years. When your story came up about the briefcase, I knew he would show up."

He studied her features. She looked a lot younger than him. When had she started to hunt this guy? As a teenager? "So his whereabouts is kept hidden?"

She nodded again with closed eyes. "It's a shame you're a one-girl guy." She stretched. "I find coition before killing rather relaxing." Her head turned toward him, and she opened her eyes. "Are you sure?"

The warmth returned to Cliff's cheeks. "I'm positive."

She watched him closely. "I was right." A chuckle escaped her lips. "You are an innocent."

"And I intend to stay that way until I marry the right girl." Cliff looked toward her and caught her eye; her eye sparkled in amusement.

The phone rang, and she answered. A moment later, it hung up. "He is willing to meet you and has asked me to bring you in. We are to wait here for thirty minutes." As her lips pursed, a frown crossed her forehead. "It sounds a little too easy, but it's all we have to go with. Can you find bay fifty-two in the warehouse area by the lake?"

Bay fifty-two, they had his family there, and he had yet to retrieve the codicil. Did that mean Fushimi had them? Something didn't fit. He turned toward Chrys. "I know where it is, but that can't be where Fushimi is hidden."

Her frown deepened. "Why?"

"Because that's where I'm supposed to find my family."

Seconds ticked by as they both considered. The assassin on the bridge had said Albert had betrayed him; he also claimed Fushimi had not taken his family. Which one was the lie, or was it both? Another possibility existed. "The cabal." He turned toward Chrys and looked her in the eye. "Who are they?"

Her frown deepened as a cold light glistened across her face. "They are power, life, and death. They protect their own."

"They are not doing a good job." Cliff waited for her to continue. "Do they have a name?"

She nodded but said nothing.

"What is it?"

She turned to the right. Cliff followed her gaze. Two similar cars headed in their direction. "Do you remember what I told you Fushimi would do if he thought he was being played?"

Cliff turned the ignition, backed quickly out into the street, and took off toward the thoroughfare. Meredith! The intersection lay empty, so he swung to the left and started a circle.

Chrys caught the wheel; for such a thin girl, she was quite strong. "What are you doing?"

"I'm going back. Meredith is inside."

"No." She pushed the steering wheel the other way.

The car jumped back and forth. The circle zigzagged. "Why are you trying to stop me?"

"Go, and she'll be safe; the others will follow us. Stop, and she'll be dead." She released the wheel. "It makes no difference to me."

The two cars accelerated toward them. He whipped to the left, straightened, and glided into his own lane. Those behind them bypassed the house.

How was this possible? Division A cars could block trackers, and they rerouted cell calls. How did these people know where they were?

It had to be the bug on Chrys. Maybe she wasn't working alone.

What if Fushimi still pulled the strings? Tish had played those mind games, too.

Those behind them picked up speed. At the next right, he swerved and narrowly missed a parked car. The gleam in Chrys' eye reminded him of Penny.

They raced through the neighborhood. Families in their yards turned to stare. Not only did they draw attention, but if they stopped, the danger would increase for the spectators.

He turned into an alley, gunned it to the end, caught the next left, and swerved past another car as its horn blared. When the cars did not appear behind, he slowed his speed to normal. A parking lot came into view. Cliff pulled toward the back.

Chrys grabbed his arm. "Why are we stopping?"

His voice was firm. "Get out."

"What?" She stared at him as one hand went toward her gun. "Are you crazy? We have to get as far from here as we can!"

"You trusted me enough to broker a deal. Listen to me now."

The hand stopped moving, and that faraway look appeared in her eyes. "All right." She opened the passenger door and stepped out beside it.

"Climb back in and watch the windshield."

As she shifted into the car's interior and the door closed behind her, a warning window flashed. Cliff didn't clear it off. She read the words on the screen and laughed hysterically until tears hit her cheeks. As her head touched the headrest, she wiped the tears from her eyes. "For five years they have known everywhere I've been and accessed my conversations."

"How does it work?"

She rolled her head toward him. "It's an implanted micro transceiver about the size of a grain of rice. It uses the body's natural fluids for power. The cabal uses them to keep watch over their own. The one I knew about has been removed. Apparently, I have two."

"But a device that small couldn't record much. Where would

the information be stored?"

"Nanites injected in the body work as a network of brain cells recording information in tiny bits. The data is uploaded when the person can be reached. Surely you've heard of this?"

Cliff shook his head. "That is science fiction."

The sarcasm stopped. "In 1990, the Safe Medical Devices Act became a law in the US. All manufacturers who placed medical devices and implants had to have a permanent method to track their product. How hard is it to jump from that technology to what I have in me?" She looked him in the eye. "How hard would it be for any country to give a vaccination and an implant? This is not science fiction; it is science fact."

It was an idea he had never considered. "And the reason Division A equips all their cars with blocks for trackers."

Chrys nodded. "I would think so."

"What do we do now?"

"Well—" Chrys raised her head up and stared at the dash. "—if we can get to my apartment in one piece, and they haven't raided it, we might be able to shut it off."

"And if we don't?"

She closed her eyes. "Someone will get to hear this entire conversation."

Cliff's jaw set. "What's the address?"

"The deeper you go with this, the more darkness you will find. It would be safer if I did it on my own." Her eyes opened.

The car shifted into reverse, pulled back, and headed for the exit. "Address."

She gave a small laugh. "Let me show you. Hopefully, they have not retrieved that information yet." Her finger pointed to the right.

Cliff did as she indicated, reached a stop sign, and went on through. The street curved, and once again she pointed. Thirty minutes later, they pulled up to a six-story tenement building in Chinatown. The nearest parking place lay at the end of the block.

Though not fancy, it sat off the beaten path. It did not fit the alluring FBI agent she played. "I would have thought—"

"I like this place." She cut him off. "It has sentimental value."

Curious, he got out of the car. The car locked as he followed her to the middle of the block. She stopped at an open door. At the front desk sat an elderly Chinese man reading a paper; he glanced briefly as the two headed up the stairs.

The boards on the stairs creaked. On the fifth floor, she stopped at a door with the number five-zero-one. A key from her pocket fit the lock and turned it. She pushed the door in.

It closed behind them with a click. They walked into the living room and moved to the one bedroom. She went to a closet and tossed a bag on the bed along with a towel.

As she unsnapped the bag, it came apart to lie flat on all sides. Various pockets held tools which ranged from guns and bullets to knives and scissors. When a flap to the side lifted, she pulled out what looked like a TV remote.

A digital readout at the top divided into four sections with several buttons in the middle and arrows on all sides. It reminded him of a stud finder. Chrys started to pull off her clothes.

Cliff stepped back. "Stop right there."

She turned away from him with a smirk but continued to remove the items. "How else do you expect to find it?"

As forward as she had been before, he should have expected this. "Surely you can keep your clothes in place?"

A laugh escaped her lips. "The static electricity in the clothes interferes with the device's electronic scan, and we need to be precise." Before she turned around, she pulled a robe from a wall hook and slipped it on. "But for your convenience, I'll wear this until you're ready."

"What exactly am I to do?"

"Get over the schoolboy mentality; this is business. Every place I can't reach, you will help me search. You'll move this device a half inch above my body, up and down, until the numbers nine-nine-nine-nine appear on the four square digital displays. When you do, you should be right over the implant. Once located, I want you to take a knife, cut a small incision, and pull it out. It will be tiny so you'll have to use tweezers. It shouldn't be more than under the skin."

Cliff nodded; he had never used a knife to cut anyone. "Okay."

A grin broke out across her face. "Surely you're not afraid of a little blood?" She reached down and picked out a utility knife along with a small pair of tweezers. Her fingers ripped open a sterilization pack to clean both tools. She placed them beside the remote. "You'll need to do the back of my head all the way to my feet. I've done the front before—" She gave a smirk. "—but if you would like to check, I'm open to the suggestion."

"No, thank you."

A grin replaced the smirk. "You're welcome. Now—" She dropped the robe and laid down on the bed with her back toward him. "—you can start at any time."

He wasn't sure where to start while attempting not to look at her. "Where are the most common places?"

"It isn't standardized. Generally, they put them in the upper body, if nothing more than for their own convenience. The transceiver works anywhere. However, the higher, the better."

He sat on the bed and leaned over but found it uncomfortable. In the end, he removed his shoes to sit on the bed. Both sides of her head were swept. "Where was the first one?"

"Just to the side of my left breast. I can show you the scar if you like?"

The heat rose slightly in his cheeks as he started on the shoulders. "I'm good, thanks."

"I thought you would be. Surely you've had biology class?"

He started on the back. "Biology is a far cry from ogling a

real woman."

"I'm flattered," she teased. "Now you want to ogle me."

His voice stayed firm. "That's not what I meant, and you know it." He became concerned when he reached her lower back. What if he had missed it? "I think I need to do that again."

"Either you're avoiding the obvious, or you really like my back and neck. Keep going. Sweep both sides. Tell me what you see."

The numbers on the device changed just below the beltline and almost directly over the vertebrae. "That doesn't make sense."

Concern entered her voice. "What doesn't?"

"It's on the vertebrae." His finger touched the spot; a tiny pucker pushed up the skin. "Do you feel that?"

"No—" She stopped and thought. "—other than the touch of your finger."

"I don't like its position. The bone is way too close."

With a turn of her head, she looked at him. "It doesn't matter; it has to come out."

He brought the tip of the knife closer and centered on the tiny pucker. "Just to let you know, having never purposely cut someone, I am having a hard time with this."

"Your opinion is noted. Now, do it; they are tracking us as we speak."

The skin split at the faintest touch, and red liquid spread. His heart beat rapidly as he picked up the tweezers and reached into the incision.

She jumped.

Eyes wide, he swallowed. "I'm sorry."

Her jaw set. "Keep going."

The tweezers hit something hard and small, about the size of a rice grain, exactly as she had predicted. When the tweezers shifted to a better position, he felt her body twitch again. As both prongs fell into place, he squeezed them gently shut and lifted. The tiny implant came out without a hitch, but the blood surged. With pressure, he halted the flow. When he cleaned the implant off with the towel, he handed it to her. "There."

Her eyes sparkled. As she pulled the robe around her, she held up the tiny device. "One implant removed; one Fushimi to go."

A knock struck the door.

"Cliff, can you get that? I'm going to take a shower."

The path to the front passed by windows which faced the street; the fire escape could be seen. He closed the door to the bedroom to give her some privacy.

The sound of moaning caught his ears, but he could not tell from where. Perhaps a couple in the room next door? If so, these walls were paper-thin.

He approached the door and spotted an eyehole. Outside the door stood a delivery woman; her arm held a package. He opened the door a crack.

"Delivery for Ms. Xu. I'll need a signature." The woman smiled and waited.

"Just a moment." He held the door lightly and turned toward Chrys' room. He called out very forcefully, "Chrys! There's a delivery—" The door knocked open. The woman raised a gun as the door slammed into the wall and bounced.

Chrys called out, "Cliff!"

Two spuds sounded as Cliff ducked to his right, grabbed the edge of the door, and flipped it back the other way. It caught the arm of the woman as she stepped forward. He threw his weight against it, grabbed the extended arm, and jerked her into the door. The gun flew free and bounced across the living room. As he flipped the door open again, he grabbed the unconscious woman to drag her into the room. She was not alone.

Chapter 27

Chrys called out again as Cliff released the woman. A spud sounded as it passed somewhere to his left. With a bound, he dodged into the hallway, knocked a gun to the side, and grabbed a man's right wrist. The man gagged as Cliff's right elbow jabbed to the throat. Cliff grabbed the man's head and slammed it into the wall.

His heart raced; sweat dropped off his brow. Despite the noise, no one had come to investigate. With a kick, the man's gun slid into the living room as he dragged in the assailants. When the apartment door clicked closed, he hurried toward Chrys' bedroom.

It stirred before he got there, and her door flew open. Still in the robe, Chrys came out with a pointed gun. Her chest heaved as she looked over the two on the floor. When neither of the two moved, she lowered the weapon. "Not bad." She used her foot to tap both. "Not bad at all."

His brow furrowed. "Are you okay?"

"You had the tough part. Mine escaped out the window."

Cliff hurried over but saw no one on the fire escape. "They must have been fast."

Chrys nodded. "Had I had the gun closer, they wouldn't have gotten away."

He left the window and stared down at what he had done. Cliff could still feel the adrenaline that had surged. His mind had taken his experiences and pieced them together in a method of defense without being trained. The realization frightened him. He rubbed his elbow. "I'm still not used to hitting people."

"Don't worry, you're getting there." She admired his handiwork as she raised the gun to fire. "In this type of job, it comes in pretty handy."

Cliff stepped in the way. "What are you doing?"

"I don't like loose ends."

"We can't kill them!"

In disbelief, she stared at him. "You don't get it, do you? If you let these two go, they'll keep coming back until they kill you. That is their purpose. Yours is to stay alive."

He stared right back. "The guy on the bridge didn't come back."

A frown creased her face. "You don't know that. He won't make the same mistake twice."

Cliff didn't move.

With a loud exhale, she stepped back into the bedroom and returned with two sets of handcuffs. She tied her robe so it would not come open and bent down next to the woman. "Drag the guy over here. If you won't let me kill them, we have to at least lock them up."

As he bent down, a pair of handcuffs flew toward him; he caught them in the air.

She smirked. "Good reflexes." With several clicks, one of cuffs attached to the woman's arm. When Cliff brought the man close, she had him place them back to back. "I want the other cuff."

He saw what she had done. The two handcuffs were interlaced to keep both individuals close together. "It limits their movement, and they can't separate."

Her eye winked. "You catch on fast. If you won't let me shoot them, then we have to keep them still." She glided back toward the bedroom. "That shower invitation is still open, if you want to join in."

He didn't answer and heard the door close. He walked to the window and stared down at the street. This was not the world he had signed up for. Kill or be killed—that was not the life he wanted to have, but every time he had an encounter, he felt the rage inside grow. Would they ever leave him and his family alone? Were the others still safe?

Time went by, and he lost track. People passed along the sidewalks going about their daily lives. His eyes followed them envious that they had no clue about the truth of their existence.

Chrys' hand gently touched his shoulder; she had changed her clothes and looked refreshed. "I felt the same way, long ago, after they killed my family."

"You think they've killed mine?"

Her shoulders shrugged. "There's no sense in guessing, and the worry will throw you off. Leave it alone; focus on the moment. You help me with Fushimi, and I will help you find them."

It was a deal with the devil, and he knew it. He stood on the edge of an abyss. All it took was one tilt in the wrong direction, and everything he held dear could be lost.

In a whisper, her lips came close to his ear. "Time to go." Her head nodded toward the door.

"Where?"

"You tell me. Before Lenord and I found you, it looked like you had a plan."

"I did."

She pointed toward the duo still handcuffed together. "I can't leave them in here. There's a garbage chute in the hall. Help me get them to it."

"Is that really necessary?"

"What do you want to do, carry them down six floors and walk them in front of the proprietor?" Her next words were laced with sarcasm. "That would keep us off the radar."

They were heavy, but between the two of them, they dragged them out into the hall and next to the garbage chute.

With unusual sympathy, she showed him how to load them.

"Feet first. We don't want them to break their necks as they land."

He held them balanced. "Will they be okay?"

She took hold of them and removed his hand. "As okay as landing in garbage will get you, as long as the bin isn't empty."

He frowned.

"Go to the car. I'll take care of this from here."

With an absentminded nod, he headed down the stairs. His plan to find Fushimi had failed. How could he locate the man now?

Two spuds sounded behind him, and the chute door flapped shut. His fingers found the handrail and gripped it tight as he slowed his walk down the stairs. She had killed them; his contract with the devil had been sealed in blood.

As the front door to the tenement building pushed open, the smell of exhaust, mildew, and sweat hit his nose. He turned toward the car, wove his way through the people on the sidewalk, and eventually found himself under the steering wheel.

Five minutes later, a smiling Chrys hopped into the passenger seat. "All tidied up."

The engine kicked over as he thought about what to say. "You killed them."

"You knew I had to." She tapped him affectionately on the arm. "Don't sound so surprised."

"But—" He gave a signal and pulled out into the traffic. It would take a few turns to get back the direction he had to go. "—I thought with the handcuffs—"

Her voice became very serious. "This is not a game, Cliff. You don't knock out assassins and let them walk away. You don't call the police, and let them go to jail. They will come back, and they will kill you." The next words came out very slowly. "That's what they do for a living."

His voice dropped all emotion. "Promise me you won't do that again."

A shocked look crossed her face. "Why would I do that?"

"Because you need my help, and I won't give it if you kill another person."

The soulless look came back, and she turned to stare at him. Her words came out slowly. "Are you threatening me?"

"I'm saving you. You're a good person, Chrys; I know you are. Don't become like them."

The car became silent. He had taken a chance making that demand but saw no choice. She couldn't kill every person that attacked them; if nothing else, it ate away at his soul.

Chinatown dropped behind as they moved into another part of the city. For the moment, Fushimi could not be reached, but Richard and Penny could. The address written on the table stirred to the surface of his mind. It was the logical thing to do.

He turned at the corner and remembered the general area from his pizza deliveries. The address lay this side of Chinatown. His subconscious mind had guided him to it.

Her soulless eyes gradually changed. Soft fingers reached out and caressed his arm. "Okay, no more outright killing until we reach Fushimi's lair."

That wasn't what he meant, but he'd take it.

West Paul Road came into view. A turn to the left took him in the right direction, and he counted off the blocks.

It sat in an industrial area formed of four blocks which stood in the middle of a neighborhood. Most of the companies were no longer doing business, but a farm supply and a radiator shop still kept their doors open. The graffiti on the red brick walls caught her eye. "Why are we here?"

The car rounded a corner and pulled down the street between two large buildings. "They have two of my friends and my grandmother's codicil."

A few feet from the corner, the numbers fifteen twenty-three appeared above a boarded up door. The lock had been broken off, and the glass pane closest to the doorknob had been busted. An available, angled parking place appeared to his right; two other cars were parked beside it.

Chrys checked the ammo in her gun. "It looks like we were expected."

His eyes threw a warning. "No guns, remember?"

With defiance in her eyes, she stepped out of the car. "The deal was no outright killing. I can shoot them if I need to." She checked the gun's second magazine. "Ready?" Her weapon dropped back into its holster as the passenger door shut.

Only the wind whistled as they approached the building; the cool air blew through the broken glass. A turn of the handle opened the squeaky door.

Crates dominated the landscape. Shelves went up at least three-stories high. A forklift stood in one corner. Despite the out of business look, someone had been very busy.

The path they traveled headed toward the center of the building. Three empty chairs sat in a row with a fourth positioned to face them. To his right, an office sat on top of a ten foot platform. A forklift stood beside it with the fork level to the platform's walkway. Footsteps echoed before they entered the center of the building, but they were not their own.

Almost there, Chrys reached toward her right side. Her voice stayed low. "Go on." With a slower gait and by himself, Cliff walked into the center.

A man's voice called to him from a PA system next to the office door; the voice matched the one on Chrys' phone. "Excellent. You did not disappoint me, Mr. Fulton."

How had this been done? He had been told to go to bay fifty-two, yet here the man stayed at an address written on Gran's table.

The door to the office opened. A middle-aged man with a balding scalp stepped out past the walkway and onto the forklift. The forklift whined as another man from nowhere operated the controls. The balding man lowered slowly to the ground with his eyes on Cliff.

"You know my name, but I don't know yours."

Nonchalant, the man strolled toward the single chair. "Sit down, please. Your friends will be here momentarily."

Another whine rose as it approached. Two crates sat side by side: seven feet long, three feet tall, and three feet wide. They were deposited to the left of the chairs.

The thumping in Cliff's chest grew; air holes were in the sides of the crates. The man on the forklift stopped and then casually walked between them. With a crowbar in his hand, he worked loose the two lids, pushed them to the side, and then returned to the controls on the forklift.

Hands appeared from the inside and gripped the sides of the crates. The faces of Richard and Penny turned to look in Cliff's direction.

"What did you do to them?" He moved toward them, but a third man stepped in his way. The man held a crowbar.

The balding man's voice stayed patient. "Please, sit down, Mr. Fulton. I will not ask again."

Others appeared to lift Richard and Penny out of the boxes. The two were ushered toward the row of three seats. Penny kept blinking and rubbing her eyes; they had been locked in darkness.

They were forced to sit on the chairs. Richard's face held no emotion, but Penny's seized fear. Her hands found the sides of the seat and gripped it until her knuckles were white.

Cliff turned away from the man with the crowbar and walked slowly toward the chairs. He purposely turned his chair so he could watch his friends and the balding man at the same time.

The balding man waited until all three sat. "Now then, isn't this more pleasant?" A smile broke upon his face as he looked toward Cliff. "As you can see, they have not been hurt."

Cliff's teeth clenched. "But you have not treated them well." Another forklift whined somewhere behind them.

Amusement spread across the man's face. "I like you, Cliff. You are terrified and brave at the same time. That's a quality rare in individuals. Usually, people are one or the other. Either fear strikes and they are paralyzed, or they are fearless and cause their own death. It is a strength I have always admired. It is a strength *our family* requires."

At the mention of *our family*, Penny's knuckles turned paler. Her wrists showed bruises. She and Richard had not only been placed in the box, they had been tortured.

The anger in Cliff grew. "What do you want? It can't be the codicil." The forklift came closer to his left from back the way he and Chrys had come.

The amusement increased as the man pulled the codicil from a pocket inside his suit. "No, it most certainly isn't. What I want requires a little more finesse."

"Finesse? As in the assassins you sent to kill me?"

"Ah—" The man smiled. "—you mean the catwalk." The man's eyes watched his. "No, Mr. Fulton, we did not send them. As you should have guessed by now, if we wanted to kill you, you would already be dead. Family is very important."

The picture of a burying beetle choosing which young to kill formed in Cliff's mind. It was paternal yet cold.

Five henchmen could be seen; they had taken equal points around them. None carried a gun. Cliff asked the question though he already knew the answer. "Then, why are you doing this?"

"Think of it—" The man's eyes swept those around him. "—as an initiation." With a wave of his finger, the five henchmen closed in; one carried a gun-shaped hypodermic needle. "Until now, you did not know we existed and would not had your grandmother kept silent." He waved a hand at Penny. "It can be her initiation, too, if you wish. She is also related to our family." Cliff caught a tremble in Penny's hand, but it stilled as the white grip tightened.

They were part of the cabal though he did not know its name. They were the ones who Doc had spoken of; they were the ones who watched Fushimi and his actions. They had put the implant in Chrys, and they were ready to do the same to him.

"It has come to our attention that you wish to kill one of our members. That, we cannot allow. If I have your word that you will drop this senseless quest, all will be forgiven." He did not have to add the *or else.*

Something snapped in Cliff. "I didn't start this. You did."

The henchmen quickened their step, but right before they reached the three, the balding man held up his hand. "Wait. Give him a chance to reconsider."

Cliff's eyes clouded in rage as every muscle prepared to move. If this man pulled Fushimi's strings, only one thing could stop him. "Consider what?"

"Consider that I hold not only your two friends, but the rest of your family as well."

The words echoed in Cliff's mind: two friends and family. Albert wasn't there.

A forklift turned the corner carrying three additional boxes. It stopped to the right of the other forklift; its payload stayed suspended twenty feet off the floor. The driver could not be seen. However, the meaning was clear.

Cliff refused to believe what his mind knew to be true. "You don't have them."

The man pulled out a cellphone. One of the henchmen came forward, took it from him, and handed it to Cliff. The balding man waited. A telephone number had been placed on the screen.

Cliff hit send. The signal shot out into the unseen airwaves. It rang once, twice, and as the third ring came, another responded from inside one of the boxes.

The strained, shaken voice of his mother answered, "Cliff?"

The phone slipped from his hands, but he caught it. "Mom?"

His mother cried.

Cliff lunged forward within inches of the bald man's neck before the henchmen dragged him back. He strained against their hold as the cellphone flew from his hands to bounce behind the balding man.

The man continued to smile. "So you see, we do have them, and if I let them go, I can get them again." His voice turned hard. "They are ours to do whatever we will. So I ask you as a gentleman, do we have a deal?"

Chapter 28

Cliff's eyes burned with fury as his mind tried to find a way out. Fushimi would never stop. This man would never stop. He and his family were pawns in a game they had never asked to play. If he gave in now, nothing good would come from it.

A third forklift headed toward them; it turned the corner with a single box. "This is yours, Mr. Fulton, should you decide to refuse our offer."

Cliff's mind stretched to the point of breaking. The lives of his friends and family were dependent upon his next words. This explained why Gran had kept his father out of it.

He spotted the fallen cellphone, and then looked toward his friends. "I'm sorry." His jaw set, and he turned back to the balding man with angry defiance. "Do your worst."

"Put them back in."

Richard stood up and gave a single nod toward Cliff. Two of the henchmen released Cliff as one went toward Richard and the other went toward Penny. That left only three on Cliff. Penny's henchman tried to get her to stand, but she refused to let go of the chair.

The balding man laughed. "Foolish youth, you think that you're invincible, but you aren't. And to think, Mr. Fulton, you could have stopped this. Lower the single box."

The forklift clicked and jerked, but instead of lowering the box, the box tumbled off in their direction. At the same time, Chrys leaped off the forklift, raised her gun and fired.

One of the henchmen beside Cliff dropped with a scream as he tried to make a fist with his left hand. The other two turned to see the box fall in a spin and leaped to the side.

Cliff lunged, caught the balding man as he tried to flee, and slammed him down on the concrete. The man's hand flew out and released the codicil. As Cliff flipped him over, he ignored the box as it crashed down only inches away. With fire behind the words, he hoisted the man up. "Get my parents out. Now!"

"No." The man's eyes became cold. "Drop them."

A shot rang out from behind and a man gasped; the forklift did not move. Chrys came up beside Cliff and pinned the balding man. "I'll take it from here." She jabbed the man with her weapon. "It's not very smart to bring a crowbar to a gun party." Her eyes weren't soulless, but they were close.

Cliff spun around and spotted Penny standing over the man who had tried to take her chair. The chair was destroyed, and the henchman didn't move. Her chest heaved rapidly as she took in the rest of her surroundings. Those eyes met Cliff's, and she rushed toward him.

His hands held her back. "Not yet."

Hurt filled her eyes, but he couldn't let her hug him. The moment she did, the anger he felt would leave, and he couldn't let it go yet.

Richard pointed. "Behind you!" A crowbar narrowly missed Richard's head; he caught the attacker's wrist and jammed him against the first forklift.

In back of Cliff, two henchmen had returned. One raised the hypo toward Chrys as the second pinned Cliff's arms. With no mercy, Cliff stomped on the foot of the one that held him, broke the bear hug, and launched his body at the one with the hypo. All three crashed to the floor. The first tried to grab Cliff's arm. The hypo flew from the second's hand, but he found a crowbar and aimed for Cliff's shoulder.

Chrys turned the gun and fired. The man on the floor screamed;

the bullet pierced his palm and the crowbar clanged to the floor. The first henchman rolled to his feet and raced toward the forklift that held up Cliff's family.

Cliff sprinted after him. His feet slipped, and he went down only to feel the sting as the concrete slapped his hands. It didn't matter. He fought back up, rounded the side, and used the step on the forklift to jump.

His body collided with the henchman who pushed the shot driver out of the forklift seat. The wounded driver tumbled out as Cliff landed on the top of the other.

The henchman elbowed, Cliff's head slammed toward the right, and the man reached for a lever. Cliff blinked back stars and then rammed his own elbow deep into the man's ribs.

The ribs cracked; the man howled in pain. As the anger boiled over, Cliff found himself hitting the man until there was no resistance.

Silence engulfed him. Where had all the noise gone? Penny's quiet voice appeared beside him as she placed a hand on his shoulder. "Cliff, you can stop."

His body shook. It took a moment for the words to sink in as he stared at the others. Penny balanced on the forklift step. Chrys stood a little way off, held the balding man, and gazed at Cliff with knowing eyes. Richard came forward and lowered the lift.

The whine brought the boxes safely to the floor. Stacked two at the bottom and one at the top, he and Richard lifted the top box off and sat it to the side. Penny found three crowbars, and in a group effort, they freed the lids.

From the first box, his mom blinked her eyes with the cellphone still gripped by white knuckles. Her arms came up, the cellphone dropped, and she hugged him tightly. "My boy! You're safe!" Tears streamed down her face.

A lump grew in his throat. "Mom!"

This was exactly what he had prevented Penny from doing. Even now, he could feel the anger drain. With gentle hands, he removed her grip, and noticed the bruises on her wrists; they had tortured her, too. "We have to get you out of here. We have to free the others."

Richard and Penny started on the second box. Cliff helped his mother to one of the chairs and then joined them to release the second lid.

His uncle blinked. The moment he saw freedom, he used his palms and shoved the lid. The wood snapped in a way that it shouldn't. His red-faced uncle rose of his own accord to meet the eyes of Cliff. With a hoarse voice, he spoke, "After we get your father out, we need to talk."

The others started on the third box. As Cliff joined in, he could feel every jerk until the lid broke loose. It had to be a family trait; his father snapped the boards in that same unusual way.

Cliff's eyes bounced from one to the other. Everyone who had been in the boxes had the same wrist marks. Had he found the codicil sooner, could he have stopped this?

His father's words were raspy as the man licked his dry lips. "How long?"

"Too long. Over twenty-four hours." Cliff looked toward the office. "We need water."

His uncle held up a hand. "No, Cliff, water can wait. We need to talk as a family."

Penny turned toward the office, but Cliff caught her arm. "All of the family."

Though his mom sat further away, she snagged every word; a twinkle appeared in her eye. "I do think it's time." She rose and picked her way toward them as they put the lids back on the crates. The crates were pushed apart so all could sit.

Richard held back, but Cliff would have none of it. "You and Chrys, too. We're all in this."

Richard took a seat. Chrys came forward with the balding man. A grunt escaped the man's lips as she jabbed him. "And what will we do with him? He's really quite soft, you know."

Cliff met her eyes. Once again, they bordered on the soulless, and he couldn't let that happen despite his own desire for revenge. "We tie him up until we're done." His next words held a sharp edge. "And then he'll give us Fushimi."

The last sentence made her focus; a slight smile caressed her face. "Yes, he will."

Richard reached over and removed the balding man's belt. He grabbed the man's right wrist and twisted it back. The man jumped but did not say a word. As the left wrist did the same, he tied them firmly. "That should hold him, but I wouldn't advise leaving him to his own devices."

The balding man glanced toward the office.

"Oh," Chrys purred, "we'll have none of that lover." She shoved him toward the floor, placed a foot on him, and sat on the end of a box. Her gun pointed down. "Don't move."

Jessie's eyebrows rose toward her son. Penny gave a frown. No one said anything until Penny snapped her fingers. "Stop it, all of you. Don't you see what's happening? They're trying to make *us* just like *them*!"

The word *us* scored like a dart. Joseph and his brother blinked; Cliff continued to stare.

Cliff's uncle inhaled. "She's right. I know these people, and I know their history with our parents." He looked toward Joseph. "We have to defeat them without stooping to their level."

Cliff found his voice. "You know these people." His head nodded. "You knew the danger."

"We all did," his mother whispered. All eyes turned to her; Cliff's held confusion. As she rubbed her wrists, she spoke the next sentence like a wish. "We hoped it would all go away."

"You too?" Cliff couldn't believe his ears and turned in a circle. "From the beginning?"

His father stared at a box. "Your grandparents hoped that by coming to America they would leave it all behind. But you can't stop rumors, and you can't run from what you've been a part of. Here your grandparents chose to make it right until the government *required* your grandmother's services."

Cliff's eyes narrowed. "They forced her?"

"That's when I met her." Richard nodded. "Not long after, your grandfather passed away. The cause was never established, but she knew why; you could see it in her eyes. She never spoke of it. She just picked up the pieces and moved on."

"They kept me out of most of it." Joseph continued. "If it hadn't been for your uncle, I would have been blindsided, too. He warned your mom and me."

His uncle put a hand on his father's shoulder. "It was too dangerous not to know. We had to stay out of the line of fire. You can't do that unless you know what you're hiding from."

Cliff's eyes searched their faces. "That was why you came to the house. You suspected—"

"That more was going on?" His father nodded. "Of course. We could never leave you alone with this though we knew you could handle it." A slight chuckle escaped his lips. "Well, maybe your mom knew first. I was a little stubborn."

Additional facts rolled into Cliff's mind: the mausoleum and the numbers with its secrets hidden in the column. "But I can't, don't you see that? I don't want to deal with it. I don't want to see people die." He looked down at his clothes. Splatters of blood from the men Chrys had shot stood out like badges. Even his hands had blood where he had hit the man in the forklift too many times. He held them up for all to see. "I don't want this."

"Nor do we," his uncle spoke quietly. "But the situation is forced upon us. Your grandmother tried to redeem our family by exposing what Gerhard had done. Fushimi—" A sigh escaped his lips. "I don't think she realized how deep that corruption went."

"No." Richard stepped in. "She knew. She would never have done it if she hadn't known. And to be honest, a lot of what you're saying has opened my eyes." His voice dropped. "I only wish I could have told her how brilliant she really was." The voice dropped completely. After a moment, it picked up again. "Two things are left: we take out Fushimi, and we let the world know the truth about those papers. We do that, and you may get your peace."

The papers were in Cliff's pocket along with the thumb drive, but the codicil had been in the balding man's hand. He turned toward the chairs, stepped over the balding man, and hurried past the destroyed box.

The ground was bare. He came back to the balding man, grabbed him by the shirt, and lifted him up. "Where is it?"

A smirk hit the man's face. "To what are you referring?"

"You know exactly. The vinyl envelope, you cold, soulless animal."

"Soulless," the balding man mocked. "You mean like her?" His eyes went toward Chrys. The man whispered to Cliff as if sharing a delightful secret. "We made her, you know. We took all that animal rage and brought it to the surface. She is a natural—" His eyes shifted back to Cliff. "—and so are you."

The gun cocked. Chrys stared into the man's eyes. "Leave him alone."

"Or what, you will shoot me?" The balding man laughed. "How will you find Fushimi then, little bird?" He spat at her. "You are pathetic. You are weak. You have been culled from the herd. By the end of tonight, you will all be dead."

By sheer willpower, Cliff lowered the man to the floor without bashing his head against it. He wrapped his hands around Chrys' hands to keep the weapon from descending toward the man. Their gazes met.

The soulless look stared back. "Let me kill him, Cliff. It will only take a second. Release me from my promise."

She was right. In all the shots that were fired, she had tried not to kill. "No." The anger felt so strong he could barely say the word. The end became a whisper. "Not yet."

Penny's voice jumped in. "Cliff, no!"

He turned on her as the rage welled up. "They will not hurt my family."

She met his gaze. "Don't you think I understand? My brother killed by my father. My brother was used to kill your grandmother, and—"

Joseph jumped to his feet. "You're Gerhard's daughter?" He started to move toward her, but his brother grabbed him. "Let it go, Joseph."

A roar left Joseph's lips. "Let it go?"

Jessie moved in front of Penny. "Let it go. This child's innocent."

"No—" Penny stared into nothing. "—I'm not. Oh God, I'm not." She dropped to her knees unable to look at anyone else. "It's all my fault."

Cliff moved toward her, torn between the need to protect and rage that had taken him. His father strained against his uncle's hold. "She killed our mother?"

Sorrow, guilt, and despair filled her face. "I—"

"You didn't." Cliff cut her off. "What you did had nothing to do with those beasts that killed my grandmother, and you know it. I will not let you take the blame."

Jessie listened to both. "The birth parents do not matter." She bent down and pulled Penny close. "She did not plot to kill Elaine; I don't care what anyone says. She and our son are in love, and I'll *not* let anyone destroy that."

The bomb of silence shook the foundations of the building. Out of the silence, the balding man laughed. "And you think you're going to take on Fushimi?" The laugh deepened as he continued. "Who knows what dark secrets hide inside your family?" The laugh became louder until it echoed across the warehouse. Unable to take anymore, Cliff turned around and hit him.

The laugh stopped. In the silence, the balding man wiped a trickle of blood off the side of his face. "You'll pay for that."

Cliff went back to the chairs. As the rage drained away, his mind became clearer. What the balding man said held truth. Unless they pulled together, they would be no match for Fushimi.

Boxes on crates existed not far behind the balding man's chair. As he remembered where the cellphone bounced, he dropped to his hands and knees.

The balding man had thrown the vinyl envelope. The small package could be anywhere within forty to fifty feet. Due to the obstacles, he doubted it would be further.

Behind him, voices resumed. The shouts were gone, and a chuckle could be heard upon occasion. One by one, he recognized his mother, his father, Richard and his uncle.

Chrys appeared to help search. Her gun sat in its holster. "She doesn't have the fire."

He looked back and saw his mother had persuaded Penny to rise from the floor; the two talked quietly. Richard guarded the prisoner.

He knew exactly what Chrys spoke of—that burning desire to see your enemy pay. He knew, but he did not want to admit it; it opened a part of him that made him doubt the person he had always been. Let it go. Yet, it would not go away. It smoldered until it could light again.

They went around a crate; a gap stood between them. At one point, the distance became so narrow that they bumped against each other. Chrys smirked. "I didn't see that coming."

He backed up, let her pass, and came in behind. More headroom made it easier to stand.

She stopped and let him bump into her from the back. "And good form, too." Methodically, she leaned forward and slowly bent her knees until she could go no further down. She touched the hand he used to steady himself, held onto it, and scanned for the vinyl envelope.

She teased him. How did she know he needed that? "Chrys, I know what you're doing." Good sense tried to return. "You know it won't work."

Her eyes batted up from between two crates with an innocent smile. "What won't work?"

Albert had been right; she really was stunning. When the soulless eyes weren't upon her, her beautiful eyes could draw him in.

As he inhaled, he fought off a smile. A stranger would have been completely fooled, but he was no stranger. "Do I really have to say it?"

Her eyes twinkled. "If it helps bring out some hidden, secret desire, why not?" As her eyes stayed locked with his, she rose slowly toward him like a cobra prepared to strike. "I know the fire. We can share it together." Her lips brushed his. They were soft and moist as she moved toward his ear. "It is a gift she will never know. It can be our secret."

Cliff stepped back from the spell and slammed into a wooden crate. What in the world was wrong with him? When he looked around, she had vanished. His mind swirled as he came out from between the crates. With Chrys nowhere to be seen, had he imagined the whole thing?

Her voice called from the right. "It's here!" With a smile brighter than he had ever seen and eyes sparkling like tiny suns, she came to him. Within the top part of her shirt, the vinyl envelope lay tucked—directly over her heart. The words she spoke were a challenge. "Take it."

Chapter 29

"Take it," she whispered. "It belongs to you, even if you never give it back."

Cliff's pulse pounded in his ears. "Chrys, I can't do that. I would never do that to anyone."

Her fingers reached down, took his right hand, and placed it on the vinyl envelope. "I know, and you don't have to. I will do it for you." One by one, she gently folded his fingers around the end, held them firmly, and lifted the envelope from her blouse.

His face flushed. Her eyes sparkled more.

As he took hold of the package, she slipped her fingers gently away. "There now, it is all complete. Our hearts are one. It is time to find Fushimi."

Richard called as they walked toward the group, "Did you find what you were looking for?"

Chrys' face beamed; the eyes were not soulless now. "Yes."

Penny turned in midsentence. Her eyes narrowed on the couple. "The codicil, I hope?"

"Actually—" Cliff's blush deepened. "—Chrys found it."

Penny's eyes became daggers. A frown formed on Jessie's face. Richard's eyebrows rose. His father and uncle were amused. The balding man on the floor said nothing.

Cliff took the last few steps and handed the codicil to his father. "I think, before we do anything else, we need to know its contents."

The vinyl envelope stared at all that looked upon it. His father turned it over several times, found no seam, and reached in his pocket for a knife. The blade caught the light and flashed as he slit the top of the envelope.

A hush fell. From the depths of the container, he slid out multiple pages. A name had been inked in cursive at the top of each one.

"They're letters," Joseph whispered, "addressed to each of us." One by one, he soberly handed them out. They all had one, including Richard.

Cliff stared at his. The signature was familiar, not only because it was Gran's. The handwriting matched the letter he had found at the bank. If that were the case, then the codicil and the letter could have been written at the same time. His fingers trembled as he read silently:

"You're alive. If you're reading this, then you have found them and know exactly to what I refer. Trust the one to whom I defer to be noble; in the end, you will not be disappointed.

"You have also stumbled upon other things. They are dangerous secrets from a time long ago, and people will kill for their knowledge. Keep them buried if you must, but learn all you can, and protect the family. It is all that matters.

"We are seven of ten in all our ways. Six medallions make the circle. Six circles will give a clue. America is the first, but not last. I dare not say more, least this letter fall into unclean hands. It is up to you to remember.

"I love you, grandson, and wish you well on your journey against the darkness. Never forget the light, for it will guide you home.

"P.S. Numbers are knowledge. Remember them well."

Gran. He stared at the letter despite having finished it. Someone cried. His father moved to sit next to his mother. His uncle and Richard remained alone, but the sadness they all showed made his heart melt.

His emotions existed in two distinct zones: he loved his

grandmother with all his heart, but he despised the world she had shown him. He loathed even more what he had to do next.

The letter should be burnt. His mind knew it, but he couldn't make it happen. Instead, he stuck it deep in his front pocket and felt the platinum ring.

The ring shouldn't be here; it should be in the mausoleum buried forever. Gran had said to learn all he could. The reason could not be missed; war had come, and he stood on the front line.

Penny's hand touched him on the shoulder; it jarred him from his thoughts. "I'm sorry, Cliff. I know it's not easy."

His taut muscles could barely feel it. In a hard voice he declared, "No—" He pursed his lips. "—but what needs to be done is clear." He turned and felt her hand fall from his shoulder. If he gave into her softness now, it would bring about his undoing.

"Dad, Mom, and Uncle, I politely request you leave—" The words of Gran came back—trust the one to whom I defer. Outside of the family, Gran trusted as noble only two people: Richard and George. George could not be found, but Richard was here. He turned to Richard. "Can you take them someplace safe?"

The meaning was clear, and it was not to a Division A safe house. The man nodded.

His father stood up, and in his raspy, dry voice declared firmly, "No, we will not. I refuse to let you walk in without us by your side."

His uncle stood as well. "Nor will I."

Cliff studied his mom's pale features; she did not look good. "And what of Mom?"

Unsteadily, she rose to her feet; Joseph caught her and defiantly gave her strength. "I am going, too," her voice remained steady. "We are the Fultons, and Fushimi is going to know it."

Chapter 30

The balding man smirked. "Pitiful."

Cliff dragged him to the top of the crate. "Just the person I wanted to hear from. Believe it or not, we had almost forgotten about you." He leaned closer to him. "Almost." Cliff's eyes glanced toward Chrys. "May I borrow your gun?"

Her eyes brightened. "Of course."

Penny tried to reach him, but Joseph pulled her back. "Leave him be."

Her eyes bulged with fear. "But—"

A grim line spread across Joseph's face. "He's doing what he must."

The snap opened as Chrys pulled out the gun. She touched Cliff's arm; he did not pull away. "I'll do it if you like."

A grim line crossed Cliff's lips. "This has to be done my way."

She deferred with a nod, withdrew her touch, and placed the gun in his outstretched palm. His heart smote him. Everything depended on if the man believed him. If not, he would have no choice but to follow through.

"Now, lets it make it simple. There will be two shots. One will be through the right foot, and the second will penetrate your left. After that, if you fail to cooperate, we will pick other targets. Do you understand?"

The balding man stared.

"Hey—" Chrys slapped him. "—a simple *yes* is polite." She demonstrated by a nod. "Got it?"

Since he didn't respond, Cliff raised the gun and fired.

Penny screamed, the balding man jumped, and all went quiet. As the shot echoed away, Cliff looked him in the eye. A hole had been blown in the box not three inches from his head. "That was to get your attention. Do you understand?" The balding man refused to answer, but perspiration ran down his brow.

He turned to Chrys. "I guess we'll have to prove ourselves. Help me put his feet up."

"Wait—" The man glared at him. "—I'll tell you where he is."

"Thank you." Cliff gave a smile and handed the gun back to Chrys. It was way too easy, and he knew it; he suspected Chrys knew it too.

A pout settled on Chrys' face. "Aw, come on. Be just a little braver, please?" She leaned near him. "You won't even feel it." Her eyes brightened. "Of course, you know I'm lying."

Sweat dropped down the man's face. "A warehouse by the lake. Bay fifty-two."

Chrys and Cliff looked at each other. That was said on the phone.

Her face brightened. "One."

The gun went off to score on his left foot. Everyone jumped except Richard and Chrys. Cliff's eyes opened wide; he really hadn't expected to do it.

The man screamed out. "You said right, right would be the first foot!"

"Did he?" Chrys' eyes brightened again. "Let me fix that."

Battle raged inside Cliff; it would be way too easy to let her. Cliff caught the hand with the gun. "Hold it. We need information." As their eyes met, she blew him an adoring kiss. His gaze fell back on the man. "Are you certain about that? You're not confused by the pain?"

The man shook his head.

Cliff inhaled. "He could be telling the truth. Maybe the

reason it went down wrong the first time was that Fushimi didn't trust us."

"First time?" Penny shook off Joseph's hold; the news had surprised everyone. "You tried to reach him before?" Her eyes narrowed. "How long have you two been together?"

Cliff didn't answer; an explanation would take too much time.

Chrys smirked, but she did not address Penny. "The implant gave us away. Now that it's removed, he cannot track me." She checked the bullets in the gun, reloaded, and placed it back in the holster. "Unfortunately, I believe him."

The word *track* stayed in Cliff's brain. He looked down at the man. If the cabal used implants in some, why not monitor them all. "He knows. We just told Fushimi everything."

Despite the pain in his foot, the man chuckled. "Indeed, he does." He looked at Chrys. "Every conversation I've overheard."

Richard stepped forward. "There's only one way to fix this. Help me get him up."

With one hand under each arm, Richard and Cliff lifted him to his feet. The man cried out and tried to keep his foot from touching the ground, but he could not; the loss of blood had weakened him.

Joseph and his brother carried the man to the entrance. The boarded up door slammed back as they stepped from the interior into the light. Smaller bits of glass tumbled from the broken pane to bounce upon the cement. A few startled sparrows leaped into the air.

Penny, Jessie, and Chrys followed behind. No one spoke. Unspoken thoughts laced the air.

As they reached the car, Cliff used the key fob and opened the door that Richard indicated. They laid the balding man's torso in the backseat but left his legs out. The windshield jumped to life as Richard's fingers went over the controls. "At least there are no new dents." His eyes darted toward Cliff. "Thanks for taking care of it."

"Thanks for giving me the key."

Joseph pointed to the balding man. "Isn't he still sending?"

Cliff nodded at the windshield. "The car notes and blocks any tracking device within."

"The car does more than that—" Richard grinned "—if you know how." A frequency scan appeared on the screen. "I would suggest anyone with a pacemaker step away from the car."

Joseph and his brother gave Richard a funny look.

"I'm joking."

Cliff pointed at the screen. "What's going to happen?"

"We're about to fry the implant."

The balding man struggled to get out of the car. Joseph and his brother caught the man's legs, and the injured foot struck the ground. The man yelped but resumed with greater force.

Frequency numbers flew by and abruptly stopped. A red light flashed beside a number as Richard accepted it. A wisp of burned flesh met their nostrils. The man went limp.

Joseph checked the man's pulse. "What happened?"

"Sometimes the nervous system doesn't like it when the implants are shut down."

"In other words—" Cliff stared at the unconscious man. "—the shock knocks him out."

"Exactly."

Chrys came near Cliff and put an arm around him. "Then it's a good thing you removed mine the old fashioned way." She casually glanced toward Penny. "Naked."

Penny glared. "Cliff, we need to talk."

Chrys turned toward her and made her face innocent. "What's a little flesh between friends?"

"Cliff!"

Chrys stepped back with a smirk. "Go on, tell her." She didn't have to add lover.

Richard cleared his throat. "I don't know what this is all about, but this is not the time to do it. We need to move this body back in the building and head out as soon as possible." He scowled at the girls. "Kapeesh?"

Penny folded her arms. "Oh, I understand perfectly." Her eyes stared straight at Cliff. "You can let that little slut put her hands all over you, but you can't let me hug you one time." Her eyebrows crossed. "One moment you push me away, and the next you call me family."

Cliff inhaled. He glanced toward the others but received no help. As a matter of fact, his mom's expression said she stood on Penny's side. He held up a hand to stop Richard. "Five minutes." He owed her that much at least. They crossed the street to the other side and sat down on the curb. From the corner of his eye, Richard, Joseph, and his uncle worked to get the balding man inside the building. Chrys leaned back against the car to watch.

Penny's arms folded. She bit her lip and refused to look at him.

What could he say? I'm sorry, Penny, but life has been treating me so bad that I've taken it out on you? I'm sorry, but I've been forced into an alliance with a beautiful woman, and oh, by the way, she's an assassin?

Ouch, for the first time he realized how tempted he had been. Chrys was a beautiful woman, but she was insane. No, not insane. She had been hurt deeply because of what had happened to her family and had determined to strike back. It could happen to him.

Tension spread across his whole body; he could not relax. The seconds ticked away until at last words came. "You can't let her get to you. We just have to make it through this."

Penny's eyes rose to meet his. "It's not her I'm afraid of." A single tear began in one eye and slowly came down her cheek. "You've changed, Cliff. In less than two days, you've gone from the boy I love to a man I do not recognize."

Her softness tried to rob him of his strength. Richard had

been correct; now was not the time. Yet, if not done now, would it be too late? His eyes looked away. "It's a world run by ruthless people, and they will do anything to stop us. Your brother did not plot to kill your father. Fushimi planned it. Tish said—"

Her eyes took a faraway look. "You've been with Tish, too?"

"She is your sister."

Venom rose in her voice. "She is the devil who wants to steal you away."

Cliff swallowed. After what had happened that morning, it couldn't be denied. "Fair enough. Yet, she hasn't, has she?"

"Has she?"

Insistence hit his voice. "No."

"And Chrys?"

"Of—of course not." The slip of the words sent him into panic. Surely she realized he could never have a relationship with Chrys? "Penny, you know I love you."

A second tear started down her face. "I worked so hard to please my father, I was willing to do anything he asked, and he never even noticed me. My brother betrayed my trust and used me. I betrayed yours. If it is my time to reap, I won't go through that pain again." She turned toward the car and caught Chrys watching them.

A plea came from his heart. "Let me complete this, and then you'll understand."

"Go to her." Cold venom laced the words. "When you figure out what you want, I may not be around."

"Cliff," Richard's voice echoed. Penny started toward the car.

"Penny, wait!" He hurried to catch her, but she did not look back.

Chrys watched her approach. When she came near, the smirk returned. "He's mine. You don't have the fire."

Something clicked, and Penny smiled brightly. "You like fire?" Her hand came up from nowhere and connected with a loud slap. A handprint flared red on the girl's cheek.

Chrys touched it gingerly and then rubbed her fingers together. The fingers transformed into a fist. "You like to hit people?" The smirk broadened on her face. "Let's see how much."

Richard caught the fist. "That's enough." With his deepest baritone voice he boomed, "Until this over, I expect us to work as a team." His arm spun Chrys around, and he caught her chin in his right hand. "If you want Fushimi, you will do as I say."

The soulless look returned as she jerked away. "I will do as you say." She stepped back. "However, make no mistake. I am not part of the team." Her hand opened the back door, and she slipped inside.

Richard turned to the others. "Cliff, I want you to take this car to the far side of bay fifty-two." His hand reached inside, pressed a button, and the trunk released. "Who knows how to use a gun?" Cliff's uncle followed as Richard went to the back of the car. Inside the trunk, the agent pressed his thumbprint on a small, circular area, and a compartment rose an inch above the floor. He caught it with his fingers, flipped it back, and revealed an assortment of weapons.

Cliff's uncle pointed, and Richard handed him one with a magazine. Richard turned toward Joseph and Jessie. "What would you like?" Both pointed. Richard pulled out their preference.

Penny stepped back. "I don't want one."

Cliff stared in horror; his worst nightmare had come true. No one knew how close he had come to shooting the balding man. "This is insane. No guns, not for us."

The magazine slid into the gun that Cliff's uncle held. "Cliff, I know how to shoot, and so do your parents."

"So, I was the only one not taught?"

Jessie stepped forward. "You were at college, and, before that, high school. Why did you need a gun?"

The absolute lunacy of it hit him. He closed his eyes. "Yeah. I'm in a family that has a history with a crazy cabal, and I'm the only one that wasn't trained to shoot. This makes a lot of sense. But that's not what I'm referring to. I don't want you here. I don't want you killed. If Gran trained me to do the job, to figure out how to do the job, then I need to do it, not you."

Everyone stopped. A car drove by the cross street. A piece of paper rustled as it blew beside them. Preparations abruptly continued.

"You're not listening to me!"

"Oh, we listened," his father assured with a wink. "We just don't agree."

Richard turned toward him. "Okay, everyone loaded?"

Cliff stared at him. "No."

"You don't have a gun. It doesn't matter."

"No, wait. Listen to me! If we go in there carrying guns, we give Fushimi every right to fight back. If I go in there alone, unarmed, I can make him see reason."

His father demanded, "How?"

"I have met Fushimi, and he said something that I did not understand until now. He can't directly kill any of us without cause, or the cabal will kill him."

Chapter 31

His uncle stepped forward. "How do you know this?" His eye held a strange look.

"I learned this from Fushimi." They weren't going to listen without an explanation, so Cliff dived in. "Fushimi likened the family to a burying beetle. Those creatures kill off their young to balance out resources for the best chance at life. With every generation, the culling begins." He stared at them, but they didn't get it so he pointed. "You see that person inside the car? They culled her family. They used it to train her to be a killer, an assassin."

Penny shook her head. "I won't give her sympathy."

"Look at her. Does she seem normal to you? Did she grow up with a fun, loving family? They killed them and then used her until she had nothing left inside."

"That doesn't excuse her behavior. Everybody has a choice."

He turned to face the others. "The way they monitor their own is through the implants. I don't know how they did it in Gran's time, but that's how they do it today. If someone in the cabal gets out of line and kills another without permission, that person is killed. It is the reason Fushimi used Gerhard's son to kill Gran. He set the boy up to stop her and at the same time wiped out his competition."

Richard thought over the words. "That still doesn't explain why he'll cooperate."

"These." Cliff pulled out the papers that Gran left him. "We do exactly what you said. We send these out all over the world to every person who will take them. We expose the trio and their revenge so that there is no longer any secret."

His uncle nodded slowly. "And once the secret is out, the reason to kill is over. By their very own code, they will not. I remember Mom mentioning the code, but I never applied it that way."

"And I will be the distraction to make sure he is not watching."

The head of his father shook. "I don't like it."

"You'd rather go in shooting guns?"

Joseph glanced at Jessie. "No, I wouldn't, but I will to save my family."

"Then give me a better option."

Leaves rustled against the sidewalk. All the emotion hit at once, and Cliff's voice shook. "Dad, Gran trained me. Let me do my job!"

Very quietly, his mother placed the gun she held back into the trunk. As she stepped back, she put an arm around Joseph. Joseph's shoulders gradually dropped as he handed his to his brother. Cliff's father's face contorted in pain and pride. "My boy, I just don't want to lose you."

Cliff moved forward to hug them, and his uncle joined the group. They squeezed each other tightly. A smaller, soft hand found Cliff's; it was Penny.

"I'm sorry. I didn't understand."

The anger drained away, and for the first time in many hours, he could think only of the moment. He released his family and hugged her. With a tight hold, he could feel every part of her press against him. Their lips met and held until she pulled apart. "You have a job to do."

"I do."

Richard wiped the corner of his eye.

Cliff handed over the papers. "You know better than I how to do this."

Gran's trusted friend gave a nod. "I do."

No more anger and no more hatred materialized—at least, not in a way to take control. His mind shifted. "I have a phone so we can communicate, but I need you to fix it." George's phone came out of his pocket, and he handed it to Richard.

"What's wrong with it?"

"Any number I dial goes to Division A."

Richard's finger felt along the battery cover, found the right place, and popped it off. He checked the battery but saw nothing suspicious. "It will take time, but I can figure out how they did it; I thought it might be a battery bug. I'll need the proper tools to go deeper. However—" He pulled out his phone, unlocked it, and adjusted its function. "—I suggest you use mine."

With the same swipe, Cliff watched the front picture appear. "How do I log in?"

The man smiled. "You don't have to. I've placed an app on the outside of the security login. Touch that—" He pointed to the icon. "—and it rings directly to George's phone which of course I'll have. If I get your call and you don't speak, we'll know there's trouble."

"Thanks." The phone dropped into his pocket. "I better get going." Without a look back, he walked to the driver's side, got in, and closed the door.

Chrys' fearful voice met him. "You're cold. The fire is gone."

The car bounced as the trunk closed behind him. The engine started. He shifted into gear and turned toward the cross street. "I know what I have to do."

Chrys moved to the right side and climbed into the front passenger seat. Her eyes were distant as she whispered, "How will you do it without the fire?"

He knew what she looked for: a way to make peace with herself. "I will do it from the heart."

Head against the seat, Chrys closed her eyes to rest. As her breath slowed, her face relaxed, and all her masks dropped away. No longer an assassin, she existed as a woman whose family had been lost.

A few blocks went by. He made his way toward the nearest thoroughfare. With her asleep, he had nothing to do, but think.

Richard would handle the details to get the papers out; of that, he had no doubt. However, what could be done with Chrys? The revenge consumed her. She was partly right; in him the fire had been doused. However, the embers still glowed. He would need to be very careful.

Gran had warned him against the darkness. It came from the world his grandparents had left behind. However, that reality could be chosen or not.

One of Chrys' hands reached out in a stretch; the back of her hand touched his shoulder. He could feel now without struggling through taut muscles. The relief flowed through him.

As she opened her eyes, her head rolled toward him. The eyes glowed with life. A smile lit her face as he turned back to watch the road.

"You must think me crazy."

The thoroughfare came, and he caught it. Bay fifty-two lay less than twenty minutes away. A slight laugh left his lips. "No."

"But I am," her voice stayed low. "I am crazy with the fire, and it is all consuming. You are the first one that could put it out—if only for a brief time."

"It is the heart that matters, not the fire. With the fire, the heart withers. Without the fire, the heart will grow."

She adjusted her clothing. "You know I must kill Fushimi."

Cliff gave a nod. "I know."

"And you're okay with that?"

Was he? The part of him that maintained the embers waited for his decision; the right spark would ignite it. "I think you have a choice. We have a plan that will destroy Fushimi far beyond mere death. If you trust me to complete my mission, you will have your revenge ten times over. The choice will still be yours."

Her hand came out and held his on the steering wheel. "I will try, Cliff Fulton. I will try."

The road to bay fifty-two appeared. Cliff turned to the right and followed it. He spotted the manhole that he and Albert had used to escape the waters. Albert had not been found, and he had no clue who took him. He pulled into the parking lot and cut the engine. "It is time."

"Yes, it is." She kissed his cheek, gave a big smile, and opened the door. When he stepped out, she had vanished.

The trunk popped open. Curious, he closed his door and walked to the back only to see Penny as she climbed out. He stared.

She folded her arms. "Well, aren't you going to say anything?"

"It would have been more comfortable inside the car?"

"Someone else's ego had filled it up."

He threw up his hands as she slammed the trunk. "Penny, you said you understood."

"I understood you, not her being with you."

With his hand on the car, he shook his head. "She has certain talents that are useful."

"I bet."

He stepped toward her. "You know what I mean."

"No, I don't. You tell your family there will be no guns, yet you bring her who carries a gun. Do you honestly think no one caught that?"

It hadn't occurred to him. However, the point had validity. "I couldn't have made her stay."

"Really? You did well with everyone else."

"That's different. Look, you didn't even stay."

"Because of her."

Cliff turned around and stared out at the lake. "I don't have time for debate, nor do I need to justify my decisions. I have to keep Fushimi occupied until those papers get out. So either you help me and stop the interference, or stay here and let me get it done."

Penny's eyes burned into him as her voice went cold. "You think I'm interfering?"

His head shook as he twisted toward her. "I didn't mean it like that."

She turned and walked back toward the road.

Exhaling, he changed directions. She approached the end of the parking lot. "Penny, stop!"

A car came down the road. She stuck out her thumb.

"Penny, please!"

He hurried toward her as the car slowed. The driver's window rolled down. "Can I help you?" The man in the car threw a look at Cliff. "Is this person bothering you?"

"Yes, but I'll be fine. Thanks for stopping."

The man gave a single nod. "If you change your mind, I'll be at the second restaurant on the left. It's called Finley's."

"Thank you."

The car drove off.

Cliff felt a spark of anger. "How could you? And with a total stranger at that?"

"Now you know how I feel about Chrys." She turned back and headed toward the boardwalk.

As the car locked, he followed behind and tried to figure out what to say. The anger drained. She was right, and that made the embarrassment worse. In her eyes, he had turned to a total stranger for help and told Penny she wasn't needed.

His heart hurt; he knew she had to be hurting, too. Though he had subdued the anger, his emotions were still on the edge.

They stepped onto the same path he and Albert had come down when they had gone to see Gerhard. The memories of it roared back. He had risked everything to take her out of danger, and now she walked into it.

Her voice was sharp. "Cliff?"

His remained cautious. "Yes?"

"Where is she?"

It would be an affront to ask her who. "I don't know."

Her eyebrows furrowed. "You don't know?"

"We stopped, and she disappeared."

Their footsteps echoed on the boardwalk. The smell of fish and the sound of water lapping against the docks reminded him once more of that fatefully night.

As Penny walked beside him in silence, Cliff wondered if Albert lay at bay fifty-two, yet, he suspected not. Whoever had sent the assassin to the catwalk remained part of that mystery.

George had remained missing, too, but Penny had seen George before she had escaped. If the facts had not changed, the rogue Division A had George confined.

Up steps, down steps, cement steps, and wood weaved the path that they followed. This time, he could see bay fifty-two from a distance. Why had Fushimi picked this place?

Pieces of the puzzle started to fill in. Gerhard and Fushimi were part of the trio; of course, he would know about this place. And why not? It had already been raided. If the rogue Division A worked with Fushimi, what better place to hide than where they would never think to look?

Penny slowed down. The four-story building stared with empty eyes as the boardwalk spread out to form the familiar second deck.

Fushimi had never said exactly where to meet him, just as Gerhard had not done the same. Nothing said the man's location, but Cliff knew they were being watched.

He took the stairs to the water and saw the familiar boat dock with the grid gate. The door beside it would not open. One of the other doors had to be unlocked.

As Penny watched, he changed directions, walked back to the boardwalk, and stepped onto the second-floor deck. All his plans hinged on the notion that Fushimi wouldn't kill him, and even if the man did, his family would be free after Richard got the papers out.

Penny's presence changed everything. Why had his parents let her do it? Then it hit him; he wasn't the only one who knew the risks.

It was funny how people caught up in their own world missed everyone else's. His parents had seen right through him. Penny's presence insured that he would do all it took to survive.

On the deck, he moved to the small door beside the larger and pulled the handle. The door did not move. If he was expected—he ran around to the right side of the building and hurried up the steps. On the platform, he grabbed hold of the door. Nothing—the door would not budge.

Penny caught up and gazed in wonder. "No one's here?"

He wiped the dust off the window. No lights were on; no one appeared within. No, Fushimi had to be here. The text message had given this address, the address had been received on Chrys' phone, and the address from the balding man matched it. Where the devil was Fushimi?

The roar of a racing boat caught their ears, and they turned to look at the lake. On the far shore were condominiums. One of the tallest could be seen easily from bay fifty-two. They reached the lower platform as the boat pulled up.

A wave of water struck the dock as the race boat turned. The driver wore a bulky, waterproof jacket and helmet. The end of the boat swung around and stopped within inches of the dock.

As the helmet came off, long, black, waist-length hair tumbled down, and a female voice with a Japanese accent asked, "Are you Cliff Fulton?"

Cliff gave a shocked nod. "Chrys?"

She returned a confused frown. "I'm Chiyo, one of Fushimi's daughters, and I have been asked to pick you up." With a polite bow toward Penny she added, "Both of you."

Penny's mouth fell open, but no words came out. The confusion on Chiyo's face increased as she waited for a response.

What choice did they have? Cliff extended his hand for Penny, helped her aboard, and climbed on himself.

Chiyo handed each a helmet. "You will need this. This boat is quite fast."

They accepted the helmets and took the seats she indicated. The idling engines roared to life and streaked across the water.

Cliff raised his voice. "You knew we were there."

With a glance toward him, Chiyo used her finger to point to a soft rubber switch on the outside of the helmet and then pressed her own. "If you want to talk, hold down the button."

He did. "You knew we were here."

"But of course. We saw you from the penthouse."

His eyes followed her pointing finger to the tall multi-storied condominium. It loomed larger as a dock approached.

The boat jumped; he grabbed hold of the handrail. Chiyo throttled back and pulled into a private dock. The stop was exact. It reminded Cliff of the way in which Chrys used her gun.

A rope was tossed upon the dock; she tied it off with practiced ease and pointed toward the building. "This way, please." Penny and Cliff removed their helmets and placed them in a storage bin. As they neared the end of the dock, they were met by three young men.

"This is Akihiko, the oldest, Eiji, our father's second son, and Diaki, the youngest. They will escort us to the penthouse."

As Akihiko stepped near Penny and Cliff, no smile showed. "We are told you are both from very old houses. It is an honor."

Cliff nodded; the note Gran had left made even more sense.

Penny's face lost all expression.

Akihiko frowned as he watched her. "Have I offended?"

She came from her thoughts. "No. No, thank you."

In low voices, Eiji and Diaki spoke in Japanese. Chiyo frowned and tapped them each on the shoulder. "Where are your manners?

We have guests."

They passed through the main door and into a waiting elevator. A key for the penthouse inserted into a slot, and the elevator rose. Eiji's voice held contrition. "It was our mistake, sister." When the doors opened, they stepped into the penthouse.

Items of Japanese origin displayed around the room. The glass exterior penthouse walls glistened in the light. Beyond the glass, a blue swimming pool with outdoor furniture sat in the sun. Three angled, metal poles adorned the edge of the building on which three flags hung.

Chiyo glanced at Cliff's and Penny's clothes. "Father suspected you would need refreshment. This way, please."

Creams and browns decorated the room they came to. A shoji screen sat in one corner and displayed a blossoming tree. American clothes in the right sizes had been laid out on a wooden bench. A smaller door on the far wall led to a bathroom. Their hostess bowed and closed a sliding privacy door.

Fushimi was right; they did need to clean up. The blood splatters and dirt stood out as a badge to the previous hours.

It seemed strange that Fushimi would go through this trouble. If the talks did not go well, Cliff and Penny might very well die. He turned to Penny and motioned toward the bathroom. "Please, you first."

Without a word, she picked up two towels, walked into the bathroom, and closed the door. After a moment, the muffled spray of water began.

As he sat on the bench, he remembered the first time they had met. It had been a rollercoaster ride until things had evened out. How they stood now, he did not know. The stress of the last two days weighed on him. The fact that they were both here did not relieve his mind.

The water stopped, all went quiet, and then the door opened. Penny came out with one towel wrapped around her body and another twisted around her head. The voice wasn't happy, but it wasn't hostile either. "Your turn."

With a nod, he grabbed his own towel, stepped in, and closed the door. Penny's clothes were still in the corner. He dropped his own, stepped into the shower, and cleaned up.

Despite the circumstance, it did relax him. The beads of water bounced against his skin and washed away the past hours though part of the tension remained. The reason they were here and whose house they were in would not leave his mind.

The door to the bathroom opened and closed, but he could not see who had entered. He stopped the water, grabbed a towel, and dried himself off. With the towel wrapped around him, he stepped out of the shower door. Their clothes were gone.

His mind panicked. Among everything else, the ring, the thumb drive, and the key to Gerhard's secret door lay in those clothes. How could he have been so careless?

The emotional turmoil with Penny had distracted him; this was why he wanted to go it alone. To call back the person who took the clothes would draw undue attention.

He stepped into the room and saw Penny dressed. She pointed to the clothes piled at her feet. "I wouldn't let them be cleaned. I suspected you might want to empty the pockets first."

"Thank you!" He grabbed them up, reached for the clean clothes, and stepped behind the screen. The towel dropped, and he began to change. "Penny, I—"

She took a deep breath and frowned. "It's okay, Cliff. I just need time to think it through."

"I did not intend to make you feel unneeded and didn't realize it came off that way. My concern was for your safety."

"Maybe that's the problem." She glanced over at him. "When we were together in the beginning, it felt like we were a team."

"Before or after you ran off?" He cringed and held up a hand. "That was unfair. I'm sorry."

She grimaced. "No, you're right. We really weren't, were we?"

Her voice went lower. "It was all a pretense."

He didn't like where this headed. "It may have started as pretend, but it turned into something great. And no matter what anyone says, I wouldn't trade our time together."

Her voice remained low. "Even if it meant your grandmother wouldn't have died?"

The words hit hard, but he pushed them aside. "That discussion is pointless, and nothing good will come from it. Even at the destruction of the briefcase, Gran would have been proud to know our relationship managed to blossom." Dressed, he went through the dirty clothes for the items.

Penny moved away from the bench and turned to face him. "How do you know?"

"You saw the way my mother reacted, right?"

Her head nodded.

"Gran would have been no different."

"But your father—"

A knock struck the door; Chiyo entered maintaining an emotionless mask. "If you are rested, father will see you now."

Cliff finished the transfer of items. "I'm ready." As he dropped his clothes near Penny's, he stepped up beside her. They followed Chiyo through a larger room and to a dark, glass door. Chiyo held Cliff back. "My father would like a few minutes alone with Ms. Von Richter."

His jaw tightened.

"It is important for good relations."

Cliff's eyebrows rose.

Penny touched his arm. "Remember why we're here."

With a nod, Cliff stepped back and watched her pass through with Chiyo. The tinted glass could not be seen through, and he did not like it. The seconds dragged by as he waited. If Fushimi did anything to her—

Chiyo returned and motioned for him to enter. As he stepped in, he saw Fushimi behind a large marble desk. Penny stared out the window as he walked into the room.

Fushimi stood as Cliff entered and extended a hand toward a chair. "Please, Mr. Fulton, be seated. Penny and I got to know one another. It has been a long time since our families shared secrets." The red carnation on Fushimi's pocket caught Cliff's eye.

That sounded odd, but he picked a chair and sat back. The chair's softness conformed to his body. Golden arms adorned the dark seats to declare its opulence. Fushimi sat in a larger chair in the same decorative style. He waited for Cliff to take it all in.

"I see you are impressed. It is good to know that one's family can appreciate good taste." Penny cleared her throat.

Cliff's eyebrows rose. "What do you mean by family? We both know what you did to my family and my friends. Why all this? What are you trying to pull?"

"Why, indeed." Fushimi smiled sadly. "I fear, Mr. Fulton, we started on the wrong foot. We were never intended to be enemies, and you showed your goodwill when I met you in the tunnel. This is my apology."

Cliff stared; of all the things he expected, that was not one of them. "You think this makes up for having my grandmother killed? You think this makes up for what you did to my parents and friends?" The very idea ignited the embers inside. "You not only killed my grandmother, but you used Gerhard's family to do your dirty work. Why should I believe anything you say?"

Fushimi turned toward the window and gazed out into a cloudless sky. "It was not I that had your grandmother killed. Think about it. What would I have to gain?"

"The papers."

"Ah, yes." He nodded. "I would like to talk of those, but not at this moment. Would you indulge an old man and let him explain a few things, first?"

In the tunnels, Fushimi had tried to say as little as possible. Now he offered to tell Cliff more? It could be a trick, but Cliff couldn't refuse. "Yes."

"I have valid investments, Mr. Fulton. My empire is here, and you are sitting in its capital. Why should you believe me? It is the very fact that all these things have happened." He squinted at the desk." We are faced with a common enemy, and they will do all to tear us apart."

"What enemy?"

"You have already met their ring leader. I believe you call her Chrys Xu."

"Chrys is our enemy?" Cliff shook his head. "I don't believe you. It is not me or my family who has to worry, but you."

"She is why I sent the cars to rescue you when she called on the cell." A sad smile appeared. "Chrys Xu is one of my daughters, Emiko Taruhito. Her identical twin is Chiyo. If you do not believe me, I can let you inspect Chiyo." Fushimi's voice held an edge as he said the next words. "From the information I received, you and Chrys have been quite close."

Penny held still. Cliff swallowed. This conversation came at the worst possible time when his relationship with Penny stood on unstable ground. His eyes centered on Fushimi. "I don't know who gave that information, but it is not true."

In a very humble tone, the man gave a single nod. "Shall I play what was received?"

Penny looked toward him with a voice bitter cold. "Yes, Cliff, I think you should listen." Her words stabbed straight to his heart.

His eyebrows wrinkled. "Perhaps, I'd better."

"Very well." As Fushimi tapped the desk, a recording played: moaning ensued, Cliff called out Chrys' name, and Chrys cried out his. Fushimi stopped the tape. "There is more."

The word *setup* stormed Cliff's mind. Who had done this? What would they have to gain? How could Penny fall for this?

Fushimi sat back in his chair. "We can always run a voice match, but I think you'll find it is your voice and hers." He let the words sink in.

Cliff nodded. "Those voices came from Chrys' apartment."

Penny inhaled sharply. "So you were really there?"

"Yes."

Penny recalled another detail from Chrys. "And she was naked?"

"Yes." His eyes drifted to Penny. Someone wanted him isolated.

Thankfully, in Penny's eyes, the recording was real. To explain it now would place her in great danger. With a lowered head, he lied. "You're right. I slept with Chrys Xu."

Penny's jaw dropped.

A knowing sadness spread across Fushimi's face. "The implant never lies."

If Fushimi believed it, then someone else had done the manipulation. If Fushimi told the truth, someone else had organized Gran's death. Chrys claimed she did not know the face of Fushimi and could not recognize him. "How is it that Chrys does not know your face?"

No longer able to fight the tears, Penny burst out, "How could you? How could you do that to me?" The room went silent as her words stopped.

Despite the pain in his heart, Cliff remained firm. He said nothing.

Fushimi's face remained without emotion. "Emiko lied; she knows my face well. I have always managed to avoid her, not because of recognition, but because, until today, I knew her location. We lost her when the implant went dead. We know she used you to remove it."

"You put it there?"

Fushimi nodded. "As a child. One is always placed for the family to watch over each other. She required two."

"Because you knew she wanted to remove it. She didn't want to be a part of the family."

Penny's eyes shot toward him, and he knew her thoughts; he defended Chrys.

The man looked off into the distance; the head tilt and the direction of the eyes were the same as Chrys. "Chiyo and Emiko were born to my first wife. She was Taiwanese, not Japanese. Purchased by a dowry, she despised the fact that her family had done it."

"Why didn't you send her back?"

"Deals are deals, Mr. Fulton, and dowry is not to be taken lightly. I thought she came to understand the arrangement. The two girls were born soon after. However, the depths of her revenge were unprecedented."

"She turned one of the girls against you?"

Fushimi nodded. "I tried to stop it. In an accident, the twins' mother died. Emiko blamed me and sought to strike back." His eyes dropped. "She has no love for me, and it is her goal to kill me. If you help her, she will destroy you, too."

The secret Tish had warned him about had been revealed: Chrys. Yet, that could not be all. "Why doesn't everyone in the cabal wear the implant?"

The look on Fushimi's face went still. "Why would you think they don't?"

Did that mean Gerhard, his son, and Tish had an implant? Was that why Tish wrote down notes? The notion of the burying beetle came to mind. They culled at every generation; they let members of their own blood destroy one another. They planned to let Chrys kill Fushimi.

Though the thoughts never left his head, Fushimi's eyes appeared to catch each one. "Yes, Mr. Fulton. The cabal will allow her to kill me, and you have opened the door."

"And that's why you want us to help you?"

A slow nod came. "With every generation, we must prove our worth."

The man had some nerve. He had used a false recording to turn Penny against him, tortured and kidnapped his family, potentially plotted to have his grandmother killed, and now he wanted a favor. Why not let the cabal kill off each other? Cliff's eyes narrowed. "Convince me why I shouldn't walk."

The answer came in a low voice. "Would you be willing to live your life with the knowledge that the true murderer of your grandmother remained free?"

"No."

"Well then—" He nodded toward them both. "—despite our differences, we are forced to be allies. You don't have to like me, Mr. Fulton. You must work with me toward a common goal."

"And what will that goal be?"

The soulless look Cliff had seen in Chrys came into Fushimi's eyes. "You have to kill Chrys Xu. You have to help me kill my daughter."

Chapter 32

Akihiko entered without expression. "Yes, Father?"

"See Mr. Fulton and his guest back to their room. They must prepare themselves."

The young man bowed and turned. His emotionless mask broke momentarily when he caught the expression on Penny's face.

They passed from the office into the living area. Akihiko's two brothers swam in the pool though they showed no sentiment either. Chiyo could not be seen. The workers who moved around the penthouse held blank looks as well.

As Penny and Cliff stepped back into the room they had been provided, the privacy door closed, and the wind flicked cloth behind the shoji. A low table with pillows on each side sat in the middle of the room.

Penny spun toward him with fists gripped tight. "How could you?"

He didn't know what to say. "It was—necessary."

"You liar. All this talk of waiting for marriage, telling me you loved me, and leading me on only to do this?" Her eyes burned with disgust as she moved. "I will never love you again!"

Cliff's mouth dropped as he looked away. The sting of those words hurt more than he thought. He wanted to come clean and tell her about the ruse, but the words would not leave his throat. In an effort to keep control, he spoke very calmly. "I understand."

With her face contorted in pain, she slid open the privacy door, stepped out, and slammed it. Cliff did not go after her. A knock followed, and the privacy door opened. Chiyo entered carrying a tray with a tokoname teapot and two cups. In a smooth motion, she placed it on the table and turned toward Cliff. Her eyes beckoned him. "You will drink tea?"

Cliff nodded slowly.

"Sit." She pointed to the pillow beside the table. "I will serve it for you."

Without too much lost grace, he sat with legs crossed; she smoothly took the opposite side. As she reached for the teapot, the poise by which she raised and poured was nothing less than art.

"Sip." She nodded toward the steam that rose off his cup. "It will be hot."

Her hand carefully picked up her cup as he did the same; her eyes never left him. He blew several times before touching it to his lips. The aroma wafted pleasantly and the tension from his clash with Penny faded. "What is it?"

"We call it tokeru ocha. In English, you would say, the tea that melts. It is like green tea."

That explained his tension leaving. Green tea with its antioxidants helped to relax the body.

The sipping continued on both their parts though no more words were spoken. She continued to watch his eyes until he drank the entire cup.

As both emptied, she poured again. A gentle smile caressed her face. "Now we can talk."

Between the hot, green tea and the quiet in the room, all the tension left. "About what?"

Her eyes were hungry. "How is my sister?"

Cliff's mind went to the implants. If she had one, nothing would be private. "I don't think—"

"Mr. Fulton, any implants in our bodies are now blocked; the effect lasts one hour after we stop drinking."

"And the nanites?"

"Additional ingredients keep the nanites from performing their function until the tea wears off. My mother passed down the secret." Her eyes narrowed. "Please, how is my sister?"

"Last I saw her, she was fine." He swallowed some tea. "She is coming to kill your father."

Her eyebrows knitted together. "My father knows she's coming."

"The implant in her body is gone; I helped her remove it." His fingers studied the teacup as he placed it on the table. "Your father wants Penny and me to help him kill her."

She sipped some more of the tea; Cliff followed her example. "Yet, you do not want to. Do you wish for my father to die?"

Fushimi had caused him and his family so much pain. He looked at his hands and remembered the blood from the warehouse. "I want your father to stop killing people—" His heart tore as it battled. "—but I do not wish him dead."

"Nor I." She looked into his eyes. "You are honorable, Mr. Fulton. My father lost his honor many years ago though he has tried to make amends. Do you believe a person can change?"

As he thought of the last two days, he nodded. "I have to."

"Then you must convince my sister not to kill him. Do what you wish to the others, but I ask you to spare both their lives."

"I do not wish to hurt anyone."

"We all have the darkness and the light. My sister and father let the darkness grow. You have felt its embrace, it is upon your countenance as we speak, and you have wrestled from its grip. Even now, it waits for you to call." She reached forward and took his hands. They were warm and soft, sculpted as if by magic. "Do this for the good of all, and your soul will return."

His soul—had he bordered on the soulless too?

Someone clapped slowly. The movement behind the shoji resumed, and Chrys walked from behind. Her clothes were identical to Chiyo's. "Very good, sister."

If Cliff had not seen them together, he would have sworn they were the same girl.

A smile broke across Chiyo's face, and she leaped to her feet. "Emiko!"

Chrys' hand moved out in front to keep her back. "Emiko is dead. I am Chrys Xu."

"No—" Chiyo shoved the hand away. "—you are my sister. You are the *smiling child* of our mother. You are my twin."

The soulless eyes turned on Chrys. "I am the bringer of death. The soul of our mother calls to me from the grave." As she turned toward Cliff, some of soullessness faded.

The war of truths raged. It threatened to steal his reason. The embers ignited.

"Yes, my love, come to me, and we will do this together."

She considered all her family dead, not because they had physically died, but because they were in the shadow of her father. His voice became emotionless. "Tell me, on your mother's grave, did you help plan my grandmother's death?"

Her ties to the cabal could not be denied, and he knew it; her response could be anything. A light sparkled into her eyes before it changed to soulless. Her voice became very distant. "No, my love. I could never do that." Her face relived the past as it grimaced in pain.

Chiyo took over in that same distant voice. "A fight occurred between our mother and father. Our mother hit her head when struck. A day later, she died."

Cliff rose as the request of Chiyo surged into his mind; he had to find a way to save Chrys. In an effort, he stepped toward her in supplication. "Chrys, to kill your father is not the way."

The spell broke on both. Chrys' face changed. The soulless turned to glittering eyes. "Spoken as my true lover, but the choice is not mine, don't you see? This is my destiny."

She stepped forward. Her body pressed against his as she took his right hand and placed it on her heart. "Even in death, it will remain yours forever."

The privacy door opened, and a stunned Penny blinked. Chiyo rose and hurried to close the door. As Penny's eyes took in Chrys and Cliff, her face reddened with fury. "How dare you!"

Chiyo tried to catch Penny but missed. Penny rushed toward the couple with murder in her eyes. As Chrys slipped her gun from a hidden place, Cliff saw it in slow motion. He grabbed Chrys' wrist, forced the gun away, and kept Penny back with his other hand.

The gun flew to the left as Chrys slipped from his grasp. A smirk struck her face as she focused on Penny. "Come."

Chiyo jumped between them. "No, Emiko, this is not the way. She is not your enemy."

Chrys tried to get around Chiyo, and both girls tumbled to the floor. Their faces contorted in effort. Their waist-long, black hair flew this way and that. Their heads swung toward the table. The one to the right stopped as the hands of the left went limp.

"Sister?" She rose to her knees and slowly checked the other's head. No bruise or cut showed, but she did appear unconscious. With grief on her face, she looked up at Cliff. "We still have time, but we must act quickly."

Time for what? Cliff stared at the girl before him, unable to tell which one was which.

"Help me," she begged, "before someone comes to see her and all is lost!"

He bent down to help her. "What do you want to do?"

"We will save her life." The girl shifted her hair. "We will keep her from killing Father."

Who was he speaking to? Cliff could not be certain. "Chiyo?"

"Yes." She smiled and then gave a small laugh. "Were you not sure?"

He grinned. "Seeing double takes a while to get used to."

Penny watched them with narrowed eyes. "We only have your word."

A knock hit the door.

"Quickly. Hide the gun with her as well." Chiyo and Cliff lifted her up and placed her behind the shoji. Cliff stepped out first followed by Chiyo as the door slid open.

Akihiko stared at the three. Penny had her arms folded with a frown on her face. Cliff sat on the bench by the shoji. Chiyo stood beside the low table. "Father waits by the pool."

Chiyo bowed. "We are ready."

"No—" Penny moved forward "—we are not, but we will go."

The boy bowed and turned. Chiyo and Penny went first. Cliff slid the door shut.

They were led to the living room, passed through a glass door, and arrived at the sparkling blue pool. The boys no longer swam.

Fushimi sat in a poolside chair in front of a table with a briefcase at his right side. Shade came from a huge umbrella that rose in the center of the table. At their approach, he looked up and smiled. "You have prepared yourself for what we must do?" He leaned back in the chair. Other individuals trickled in around them. Workers stood in front of the entrance to the sliding glass door. Cliff watched him carefully.

"I have great admiration for your family, Mr. Fulton. Their guidance throughout the ages has been most important to our cause. What we desire is peace, not war. If you choose peace, we will be friends, but that friendship must be proven." He gave a nod, and a young man stepped up with two items: a metal case and a small paper bag. Both were placed on the table. Fushimi pulled the bag to himself and turned the front of the case toward Cliff. "Open it."

Chiyo spoke softly, "No, Cliff. If you do not know its secret, you are not required to partake."

Her father folded his hands. The workers who had come in made a hole and allowed others to join. These were dressed in black and wore masks to hide their faces. "Mr. Fulton, the decision is yours. Do you want peace or war?"

"I want you to leave us alone—" Cliff turned toward him. "—but if that's what it takes to stop this feud, I'll open the metal box. May I call my family first?"

Fushimi gave a respectful nod.

As he pulled out the phone, Cliff's swipe cleared the screen. He tapped the icon and waited. A brief pause held silence as a tower picked up the signal. Richard's instructions were clear; if you call and don't speak, we'll know there's trouble.

The sack on Fushimi's table rang. Without a drop in his smile, Fushimi's hand reached over and pulled out George's phone. "Shall I answer it, Mr. Fulton?"

Cliff's face fell as the phone ceased to ring. His heart beat loudly in his ears.

The man reached down and lifted the briefcase. With a click, the latches released. He pulled out a set of papers; Gerhard's seal could be seen. "Remove the masks."

As Cliff turned, he noticed two workers beside every person in black. One worker removed the masks of the black-clad person between. The face of Richard, his uncle, his father, and his mother appeared. His eyes narrowed. He turned back to Fushimi. "How?"

"Do you really have to ask?"

The voice of Cliff became very hard. "You implanted someone."

Fushimi's eyes turned to smile at Penny. "You have been most helpful, my dear."

"No!" Penny's eyes opened wide as she shook her head and glanced at her body.

"They have all been initiated." He turned back to Cliff. "And you will be the last."

Cliff's jaw set.

"Brave antics will not save you this time. For you, we are adding a little gift."

Cliff eyed the papers on the table as the wind ruffled their edges. The plan to reveal Gran's secret had been shut down cold.

The sliding glass door whooshed opened. In walked Chrys accompanied by two workers. Her face swept the area around them peacefully as her gaze caught Fushimi's.

"Well now—" Fushimi smiled. "—we are once more a family. Please, look upon our newest family members, and say hello, Emiko."

Chrys stared.

"No words of welcome? No hugs for the father you have not seen for many years?" He glanced down and inhaled. "Perhaps it is just as well. You won't be staying long."

His hand beckoned; a worker shifted to the front that held a translucent, amber case.

"You see, Mr. Fulton, when someone demonstrates they cannot be trusted, we do have ways to deal with them." Fushimi accepted the amber case and pressed a thumb on the top. As red and blue lines flashed within, the top popped up. Glittering lights danced in one corner of a large touchscreen tablet. When he tapped the appropriate app, the screen cleared, and he entered Chiyo's name. As the personal details were verified, he touched the word *locate*.

The screen showed a spinning globe. The view zoomed down, focused on North America and then the United States. It dropped until it gave a single point on the screen. At the top, it flashed the words: last known coordinates only.

He stared at the screen. His gaze rose to look at Chrys. "What have you done?" With a finger, he adjusted the search. Rather than show a single name, he set it to show everyone around him. Dots appeared and defined the signals of various people.

Cliff knew what Fushimi looked for. If he could locate Chiyo's trace, then the other girl had to be Chrys. However, if the trace did not show, he could not tell them apart.

"It is a present, Father." The one called Chiyo smiled. "One of us is Chiyo, and one is not."

Fushimi's nostrils flared. "You have betrayed me."

"No," she spoke calmly. "If you cannot tell us apart, you will never know who to kill."

"Your words betray you." He studied the one labeled Chiyo. "I know it is you."

The one labeled Chrys smiled in the exact same way. "Do you? Even these two could not tell." She pointed to Cliff and Penny. "Perhaps you should kill us both?"

Fushimi's face turned red with anger. "You will show me respect. You will reveal who you are, and Emiko will die." The dots in the amber case mocked him. "How have you done this?"

The one labeled Chiyo stared into his eyes. "The voice of our mother calls to us from the grave. She demands vengeance to free her soul."

Fushimi struck his fist on the table. "Tell me! Tell me which one, or I swear you both will die!" His hand shifted into the briefcase and rose with a gun. "I will have the truth." The gun pointed toward Cliff. "And you will find it for me."

Despite the gun pointed at him, wonderment crossed Cliff's face. "Family—that is the key." All eyes turned toward him as he changed directions so he could see everyone. "That's why you wanted Penny and me. That's why you implanted Emiko twice. You can't kill either daughter. If you do, the cabal will know. And a leader who kills without authorization is culled."

Cliff turned on him with a vengeance. "You are a murderer. You killed your wife, Michael Bishop, and my grandmother. You killed Gerhard and his son. Even though your children walk around you, you have already killed their souls. Do you honestly think I will help you now?"

Fushimi's face turned blood red. "Then perhaps you will need some persuasion." The gun shifted to the right and stopped on Penny. The finger began to squeeze. Cliff leaped forward, threw himself at the seated man, and chaos broke loose.

Chapter 33

His hand smacked against Fushimi's gun as the trigger reached its peak. An explosion of sound slammed his eardrums as his body weight crumpled the chair Fushimi sat on. Both crashed to the ground. The table jarred to the right. The briefcase, the metal case, and sack flew from the table. As the briefcase slung further open, papers shot into the air.

One of Fushimi's daughters barreled toward them while the other pulled Penny out of the line of fire. Most of the workers around them stood stunned, but a few rushed forward. The daughter nearest to Cliff pulled a gun and fired. Two spuds dropped two workers. A third worker leaped to the right behind a table. Those inside the penthouse rushed away.

Cliff's eyes riveted to Fushimi as they fought for control of the gun. By inches, it moved in Cliff's direction as it teetered back and forth. His muscles strained to hold it, but he could not break Fushimi's grip. Fushimi, with his free hand, latched onto Cliff's throat.

The viselike grip squeezed. Cliff's pulse quickened. As his right hand fought to peel off the man's fingers, his reserve air drained away. A strange, chopping sound filled the air.

Tables blew over. Benches lifted up. The pool water pressed down until the waves crashed over the sides. Gran's scattered papers flew and plummeted off the building.

Fushimi shoved Cliff as the water sprayed; he released his grip on Cliff's throat and broke Cliff's hold on the gun. While

Cliff gulped for air, Fushimi grabbed the amber and metal cases. The red carnation tumbled of his jacket as his foot stepped forward. The wind whipped it under his sole, and he crushed it.

The workers dashed for the sliding door. Fushimi raised his gun and fired a circular pattern. A glass panel shattered; the man bolted through.

One of his daughters broke free of the chaos and raced after him. The second chased them both. Ropes fell down around the pool. Black ops dropped toward the patio. Richard pulled Cliff's family into a contained area. Cliff started toward Penny.

"I'm fine," she shouted above the helicopter blades. Her voice became hard. "Go after him."

Cliff turned, passed through the shattered glass panel, and raced into the penthouse. His eyes swept the room and saw a shadow reflected in a full-length mirror with a golden frame. It rushed down the hall to his right. He bolted after it.

At the end of the hall, he came to a T-section. Though the sound of running could be heard, its direction was not clear. His eyes dropped to the floor and saw wet footprints to the left. His feet raced down the hall.

A wide area appeared with three elevators; each elevator had a single button that pointed up. The first and second elevator had ascended. The third began to close its doors. "Wait!" The face of one of Fushimi's daughters appeared; no gun sat in her hand. "Chiyo, wait!"

"Get in." Her hand grabbed his wrist and pulled. When he passed the doorway, she hit the button to ascend. The elevator climbed past two floors. When it opened, they stood at the entrance to a huge botanical garden.

A shot rang out; a glass wall plate shattered. Chiyo pointed to a bridge above their heads. "Up there. We must stop them before they reach the helicopter pad!"

His eyes traced the bridge; Fushimi raced toward its end. "Show me."

They weaved down a trail designed with small bridges, fish, and trees. Fragrance wafted toward them as they hurried past the plant life. A rock face loomed with stairs at its base.

The handrails helped as they raced skyward. Observation points were bypassed as they worked their way to the top.

Fushimi's footsteps became louder with Chrys on his heels. She raised her gun and fired. Another plate shattered; pieces of glass sprinkled down. Fushimi vanished up a staircase, and Chrys disappeared after him.

When Chiyo and Cliff knocked open the outside pad doors, a helicopter's blades screamed. Fushimi raced toward it. Chrys took aim and fired.

Fushimi jerked as the bullet pierced his left arm. The amber and metal cases flew from his hand to skate across the landing. His body spun to face Chrys as he fired. It ricocheted off the entrance to the botanical gardens.

The man backed up until he bumped the helicopter. Toward the front of the craft, a door popped open. The pain in his shoulder contorted his face. He threw down the gun and shouted over the sound of the engine. "Emiko, come with me! You are my daughter! Come with me, and all will be forgiven!"

Chrys' eyes went soulless. "Emiko is dead!" Her finger tightened on the trigger.

Chiyo raced forward and stepped in front. "No, Emiko, please!"

Cliff went to Chrys' right side. "This is not the way. He is still your father."

Fushimi leaned toward the cases, but a spud from Chrys' gun made him jerk back; the wind pushed the amber case further out of reach. He spun toward the helicopter's door.

Chrys fired. The gun spudded three times into the helicopter's body right behind her father. He scrambled inside. Another spud slammed through the door's window. The helicopter lifted.

Cliff had never seen her miss before; maybe they were getting through. He grabbed her. "Chrys, I want him to pay for his crimes, but killing him won't bring her back!'"

Her eyes focused on him as she held perfectly still. The gun dropped from her hand and clattered to the pad.

A scraping sound caught their attention; the wind from the helicopter blew the cases toward edge of the pad. Her eyes darted to the tie downs which had been used to secure the craft. "Thank you for believing in me." She leaned forward and kissed him. As his grip relaxed, her body broke free. "But I cannot let him go." With the grace of her sister, she spun and rolled, snatched up a tie down, and swung it toward the back of the helicopter.

A terrible screech met their ears as the blade attempted to slice through the cable. The back blades jammed. The helicopter spun toward the side of the pad as the cable whipped past.

She dove again, rolled, and snatched up a second tie down. As the helicopter neared the edge of the pad, the second tie down swung into the primary blades.

The lifters sliced the cable. The cable damaged the blades protective coating. A loud hum grew as the operator struggled to balance the craft.

A third tie down reached her hand, but as she threw it, the tail end of the helicopter swung her way. The first cable tagged the third in the air, tangled around it, and jerked.

Chrys flew forward as the helicopter moved off the top of the building. The hum grew worse as the blades vibrated out of sync. Chiyo and Cliff raced to grab her but caught only empty air; she swung off in a wide arc. The helicopter headed out over the lake.

A black ops helicopter spotted the fleeing craft. In slow motion, it turned. With a burst of fire, two rockets ignited, but before the rockets touched, Fushimi's helicopter ripped itself apart.

The pieces exploded in a ball of fire. Smoke billowed as fragments plummeted into the lake.

Chiyo's mask broke; tears poured down her face. Cliff put his arm around her as she buried her head in his shoulder. She finally backed away. "Thank you. I am in your debt."

He turned back to face the doors and spotted the metal and amber cases on the landing. The function of the amber case he knew, but what was the metal one? "What is it?"

Her eyes traced his and stopped. "It is a curse, but it is yours if you wish."

His grandmother's words came back to him, "Learn all you can." He walked over and picked up both cases. The metal one wasn't large; it could fit in his back pocket. However, the amber one at seven inches could not be hidden.

He tucked away the metal one and held the amber as he turned toward Chiyo. "Thank you."

Doors pushed open to their right. Three black ops approached with weapons. The man in charge asked, "Cliff Fulton?"

"Yes."

Though the words were spoken amiably, the command held warning. "Come with us."

Two of the black ops stayed on the pad. The third led them through the botanical gardens, down the elevators, and to Fushimi's penthouse living room.

Broken panels littered the floor. The bodies of the dead lay beside the pool. A group of workers were herded inside the penthouse. The man they followed waved over two personnel and had them follow. Chiyo and Cliff came to the same room he and Penny had used.

"Our commander will speak with you in a moment." As the man turned to leave, he posted guards outside the door. The door slid shut.

Cliff turned and looked into Chiyo's eyes. "If you have any way out of here, you should go now." He handed the amber case to her. "I cannot hide this from them."

Without hesitation, she nodded. That same sparkle he had seen in Chrys appeared in Chiyo's eyes. Her lips reached up to his in an affectionate kiss. "Thank you."

The familiarity was uncanny.

A knock rapped the door. As Cliff turned toward it, the door slid back, and his mouth fell open. Karl Duncan stepped in.

The man walked slowly. One arm lay in a sling, but the Division A leader paid it no mind. "It seems we've both survived, Mr. Fulton. It is good to see you again."

Cliff's mouth closed, but his eyes remained open wide. "I thought you died."

Karl looked around the room and spotted the bench beside the shoji. "May I?" As Cliff followed him with his eyes, he noticed that Chiyo had vanished.

Karl dragged him back from his thoughts. "Richard informed us that the codicil was lost." The man frowned. "I am sorry that happened. From experience, I am familiar with losing loved ones and the things that they owned."

Cliff didn't blink. "Thank you. I wish there could have been another way."

Karl nodded. "My men informed me that they shot down a helicopter while it attempted to escape. You wouldn't happen to know who it carried?"

"Fushimi Taruhito. I followed him up to the pad." His thoughts went to Chrys. "Apparently—" The explosion still burned in his memory. "—he had planned his escape."

"Not well enough. My men will be going through the wreckage. If we find anything in one piece—" He frowned. "—I may ask your help to identify it. The workers appear to know nothing, the other family members have vanished, and every computer has been wiped clean."

Cliff put his thoughts in order. "What of the rogue Division A?"

"They are gone." Karl assured. "Those captured are under interrogation."

"But some are still out there?"

Karl nodded. "Their threat has been minimized."

The word *minimized* held Cliff's attention. "Did you find George and Albert?"

"George Sealman is in a hospital recovering quite nicely. Albert has not been located, nor has the car he drove been found. Any information you have would be of great help."

"So you don't know?"

"Know what, Mr. Fulton?"

Cliff looked into the man's eyes. Was this man telling the truth? "About the assassins? About the group that attempted to kill us?"

The door slid back and in walked Richard with the rest of Cliff's family. As if he had listened to the whole conversation, Richard responded. "I've reported everything to him. Do you have anything to add?" His eyes matched Cliff's, and Cliff took the hint.

"No."

"Don't worry, we will find Albert."

The implants came to mind as his mother and father hurried toward him. They had to be checked, or the cabal would know everything.

Penny came in behind them but did not approach; the hurt still showed in her eyes.

"Cliff!" Jessie threw her arms around him. "No more, do you hear me? Next time someone else can do it!"

"I agree with your mom." Joseph hugged them both. "No more taking risks."

His uncle stepped up beside them; his voice remained sober. "That may be out of our control. Until Fushimi is gone—"

"Fushimi is gone." Cliff refused to believe anything else. "We saw his helicopter explode."

A frown crossed his uncle's face. "We?"

"Chiyo and I."

Cliff's black ops guide stepped into the room. "I'm looking for a girl named Chiyo." His eyes stopped on Cliff. "She came in with you."

Cliff shrugged. As the black ops man left, Cliff motioned toward Richard. The man stepped closer to the family with a smile on his face. "It's good to see you too, Cliff. For a moment, I thought this would come out badly."

Confusion filled Cliff's face. He stared at Richard and tried to keep his question vague while lowering his voice. "Implants?"

Richard pulled a small device from his pocket and handed it to Cliff. "This is a miniature version of what the car can do to remove them. You have to know where it is, but once you locate it, it will zap the bug."

The balding man's reaction in the back of Richard's car hit his thoughts. Cliff cringed.

"I know. It can be unpleasant, but it is fast. I've taken care of your parents and uncle."

"And Penny?"

"She came to us while you were gone."

A frown took his mother's face. "Cliff, I don't understand. Why is Penny so standoffish?"

The faces of those around him waited. "Mom—" He swallowed. "—I told her a lie to keep her safe. The people who know the truth are dead."

Jessie glanced at Penny. Penny's eyes had never left the group. "What lie?"

"I told her I slept with Chrys."

Shock spread across Jessie's face. "Did you?"

His eyebrows rose. "Of course not! But at the time, Fushimi had demonstrated false proof." The rest of the details came quickly.

Joseph whistled. "You've got to come clean."

"She'll never believe me."

"You've still got to try."

Chapter 34

With rampant emotions, Cliff nodded. "I will try." He squared his shoulders, moved toward Penny, and prepared for battle. She saw him approach and stepped back, but her retreat came slower than his advance.

A member of the black ops opened the door and headed straight for Karl. As they talked, they walked toward Cliff. Karl put a hand on Cliff's shoulder. "I need you to come with me."

The look on the faces of Cliff's family said otherwise, but Karl remained firm. As he led Cliff from the room, he gave a single nod to the guards. "Nobody leaves this room without further orders." Richard turned to follow, but Karl shook his head. "Nobody." The door closed behind them, and Karl turned toward Cliff. "Someone wants to speak with you."

"Who?"

They reached a room set up as a command post. A black shelter had been constructed with a zippered access guarded by two personnel.

As they approached, one of the guards unzipped and tossed back the flap. Cliff ducked in with Karl. Darkness met them as the guards secured the outside until Karl reached over and opened a second inside flap. Dull lights glowed to life.

"This is a blackout tent. It is designed to stop known frequencies from penetrating its outer skin. A hardline leaves through a special scrambler so that no communication can be intercepted between here and the transceiver. At the same time we communicate, we have multiple dummy sites doing the same thing to keep our location obscured."

The man's hand waved toward a seat; Cliff took it. Something appeared on the display.

"The message received was simply this: Cliff Fulton—alone—twenty minutes. All our monitoring stations recorded it at the same time. It took five minutes for it to be relayed to my headquarters, five minutes for them to find me, and five minutes for us to get here. As I finish this explanation, the time is almost up. Whoever they are, they know all about us and our procedures. I hope I don't have to remind you how important it is to discover who these people are." He raised a hand up and counted off. "Five, four, three, two, one."

The display flashed, and a man in his late fifties appeared on the screen. Graying hair with a beard neatly trimmed adorned a face with no mustache. The deep black eyes focused on Cliff.

A garbled voice demanded, "Tell the man with you to leave."

Cliff looked toward Karl and shrugged. "It's up to you."

"No, Mr. Fulton. If he doesn't do what we say before one minute, we will destroy the penthouse." A timer appeared on the screen. "Don't make me say I told you."

Karl headed toward the flap. The light dimmed as he passed through.

"Now we can talk."

Pixels flashed on the screen; the computer generated image altered and jumped.

The person paused as he focused on Cliff. "It seems you have created a conundrum for us, Mr. Fulton. You have succeeded in killing the head of one our families. That in itself is not a crime; it is a matter of succession. As a member of our cabal, it would be your right to take on that family's assets and responsibilities. This is provisional, of course, based upon the fact that no legitimate heir chooses to oppose you."

"Then what's the problem?"

"Fushimi knew of his coming death. He knew his daughter would not stop, and none of his heirs could take his place. You are from an old house, and though they are not active, no one ever leaves. When you refused to join, you refused to be adopted."

Cliff blinked. He remembered his studies in Japanese history. Males between the ages of twenty to thirty were routinely adopted so that the family name would not be lost. He stared at the screen. "Fushimi picked me to be his heir?"

"Like it or not, you are qualified. You have shown spirit and determination. You have shown resilience under pressure. You learned that nothing is black and white. You followed every hint we gave to the point of alienating your girlfriend, Penny 'Mayeth' von Richter. You were Fushimi's ideal replacement."

Cliff's jaw tightened. "You doctored the recording."

The eyes of the image bore into his. "Nobody refuses the cabal, Mr. Fulton. It is a privilege not to be taken lightly."

He watched the avatar's face but could not read it. "What do you want from me?"

"You have two choices: you will join the cabal and assume your place in the organization, or you will be terminated along with your family. To prove our good intentions, I offer two gifts. One, proof will be provided that you have not been unfaithful to Penny. Two, we will give you a chance to save your friend Albert."

His relationship with Penny laid rocky at best; even proof might not save it. On top of that, a chance to save Albert meant his friend could still die. "There's no guarantee that either will work."

"We do not control the heart or will, Mr. Fulton. We only offer information."

"You set me up."

"Agreed."

"You burned down the church."

"We did."

"You arranged the ruse about my grandmother's codicil."

"Of course, Mr. Fulton."

"All this—" As the words sank in, his face flushed. "—just to get me to join the cabal?"

The face stared.

"Why me?"

"We sit on thrones, not pedestals. We are kings, not heroes." The connection jumped and the garbled voice faltered to sound almost real. "Our time is up. Tell Division A that their trace will be ineffective. Tell them we are watching. Tell them—" The avatar smiled. "—the countdown has begun." The connection dropped.

Karl reentered. "What was that about?"

Cliff's eyes narrowed. "You mean you weren't listening?"

The man cleared his throat. "An attached carrier wave fried the circuits of every listening module we had."

The last four words came back to Cliff's mind, *The countdown has begun.* His eyes opened wide. "We have to get everyone out; they are going to blow up the building."

Karl turned, pushed through the last flap, and stared at the commotion. A black ops member came to attention. "Report."

"A secret door opened in the hallway. We are uploading to the satellite now."

"Show me."

They hurried back to the penthouse living room. Around the corner, where the hall began, the large, full-length mirror with the golden frame hinged outward from the wall. Within lay a passageway, and inside the passageway lay a large media storage device with a single interface. Division A had attached a hardline to download the information.

The terminal's screen showed a data bar. It filled with color as the upload continued. In the upper right corner sat a three-digit number. It counted down.

Cliff didn't blink. "We have until the counter reaches zero."

Karl nodded. "And it will reach zero when the data is complete."

"They are giving you data." Absolute certainty entered Cliff's voice. "I would ask why."

Karl's eyes opened wide. "Another carrier wave." He tapped something in his ear. "Everyone clear out of the building, and stop that download. Code nine-one-three." He addressed the man with him. "Take the civilians to the helicopters. Get them to the far shore. You have ten minutes." Karl pushed Cliff after the man. "Go!"

His family stood outside. With no room for landing, helicopters took turns hovering a few feet over the patio as guards helped people in.

Cliff's father turned to him as they waited in line. His voice rose to a yell as he tried to be heard over the sound of the twirling blades. "What's going on?"

"The building is going to blow."

The helicopter in front lifted toward the lake. A second came down to take its place. The front of the line came closer.

Narrowed eyes and stern glances filled the view. Richard tapped his earpiece and gave a nod. "The data upload to Division A's system has been stopped, but the countdown is ongoing. Karl wants everyone out of here in five minutes. He doesn't trust the countdown." The personnel began to help his family onboard.

A flicker caught Cliff's eye; it came from the living room. Its occupants had been reduced, and all the workers were gone. What had caught his attention? In the angle of the full-length mirror, waist-long, black hair could be seen. "I'll be back!" He slipped through the crowd.

Richard's voice rose. "Cliff!"

The noise of the helicopters muffled as he raced into the building. He turned down the hall only to find the image had vanished.

At the first T, the flicker of Chiyo's dress caught his eye, and he sped up. As the elevators came into view, one headed toward the botanical gardens. The countdown hit his mind, but he could not halt now. He took the first available elevator and headed toward the top.

The doors slid back to greenery. To his right, the other elevator sat open and empty.

"Chiyo!" Surely she knew the building would be destroyed? "Chiyo, the building is about to be blown up!"

Nothing answered. Was he hallucinating? He didn't know how many helicopters were left and knew his family would be frantic. As he turned back toward the elevator, a hand touched his shoulder. He almost jumped out of his skin.

Chiyo put a finger to her lips and motioned for him to follow. She stopped at a narrow entrance to a small artificial cave. A large rock sat in the center of the alcove.

When one of the stones on top reversed, a piece of the rock hinged backwards to expose a small glass panel. She touched the panel. With a slight click, the large rock slid back. It revealed a ladder that went down into the heart of the building.

Voices sounded outside the small alcove; orders were issued to stop the search. Chiyo pointed for Cliff to climb down the ladder. When he had descended to the first platform, she dropped in beside him, touched a second panel, and the large rock slid closed.

Her eyes filled with fear. "Choose wisely."

The words she spoke were all about the implants; the tea they had taken must have worn off. He removed Richard's device from his pocket, turned it on, and scanned her body. A curious look crossed her face as she watched him move the device down to her feet.

With nothing on the front, he walked around behind. As he worked his way down, a point of light appeared on its display. The closer he came, the brighter it grew.

Past the small of her back, its brightness dimmed; he verified it twice. Of course it would there. Low-key, difficult to remove, and directly over the vertebrae matched her sister's. The word *terminate* appeared on the screen. He tapped it.

Chiyo's knees buckled, and he caught her. As her eyelids fluttered open again, she gazed up at him with large round eyes. "Is it gone?"

"That's what Richard said. Something in the device gets shorted out."

Her strength came slowly. She stood though her gaze turned toward the wall. "I am grateful, Cliff, but I must know, why did you follow me?"

"I thought you had gone, but when I saw you watching, I could not leave you to die."

Her head dropped. "The Taruhito family is over. The cabal has chosen our fate. We are not to leave the building."

Part of him said he could have prevented this by joining the cabal. The other said that was insane. Fushimi had helped to kill his grandmother. Why should he care if these others died?

In his mind, Chrys' actions were burned. As an assassin, she had killed her father. How many more had she killed as well? His eyes went to Chiyo. "They want you to die?"

She gave a slight nod.

"Why? There is no reason. Just leave. They do not own you anymore."

Her voice stayed patient. "And where would we go? We are wanted by your Division A, and we would be hunted by the cabal. The world you ask me to flee to does not exist." Her eyes focused on him as if she looked for something within his eyes. "Does it?"

Cliff took a deep breath. The meaning was clear, but he had no time to deal with it. The words of his grandmother came back. The choice he had been given did also. "Your family must not die. I can't guarantee anything beyond the now. Do you understand?"

Though hesitant, she gave a slight nod.

"Please, take me to see your family."

"They will never trust you with this device. I must do it myself."

He handed the device to her.

She led him down a small maintenance tunnel to a second hatch. Again, a tiny panel gave access. They descend past wires into another room that branched out in other directions.

"Wait here."

She passed through a door; it slid shut behind her. The equipment around him hummed. Displays attached to selected walls showed real-time status. A utility panel lay on one wall. The word 'tube' labeled another. He moved to the panel labeled 'tube' and studied its configuration.

Time ticked away. He glanced at his watch, but it meant nothing; the countdown could end at any moment.

The door Chiyo had walked through opened; no else came with her. Had they even listened?

"It is done." She nodded. "The implants have been neutralized. My brothers have voted to defy the cabal. It is time for you to go." She pressed her index finger against the panel labeled 'tube'. The panel slid back to reveal a series of flashing lights. As she touched them in sequence, a door to their right opened. Inside sat a small, oval vehicle with a single seat.

His eyebrows narrowed. "You are leaving?"

As she nodded, a slight smile crossed her lips. She placed a knapsack strap over one of his arms. "Take this; it will help you find your friend."

He hurried past the hatch and dropped into the seat. A glass window descended.

"Thank you," she called behind him. He could see her reflection in the window as it locked in place. "May your journey be swift, your feet sure, and your house blessed."

She touched a light on the panel; the hatch sealed. The moment it locked, a countdown started on the screen. He grabbed hold of a safety belt, stretched it across, and heard the click.

The vehicle launched. It slammed him back as he struggled to breathe. A roar built up behind him as flames licked at the sides. A glass panel at the end of his launch tube melted as super-heated air struck. The craft passed through the hole and soared away from the building.

The trajectory swooped toward the lake, curved slightly, and approached the far side. The power cut over the water, and the craft dropped. Huge waves shot up. The water boiled as the heated craft bobbed back to the surface.

As it settled, the water lapped at the sides just beneath the window. He gazed down at the controls and touched the word *exit*. The window shot off. The motion caused the craft to turn toward the condominium. The building blew up.

Chapter 35

The explosion started at top and ripped down through the levels. Orange bursts shot out on all sides, glass shattered, and floors collapsed. In one smooth motion, the top part of the building built up speed and fell in a shower of debris and violence. Waves of black dust billowed away from the scene. It struck the nearby buildings and shot out over the lake. As the black dust curled toward him, he undid his safety belt, balanced in the center of the craft, and jumped.

The cold of the lake slapped him as he dropped beneath its surface. The light dimmed; he could not tell the way up. His head struck something hard. Water absorbed into his clothes and dragged him toward the bottom. The distorted water lost its glow, and everything went black.

Undecipherable sounds met his ears along with oars in the water. Water lapped metal. A muffled splash called. The pressure of an arm wrapped around his chest. The sound of breathing caught his ears. Small fingers pulled him to the surface.

His eyelids blinked; they burned so he closed them tightly. The crackle of a fire caught his ears as the smoke reached his nose. Someone lay beside him; he could feel their warmth against his body. When he woke again, the person had disappeared. He lay on something solid.

His fingers felt muck. The debris coated everything in a wet, dirty, filthy sludge caused by the building's destruction. Whoever had helped him had cleaned his face; when he looked at the gray sky, his eyes no longer burned.

"Son!" His father came through the foliage. Other voices called out: his mother, his uncle, Penny, and Albert. No, not Albert. The voice belonged to someone else.

Richard's voice appeared near him, and Cliff jumped. "He's fine. He hit his head. Someone must have brought him ashore and hurried off to help others."

They carried him but distance had no meaning. Flaps brushed his arm on a tent door. The cot they placed him on felt soft. "Get him undressed. His body is cooling."

Covers were thrown over him, and for the second time, he could feel warmth. When he opened his eyes, Penny sat on a cot next to his and stared.

"Do I look that bad?" He felt much warmer and tried to sit up. The base of his skull pounded. With one eye squinted shut, he turned toward her. "Hey, cheer up." A smile half-formed on his face though it looked more like a cringe.

She pursed her lips. "You're a liar, Cliff Fulton—" A tear dropped from one eye. "—and I love you more for it."

Both his eyes shot open despite the pain. "I am? I mean, you do?"

Through sobs, she nodded without words and put her arms around him. The pain decreased.

"So—why am I a liar?"

"Because you told me you had slept with Chrys."

"And—why am I loved?"

"Because you did it to protect me."

The proof the cabal had promised had arrived, but how had they done it?

The tent flaps opened, and Richard entered. "So that's your secret: get shot out of a building that blows up and anyone can get the girl." He clapped him on the leg. "Feeling better?"

Cliff's voice was muffled; Penny had tightened her grip.

"Penny—" Richard laughed. "—let the boy breathe."

The grip loosened, and she sat back wiping the tears from her cheeks. "I'm sorry."

Cliff's eyebrows furrowed. "What happened?"

Richard chuckled. "The information we uploaded. The carrier wave it brought installed a virus and wiped out every piece of data in our computers."

"That doesn't explain—"

Richard held up his hand. "It seems our benefactors only left two pieces of information after the transaction. One detailed how a certain recording had been made—" He threw a glance at Penny. "—which might explain why a certain girl has changed her opinion of you. The other stated Albert is alive, and that the coordinates would be relayed." His eyes watched Cliff.

Cliff rose despite the headache. His voice strained, "We've got to go find him."

Richard forced him back. "You're not going anywhere. Until the doctor clears you, you're staying right here."

Cliff stared at him. "But—"

"Here." Richard pointed to the cot. "You're in no condition to go running anywhere."

"Can I at least have some clothes?" He looked down at his covers. "I don't mind the blankets, but I'm really not ready for a toga party."

A grin crossed Richard's face. "I'll see what I can do. In the meantime—" He got up and strolled out the door. "—enjoy the privacy." The tent flaps closed.

"I've got to get out here." He pushed the headache to the back of his mind. "They don't understand who they're dealing with."

Penny bit her lip. "I thought you might say that." From under his cot, she slid out a small bag. "Think of it as a peace offering."

A smile broke out on Cliff's face; he reached over and kissed her. "That will come later—" He winked. "—for both of us. Where did you get the clothes?" He started to dress.

"From your house, of course. I have a key." Her frown returned. "Cliff, we found a woman tied up there. She babbled about an assassin—"

"Chrys." He continued to dress. "Meredith is okay?"

"She was scared out of her wits. She claimed to be a teacher at the university."

As he tied his shoes, he nodded though his head throbbed. "Do you know Albert's location?"

Penny shook her head. "I only know what Richard said."

One by one, he transferred items from his soaked clothes. Until now, he never realized how full his pockets had become. He counted out the items when his eyes spotted the knapsack on the floor; Chiyo's words came back. Did Chiyo and her brothers get out before the blast?

Penny caught him staring. "Cliff?"

His fingers snagged the knapsack's strap and hauled it to the cot. As he unzipped the opening, the bag revealed a waterproof interior. Within the pouch, he spotted the amber case and the implant detector. Which one had Chiyo meant?

Penny's eyes opened wide as she spotted the amber case. "Can we use that to find Albert?"

Cliff tried his thumb to open it, but the device remained locked. Penny reached over and tried as well, but it did not respond. His hand placed it back into the knapsack, and he removed the implant detector. It didn't make sense. If the amber case couldn't help him, how could the detector be any better?

He pressed the *on* button; the unit hummed to life. Instead of a blank screen, a set of coordinates in longitude and latitude glowed up at him. A few seconds later, they vanished. He turned to look at Penny. "I know where Albert is."

A frown crossed her face. "Cliff, you know you can't trust them—any of them. If they have an agenda, it will be for their own gain."

"If the agenda saves Albert—" His eyes became distant.

"—it's a chance I'm willing to take."

Richard's phone had been soaked. "Penny, where's your phone?"

The frown deepened as she held it up.

"Find an app that will guide us with GPS coordinates."

Her finger flicked over the screen. "Now what?"

He recited the coordinates. As Penny finished entering the information, the app showed a map. "We're fifteen minutes away by car. To walk will take more time."

"Then we'll have to find a car. Give me a moment to finish." His fingers dug into his wet pants pockets and transferred items to his dry clothes. Two items were missing: Gran's codicil note and the thumb drive. Either they had fallen out or someone had removed them.

A glimmer of memory hit him. He lay on the shore after being pulled from the water. A hand had reached into his pockets and looked at what he carried.

"Cliff?"

"Sorry, something is coming back to me."

"You hit your head pretty hard. Give it time."

As he forced a smile on his face, he put up the detector, closed the knapsack, and dropped it on his back. With a lean toward her, he gave her a kiss. "You're right. Let's go get Albert."

The grounds were nearly empty as twilight descended; lights danced across the shore next to the exploded building as people concentrated on the rubble.

"Penny, how did you get to my house?"

"Richard had someone pick me up and take me there. Why?"

"We need transportation."

"According to the map, we have to head away from the lake."

Cliff snapped his fingers. "That's it—the lake. Come on!"

Penny stayed beside him as Cliff sprinted. "But you're going the wrong way."

"To the lake." He nodded. "Someone pulled me from the

water. Do you remember where?"

"Sure."

They found the remains of the campfire. He remembered this; the idea of small hands played at the edges of his mind. The items taken would not be here, but something else would.

Penny could not help but notice. "You are looking for something."

"Yes."

Though difficult to locate, he found the markings of where he lay. The noise of lapping water as it struck metal hit his ears. He turned toward the lake. Two large trees sat near a small alcove. A rowboat floated in the water. The key to their transportation had been found.

A difficult journey lay before him. Adrenaline had pushed his headache away, but as he started to row, it all came back. The rhythm of the noise made it worse as it amplified the pain.

Warehouse restaurant lights danced across the water. The lights teased him like a mirage. His patience grew thin, and he felt tired, yet he had to find his friend.

He refused to believe Albert had betrayed him. If he had done such a thing, it could only be coerced. What if they had implanted him, too?

The stroke of the paddles became stronger. A fish jumped to his right. The lights grew larger, and the boardwalk could be seen. The boat adjusted direction as he picked up speed.

Penny's voice broke his thoughts. "Cliff, why do you love me?"

His brow wrinkled. Between strokes, he spoke, "Do I have to have a reason?"

"No, but—" A sigh escaped her lips. "What if it's the wrong reason? What if it's a perception that is not true, and one day you find out it is not real?" She shivered. "After all, our whole relationship started on a lie."

"No, the lie brought us together, but it was not the reason we stayed. We saw something in each other, something that went beyond words." He raised the oars and let the boat coast toward a dock. On it, a single light glowed in the darkness.

"If I say I love you because you are thin, and you gain weight, all would be lost. If you say you love me because I tell the truth, and I am forced to lie, then all would be lost, too. That almost happened today." The row boat bumped the dock. "Careful." He stepped off the boat, tied it to a pole, and extended his hand to help her out. "The car should be this way."

She caught her balance and walked beside him. Ropes and small fishing articles lay upon the path. "It did happen today, and that's part of the problem."

Despite the low light, Cliff could not miss the frown on her face. "You doubt our relationship?" A sinking feeling hit his stomach.

"Yes. No. I don't know."

The parking lot came into view. Richard's car sat parked and unchanged. Was the key fob watertight? He tapped the unlock button and pulled the door handle on the passenger side. Relief washed through him as it opened.

Penny stepped in, and he closed the door. The last two days had been merciless on his psyche. Could he handle dealing with this conversation now? As he slipped into the driver's seat and closed the door, she continued.

"You've changed in only two days. One moment you are hard and aloof; the next you are soft and open. I don't know what to expect from one moment to the next."

The key slid into the ignition, and the car started. "How about the previous month?" The car made a U-turn and headed toward the road. "Let me know what the next turn is."

She nodded. "Left at the exit. We'll follow it for about five miles, and then make a right."

They headed into thicker woods. Homesteaders owned large plots here.

"The previous month was fantastic despite the brief times you closed off. Don't you see? The detachment is within you; it's a shield you raise in defense."

He followed the curve. His voice became firm. "I can't survive without it."

Her voice faltered for a moment. "Th—That doesn't bother me. What bothers me is when you direct it toward me." She stared at him while he drove. "I am not your enemy."

The word made him think of the cabal, and the embers in his heart yearned to burst into flame. In a distant voice, he spoke, "I know you're not."

She shivered; her attention went to the phone. "Go right." Her finger pointed. "We're looking for the next farm-to-market road." She looked down at the phone again. "At FM two-twelve, we'll turn to the left."

Their headlights stabbed the darkness as the road curved. Out here, streetlights had not been installed. They reached a gap in the trees, and Cliff hit the brakes.

A construction sign stood in the middle of the road. Penny moved the map around and studied their projected course. "There's no other way."

He threw her a glance. "Then there's no other choice."

The car drove past the barricade. The road ahead changed from blacktop to gravel. He remembered the gravel road up to Division A's safe house and wondered if these people were doing the same type of monitoring. A sigh escaped his lips. "I— I can't be open and closed at the same time. I can't let them know you are my weakness."

Her eyes narrowed. "How am I weak?"

A dim light bounced through the trees. A metal, two-story barn nestled in the foliage.

"You are not weak, but you are my weakness. Don't you realize that after the implants had been placed in everyone, they knew exactly what we talked about and how to use it against us?"

Anger came into her voice. "You didn't know that at the time; you didn't find out until later. Yet, you cut me off."

As the car continued straight, a small side road appeared that led to the lighted barn. The emotions of their past debate surged back, and his voice rose. "I explained that. For your own protection, it had to be done." No, his mind told him, it was for mine; I can't let her distract me and do what I must do. As they pulled up to the barn, no other vehicles were about.

"Maybe I don't want to be protected." Her voice shook. "Maybe I just want to be with you."

Silence dropped as Cliff's stomach knotted; his jaw clenched. In a low voice he answered, "You're here now."

"Am I? Am I really? Or did you bring me along just to humor the girlfriend?" With a glance away, she stopped a tear from falling, looked at the GPS on the phone, and turned it off. "We're here. We need to find Albert."

Chapter 36

His fist tightened on the steering wheel. "Penny—" A flicker caught his eye from the trees around the barn. All his senses went on alert. "—we're being watched."

The faint image of a human being stood out to his left; the person stood between two trees. In the rearview mirror of the car appeared a second. A third lay to Penny's right. In front of them, a small, tin door stood in the side of the barn about three feet from the car's passenger's side.

Her voice went low. "What do they want?"

"What do you think?"

"This is a trap."

He nodded while debating what to do next. A warning window bounced on the windshield.

"We could pull out and leave. We could bring back reinforcements."

"I can't leave. If Albert is here, they might move him. No—" He shook his head. "—I need you to drive away and find reinforcements. I'll go into the barn."

Her face narrowed. "We just talked about that. Why don't we try the phone?"

"Try it."

She stared. "No signal."

His head nodded. "I bet the GPS doesn't work either."

Her finger tapped several places on the screen. "How did you know?"

He pointed at the windshield. "The car told me. Penny, this is real, not some made up adventure story. If you don't leave, you could get hurt."

"I'm not going anywhere."

His voice tried to rise, but he stopped it. "You don't have to be by my side to help me. We all have a role to play." From the corner of his eye, Cliff caught the image to his left move closer. "And just to let you know, I'm about to play one now." He looked her in the eye. "Don't take this personally."

As he threw the door open, he turned toward the car and yelled, "Leave! Just leave me alone! I can't handle it anymore!" The motion to his left stopped. Tears started down Penny's face. He hoped to God she understood what he did. With one smooth shift, he slammed the car door and moved toward the barn.

The barn door lay unlocked. Through the cracks, dim lights glowed inside. As he opened it, the angle gave him an excuse to watch the car.

Penny shifted to the driver's side and put it in gear. The light reflected from the tears on her cheeks as the car pulled back. His foot stepped into the barn, and he closed the door behind him.

His eyes adjusted to the gloom. Stalls for horses and hay bales divided the interior. To his right, a tractor stood parked. A hook and chain hung from the rafters, and a ladder went up to a loft. Where was Albert?

The hay on the floor muffled his footsteps as he stepped lightly into the interior. Both ends of the building had two large closed sliding doors. As he rounded the shoulder high fence which guided him in, he noticed a low table with two pillows sitting on the barn floor. On the table were five pieces of fish; each had been carved in the shape of a chrysanthemum. Chrys' had taken her name from that flower. She was an assassin; the flower represented death.

"Have you ever tried fugu, Mr. Fulton?" The distinct male voice came from everywhere at once. One by one, he found the speakers along with the cameras.

Cliff shook his head. "I don't believe I have."

"Of course you have. You just didn't know it. She was the flower of our collection."

Cliff's head jerked as the words hit home. "Chrys was your agent?"

"We trained her to be the woman she was. Like the fish you see upon the plate, death lay within her. We brought it out by shaping her into a chrysanthemum. Was she not delicious?"

Cliff shook his head. "I wouldn't know."

The voice held laughter. "You were drawn in by what gives us our strength. You touched the dark and found it powerful. You were tempted to make her your own. You were desirous because of a family trait."

Cliff remained firm. "No."

"What if four of the five pieces on that tray contained deadly poison? Would you try it?"

The meaning rang clear. Chrys did have a side not dark, but how much would remain a guess forever. As he walked closer to the plate, his thoughts shifted to an unusual apparatus. "No."

"And I would say good choice—if you meant it. What if it were three or two or one? Would your answer be any different? You sought the good in Chrys. Why not take the chance now?"

"No."

A hologram flashed into existence. It stood about five foot nine and wore a dark suit with gray pinstripes. Dark glasses covered its eyes, and the skin tone matched Albert's. Even the bone structure had a startling resemblance. "As I would expect from any who had never experienced the delicacy." The image looked down at fugu.

"You see, Mr. Fulton, you have no clue whether the meal is deadly or safe, but I do. I understand the game, and I know what risks are worth the effort. At one time, you felt they were acceptable when your family lay on the line."

The man pursed his lips. "You beat my assassins at the café

and catwalk. You took one of their cars. You didn't know how this might connect you to the murdered man in the trunk or how this might make you a fugitive from justice. You believe in justice, don't you, Mr. Fulton?"

Cliff kept his eyes on the hologram as he walked about. He took everything in. "Of course."

The image grinned. "Yes, I can see you do, but it conflicts with your basic choice for mercy. That makes you weak. Shall we see if you are weak, Mr. Fulton?" The man waved at the table.

"It has been reported to me that the codicil stood as a ruse to bring my people out of hiding. I don't like being played; I like to manipulate. However, with the codicil destroyed, I no longer have a reason to kill you—" The image inhaled. "—and no money to collect if I do."

Cliff stopped. "Then let Albert go." He studied the projectors.

"That is mercy, Mr. Fulton, and I believe in trade. I need something out of my investment, if only to have some sport. So here's the deal: you can walk out and leave your friends, or you can choose to eat one of the fugu pieces. The odds are good as only two of the five pieces are poisoned. Is that not better odds than your dealings with Chrys?"

Cliff frowned; the man had said friends. Who could he have other than Albert?

"Yes, there must always be an incentive to make one play with the dark, should there not?"

With a screech, the large barn door furthest from him slid open. Footsteps approached. As they moved toward the plate of fugu, two people were pushed in front. Albert's hands lay tied behind his back with a gag stuffed in his mouth; Penny stood bound in the same way.

Albert's round eyes studied the room. Penny looked down at the plate. As she met Cliff's eyes, she shook her head slowly.

"Well, Mr. Fulton, what is your decision?"

The embers ignited. Cliff compressed his anger into a cold

ball of flame. The man liked games; Cliff would see how much. "Wouldn't it be more sporting if you joined me?"

A strange smile crossed the hologram's lips. "Perhaps it would."

As the man's image vanished, a hydraulic pump began. In one of the horse stalls, a light turned on as a large box rose from the floor. The pump stopped, a door opened, and the man who had been a hologram walked out.

"Now then—" He grinned at Cliff. "—shall we begin?"

"The rules?"

"We each take one piece until someone is poisoned."

Cliff's jaw set as he nodded. "I have one condition."

"Which is?"

"Regardless of what happens, Penny and Albert go free."

Albert shook his head violently. Muffled words were heard, but nothing made sense. Penny stared at Cliff's face, but he did not meet her eyes.

"It seems your friend wishes to speak." The man waved to the guards. "Remove his gag."

Albert's words leaped out. "No, Cliff! No antidote exists for the poison!"

The man looked at Cliff. "He's right, but you already know that; you've experienced Chrys."

Penny's eyes narrowed.

"Unless you can get to a hospital, odds are you won't survive."

Cliff wrinkled his brow. "Then why are you willing to take the chance?"

"It is the thrill, but surely you knew that?" His grin grew in intensity. "Ah, now I understand more of the codicil ruse. They have chosen *you* to be a part of the game."

Penny struggled against the gag and bonds. One of the guards grabbed hold of her.

The man in charge studied Cliff with merriment in his eyes.

"Have you taken up their offer?"

Cliff said nothing, but he could see the questions in his friends' faces.

"You haven't?" The man laughed. "They will force you, you know. It is inevitable. Perhaps I am doing you a favor." With a grin at the fugu, he waved a hand. "By all means, Mr. Fulton, go first. The odds are better."

Cliff looked down at the fugu. The game was stupid, but how could he stop it? No guns could be seen, but he knew that meant nothing. In addition, seven guards existed if the three outside were included, and maybe more were strategically placed. With Penny here, no reinforcements would come. He reached down and picked up a piece.

Albert exhaled, "Cliff, no!"

In one deft move, he placed the white flesh in his mouth and started to chew. It had a very light taste—somewhere between yellowtail and salmon. His thoughts drifted back to the helicopter that had exploded. As he swallowed, he stared into the man's eyes. "Your turn."

Two pieces poisoned out of five gave a sixty percent chance of success. Two out of four moved it to fifty. The man smiled, raised a piece to his mouth, and did the same.

"Now what?"

"Patience, Mr. Fulton. It takes about five minutes for the poison to affect the system. Please—" He motioned to a pillow beside the table. "—sit. We should both be comfortable."

A teapot came. Steam rose from the cups as tea poured in. His conversation with Chiyo came back as she pleaded for him to help.

The man sipped his tea. "Here is what to expect from the poison. You may feel a trembling in the lips. A lightness may take you. Your extremities will go numb and in some cases, the arms and legs as well. If the poison is strong enough, your chest muscles with cease to move your lungs. You will be fully awake as you asphyxiate without the ability to breathe."

The minutes passed. A glance at Cliff's watch showed the time had arrived.

"Again." The man motioned to the plate in front.

Albert shifted forward but the guards pulled him back. "Stop!"

The odds hit Cliff's mind. Neither he nor the man had shown any ill effects. With three pieces left, a thirty percent chance existed; one of them would be poisoned.

His heart beat wildly as he selected another. The taste did not change. The man did the same. This was it; one of them would die.

The watch stared up at him. The last two days flashed into his mind. It all came down to—

His lips trembled, and his eyes darted to the man across from him. The face of the man brightened as if a cosmic joke had just been told. "It seems we have both played and lost. Is that not the way of the dark?" The man took a deep breath and closed his eyes. Two of his men reached down, lifted him to his feet, and took him back toward the horse stall. Slurred words called, "Till we meet again, Cliff Fulton."

One of the men cut the ropes off his friends. Albert and Penny rushed to him while Penny pulled the gag from her mouth. Cliff could feel the numbness. His legs did not want to work. From the corner of his eye, Cliff caught the back of a thin framed woman carrying a whip.

Albert swallowed. "We've got to get you to a hospital!"

Cliff stood up awkwardly while his friends grabbed both arms. He tried to swallow, but it wasn't working well. A strange lightness hit into his body; he thought it would float away.

The two slammed open the sheet metal door. They carried him from the building to the car fifty feet away. Penny had made it that far before they had stopped her.

The key fob fumbled in Penny's hand as she pressed the unlock button. The back door opened, and they laid down Cliff on the backseat. With a turn, she tossed the keys to Albert. "You drive. I'm riding with Cliff."

Cliff's lungs still moved, he could feel them, though his arms and legs were completely numb. The idea of being asphyxiated, while not comforting, did not feel unpleasant. He floated in clouds devoid of all feeling. His heart still beat, but it had begun to slow. He could hear the drop as the blood rushed through his veins.

Strange images swam before his eyes. Penny's face appeared, but it kept changing. It would have brown hair one time, dark hair the next, and then white. Was it really Penny or Tish staring down at him? Was it really Chrys or Chiyo?

He closed his eyes; it was easier not to watch. His body bumped. He could hear metal strike metal. Wind whipped by his ears. Voices. Many voices called all at once, but the words became garbled. The garbled voice of the avatar came back, and he felt his heart stop.

Chapter 37

His lungs didn't move of their own accord, yet somehow he could breathe. His eyes struggled to open and gradually did. He lay on a bed with a ventilator. It pushed the air into his lungs, stopped, and allowed the carbon dioxide to leave.

A nurse walked in, saw his eyes open, and smiled. "You're awake. Let me get the doctor." His eyes closed, and the dreams came. His grandmother called, "Learn all you can." The avatar floated, "You will join the cabal." His mind reacted in anger, "Leave my family alone!"

With a jump, he surged forward to sit up and opened his eyes. The ventilator had vanished. The hospital room held silence. How had he gotten here?

A nurse worked at the side of his bed with her back to him. The long black hair caught his attention, and he heard a familiar voice. "Welcome back from the dead, Cliff. Your journey has just begun."

Epilogue

The metal box stared up at him cold to the touch. Ever since he had come back from the hospital, he couldn't shake the feeling.

Fushimi had wanted him to open it; Chiyo had said no. The cabal had demanded he join them, or his family would die.

No one watched; he sat alone in his room at Gran's house. The downstairs clock disturbed the silence as it chimed the current hour. The time had come.

His fingers fell over the latch. How could it be so important that one look would commit him forever? As his thumb increased the pressure, a slight click sounded. The latch flipped up.

"Cliff?" Chrys walked into his room as her long black hair sparkled in the light. The smile that met him had soulless eyes. "You're dreaming, love. This is all a dream."

Penny's voice shook his thoughts, "Cliff?"

His hands were empty, and he sat on the sofa downstairs as he eyed the clock on the mantel.

"We're still going out, right?"

"Of course." He stepped into the dining room and passed the china cabinet where his grandmother's picture sat. Beside it lay the metal box though very few knew what it was. He took her hand and pulled her toward him.

"Not too frisky." She laughed. "You know you're still in recovery."

"I'll be fine," he whispered. "Let's head out to the car."

Outfitted in a beautiful dark dress, she moved toward the front. It accented her face and eyes.

He made it there before her and opened the door. "After you."

"Thank you."

A darkened sky stared down as evening dropped its veil. The touch of winter had begun, and a light frosting lay in the forecast.

The phone in Penny's purse rang. She stared at the number as she pulled out the cell. Leeriness filled her voice. "Hello?" The other side, though familiar, was not loud enough to catch. With rounded eyes, she turned toward him. "Cliff, something terrible has happened, and Tish needs to see us right now."

. . . Thought That's Thin . . .

About the Author

J.W. Peercy spent his early years in California, (fifteen minutes from Disneyland!). As to the effect of this experience, we can only guess, but imagination seems to make the top of the list. His later years in Texas, he holds a BA in Computer Science with a minor in Math. Although analytical, the creative side has to find a way out. To ease the pain, he writes fantasy, mystery, and sci-fi. If you like the book, please drop him a line. If you don't like the book, drop him a line anyway. He will appreciate the feedback. As in the words of J.R.R. Tolkien, 'May the hair on your toes never fall out!'

Visit his website at www.JamesWilliamPeercy.com

www.ingramcontent.com/pod-product-compliance
Lightning Source LLC
Chambersburg PA
CBHW071118180726
48291CB00007B/2084